D1424206

THE SATISFACTION HOUSE

Ray Bryant

A *Warner* Book

First published in Great Britain in 1997 by Warner Books

All characters in this publication are fictitious and any resemblance to real persons, living or dead, is purely coincidental.

A CIP catalogue record for this book is available from the British Library.

ISBN 0 7515 2049 7

Typeset in New Baskerville by M Rules
Printed and bound in Great Britain by
Clays Ltd, St Ives plc

Warner Books
A Division of
Little, Brown and Company (UK)
Brettenham House
Lancaster Place
London WC2E 7EN

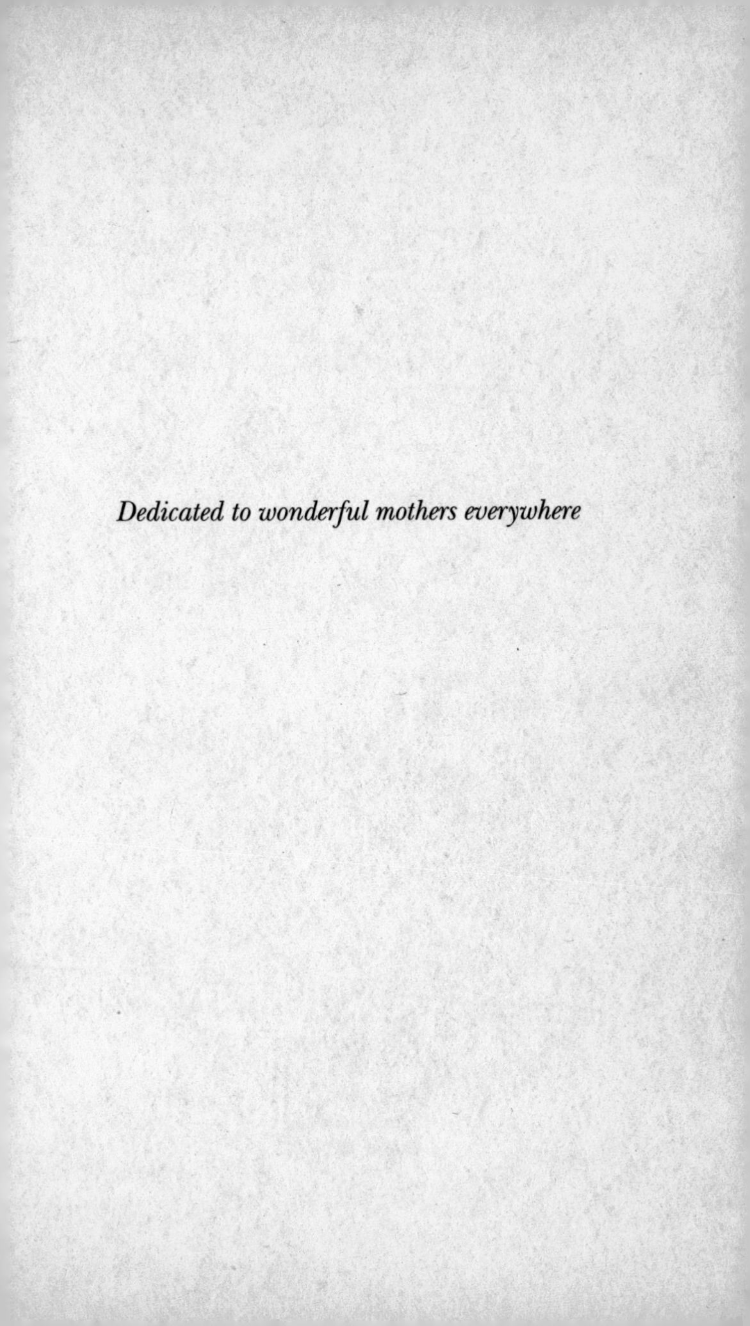

Dedicated to wonderful mothers everywhere

BROADMOOR
HOSPITAL AUTHORITY

To all the kind readers of my story

More than twenty-four years have now passed since I was first committed to Broadmoor as a patient. A patient! Yes, that's what they call me in here - a term normally applied to someone who is in distress, someone who exacts the help and compassion of others, someone normally the recipient of kindness and sympathy. And, don't get me wrong, for that is indeed how I am treated by the staff at the hospital. I would like to say I have nothing but admiration and praise for the kindness of them all; especially Dr Sigmund who even lent me his old but much-loved electric typewriter so I could write my story (its row of curved silver teeth - with a gap where the missing 'eye' tooth should be, the result of a little accident a few months ago apparently - grins up at me now as I sit here and stare at it, waiting for inspiration to strike, mindful that I have only yet half-peppered its white paper tongue with black indelible letters).

But I know that many people outside of here have other, less enlightened, words to describe me; words more disposed to the sentiment that I should mercilessly have been put down rather than committed for treatment. In the press I have often been referred to as a

'Monster' a 'Twisted Pervert', and many of the tabloids have gone even further, calling me names like 'The Witch-Hazel Nut', 'The Nutty-Bar Kid' and 'Squiffy Smiffy'. I am not damning them for that and neither do I really blame them. But, as the saying goes, sticks and stones may break my bones but words can never hurt me. And I suppose some will always hold the opinion that the things I have done deserve that kind of condemnation. After all, they reckon I am now the most celebrated serial killer in British history, my name transcending even those of Crippen, Jack the Ripper and, more recently, Brady and Hindley, Sutcliffe, and Frank and Rosemary West in the darkest depths of the blackest rogue's gallery of them all. I am not saying that with any sense of pride. I did not seek the notoriety that has been heaped upon me. I swear I did not do the things I did to achieve publicity for myself. All I ever wanted was to remain in the obscurity of my ordinary life, nameless and unknown. But She had other ideas about that.

Twenty-four years! I've lived here longer than I lived in the world outside. Though, sometimes, it seems like only yesterday I was standing in the dock of that big hushed courtroom waiting for Judge Cattermole to sentence me. I know I will never forget his words.

'You have been found guilty of the cold-blooded

BROADMOOR
HOSPITAL AUTHORITY

slaying of twenty-six women. In all my years on the bench, I have never had to preside over a more hideous and macabre case. To kill one is outrageous; to kill twenty-six is carnage. But your counsel has submitted a plea of diminished responsibility and I admit it is with reluctance that I have to accept that submission.

'Nevertheless, the fact remains you are a danger to innocent women everywhere and your reasons for committing these atrocious crimes are of no consequence to the way I must deal with that. I can never allow you to walk the streets and endanger the lives of decent law-abiding citizens ever again.

'My one concession to your counsel's plea is to accept the fact that, for the time being at least, you need constant psychiatric attention. You will therefore be taken from this place to a high-security institution for mentally-ill offenders where, for as long as is deemed necessary, you will spend time in their charge. But that does not mean I can put any time limit on your sentence because, if the day ever dawns when it is felt you can be transferred from the hospital to a prison, I intend to see to it that you remain locked up for the rest of your life. And rest assured, Smith, when I say life I mean just that. You will spend the remainder of your natural days safely secured behind bars where you

BROADMOOR
HOSPITAL AUTHORITY

will never again be given the chance to commit the kind of atrocities we have heard about in this courtroom over the past few weeks.

'I can find no more words to say on this matter. I suspect the entire court is glad this case is finally over. Just thinking about the appalling deeds you have done makes me feel sick in the pit of my stomach.

'Take him down!'

They have often asked me how I felt when I heard those words, and to be truthful, it is hard to explain my feelings precisely. If I say I felt a strange sense of exaltation, I know that would give the wrong impression; that I viewed my acts with virtuousness and that I was unrepentant. But it would be quite wrong to claim that. Yes, I considered I was condemned unjustly but in a way more akin to the likes of Shadrach, Meshach and Abednego in the Bible, sentenced to be cast into the fiery furnace of Nebuchadnezzar for remaining faithful to their God by refusing to commit an act of worship to the profanity of the craven idol. You see, I felt I was sentenced similarly, because of my faithfulness to Someone who, to me, was just as omnipotent. Someone who had to be obeyed at all costs - regardless of the consequences of that action. And fear? Yes, of course, I felt fear just as I am sure even Shadrach, Meshach and Abednego felt fear when they learnt of their gruesome fate. After all, we can still fear the consequence of obedience even though we may fear the consequence of disobedience more. Fear, even that fear which comes as the price of faithful service, is not mysteriously eradicated through the grace and mercy of the One you strive to serve. Facing your fear is a test of your conviction but its edge can be softened if your faith is strong enough. Truly zealous faith can even turn fear into exhilaration. And my faith was very strong. It had been instilled in me from a very early age. That is why I say I felt exalted - because She made the exaltation of serving Her override my fear. And, just as in the analogy I have mentioned from the Good Book, not only has not one hair of my head been harmed in the twenty-four years from that day to this, but She has rewarded me for my obedience by allowing me to find contentment, even here, inside this grim and dismal place.

Can you understand that, I wonder? No? Well, perhaps it doesn't really matter. After all, I am but a common or garden psychopath. Would you expect the things I say to make sense? But wait, please wait! I beg your indulgence just a little longer. My tale is bizarre. It is utterly incredible. It may seem unbelievable. Yet I swear every word of it is absolutely true. And I ask nothing of you except that you hear me out, that you judge me for yourself; not only from the prejudiced words you may already have read about me in the press or heard on the television or radio, but also from the truths I am about to tell. Truths I can now recount without the fear I once felt because She has granted me the sanction to tell it all - complete and unabridged, to leave nothing out, to tell it just as it was and as it truly happened.

They say there are two sides to every story. And surely everyone has the right for his side to be told. Even a Monster! A Twisted Pervert! A Witch-Hazel Nut! A Nutty-Bar Kid! A Squiffy Smiffy! Perhaps, even a Broadmoor patient!

And who knows - one day, you might even begin to believe the things I am about to tell you. Because, as time goes on, it seems that even stranger events are happening in the world outside than are happening here in this loony-bin I call my home. But I will leave you, my kind readers, to be the judge of that, just as I hope you will judge me from the truths I will tell and not from the misconceptions others may have voiced. I am not seeking your forgiveness. What's done is done and can never be undone. I accept I am where I deserve to be - and here is exactly where I desire to be - for having done those things. No, my dear readers, all I ask

BROADMOOR
HOSPITAL AUTHORITY

is that you do your best to understand and, if you read my tale with an open mind, I know you cannot fail to see how it was I had no choice but to strive to serve Her then, just as I strive to serve Her now, and will continue to do for the rest of my very ordinary and unremarkable days.

John Smith

John Smith

24 December 1996

Part One

The Tree House

There's a house up in a yew
That me and Ben climbed to
One night
When we should have been in bed.

On her broom the witch did fly
When she heard us tell that lie.
She took poor Ben
And gobbled off his head.

by Johnny Smith (aged 11)

Chapter 1

This is my story. Not my complete story, you understand. Most of my life has been much too ordinary to recount. I was born forty-five years ago and christened John Smith. A very ordinary name for a very ordinary boy. I would still say I was born of ordinary parents of ordinary status with ordinary looks and ordinary intelligence despite what I later discovered. When I recall my childhood, I remember it as nothing but ordinary; a totally unremarkable time. My most traumatic recollections are falling off my bike and fracturing my leg rather badly at the age of ten and a severe case of acne in my early teens which I feared, and in the confusion of thoughts of those formative years, sometimes even hoped, would leave my face permanently scarred to render my countenance less ordinary and more noticeable. But neither of these things left me with any permanent disfigurement to encroach upon my otherwise ordinary and unremarkable existence.

My progress at school was not marked with any special distinction either. There was nothing at which I excelled. I enjoyed reading but not the literature of the school curriculum. My mother used to read to me. One Christmas, she gave me a huge book of fairy tales and if I am asked, as I often am now, to recall but one delight of my boyhood, I would unashamedly have to say it was excitedly snuggling under the bed covers on cold winter's nights, sweating with cold anticipatory shivers, waiting for my mother to come in and read to me from that book.

It was the excitement of fear I felt. I remember. I would turn out the light and pull the covers up over my head. There was a kind of cold comfort in the warmth of that darkness. My mother would enter quietly and creep up on me; just like the wicked old witch who, in the stories she would read, would creep up on the little boys She wanted to eat for her supper. My mother would pretend she was that wicked old witch and tickle me through the quilt.

I remember. She used to speak in a strange voice; a gnarled and haggard voice. A voice which, like the wicked old witch she was trying to portray, almost seemed to have hairy warts growing on it. She would say, 'The wicked witch is coming to get you!' Then the tickling would start. I used to laugh. But it was not the laugh of a happy game; it was a frightened laugh which begged for comfort. Why did my mother never recognise that my laugh was nothing but a mask disguising my fear and that it was really entreating her, 'Please tell me you're not the wicked old witch! Please tell me you're my mummy!'? But she never did. She just went on tickling. I remember it was a tickling which became more intense until it grew into a hurtful kind of pinching – just like the wicked old witch in her stories who used to pinch the scrawny arms and legs of the little boys She took away. I knew what the witch was thinking. 'What a skinny little boy! I shall have to fatten him up before I can eat him for my supper!'

But, in the end, after she had often pinched me till tiny dull yellow bruises appeared on my flesh, she would pull back the covers from over my head and, when I dared open my eyes again, the witch would be changed back into my mother. She would be smiling; a kind of mocking sneer. I used to try to pretend it was all a game but, even then, I think I perceived something sinister in the way she behaved. It's hard now to explain exactly what I mean. But sometimes her eyes expressed a look which was almost sadistic pleasure as she picked up that big old book of fairy tales to read me another gruesome story about another wicked old witch who lived in another forest and ate other little boys. And all the time, she seemed to be watching me, gleefully, as I slithered down the bed in yet another cold comber of fear.

I didn't feel sorry for those 'other little boys'. I just felt glad I didn't live in that strange place called fairyland where everyone seemed to be poor and every little boy's father seemed to be a woodcutter. Strangely, I remember thinking that if every daddy cut down trees, how come there were any forests left for the wicked old witches to live in?

But these thoughts came to me only in the warm light of morning. When my mother was reading me the story, putting on that 'hairy, warty' voice, and even after she had left me in the wonderful loneliness of my darkness – always without ever tucking me up or giving me a good-night kiss, as I recall – I *was* those other little boys and my bed *was* that cage those other little boys were kept in while the witch was fattening them up to eat.

They often ask me if I loved my mother. I think I always knew I hated her. I wanted to love her and I really did try, but how can you love someone who doesn't love you? I know I didn't cry when she went away. That may seem strange when I tell you she left me all alone and I knew she would never return from the place she was going to. But, even so, I didn't feel sadness, so I guess I couldn't have loved her, could I? I did love my father though, until he was taken. I dearly loved him. I was eleven then. I will never forget that day. I think it was the only time I ever cried because the agony inside me was too illimitable to bear. I didn't even cry when I fell off my bicycle and broke my leg. I wanted to, but the kids I was with went and got my mother. I remember her apathetic face staring down at me through the twisted spokes of my bike's wheel as I was writhing about on the road in terrible pain, and her indifferent voice asking, almost with a joyfully informing tone, 'Going too fast, were we, Johnny? Didn't I warn you about that when your father bought you that stupid bike? But you never listen to your mother, do you, Johnny Smith? Oh no, you never listen to your mother!' Those 'other little boys' never cried in front of the wicked old witch, did they? They were always brave so I tried to be like them.

Come to think of it, I didn't even cry when Ben was taken. Ben . . .Funny I should suddenly think of him now. I haven't remembered Ben in ages. I haven't even told them about Ben.

Ben was my best friend; my very best friend. We shared the same passion. We were collectors. Not of stamps or caterpillars in matchboxes stuffed with leaves. No. We were collectors of the strange and the macabre. We lived in a bizarre world of the supernatural, fashioned by horror comics and the ghost stories of Edgar Allan Poe. These things were sufficient for our weaning but our obsession soon craved a stronger stimulant. So we would hang around the rear exits of cinemas showing the latest Hammer House of Horror movie, waiting for someone to leave when we would sneak into the darkness before the doors sprang shut. Those movies were fun but innocuous. But I am talking of the days which began right at the start of the new decade. No one yet knew the Sixties were swinging. They were the days before video nasties. Days of innocence, of rock 'n' roll and the pursuance of pleasure. They were the days before people became hardened to authentic horror; the horror of man's atrocity to his own kind, like the graphic scenes of those sad little kids hideously burnt by napalm in Vietnam, nightly serialised on our television sets.

They were also the days of the awakening of our innocence; the days when Ben and I realised that real horror – the kind which makes you cringe from the hair on your head to the toes in your boots – doesn't come from inanimate words printed in the pages of books or even from transient images flickering on a screen. No. Real horror comes from an imaginative mind which takes the glowing embers of these things and fans them into an all-consuming fire. They were the days of long hot summers when the searing sun turned everything tinder-dry and ready for ignition by any stray spark.

Yes, I remember Ben. And I still say we were just ordinary kids. After all, show me a kid who isn't fascinated by feeling the clamminess of terror envelop him and scare him witless. That's why they wrote fairy tales, isn't it, to cater for that need in kids to feel the excitement of fear? But that's not what my mother used to say. She said they were written for children as a warning.

'Johnny!' she would whisper with that inflection in her voice that told me the warning was coming. 'You know what those little boys in the stories were, don't you? You know, the ones the horrible old witch ate for her supper? Well, they were naughty little boys, Johnny – yes, *very* naughty little boys. So what must you be if you don't want that wicked old witch to take you away and gobble you up? What must you be?'

I can still hear myself whisper, 'Good, Mummy! I must be good! I will be good, Mummy, I promise!'

'That's right, Johnny,' she would answer, 'you must be good, 'cause the wicked old witch knows when you're not. She knows when you're being naughty. And even if you're not being bad enough to deserve being taken away and gobbled up, she'll still make something nasty happen to you! You know that, Johnny, don't you?'

When she gave me that warning, I knew real terror. And I would be good for as long as I was able; till my boyish impulsiveness finally overthrew the abject dread reigning in my mind. But I learnt that, sometimes, that wicked old witch, despite my mother's contestations that She is infallible, makes terrible mistakes. I was being good – very good – when I fell off my bike and when I got my acne. There was no need for her to make those things happen to me.

Then there was the time that wicked old witch proved just how unfair Her so-called justice really is. I was guilty too but I got off scot-free while Ben was . . . taken. It happened during one of those long hot summers, the year after I fell off my bike.

My father had built me a tree house in the big old yew that grew at the bottom of our garden. My mother didn't want him to. She never wanted me to have anything I would really enjoy. But Daddy got his own way that time and built me that tree house anyway. It was fantastic. He was so clever at things like that. He built it between two huge branches of that big old yew which grew off the main trunk about fifteen feet off the ground. It had a rope ladder you climbed up through a hole in a big planked platform like a railed balcony. The house was built in the middle of that platform. It had a door, two glazed windows and an apex roof just like a real house. Daddy had put roofing felt over it to keep out the rain. Funny, I never remember it raining in the summers back then – except that once, of course, the night Ben was taken.

I don't know what games other kids would have played in that tree house if they'd had the chance, but Ben and I didn't really play in it at all; not in the true sense of the word, anyway. You see, that tree house was our deliverance; a release from life's ordinariness. It was our own special place. A private and magic place which stood perched on the crossroads of two worlds. Down below was the world of mums and dads and ordinary houses in ordinary backyards, a world which slept when the sun went down. But our tree house somehow floated in the same nebulous ether as that other world; the world of an unknown dimension. A world of eeriness, excitement and fear. A world which woke up when the ordinary world slumbered. And our tree house was the gateway to it.

We would lounge in that tree house on the cushions Ben's mum had given us and recount stories of that other world, not read from books or comics now, but concocted with that unique revulsion – that ridiculous but somehow plausible source of graphic inventiveness – nestling in the recesses of every small boy's mind. But, no matter how grisly and macabre our stories became, the threshold of that ecstatic fear always eluded us. Ben and I knew we needed more kindling to fire the red-hot embers of our imagination. Wouldn't it be wonderful, we thought, if we could be at our magic place where this other world began, at the very moment of its wakening; the bewitching hour – midnight – which, as every small child knows, is when every gruesome ghoul and ghostie is loosed to stalk the world of banality?

All that day we made preparations for our vigil, the excitement of delirious expectation beaming on our faces. We smuggled up candles and put them in empty Coca-Cola bottles (which were made of glass then). We smuggled up some matches and a supply of food and drink. I remember the day was hot and humid. The air inside the tree house was rank with the sweat of our exertion and trepidation. But we didn't care.

We planned things as meticulously as two generals planning a decisive battle. I would tell my mother I was staying over at Ben's and he would tell his mum he was spending the night at my place. We chose a Monday because both our mothers usually spent that day doing the family wash and were less likely to bump into each other at the shops to compare alibis and discover our connivance.

I even remember telling my mother that Ben's mum wasn't feeling too well. In my impulsive enthusiasm to construct a watertight plan, I thought this news would reduce the risk of her phoning the other on the off chance. It was only later that I considered this further intrigue could be the plan's downfall; that it might, in fact, increase the risk of contact between the two mums to enquire about the indisposed one's condition or to question the wisdom of putting up with me if she wasn't feeling well enough to cope with the extra aggravation.

My terrified mind was buzzing with the imagined telephone conversation I was convinced they would have. 'Are you sure you want Johnny to stay tonight, Hilda? He can be a bit of a handful at the best of times but when you're not feeling well—?' 'What do you mean, Helen?' Ben's mum would reply. 'I'm feeling fine and, anyway, it's Ben who's staying at your house tonight, isn't it? That's what Ben told me!'

My mind refused to continue that thought beyond its humble beginnings of our duplicity being discovered. It was all too frightening. But, as it turned out, my fears were unfounded. That Monday was a very busy day for my mother, and Ben's mum's concocted illness passed the same way of inconsequence as most other things on hectic washdays and we were left undisturbed in the tenuous comfort of the tree house to continue planning our great adventure.

At last, we felt our plan was honed finely enough to cater for every possible contingency. After supper we would politely ask if it was okay now to go over to the other's house as agreed. If my mother asked about Ben's mum, I was to say, 'Ben says she feels a lot better now!' Then we were to collect our pyjamas and toothbrushes and display them to our parents to prove that nothing essential had been forgotten and walk round to the alley at the bottom of the garden and wait for the other by the back fence.

I could hardly contain myself as I ate my supper that night. It was really difficult to curb my excitement, bolting down my food and sensing the minutes pass like hours. But at last, clutching the plastic bag containing my 'necessary' overnight things, I was allowed to leave, only to be recalled before I was halfway down the garden path. I was sure my sheepish look had condemned me as guilty of something even if the crime itself was unidentified. 'Haven't you forgotten something?' my mother said with her hand on her hip and that expression in her eyes of the exasperated martyr.

I looked at her, down at the plastic bag, then at her again, a stare of bewilderment on my face. I was sure that visible contrition was mingling with the sweat oozing from every pore of my body.

'Johnny! Show your wonderful mother the respect she deserves!'

With some relief, I realised what it was she expected me to do and pecked her on the cheek. Then I was walking back down the path again, trying hard to suppress my pace; trying to stop it becoming a run.

'Be a good boy, Johnny—' she called out after me. 'Remember, Mrs Jenkins has been poorly today. Don't play her up tonight, will you? Remember, Johnny. Remember what happened to those other naughty boys! You know, the boys in the stories Mummy reads to you.'

It was the first time her warning about the wicked old witch's retribution was implied rather than actually stated. It was also the first time it did not fill me with obeisant dread. But too much adrenaline was flowing now for me to fear anything. I remember hearing the front door close. My walk immediately became that run. My energy was boundless; I felt I could run for ever.

CHAPTER 2

I hadn't realised that dusk had begun to cast its tawny cloak until I ran into the alley. Quite suddenly, I was conscious of a delicate penumbra running beside me, its scrawny legs pounding the ground with my own in a silent synchronous frenzy. I looked up at the watery moon and seemed to see a chiselled face beaming an enchanted smile. It was a mystical, enigmatic face shrouded with a diffuse halo; a face as old as time itself which whispered recondite secrets of incomprehensible things. It was a night when the very air seemed charged with mystery and magic and I knew that, on such a night, Ben and I could not help being consumed by its enchantment.

My mind was so exhilarated with the anticipation of these things, I didn't immediately notice Ben standing by our fence. It was the movement of his own white plastic bag, reflecting the phosphorescence of the moon's eerie yellowness, which first caught my eye. He was using it to batter a poor, defenceless cow parsley to death. Its movement stopped when he discerned my running footsteps.

'Halt! Who goes there? Friend or foe?' he said in a

subdued whisper. It was part of our plan to use the archetypal military address. It seemed appropriate at the time; the whole operation had, after all, been schemed with absolute military precision.

I stopped running. 'Friend!' I answered.

'Advance, friend, and be recognised!'

So I advanced to be recognised and Ben was given the opportunity to discern at close quarters what he had already discerned at a distance of some fifty yards – that it was one Johnny Smith who was running down that alley at the back of that row of suburban gardens.

I took hold of Ben's free hand and shook it. To this day, I don't really know why I did that. It may have been because, at that moment, the prearranged 'Halt! Who goes there?' routine had seemed such a puerile act to perform at the onset of such a great adventure although, more probably, it was an expression to Ben of the closeness I felt to him; a kind of confederacy which seemed an adult thing to feel so perhaps I needed to demonstrate it with a seemingly adult gesture.

I remember clearly though that Ben seemed confounded by my action. He gave an embarrassed kind of smile, immediately withdrew his hand, turned towards the fence and hauled himself up so his head was peering into our backyard.

He lowered himself to the ground and turned to face me. 'It's okay! Your mum's pulled the curtains on the back windows!'

The coast was clear. It was time to begin. We clambered over the fence, desperately trying to make as little noise as possible. From somewhere a dog barked. In mid-straddle, we turned and looked at one another, fearing the disturbance would provoke an investigation by my father. Then the barking stopped and all was quiet again.

We slithered down the other side into a wild area of our garden, affectionately referred to by my mother as 'the forest'. This was a sacrosanct patch she forbade my father to cultivate, insisting that the garden should have a natural tract dedicated to the attraction of wild insects – butterflies, and such like. Whatever else I thought of my mother, I will credit her with one virtue. She was a perceptive, forward-thinking woman who felt a passionate concern for issues like the environment long before it became fashionable to do so. And, as a very small boy, I must admit to spending many a delightful hour there at the forest's edge, gazing in awe at the multi-coloured profusion of tiny fluttering wings.

On that night, however, the forest was anything but a delight. I landed in a thick patch of bramble which tore both my trousers and my legs and Ben stumbled headlong into a luxuriant growth of nettles. We picked ourselves up, both trying to stifle a cry of pained surprise and rub an abundance of smarting places all at once. I remember we both dropped our plastic bags containing our overnight things so, after extricating ourselves from its painful clutches, we had to scamper around in that dense and dangerous undergrowth again to recover our belongings, acquiring in the process more gashes and stings to the already inflamed flesh between our short trousers and rolled-down socks.

In a strange way, that painful experience increased the camaraderie Ben and I felt. Our injuries were battle scars willingly endured in the pursuance of our passion; a passion for which we had suffered together. I felt closer to Ben that night than I have ever felt to anyone in my whole life. It was unfair that the wicked old witch separated us. We should both have been taken. For months after it happened I used to wake up at nights and scream and scream. I think I knew why, even then. It wasn't so much my sadness for Ben; it was the unbearable feeling of desolation and guilt that I was left as the living testimony of that inequitable verdict.

But, of course, when I was standing with Ben at the edge of the forest, both of us rubbing our wounds, I was unaware of the events that were to come, just as I was unaware that that was the last time I would ever see Ben smile. We ran to the yew. As I began to climb the rope ladder, an owl hooted. I remember it made the hairs on the nape of my neck bristle and stand on end. I pulled myself up onto the platform and waited for Ben to join me.

Until that moment, not one single breath of air had disturbed the clamminess of that hot and sultry July day. But, as we reached the tree house door, a stiff breeze sprang up from nowhere, inciting the luxuriant foliage of the yew into a fervent rustling and, from high above, a bough wheezed a weary creak. It was a steely wind that caused goosebumps to instantly form on our exposed flesh; a wind that seemed dedicated to a singular purpose. I swear that wind followed us in through the door of the tree house. Then, having achieved its design, the air outside was left to resume its untroubled and stuffy tranquillity.

I shut the door and Ben and I settled down on our cushions. For a while, it was like sitting inside a refrigerator; we just squatted, huddled up in our respective corners, waiting for that icy chill to pass. To this day, I believe that wind was an emissary of the invidious spirit of that wicked old witch. I remember looking out through the window at the chiselled face of the watery old moon.

I thought I saw a dark shadow pass across it. I think I knew then that She was coming.

I found the matches and lit the candles, more for the meagre warmth they might provide than for light. Even though the moon was enshrouded in a miasma of haze, it was still full enough to cast sufficient jaundiced beams through the windows for us to see quite clearly.

The flickering candles did induce a certain cosiness. Soon, the sinister presence carried in by that icy blast seemed to dissipate and the numbness we felt was gradually coaxed into the warm inner glow of a vibrant expectancy.

Ben spoke, 'Aw, Johnny! We forgot to bring a watch! How we gonna know when it's midnight?'

With all our meticulous planning, we had forgotten something which now seemed fundamental. It was only then I recalled that it had passed through my mind during a mental cataloguing of things to remember. My father had an old fob watch which used to belong to his own father. It was still in perfect working order and would have been ideal; he never used it so it wouldn't have been missed. And I knew where it was kept. I guess the reason it slipped my mind again was that it didn't seem as crucial as the candles or the matches or the food or the drink. I thought of the watch more as a desirable element than a necessary one; that we could do a 'Ten! nine! eight!' countdown to midnight, like the grown-ups did on New Year's Eve, to heighten the thrill of anticipation as the bewitching hour approached. Then I remembered that eerie shadow I thought I saw pass over the moon.

'I guess they'll let us know when its midnight, Ben!' An icy shiver ran up my spine as I said those words.

Ben looked sullen. I threw him a Coke and the bottle opener. 'You wanna start?'

Through the fizz of the escaping gas, I heard him say, 'Yeah, okay!' I remember he took a long swig of his drink, let out a loud burp and wiped his mouth with the back of his hand. His voice sounded more cheery as he began the first tale.

'Right!' he said. 'This is a story of the phantom of the foggy moors – about a grisly, 'orrible, disgusting thing which used to jump out on people an' rip their eyes out of their sockets 'till they were just hanging there restin' on their cheeks on grey, slimy stalks with blood oozin' everywhere!' Ben seemed to be feeling much better.

He recounted a tale based on the Arthur Conan Doyle classic *The Hound of the Baskervilles*, with suitable embellishments only Ben could endorse. For the first time in the history of our little elitist club of horror, a tale had provoked that all-consuming tingling shiver which froze my senses into obedient attention. I could tell that Ben was feeling the same sensations too as he launched himself into the tale's narration with a devotion that could only be described as total.

I tried to convince myself it was only the spooky ambience of the tree house which had caused us to be incarcerated in this grip of energised terror; our isolation, the darkness outside, the eerie moonlight slithering its yellow tentacles through the windows and the flickering candles placed at strategic points about our feet.

After all, creeping up there in the black of night to create the right atmosphere was the whole idea behind our little escapade, wasn't it? But, in my heart, I knew the truth. The biting emissary of the wicked old witch had made the silent message of its mistress unmistakably clear. She was coming!

Ben finished his tale. We sat motionless and speechless

for a while, then we had another Coke. It was my turn to recount a creation of equal gruesomeness.

I can't recall now the gist of that story but I guess it is really inconsequential. To be honest, I can't be sure I was conscious of the words I was speaking even at the time of their telling. But I can vividly remember a penetrating coldness devour me. I was numb; enveloped completely in a stupor of ecstatic fear.

Now and again, my awareness of the real world would momentarily return and I would glimpse a fragmented image of Ben's face, lit by the spooky glow of the flickering candles, transfixed in a motionless stare, his mouth wide open.

We were much too engrossed fanning the hot coals of our imagination to notice that the moon had drawn a veil of thick impenetrable cloud over its ancient chiselled face, or to feel the wind rock the very foundation of those immovable boughs on which our tree house stood.

Yes. I can remember now. There was a point in my story where some of the words I spoke are not filed away in those unreachable parts of my memory. I can precisely recall those particular words because their very speaking seemed to fuse together the dimensions of imagination and reality. It was the climax of my tale.

'—then, the thing, covered in this dripping, gunky, green sludge rose up from the pit and opened 'is 'orrible gungy, slimy mouth—'

At that precise moment, it happened; like a sound effect worked by some all-seeing deity dedicated to the production of realistic drama. The noise was deafening and the flash blinding.

There is this image in my mind of Ben's face frozen in a tomb of petrified whiteness. I could only have witnessed it for an instant but I know it will be etched on my mind for ever.

I am trying to recall what happened next but that vision of Ben's horrified face remains. I know I was conscious of nothing until I felt a searing heat. I blinked my eyes. When I opened them again, Ben's head was gone. His body was there, I remember it twitching. But his head was gone. In its place was a wall of flame. It was as if someone had lit a fire in the grate of his shoulders.

I remember looking up, above the place where his head used to be. I saw a huge hole in the roof and flames were licking the charred edges of its blackness.

Ben's headless body jumped up. It was sudden and unexpected. His feet were running, knocking over candles in their wake, and his hands rose up as if to lift the wall of flame from his shoulders. He made no human sound. All I could hear was a hideous, unholy hissing, the sharp crackle of the flames and the clinking of Coke bottles bouncing around the wooden floor.

But it is the smell – that sickening, odious smell – which, of all the sensations of that night, is the one which can be recalled with the most crystalline clarity. That smell is in my nostrils now. It is indescribable. It is obscene. In all my years since, I have never smelt anything as vile and I know I never will.

Ben ran to the door and crashed through it. It was only then I was conscious of the rain lashing the wooden balcony outside. It was so heavy, it stifled the sound of Ben's body toppling over the rail and crashing to the ground below, into a muffled thud.

By this time the complete roof was ablaze. The heat was so intense, it was unbearable. I ran out onto the balcony and screamed. I remember looking down into the blackness. I didn't want to but I felt drawn by some strange compulsion. All I could see was an eerie glow lying at the base of the tree and the faint outline of Ben's lifeless shoulders, illuminated by an incandescence that was once his head.

Then, above the sound of splashing raindrops and the crackling of flames, there was another noise; a commotion of shouts and soft running feet. I saw a zigzagging pinpoint of light which drew closer.

There was a boom of thunder and, instantly, there came another light; a flash of lightning so intense it lit up the whole sky and froze the garden, and the running figures of my parents, in a glacier of dazzling brilliance. I remember my mother's emotionless voice shouting 'Oh, my God!', then my father shouting, 'Jump, Johnny! Jump! Jump, son! I'll catch you!'

Then I saw that etched vision again; Ben's face frozen in that tomb of petrified whiteness. And I smelt that odious smell. It was entrenched in my nostrils.

Chapter 3

'Johnny Smith, how I wish you were born a girl! You know what little girls are made of, don't you, Johnny? Yes, Johnny, sugar and spice and all things nice! But, I'm afraid you were not born a girl, you were born a boy. And we know what little boys are made of, don't we?'

I was forced to recite the words with her. 'Slugs and snails and puppy dogs' tails! That's what little boys are made of!'

She looked at me, her lean and contemptible face displaying that pained, disdainful countenance she was so fond of wearing, and paused before continuing. 'I once thought you might be a special little boy. A boy made of nicer – more wholesome – things. A boy who might grow up to do something extraordinary with his life. But I know now, with absolute certainty, you are a very ordinary little boy. Yes, a very ordinary little boy indeed, destined to spend the rest of his ordinary little life among the ranks of those other ordinary little boys who have grown up to be layabouts and wasters. I see them wearing those ridiculous drainpipe trousers and huge quiffs in their hair, hanging around coffee bars doing nothing but cause trouble.'

Her eyes pierced me with the searing coldness of her anger. 'Johnny!' That inflection was back. The warning was coming. 'That is, Johnny, assuming that wicked old witch doesn't take you away and gobble you up before you have a chance to grow into one of those ridiculous teddy boys. Do you know what they are, Johnny? Those layabout teddy boys? They're just very ordinary, naughty little boys who have grown up into bigger and more repulsive slugs and snails and puppy dogs' tails. That's what they are, Johnny!'

My mother took great delight in saying such things to me. The words might sometimes change but the portent was always the same. I was just a disgusting and apparently inferior male, destined to live in a world of useless ordinariness. After such an indoctrination, it is hardly surprising my life turned out to be so unremarkable.

I distinctly remember her giving me the warning I have cited. I was nine years old and had been caught red-handed, scrumping apples from Mrs Jessop's garden. I knew it was a naughty thing to do but my boyish enthusiasm to sample the delights of their rosy red succulence temporarily overrode my fear of the wicked old witch's retribution.

I remember my father looking over her shoulder while she was berating me. He would always be smiling a sympathetic fellow-sufferer's smile until she turned to him, when his countenance would immediately change to one of stern consternation and he would nod his head in a hearty gesture of agreement.

He would never say anything; not in my mother's presence, anyway. Sometimes, after she had left the room, he would come over to me, look into my dejected face and smile. 'Your mother doesn't really mean those things she says to you, Johnny. It's just that she wants you to make something of yourself. She wants the best for you but all you seem to do is get into mischief. Why can't you be a good boy, Johnny, for your mother's sake?'

When the immediate fear of the new warning had subsided, I remember thinking that if little boys were really made of slugs and snails and puppy dogs' tails, how come witches found them so tasty? But then, wicked old witches were always brewing up revolting things like 'ear of newt and eye of toad' in their cauldrons so I concluded it was *because* little boys were made of such nauseating things that witches thought them such a delicacy. And since the naughtier they were the more repulsive the things they were made of became, naughty boys were even tastier which was why witches only took the very naughty ones away. With the hindsight of these thoughts, I remember wondering what particularly naughty things Ben had done to make him so desirable as an item on the witch's supper table.

Then my mind aimlessly meandered again to thoughts of my father. He was a wonderful, kindly man. He was always sympathetic to me and I loved him dearly. But he never put his arms around me or displayed physical affection of any kind. I wanted him to. Sometimes I needed him to take control and tell my mother to leave me alone and accuse her of being the wicked old witch I knew she was. But he never did. I suppose that was why he tried to make up for things in other ways, like building me that tree house. But I didn't have the tree house any more, did I?

All these things drifted through the woolly locus of my consciousness as I lay tucked up in bed, idly watching the blue lights of the police cars and fire engines in the street outside pulse little cyclic flickers on my bedroom walls and ceiling. The gyrating reflections were strangely hypnotic and mesmerising. I didn't cry. I didn't feel emotion of any kind, only emptiness and exhaustion. My mind was being transported in the curious macrocosm of sedation. I was vaguely conscious of instructions being shouted from the street below, then I felt a peculiar floating sensation. I remember wondering if the wicked old witch was taking me away after all . . .

But I was transported back to the tree house. Ben was there and everything was just as it was before he was taken. I could hear myself saying those same words; those words of harmless innocence, the climax of an asinine ghost story conjured up from a no less innocuous source than the vivid depths of a boy's imagination. Yet the words I was speaking now sounded hollow and sinister; they made the whole tree house rock with their ominous portent. They were a benediction summoning up a dastardly force, spoken just as I began to hear the town hall clock chime out its twelve sonorous bongs of midnight. '—then the thing, covered in this dripping, gunky, green sludge, rose up from the pit and opened 'is 'orrible gungy slimy mouth—'

The booming cacophony of its presence was ear-splitting and the light heralding its power was so brilliant, the creosoted walls of the tree house were instantly bleached. This time I was aware of it. I heard the crunching of its teeth bite a cavernous hole in the roof above Ben's head. I saw those yellow, drooling fangs chew the timbers and swallow them whole, as if they were matchsticks. I saw the rest of its enormous, hideous face grin at me through the hole it had made.

It was the most repulsive thing I have ever seen. Red, beady eyes that scorched you with their very gaze. A long, hooked nose bearing three huge warts growing a profusion of stubbly hairs. A gnarled and haggard face showing the wrinkles of millennia.

The roof was burning around the hole it had made and, through this ring of fire, the abhorrent mouth plummeted, opening as it did to reveal a bottomless cavity. Its teeth snapped shut and I heard the crunch of bone, and a belch like the eruption of a volcano.

Then came the smell. That hideous, repulsive smell, emanating from the very foulness of its flatulence. And a laugh; a raucous echoing snigger. The witch stared at me cowering in the corner.

'*Mmm! That was tasty! Like slugs and snails and puppy dogs' tails, done to a turn and twice as lovely! – I'll save you for later, Johnny Smith. I'm waiting for you to get fattened up with a little more naughtiness – waiting for you to get a little more tasty, then I'll be coming to get you! To gobble* you *up!*'

Her voice bellowed out in a gnarled and warty tone that personified Her gnarled and warty ugliness. Then I remember She puffed up Her old haggard cheeks and blew. There was a wind; a callous, icy wind which rose up from the floor of the tree house. It coursed around the centre of the floor like a tornado, dragging up Coke bottles into the vacuum of its core.

It circled around Ben and lifted him up. I saw his lifeless limbs and headless body twirl round in the twisting force, then he was gone within the vacuous wastes of its centre.

'*I'll have the rest of him later for my supper! Mmm. Scrummy!*'

The witch laughed that heinous howl once more, then Her head withdrew and the wind, carrying Ben's headless body within it, followed it through the hole in the roof. I heard a roaring, gushing sound and saw the force of that wind fan the flames into a fervent conflagration.

I could still smell that smell; that odious smell entrenched in my nostrils. I screamed and I screamed and I screamed . . .

I remember another face staring at me. It was just a shape of blurred fuzziness but I knew it was a face; a face of warmth and kindliness. I felt a cool soothing hand on my forehead and heard the soft compassionate voice of Dr McDonald.

'Bad dream, laddie? Never mind, it's over now. All over now.'

The coolness left my brow and the voice became more subdued, as if spoken to another part of the room.

'I'll leave you some sedatives. Give him a couple of these if he gets this restless again. But no more than four a day, mind. His body's as fit as a bell but his mind is troubled. Not surprising after what he's been through. I'll pop in and see him again tomorrow but if you need me to come in any time, night or day, mind, you just let me know.'

There was a pause. 'If – if things don't improve in a week or so, I think we'd better see about letting a child psychologist have a look at him. Nasty things, shocks like this. But Johnny's tough—'

The face turned and was looking at me again. It smiled.

'You're as tough as old boots, aren't you, Johnny m'lad?'

I peered beyond the face. My parents were standing at the foot of the bed. My father was smiling a weak but genuinely compassionate smile. My mother just regarded me with a look of cold indifference.

Dr McDonald picked up his bag.

'I'll see you out, doc.' It was the voice of my father. He shook Dr McDonald's hand and the two men disappeared, Dr McDonald nodding politely to my mother as he left the room.

My mother and I were alone. I closed my eyes tightly but I could still feel her frostiness approach me. I knew I would soon hear her voice with that inflection preluding its admonition.

'Johnny! You were lucky this time.' Her words cut through me like cold, piercing icicles. 'Look upon this as a warning, Johnny. Next time – if you're ever this naughty again, that wicked old witch will get you, my boy, sure as eggs is eggs and—'

I had to shut her up. This time I could not suffer the heartlessness of her words in my customary submissive silence. And I had to know. I had to have the truth confirmed to me.

'Ben? – Ben? Please tell me!' I stuttered.

There was a long pause. Although I couldn't see her, I knew she came close to me for I could almost smell her bitterness on the frosty fetor of her breath.

'Ben?' she answered with the exaggerated sarcasm of feigned surprise. 'Oh, Ben's been taken, Johnny, He must have been a very naughty boy, mustn't he? A very naughty boy indeed!'

Still I didn't cry. I didn't feel sadness or fear any more. These things were replaced by another emotion. Anger; an anger which forced my ears to shut out the rest of her cruel obnoxious words.

In the silence of my mind I vowed, there and then,

that I would avenge the taking of poor Ben. My anger rose in me till it could not be contained. I opened my eyes and saw my mother staring at me with her obdurate frigidness, her eyes giving out little frosty glints of derision.

'I hate the wicked old witch and I hate you! I'll send away the witch who took Ben. I'll send Her away, back to where She came from. I'll send Her away, do you hear me! I'll send you all away! Because I hate the wicked old witch – I hate you all!'

I was screaming out with the frenzy of my anger. Suddenly, I heard my father running up the stairs. I remember him coming into the room and looking dumbfounded at my mother's cold and vacuous stare. He put a wary restraining arm around her and led her away.

I was alone again; alone with nothing but my vision of Ben's paralysed face frozen in his tomb of petrified whiteness.

CHAPTER 4

On the orders of Dr McDonald, I spent the next three days in bed. But I didn't mind. The harrowing events of that night had temporarily restrained the natural exuberance of youth. I was content to exist in my own world of introspection.

Dr McDonald would come to see me every day. He would always ask me how I was feeling and I would always answer, 'Okay.' He belonged to that kindly old breed of family practitioners which now sadly seems to have disappeared off the face of the earth. I liked Dr McDonald. I remember he would look at me with that shrewd and knowing smile of his and say, 'Is there anything troubling you, laddie?'

When I shook my head, he would lift his bushy white eyebrows and look me deep in the eyes. 'Johnny, you would tell me if there was, wouldn't you? That's what I'm here for, laddie, to help the unburdening of troubled young minds. Believe it or not, I was your age once. I know it's not easy growing up, Johnny, having to face the tragic things that sometimes happen in life. But this was an accident, y'know, laddie. Not your fault. If you're blaming yourself, you mustn't!'

He looked at me and grinned. 'I insist on seeing my patients smile. So let me see one. Now! And that's an order!'

I smiled. Because I liked him, not because I felt like it. I wanted to talk to Dr McDonald but he could never have understood the truth. This truth could not be identified etched in the silver nitrate image of an X-ray film or read from the mercury of a thermometer. For all his abundant knowledge tempered with kindly compassion, this truth was not part of his perception.

Only my mother had the insight to behold this truth. It was an insight she had cunningly used to her advantage all my life, like a cruel despot waving the deterrent of abject fear to goad a subject into loyal and obedient submission. And she was a master at it.

In my understanding of these things, I wasn't blessed with the blinding light of revelation like Paul on the road to Damascus. Its dawning was slow and gradual and only fully came with the erudition and maturity of years.

At the time, I suppose I only really understood that I hated my mother because she hated me. But I couldn't understand why she hated me so much. I knew I was naughty sometimes but even my childish wisdom perceived the degree of her hate to be disproportionate and inequitable for such minor misdemeanours. I supposed it might be because she blamed me for being born a detestable boy. But the unfairness of such loathing for something outside of my control was difficult for me to perceive.

I wanted to ask her, 'Why do you hate me so much? Why do you want that wicked old witch to take me away?' I wanted to please her. Even then, I would have done anything to make it all right again; to make her love me and make the guilt of my hating her go away.

But I had acted unforgivably by my audacious display of arrogance and anger in the face of her reprimand. To my mother, such things were viewed as an undermining of her authority and were totally indefensible. From that time on, I was unworthy even of receiving her admonition. I was a lost cause; totally and irrevocably.

During those days of confinement in my room, I would see her only three times each day. When she graced me with her presence to bring me food and drink, she didn't speak, she didn't even deign to look at me. She simply brought in my tray, set it silently down on the table beside my bed and left again.

That is, except for two occasions. The first was the morning after my impertinent outburst. By this time my anger had cooled and I wanted to tell her I was sorry but she never gave me the opportunity. I remember she came into my room with my tray bearing a covered tureen from her Sunday-best china. There was a smile on her face and my heart leapt with joy with the thought that, perhaps, I was about to be forgiven.

'I've prepared you something special for your breakfast, Johnny!' she said, setting the covered dish down on the table. I stared at her, trying desperately to discern a hint of warmth in her words. Instead, there was something in her manner that forewarned another act of cold-heartedness but which, in my desire to perceive clemency, I suppose I chose to disregard.

As my hand went to lift the lid from the dish, I remember thinking that my 'special' breakfast didn't have that wonderful smell of freshly cooked bacon and eggs or sausages; in fact, it seemed to have no smell at all.

I lifted the lid and peered in. I wanted to vomit there and then but was determined not to allow her the satisfaction of witnessing my weakness. It was the silvery slime of their trails I first noticed; then their glistening blackness.

My mother gleefully observed my expression of repulsion. 'What's the matter, Johnny?' The coldness of her sarcasm struck like daggers into my heart. 'Are the slugs and snails not to your liking? Or is it because I couldn't find any puppy dogs' tails to go with them? I am sorry about that but puppy dogs' tails are not easy to get hold of. I think they must be out of season!'

She took the cover from my trembling hand and replaced it on the tureen, almost joyfully observing the repulsion conveyed in my eyes. 'Never mind. I'll leave it here, shall I? You might fancy your breakfast later!' With that, she laughed, a cold callous laugh, turned her back on me and was gone. I waited for her footsteps to descend the stairs and then I rushed into the bathroom. I threw up till there was nothing left inside me.

I think it was on that night I first had that dream. It was the first of countless visits to that bizarre courtroom. It was a court similar to the ones I had seen on the *Perry Mason* series on television. I could clearly see the spectators in the public gallery, the jurors on their benches and the judge sitting on Her lofty chair. At the onset of the dream, they were all just blurred unrecognisable faces but, as the dream progressed, those faces took on real identities.

I saw the judge transformed into the repulsive figure of the wicked old witch, as beheld in my nightmare the night before, but dressed appropriately in the garb of office. She still wore Her shabby black cloak and a black conical hat with straggly strands of filthy white hair poking down from it. But now, perched on top of the hat, sat a judge's wig, its sides flopping down, looking more like the ears of a sad spaniel dog. She was an indecorous sight and I suppose that most would have considered the way I envisioned Her nothing short of ludicrous and laughable. But, I remember distinctly, She struck abject terror into my heart; a terror which increased even more when I saw my mother's face among the jurors. Then that face, looking austere and grave, was replicated on the shoulders of each of the other eleven. Each juror became a living, breathing clone of my mother. They all moved together. They all blinked their eyes together. They did everything together just like glove puppets worked by a puppeteer with twelve hands.

I looked at the faces in the public gallery. Again, each one became that same face; my mother's face, wearing the same expression, identical in every detail.

The judge banged Her gavel. Except it suddenly wasn't a gavel. It became a stuffed black cat. The witch was holding it by its rigid tail and was banging its head on the desk. I remember seeing Her broom, an old-fashioned besom, propped up against the wall behind her.

Bang! bang! bang! '*This court is now in session to hear the evidence in the case of one Johnny Smith, an extremely naughty and very ordinary little boy! Who is the counsel for the defendant?*'

In my dream, there was a prolonged silence.

'*Is there no one who will defend Johnny Smith against the naughtiness and ordinariness of which he is accused?*'

I scanned the courtroom for my father. But his face was nowhere to be seen. Where was my father? Why wasn't he here now to defend me and protect me?

'*Ah well. Never mind!*' sniggered the old witch, '*It would only have wasted time. You only have to look at him to see he's guilty!*'

My cloned mothers rose from their seats on the jury benches. In one ensemble voice they shouted, 'Guilty!' Then my mothers rose from their seats in the public gallery. Again the shout, 'Guilty!'

'*Guilty, eh!*' sniggered the judge. '*Ah well. As I said, guilty written all over his face! Do you, Johnny Smith, have anything to say before I pass sentence?*'

I found no words to reply, which was just as well because She gave me no opportunity. The judge carried on without a pause. '*You have been found guilty of being an extremely naughty and ordinary boy! But you are not yet quite naughty or ordinary enough to be taken away and gobbled up! Your slugs and snails and puppy dogs' tails are not yet ripe enough or juicy enough for gobbling! But give it time, Johnny, give it time! I know I will see you standing in the dock again and, next time, my verdict may be different. But, for now, I will have you bound over to your mother's custody to be dealt with as she wishes. When you become as naughty and as ordinary as your friend Ben Jenkins was, I will certainly take you away and gobble you up. Now, he was scrummy! He was very, ver-ry scrum-my indeed!*'

As the dream faded from my perception, the last three words of the witch's judgement seemed to reverberate around my mind and, somehow, their sounds became indelibly fused with my own real screams of terror. It was always my father who rushed into my room when I started screaming; never my mother. He would pour me a glass of water and take out two of the sedatives from the bottle. My hands would be so sweaty and trembly, it was sometimes difficult to pick the tablets up out of my father's palm.

It was then, more than ever, I wanted my father to put his arms round me; to comfort me. But he would just sit there on the side of the bed, looking sad and dejected, and stay with me until he was sure I had drifted back into the comfort of a sleep which was dreamless.

I was in one of those deep, restful and untroubled sleeps that morning when I was awoken by my mother roughly shaking my shoulder. There was no smile or softly spoken expressions enquiring after my welfare. As I rubbed the sleep from my eyes I saw the back of her walking out through the bedroom door and heard her emotionless voice addressing someone in the hallway.

'You can go in now!' it said. Then, without turning round, without even a word of comfort to me, her slight bony figure was gone. I heard her footsteps walking back down the stairs.

A man entered my room; an enormous man wearing a three-piece suit and with a bushy black moustache. He smiled, walked over to my bed and sat down on its edge.

'Hello, son!' His voice was as enormous as his girth. It was the kind of voice which, in those tender years, would have coerced me into immediate attention. It was a voice of authority and influence.

The man stared at me for a while, then he took out a small notebook from the inside pocket of his jacket.

'I just want to ask you a few questions – let me see—' He referred to a page of writing in his notebook. 'Yes! It's Johnny, isn't it? Just a few questions, Johnny.'

I knew immediately what he was and my mind was filled with dread. I was convinced my mother had called him in to investigate one of my, as yet, undisclosed misdemeanours. I searched my brain in an attempt to identify what particular bit of mischief this might be.

'You – a policeman?' I stammered, desperately hoping my fears would be allayed.

The man studied the anxiety on my face for a while. 'That's right, son!' he boomed.

I felt sick. I could actually feel my face physically drain of colour.

'Name's Dixon. Sergeant Dixon—' the booming voice continued. 'You can imagine the jibes I get back at the station about a name like that with Jack Warner still doing his *Dixon of Dock Green* on the telly! But why don't you just call me Ted? Okay, Johnny?'

But I wasn't going to call him Ted. I'd made up my mind I was going to call him sir; showing grovelling respect, I reasoned, was the only chance I had.

'What – what questions? You – you said you wanted to ask me some questions, sir?' I managed to splutter out.

Sergeant Dixon observed my sullenness. 'Dr McDonald tells me you've not been feeling very well after the incid – after what happened in the tree house that night. That's why I've left it a few days to come and have this little chat with you. I'm sorry to ask you questions about what happened but I'm afraid I have to. It won't take long, Johnny. Then I'll go and leave you in peace.'

I didn't know whether to feel relief or not. For some reason, I wanted to cry but I didn't. In an effort to restrain my tears, I remember lowering my gaze to the bedclothes and concentrating my mind on that vision of Ben's face paralysed in its shrine of whiteness. Its image made my sadness turn to outrage.

'You going to arrest Her, sir?' I suppose I blurted that out in my exasperation that the taking of Ben would never be avenged, but as soon as I'd said those words, I regretted it.

Sergeant Dixon's face looked puzzled. 'Arrest who, Johnny?' His voice was softer now. Not booming like before but suppressed as if uttered in a confidential whisper.

I looked into his eyes and inhaled sharply, almost as though I were trying to suck back my words into unspoken thoughts.

'Arrest who, Johnny?' The confidential whisper was repeated.

'I – I dunno, sir! Just confused about things, I guess.'

There was a long pause while Sergeant Dixon assessed my disorientation. I remember expressing a silent prayer of gratitude to Dr McDonald for his counsel to the sergeant about my 'not feeling very well'. Sergeant Dixon let the question drop.

'What were you and – and – er,' he examined his notebook again, 'Ben – doing up there in the tree house at that time of night, eh, Johnny?' The booming voice was back.

'Just talking, sir.'

'You told your parents a lie, y'know, son.'

I looked ashamed and nodded my head.

'A midnight feast, was it?'

Again I nodded. Sergeant Dixon smiled. 'That tree house looked a great place.'

I nodded for the third time.

'Have matches up there, did you?'

I looked culpable. It was the first time I had even considered that our other offences, like the things we 'borrowed', would ever be discovered and added to the irrefutable transgression of lying to our parents.

Sergeant Dixon's voice sounded more compassionate. 'Don't worry, son. We already know you took a box of matches and some candles up there. We also know you didn't start the fire. But it's part of my job, Johnny, to warn boys like yourself about playing with dangerous things like matches. Now, you won't do it again, will you?'

I shook my head in a firm gesture of confirmation that I wouldn't.

Sergeant Dixon got up to leave just as my mother brought my breakfast tray into the room. This time the air was filled with the sudden and wonderful aroma of bacon and eggs. She nodded at the policeman, silently set the tray down on my bedside table, turned, walked out and waited on the landing to show him from the house. All this was performed without even giving me the courtesy of a glance or a smile.

The sergeant began to walk away, then he stopped and turned again to face me. 'Something smells great, Johnny. I always think that's the one good thing about not feeling too well – being waited on in bed. Enjoy your breakfast, son.'

He got to the door, then he stopped and turned again. 'Oh, Johnny! Your best friend was he, this Ben?'

I nodded.

'I know it seems hard on you now but you're young. You'll get over it. You'll get over it, son.'

He smiled and left. I knew he was wrong about that. I would never get over it. I would never forget that harrowing image of Ben's face frozen in his tomb of petrified whiteness. But Sergeant Dixon was right about one thing. The wonderful smell of my breakfast made me realise just how hungry I was. For the first time in three days, I felt I could actually enjoy a hearty meal.

I began to eat. Then I heard my mother's footsteps coming up the stairs after showing Sergeant Dixon out. She came into my room.

'Johnny Smith—' she began, in a voice dripping with patronising contempt, 'you mark my words, Johnny Smith, and you mark 'em well. If the wicked old witch doesn't get you, then one day, that policeman will. One day, and I don't think it is too far away now, you'll be naughty enough for one of 'em to get you. It's what you deserve, Johnny Smith! It's what you deserve!'

I said there was a second time she spoke to me. And that was it. Suddenly, I didn't feel hungry any more.

CHAPTER 5

Dr McDonald came the next evening and I was pronounced well enough to be allowed out of my bed. First, we went through the usual routine of 'How are you feeling today, laddie?' and me answering, 'Okay.'

'You're not to go outside yet, mind. But, you can sit downstairs and watch some TV. That should cheer you up a bit, eh?'

To be honest, I wasn't sure if my emancipation from my sickbed was a blessing or a curse. For one thing, being downstairs would bring me into closer contact with my mother and subject me to more of her animosity. But, for Dr McDonald's sake, I had to feign a pleasant smile of gratitude at hearing his 'good news'.

'Your daddy tells me you're still having those bad dreams though, laddie. I think we'd better arrange for you to have a wee chat with a friend of mine at the hospital. What do you say?'

'Is he a psych – a psychol – 'gist?'

Dr McDonald looked at me with a surprised grin. 'A psychologist. Aye, that he is. You do know some big words, don't you, laddie? Tell me now, do you know what a psychologist does?'

I shook my head.

'Well – How can I explain this? A psychologist, Johnny, is a doctor who sorts out people's problems, things that are worrying them, like bad dreams and such. He'll just ask you lots of questions and try and find out why you're having them and then – well, try and put your mind at rest so you don't have them any more. That sounds okay, doesn't it, laddie? There's nothing to worry about. He'll do nothing to hurt you.'

'S'pose not,' I said, demonstrating a certain apprehension.

Dr McDonald's grin grew wider. 'Och! You'll be all right, Johnny. A big, strong laddie like you.'

And so my visits to the child psychologist were arranged.

During my days downstairs, I grew restless. The time spent with my mother passed in the condemning silence of her rancour. Mostly, she ignored me completely. At meal times, she would slam my plate of food down on the table, without a word, without even looking in my direction.

I looked forward to my father coming home from work. But there was something strange about him now; he seemed different, no longer that same smiling, kindly man he used to be. There was a sombreness about him; dolorous and gloomy. He became intolerant of my boyish chatter and had lost his enormous appetite. At supper time, he would merely pick at his food, push his plate away and go and sit in his favourite chair and suck on his old pipe, lost in his own private thoughts.

It was not a happy time in the Smith family home but,

after a while, I realised it would not improve. It had become the new standard by which I now judged life. My former ordinariness was replaced by a banality even worse.

I began my visits to the child psychologist. My father arranged to have time off work to take me. I started to look forward to them. It seemed the doctor was the only person in my life who actually wanted to talk to me.

He asked me lots of questions; questions about Ben and that night in the tree house; questions about my parents; questions about the recurring dream, which was still making me scream out at night. I wasn't always truthful with my answers.

Sometimes, he would show me funny pictures, like big ink blots, and ask me what they reminded me of. One of them reminded me of the wicked old witch but I didn't tell him that. I told him I thought it looked like a butterfly. I think he knew when I lied to him because he would always look at me with a strange quizzical expression, curl up his bottom lip, and exhale a curious gasp which sounded something like air being let out of a balloon.

Somehow, the days passed. Eventually, I was allowed outside in the garden to play in the decaying embers of the late summer sun. I remember looking up at the charred blackness of that old yew tree. It looked so sad; only a few wisps of its once lush foliage were left, struggling to survive. Every vestige of the tree house had been removed; that is, of course, if any of it had remained undestroyed by the fire. I never asked. That night was never spoken of at home and I had no inclination to mention it.

Even the forest looked sorrowful. There were no butterflies to grace its shabbiness with their beauty. And leaves were already beginning to fall from the deciduous shrubs at the forest's edge.

My eleventh birthday came and went. I received a card from my Auntie Pat and one from my father who, I'm sure, without even mentioning it to my mother, had written 'from Mummy and Daddy' on the inside. He bought me a construction set and a comic book but, otherwise, the day was not made special for me. My mother didn't bake me a cake or even wish me 'Happy birthday'. She spoke to me only when she absolutely had to; always curtly, never once lovingly.

I was glad when late September came and it was time to go back to school. I even began to enjoy school, especially English. I suspect my newfound studiousness was due to my enforced solitude during that summer of imprisonment. I started reading a lot then, you see, as a release from the boredom of silence. But one book I never read for myself was that big old book of fairy tales my mother used to read to me. As I have said, by this time I had become a lost cause to her. She didn't read to me from its pages any more, so my big old book of fairy tales remained firmly shut, gathering dust on the top of the tallboy in my room.

I began to write essays and poems, much to the delight of Mr Anderson, my teacher. I know he didn't regard my talent as exceptional – as I have already said, there was nothing at school at which I excelled – but he actively encouraged my interest.

But, at home, nothing changed for the better. In fact, things got steadily worse. To say my mother was indifferent towards me is the understatement of all time. As far as she was concerned, I didn't really exist.

I remember the excitement and pride I felt bringing

home a school report giving me an 'A' for English. Mr Anderson had written the comment, 'Excellent work. John has shown much dedication and promise this term and has produced some admirable and imaginative essays and poems.' But my mother refused even to look at it.

And, as autumn transmuted itself into the chilliness of early winter, I began to notice a serious deterioration in my father's condition. He hardly ate at all and, with the waning of his strength, there seemed to come a decline of his will.

He had always been a powerful man. I remember him building the tree house, effortlessly carrying up bulky planks and nailing them to the yew's boughs, whilst being precariously perched on the upper rungs of that huge ladder of his. It had all seemed so easy for him then but now he began to look wasted. All he wanted to do was sit in his favourite chair, sucking on his old pipe, staring into the dancing patterns made by the coals on the fire.

One night, while my mother was in the kitchen doing the dishes, I sat on the floor by his feet staring up into his sorrowful blue eyes. He looked at me and seemed to read the unstated question written on my frown.

'Don't you see, Johnny?' he whispered; his voice was so anguished it was almost a whimper. 'It's that bloody tree house! If I hadn't built it, none of this would have happened. It's my fault, Johnny! All my fault!'

Then he did cry; great lamentable sobs. It was the only time I ever heard him cry. It was the only time I ever heard him swear. It was the only time the tree house was ever referred to after that night Ben was taken.

Soon after that, he didn't come to the supper table any more. My mother would take a tray up to their room every night and bring it back down again, the food virtually untouched.

Often, after I had gone to bed, I would lie awake listening to the muted footsteps of my mother going into their room and coming out again. Sometimes I would hear a whispered conversation on the landing outside. I could never grasp the words being spoken but I recognised the kindly strains of Dr McDonald's voice.

I didn't see my father again.

One night, when I was in bed, my mother's footsteps seemed to be rushing to and fro outside with a greater urgency than usual. Later that night, I heard Dr McDonald's voice again from the hallway. The whispers continued for a long time, then there was silence. I knew that silence was a prelude to sadness.

I lay awake, waiting for that inevitable something to happen. After a while, the door suddenly opened and my mother stood silhouetted in the doorway. She looked at me, just long enough to say, 'Johnny, your father's been taken.' Then the door slammed shut, enclosing me in the warmth of that iniquitous blackness.

I welcomed my solitude then. I could cry without displaying my weakness to my mother. And I did cry; piteously. I cried myself to sleep. Up until that time, my bad dreams had left me. But that night, they were to begin again; another recurring dream, different but no less disturbing.

It was the same court, with the same wicked old witch as the judge, the same twelve clones of my mother as the jurors and the same uncounted replicas of her stern, unyielding face present in the public gallery. But it was my father in the dock. I was just an unseen observer to the proceedings.

My mothers were shouting, 'Guilty!' and I remember clearly reflecting that the court had not even heard the charge or the evidence.

The gnarled and warty voice of the wicked old witch was now speaking. '*You have been found guilty of being a very ordinary and naughty father! Very naughty and ordinary indeed! But – as you are much too old to be taken away and gobbled up – as your slugs and snails and puppy dog's tails have long since lost their prime tenderness for gobbling, you will be taken from this place into my forest and work in my service as a woodcutter, chopping up firewood for me to cook those very naughty and very ordinary little boys whose slugs and snails and puppy dog's tails are tender enough for gobbling! – I like those little boys! They're scrummy! Very ver-ry scrum-my indeed!*'

She banged Her rigid stuffed cat down on the desk three times, then came the raucous howl of Her heinous snigger.

I awoke in the sweaty clamour of my terror but, this time, there was no one at my bedside to hear my screams, no one to stay with me till I drifted back into the comfort of a sleep which was dreamless. This time, I was totally alone.

Chapter 6

Harry Smith, the father I loved, was taken on the night before Christmas. I will never forget that night. I finally stopped screaming but I could sleep no more. When the fear of my nightmare finally receded, a terrible coldness devoured me. There is no other way I can describe it; a soggy iciness slithered its way under my quilt into the very sanctuary of my bed and physically nibbled away at the warmth of my substance.

I was encased in a shroud of penetrating dampness which rendered me powerless. I was unable to move. I couldn't even cry any more. I just lay there listening to my teeth chatter. The vibration seemed to rock my brain and assuage it into a numbness which anaesthetised all thought.

I remember the night seemed endless. Its darkness was so complete and the dawn so gradual, I was staring into its emptiness with an abstraction of eternity until finally becoming aware of the dinginess of that cold and frosty daybreak dappling the curtains with smudges of sombre grey.

There were no sounds to herald its dawning. No birds

sang their hymns of praise. This day awoke with a despair which seemed an apt and proper acknowledgement of my own.

But, as miserable as I felt in the chill desolation of my lonely room, I knew it was preferable to the frostiness of the world downstairs which even the warmth of a roaring fire could not pervade.

It was Christmas day but there would be no tree standing in the bay window with its twinkling lights and presents wrapped in brightly coloured paper stacked beneath it. There would be no decorations to enliven the drabness of the faded flock wallpaper in those dreary alcoves of the living room. And I guessed there would be none of the delicious aromas of turkey and chestnut stuffing basting in the oven.

But I was not really concerned at the absence of these trappings of merriment and cheer. In fact, my despair welcomed their absence. My one real sorrow on that Christmas day was that there would be no holly wreath on our front door declaring to all the world that Harry Smith wished goodwill to all men!

That thought made me cry again because Daddy would have wanted that wreath on the door. The tears came easily and in floods. Then other thoughts came crowding in to consolidate my melancholy. I could not give Daddy the new pipe I had bought him and which I had carefully hidden under the socks at the top of my wardrobe in late September, and I would not see him wearing his funny paper hat, carving the turkey at the dinner table. But all these separate reflections of grief became united in one underlying anguish – there would be no goodwill for me this day, either given or received. This Christmas would be spent in a house without love.

I can't be sure now whether it was the intense cold or hunger which finally drove me downstairs. But it was well into the afternoon when I ventured out of my bedroom. I remember I couldn't find my slippers and was wearing only a dressing gown over my pyjamas. My feet were so cold, I had no sense of awareness of them on the hallway carpet as I compelled them unwillingly to carry me down to the antagonism I was sure awaited me.

My journey down those stairs, clutching my mother's present – a pair of woollen gloves wrapped in paper printed with the words 'Merry Xmas Mummy' – was filled with trepidation and fear.

When I first noticed her she was sitting, staring vacantly into the fire. I felt a strange ambivalence. I remember she looked even more slight than ever, her body hunched, her elbows resting on her knees and her hands pressing into the hollowness of her cheeks. There was sadness in her face which somehow evoked compassion, yet a powerful feeling of indignation abruptly rose up and smothered it. I think it was because she was sitting in my father's chair and my immature mind perceived that as an act of unworthiness. But my resentment was somehow restrained by the depth of my sadness.

I cautiously approached her, silently offering my little gift. She was unaware of me at first but, slowly, her hands disappeared from her cheeks and folded into the shadowy hollows of her lap. Her face turned towards me, her gape absent-mindedly finding my outstretched hand. Then her eyes lifted and she scrutinised me with a cold, indifferent stare. I gazed into those eyes but saw no real sadness, just a greater sense of impassivity. She didn't look at me for long, her eyes drifting downwards, following the slope of my shoulders and my outstretched arm, and coming to rest again on the little package I still held out to her in my trembling hand. I didn't exactly see or feel her snatch it from my palm and throw it onto the fire. That seemed to happen so quickly. But, as I stared into the fervour of the flames, watching their dancing yellowness lick the words 'Merry Xmas Mummy' before devouring them with a voracious, ravenous frenzy, I recall thinking only that she had destroyed my gift without even a word of explanation or a glance in my direction.

My father had always told me that the true pleasure of Christmas comes from the joy of giving, not receiving. And I truly think I understood what he had meant. From early January, I would save up for the purchase of my humble gifts, putting every spare penny I had from my pocket money into a large ceramic pig. For me, that pleasurable feeling started when I felt the weight of those pennies grow into a measurable heaviness.

It was wonderful to watch the look in my father's eyes as he tore off, in seconds, the wrapping paper it had taken me hours to apply. His face would beam as he said, 'Johnny, it's just what I've always wanted!' Whether that was true or not didn't matter at all. He knew how to make me feel joy and my heart swell with pride. But now I wondered if that same spirit had ever consumed me when giving to my mother. This year especially, I knew I had bought her gift grudgingly; rather, I supposed, it was done out of a sense of duty or perhaps I was still vainly trying to gain her approval.

It was only by thinking deeply of these things that I restrained my tears while watching the charred embers of her woollen gloves disintegrate to nothing on the red-hot coals of the fire. At that moment, every last vestige of hope at reconciling things with my mother disintegrated with them. I knew then she would always hate me.

I tried to tell myself it didn't matter what she had done with a gift that wasn't given with that true essence of joy but my heart was untouched by logic. It still beheld her action as a cold and callous act of cruelty. My tears could be repressed no longer.

I rushed from the room, into the kitchen and out through the door leading to the backyard. Though I was barefoot, I was oblivious of the biting cold. The day was dull and gloomy and a hoarfrost was forming like fine powdered snow. I ran to the bottom of the garden, knelt down on the frozen ground, and looked up at that sad old yew tree.

Then I howled, 'No, Daddy! It wasn't your fault! I was the naughty one. I caused you to be taken. I caused Ben to be taken. Don't blame yourself, Daddy! Please, don't blame yourself!' I cried till I had no more tears left.

I would have run away there and then except I knew that if I did justice would be served. I believed I would not have escaped the ultimate retribution of a wicked old witch whose all-seeing eyes were constantly roving about the entire inhabited earth just looking for very naughty, very ordinary little boys like me to take away and gobble up.

So, when I could stand shivering and trembling in that bitter cold no more, I summoned up my courage and passively went into the house again; back to my mother's sadistic reign of silence.

I retreated into my misery and, that night, I visited the courtroom to witness, yet again, my father being sentenced to his eternity of servitude, cutting down trees in the old witch's forest. I became a regular visitor to that parody where it seemed, more and more, my mother's derisory roars of 'Guilty!' were directed at me. They became a constant reminder of my own denunciation and shame.

When I could stand my guilt no more, I would scream out my remorseful confession and offer myself up to the old witch's justice to be taken away and gobbled up in return for clemency for my father. I would plead his innocence passionately. He was a good man and I will always love him.

For the next few days, nothing changed. My mother spoke not one word to me and I could never pluck up the courage to say anything to her. More and more I would seek the sanctuary of my lonely little room where I would ponder the mysterious things of witches. Every night I cried for the memory of my father and grieved at his harrowing sentence in the service of the Mistress. I asked that he might be delivered from his ordeal but all I witnessed in my dreams was the damning judgement against him and the heartless delight of my mothers as his sentence was pronounced. His condemnation was also mine. I was just an ordinary, unremarkable and naughty little boy who would, one day, suffer the same fate as his best friend Ben.

I had often wondered how the wicked old witches kept their beady red eyes on all the very naughty boys of the world in order to dispense their justice. According to my mother, there are so many naughty little boys deserving of being taken away and gobbled up, I reasoned there couldn't possibly be enough proper witches to keep their beady red eyes on all of them. All this was made even more obvious when Mr Anderson informed us there were probably around one and a half million little boys in China alone. All these, I believed, needed to be constantly surveyed so the naughty ones could be punished. The thought did occur to me that witches might enlist the help of long-suffering mothers as cohorts in their campaign. Some mothers, I supposed, might even enjoy the work so much they themselves would apply to become apprentices, and eventually full-blown witches, to help redress the balance in ridding the world of boyish naughtiness.

It was my mother's overt and vehement hatred of me which first made me suspect her collusion. But my suspicions were confirmed when, just three days into the new year, I saw her one morning dressed entirely in black. Even her legs were black; blacker, in fact, than the legs of Mrs Jessop's cleaning lady who, my father had said, came over to this country from a small island in the West Indies.

She had never worn black before, especially ebony opaque stockings. In fact, I once remember my father buying her a black dress for her birthday. She had angrily remarked that she would never wear black. 'Take it back where you got it from, you stupid, stupid man! Do you really want me to look like a beanpole's shadow!' So I knew there had to be an extraordinary reason for her to wear it now. She had to be going somewhere special and I thought I knew where that was; to a coven in some deep, dense, dark and unknown forest to meet with more of her kind. Witches always wore black; I knew that from the pictures my mother had showed me in that big old fairy tale book.

When I thought about it, her face had looked more gnarled and haggard lately, especially since the taking of my father, and a big red swelling had formed on the side of her nose. She had told Mrs Jessop it was a large carbuncle. But I knew the truth; I knew it was the beginnings of a big ugly wart which would soon grow a profusion of thick, stubbly black hairs.

*

Auntie Pat was expecting us. She was waiting at the door as we walked up her garden path. She crouched and hugged me.

'Johnny, you poor boy! You poor, poor boy!' she cried as she cuddled me harder and nestled my face into the hollow of her shoulder.

Then she spoke softly to my mother for a while on the front doorstep and, when my mother left to keep her assignation, Auntie Pat took me into the house and sat me down in her big kitchen with a glass of warm milk and a slice of chocolate cake. There were tears in her eyes as she cuddled me again.

'He was a kind man, y'know, your daddy. A very kind man. I loved him! Poor Harry! That's why I couldn't go today, Johnny. Do you see? Can you understand that? I know he was my brother and I don't want to be disrespectful but I'd sooner remember him just the way he was.'

My mind replayed some of the words she had said. '*. . . That's why I couldn't go today . . . I don't want to be disrespectful . . . I'd sooner remember him just the way he was . . .*'

It hit me like a thunderbolt from the blue. Not only did I know where my mother was going but also why she was going there. She had never loved my father. She would enjoy being where he was, to gloat; to bask in her contemptuous delight at his unjust sentence. Yes, that was it, of course. It all suddenly became so clear, it was patently obvious. My mother had been granted visitation rights by her mistress to witness my father's servitude. I could picture her at that very moment, sniggering at him with those cold and hurtful sneers of derision, gleefully watching the sweat run from his brow as he bent his back and chopped those countless logs for his mistress's interminable fires where She would cook those naughty little boys She took away and kept in that cage, fattening them up to eat at a future suppertime. That realisation made me despise and loathe my mother even more.

I knew she would be back; Auntie Pat had told me that. But I would make her go away again; soon, I would make her go away again. Back to that deep, dense and dark place of witches. And this time it would be for good. With all my heart and soul, I vowed that, somehow, some day, I would send her back to the secret forest of her mistress, and that she would never return to hurt me ever again . . .

But the months passed and life went on; a life of silent existence and unremarkable ordinariness. It could almost be said that my mother and I lived separate lives under our one shared roof. It was true I still depended on her and, to give my mother her due, she continued to feed me and clothe me. But, in all other things, I was ignored as if I simply wasn't there.

I was made to feel insignificant; worthless. My hatred for my mother grew but, to tell you the truth, I almost forgot about the vow I made that cold winter's day. Until, that is . . . I remember it was late spring. The days were warm and the garden blossomed. I came home from school one evening to find my mother standing by the edge of the forest.

'Aren't they lovely, Johnny? Look at their graceful little wings, fluttering them about on nature's business. They are dedicated to that cause, Johnny. Dedicated to it! And they hurt no one, do they? Butterflies are so beautiful – they're not made of horrible slugs and snails and puppy dogs' tails, are they?' She smirked at me, then screwed up her thin, angular face in a gesture of abhorrence. 'Not like you, Johnny Smith! When I look at you I still see a detestable little boy made of detestable little things. And, do you know, Johnny Smith, I know I always will!'

It was the first time she had spoken to me in months. I was maddened by her patronising voice. I looked up into the dead branches of that big old yew tree and remembered Ben's face frozen in his tomb of petrified whiteness and, instantly, that same odious stench was entrenched in my nostrils.

I remembered my vow. It was then I knew with certainty that my mother would be going away soon. Very soon indeed.

Chapter 7

Mr Anderson once read us a poem. I can't remember now who wrote it but it was called 'The Satisfaction House'. One verse sticks in my mind; I don't know why. Perhaps because I liked the feeling it evoked; qualities of comfort and peace which somehow seemed eternal.

. . . It has a 'Welcome' mat
where sits a big fat cat,
which grins, 'come in and have a gin,
It's warm inside, I won't deride.
For I'm a place that's special,
I wasn't built with wealth.
Love is me, in me you'll see
That you can be yourself.'

I suppose I once thought of my tree house as that special place; my 'Satisfaction House'. But life's experiences have taught me that nothing is eternal. And even comfort and peace can be cruelly taken away from you when you least expect them to be.

The question is, now I've remembered the tree house, now I've remembered Ben and the events that followed, should I tell them? They probably know most of it already. So perhaps it's best to leave it that way.

I know what they'll say if I do tell them. 'That's a sad story, John! But why didn't you tell us about it before, when we asked you to recount your most perturbing recollections of childhood? It seems much more traumatic than falling off your bike or getting acne.'

They wouldn't believe I simply didn't remember it until now, that my mind had blocked out the terrible pain of remembrance. And, anyway, they wouldn't understand. They couldn't accept what happened as something I should have foreseen; the predetermined consequence of disobedience. They would never believe it was the wicked old witch's punishment for naughtiness. They would never be able to grasp why I thought those other things – fracturing my leg and getting acne – much more traumatic. I didn't deserve those punishments, you see, that's why.

I was simply a very ordinary boy. I was no angel but, looking back on those times now, I don't believe I was really a bad boy – especially when compared to the dreadful things I've heard kids get up to nowadays – except that once, of course. And I've had to live with the guilt of that naughtiness all my life. Because it caused the taking of the only two people I've ever really loved.

No. I won't tell them. It will be our secret.

Part Two

The Halfway House

A halfway house is my abode
My mother chose the witch's road
She went away to that dark domain
Where our paths will never cross again

by Johnny Smith (aged 16)

CHAPTER 8

I stopped having those bad dreams when I went to live with my Auntie Pat. No, actually, I stopped having them before then – they went as soon as my mother went away. It was as if her presence was the umbilical cord which linked me to the witch's spell and, when she left, I was released from that incantation. If I had any doubts about my mother's collusion before, it was now confirmed to me.

I wasn't sure whether the wicked old witch was still able to spy on me without the complicity of Her agent; my mother had told me that witches used their bubbling cauldrons to peer into the nefarious activities of naughty little boys, so I made sure I was good – very good – just in case. But at least I wasn't constantly condemned by my mothers' shouts of 'Guilty!' in my nightmares.

I enjoyed looking after myself for as long as I was allowed to. I found some money in the house and I would go and eat at the coffee bar where I made friends with some of the teddy boys my mother was always deriding. I liked them. I also found out there were such things as teddy girls; it's strange my mother never mentioned them.

My life of being home alone went on for eight days before Mrs Jessop told Dr McDonald she hadn't seen my mother for a while. Mrs Jessop always liked to keep an eye on the goings on in the neighbourhood and, one evening, Dr McDonald knocked on the door. He asked me where my mother was. I told him a lie; I said I didn't know. I just told him she had gone away. I was so worried my iniquity might have been envisioned in the bubbling cauldron of the old wicked witch but it appears She wasn't staring into it at the time; which is just as well, I suppose, because I told the same lies to Sergeant Dixon when he called on me later that evening.

The sergeant asked me lots of questions like, 'When did you last see your mother?' and 'Did she say where she was going?' but I just said, 'I don't know, sir!' I remember he looked at me oddly then took me up to my bedroom where he helped me pack a few things into a suitcase. He asked me if I had any aunts or uncles and I told him about my Auntie Pat. He took me round to the police station first where he asked me more questions and filled in a lot of forms. Then he made some telephone calls and a young social worker called Miss Ramsbottom, who looked straight out of college and had piercing beady eyes which reminded me of the wicked old witch, came and asked me even more questions. She filled in lots of forms too and asked me if I'd like to stay with my Auntie Pat and, later that evening, they took me round to her house in a police car. They said it would just be till my mother came back. I wanted to tell them that she wasn't coming back; in fact, I nearly let it slip out but stopped myself just in time.

'Oh, Johnny, you poor boy! You poor, poor boy!' Auntie Pat cuddled me. She was always cuddling me.

I thought it strange that she wanted to do such things to a loathsome, ordinary boy made of nauseating things like slugs and snails and puppy dogs' tails, but Auntie Pat didn't seem to mind. She actually seemed to enjoy cuddling me.

I remember she tucked me up in bed that night and gave me another cuddle before she turned out the light and, when Uncle George came home, he came up to see me and told me a few jokes. I liked Uncle George. He was a funny man. I liked them both. They were nice people. And, of course, they still are, though I haven't seen them in a long while now. My father once told me that they couldn't have any children of their own. Maybe that's why they liked having me there so much.

Some weeks later, as Auntie Pat cuddled me, she said, 'Now, Johnny. What are we going to do with you if your mother doesn't come back? After all, it's been some time now, hasn't it.' She looked at me and smiled. 'Would you like to stay with us, Johnny? Would you? I mean live here with Uncle George and me?'

There was a wonderful look of warmth and tenderness in her eyes as she asked me that. I nodded my head, unable to remove my gaze from the sincerity written on her face. But, as I continued to look into the depths of her love, pondering an emotion previously unknown to me in all of womankind, her expression abruptly changed to one of thoughtfulness. 'Do you miss your mummy, Johnny?' she asked me, suddenly and without warning.

I didn't have to think about my answer. 'No! But I do miss my daddy.'

Auntie Pat saw the tears in my eyes and she cuddled me even harder. She didn't seem surprised by my reply. In fact, she seemed to sense my response beforehand. She smiled a knowing kind of smile and whispered sternly, almost indignantly, 'I understand, Johnny. I know your mother was hateful to you!' Then, within an instant, that same tender warmth was back in her voice. 'Your father was a kind and wonderful man though, wasn't he?' That marvellous smile returned to grace her face again and, without another word being spoken, a binding contract of attachment was decided between us. I would continue to live with my kind Auntie Pat and her nice funny husband, the man I knew as Uncle George.

Life with Auntie Pat and Uncle George was, I suppose, nothing more or less than ordinary. But I began to understand there are different kinds of ordinariness. And this new kind was nicer. Auntie Pat took a real interest in my school reports. She praised and encouraged me. She would read my poems and essays and when I passed my exams and was accepted at the local co-educational grammar school, they were both really proud of me. I remember they bought me a brand new bike. If only my daddy could have been there, I think my life would have been complete.

I didn't see Auntie Pat much when I lived with my parents. Till then, my mother was the only woman I had really known; she was my one and only reference to this superior gender of beings known as womankind. Now I began to wonder why Auntie Pat treated me so differently, why she was so much more tolerant and why she didn't seem to regard me as something lowly and detestable.

It was a warm afternoon in early summer when these things were, at least, partly answered. I was thirteen then. I had been out on my bike, with a group of kids I used to hang around with, and was putting it away in the shed.

The kitchen window was open and I clearly overheard the conversation coming from inside the house.

'What are we going to do about Johnny, George?'

'He seems happy enough, why should we do anything?'

'What do you think happened to Helen? Is she going to turn up suddenly one day and spoil everything for us? We're only his legal guardians, y'know. We'd have to give Johnny back to her!'

'Gracious, I dunno! Maybe she found some ninety-year-old millionaire and is sailing around the world on his yacht – hey! I wonder if he's got an older sister for me?'

'For goodness' sake be serious, George! There are – there are things about Helen you don't know; things Harry told me in confidence. He told me not to tell a living soul, poor man! But now – well, he's gone and no one knows where Helen is and – well – now things are different somehow, aren't they?'

'Spit it out, ol' girl. Let's hear all the scandal!'

There was a long pause.

'Helen hated Johnny, y'know!'

'Aw, that's a bit strong, isn't it, Pat. I know she was a strict disciplinarian, but hate – aren't you exaggerating just a little bit?'

'No I'm not, George! Hate is not too strong a word for it. Hadn't you noticed the way she treated him?'

'Well – as I say, she was certainly strict and I know she sometimes seemed a bit cool towards him but – we didn't really see them that much for me to form an opinion—'

'Come off it, George, Johnny was scared stiff of her. He was terrified, especially after that night – you know, up in that tree house when his friend Ben was – oh, George, I felt so sorry for Johnny then!'

'What's all this leading to, ol' girl?'

There was another pause, even longer.

'Johnny is not Harry's child.'

'What! Whose is he then?'

'Oh, George – Harry came round to see me one night when you were on night work. It was soon after the accident. He was at his wits' end. I think he just needed someone to talk to; someone to confide in. He could see what Helen was doing to Johnny but he didn't know what to do about it.'

'What do you mean?'

'Helen was abused by her father as a child. He led her a terrible life, apparently. Used to rape her frequently – she ran away from home and got in with a bad lot, a gang of those teddy boys. She was raped again and – well – Johnny was the result!'

'So – where did Harry meet her?'

'It was soon after Johnny was born. She was living at that home for unmarried mothers. You know, that one in Addlestone. Harry was doing some contract work there. Took to the boy straight away. He really loved Johnny, y'know. Offered to marry Helen just to give the boy a proper home and a proper name. Never loved her though. It was a loveless marriage right from the start. Do you know, he told me he never once slept with her. They had single beds in their room. Always had from the beginning. After her experiences, she never wanted to know another man in that way again – can't say I really blame her for that, I suppose. But it left her with a hatred of men – all men! Young or old, it didn't matter. She only tolerated Harry because he provided for her. And he only stayed with her for Johnny's sake.'

'But – then why didn't you tell me all this before, Pat? Johnny's been with us over two years now!'

'Oh, I don't know, George. I suppose because I promised Harry I wouldn't. But anyway – it was Johnny she really vented her hatred on. Harry said she tried to give herself an abortion when she first found out she was carrying and when that didn't work, poor Johnny became a constant reminder of her painful past. When he was born, apparently, she wouldn't even look at him. And Harry said she never spoke to the boy. Wouldn't even give him the time of day except to berate him and scare him silly with stories of witches coming to take him away for being naughty. Poor Johnny! Poor little soul! It wasn't his fault, was it?

'Poor Harry didn't know what to do. When he spoke to her about it she would tell him to keep his nose out of things because Johnny wasn't his child and he had no right to interfere. What a thing to say to him! Poor Harry! She led him a dog's life too. He was too kind a man, not strong enough for the likes of her.'

'Hmm! Sounds like she was a bit of an old witch herself.'

There was a moment's silence before Uncle George continued.

'But – how did Harry fool the family? I mean, if Johnny was born before they got married, you must have known, mustn't you?'

'No! No one was invited to the wedding. No one even knew about it. Harry moved away. Said he was going to work down in Kent for a while. Didn't come back for five years or so. Didn't even keep in touch. When he did come back, he had Helen and Johnny in tow. That was about a year or so before I met you. We all just assumed Johnny was his. Well – why wouldn't we? But Mum and Dad didn't like Helen. Wouldn't have anything to do with her before they died.'

'Hmm! Did Harry legally adopt Johnny?'

'Yes. He was a good man, George. Harry did everything that was right for the boy; everything he could, and more. Oh, George – I feel so sorry for Johnny. First his mother, then that terrible thing that happened up in that tree house, then Harry. He seems so sad sometimes, lost in his own little world. What are we going to do? And what has happened to Helen? Is she dead, do you think?'

'I dunno, Pat. I guess that's a matter for the police to sort out. But after what you've told me I think it might be best if she is, or at any rate stays wherever it is she's gone and doesn't bother the boy again. What are we going to do? We're going to make life as normal as possible for Johnny, that's what we're going to do. Poor little bastard – sorry, I didn't mean that. If you're thinking of telling him any of this, don't! Even though we can't adopt him, we're acting in, what is it they call it? Yes! *Loco parentis*! That means he's practically ours anyway. We love him like he was our own son, don't we? And he seems to be getting on all right, at school and such. He's a bright lad, I'll say that for him. All these experiences don't seem to have affected him too much.

'Listen, Pat, I know you're worried about Johnny and now, of course, I can understand why. But kids are resilient, y'know. He'll bounce back! Do okay for himself! And we'll be there for him, won't we?'

'Oh, George. It will be all right, won't it?'

''Course it will, ol' girl. 'Course it will.'

I stayed in the shed for ages. For some reason, I felt ashamed. I didn't want to come out and face them. I had heard of words like abuse and rape and abortion, of course, and, at the age of thirteen going on fourteen, I was egotistical enough to think I knew everything there was to know about almost everything – especially sex. That particular topic, and all its related matters, was the constant playground talking-point and there was a rumour about a girl at school whose name was Joan Foster, as I recall. She was in the fifth form and no one had seen her for some time. It was said she was raped and had to leave school to have an abortion. I used to see her female friends huddled in groups in the playground. They talked about Joan all the time. Some said they felt sorry for her, others said she was a tart and deserved everything she got.

My perception of the feminine gender was now more confused than ever. The way my mother used to expound their 'sugar and spice and all things nice' qualities, I was convinced girls could never be naughty. My indoctrination made me perceive them as paragons of virtue and light. But, at school, I had seen the older girls with boys behind the bike sheds, kissing and touching their bodies in naughty places and making those funny little sighs and moaning noises. I realised they were sounds of pleasure and I could only conclude that the girls seemed to enjoy doing those things just as much as the boys did.

I remember the headmaster saying in assembly one morning that '. . . the practice referred to in the current vernacular as snogging—' He coughed. '—has reached epidemic proportions and has to stop! We have had complaints about our pupils unashamedly doing it in public places, whilst still wearing enough of their uniform to be recognised. It is bringing the fine name of Compton Grammar School into disrepute and anyone caught will be punished severely!' I remember his face went bright red when he said that and some of the girls were sniggering at him. He tried to allay his embarrassment by adding, 'In my days in the army, we were told that a cold shower would help stop the sap from rising – it worked for us lads back then, it'll work for you lads now. And, I presume, it will dampen even a young lady's ardour too!' Nobody laughed at his joke but those same girls whispered and sniggered again and Mr Hacker went even redder.

But his warnings didn't stop them. I used to see them in the park behind the bushes by the playground. They were so engrossed they didn't even notice me. I didn't watch long; I used to get strange feelings and my willy went hard so I would run back home and take a cold shower. But even cold showers didn't make the strange sensations go away. I was scared the wicked old witch could see my penis stiffen in the sapient abyss of Her bubbling cauldron. I thought it was unfair that girls could seem to do anything they liked without fear of punishment while boys were always risking Her retribution; of being taken away and gobbled up. But such was the inequitable unfairness of being born a boy. I could do nothing but make the best of it.

Often, at night, I would think about those girls and those same nice feelings would sweep over me. Once, I felt a stickiness in my pyjamas. It was a pleasurable sensation but afterwards I was scared. I knew what I'd done was naughty and I was sure that, this time, I would finally be adjudged guilty enough to be taken. But I wasn't taken. And, after the fear subsided, the dread of the wicked old witch seemed to subside with it. Yet, I still tried to suppress those feelings as much as I could, just to be on the safe side.

I had some idea why these things were happening to

me. A short while before, the boys were segregated from the girls one day at school and our Biology teacher, whose name escapes me now, told us about sex and the changes happening to our bodies. We were all trying hard not to snigger. He had said that sex was a beautiful thing in marriage where two people loved each other but he then warned us boys '. . . not to take advantage of girls at a time when they are at their most vulnerable'. I didn't really understand that. From what I had seen in the park, it had not seemed to me that the girls were being 'taken advantage of'. More often than not, it was them doing things to the boys rather than the other way round.

I suppose my juvenile mind chose to ignore the concept of my unknown grandfather's incest with my mother as being too onerous to contemplate. Instead, my thoughts concentrated on the rape which had led to my conception. My naiveté made me ask myself if girls could ever be completely blameless in a case of rape. There seemed some diversity of thought on that subject even amongst females themselves; at least, that was what I discerned from listening to Joan Foster's peers. But, Auntie Pat seemed to feel my mother was innocent, on that issue anyway. And I didn't think she would have defended someone she didn't seem to like very much. I remember thinking of these things and wondering whether I did right in making my mother go away.

I knew only I felt sad and confused. I was certain of only one thing; that the main reason for my sorrow was the knowledge that the man I had known all my life as Daddy was not my real father after all. It wasn't his fault I was a bastard. In some ways, this new insight made it easier for me to understand why he found it so difficult to express his love for me. I desperately wanted to tell him that I understood and that I still loved him. But I would never see him again; the wicked old witch and my mother had seen to that. No, I could not feel sadness for my mother even with this fresh enlightenment. There was still no compassion for her in my heart. I was glad she had gone away and wouldn't be coming back. After all, hadn't Uncle George confirmed my suspicions by saying that she sounded '. . . like an old witch herself'? No, I felt no guilt over what I had done. It was just. It was deserved.

In my deep contemplation of these things, I had inadvertently leant back against the shed wall, knocking a hanging rake from the precarious support of its rusty nail. The rake dislodged a spade which dislodged a hoe, producing an almighty clatter. The noise roused me from my introspection. Suddenly, I saw Uncle George was standing in the shed doorway.

'Hello, Johnny. Scaring the rats away, are we?'

I tried to smile but, somehow, seemed unable to. I could feel my face blush to a bright crimson.

Uncle George smiled a puzzled sort of smile. 'You okay, lad?' He didn't wait for any kind of answer. 'Why don't you come into the kitchen? Auntie Pat's made a lovely chocolate cake.'

Chapter 9

'Oh, Johnny! You poor boy. You poor, poor boy!'

Auntie Pat cuddled me as she peered into a pock-marked countenance resembling something more like a relief map of the moon than the ordinary, unremarkable face I remembered staring back at me from the mirror just two days before.

She cuddled me harder as she administered her own brand of genuine, if somewhat overstated, sympathy. 'I'm afraid it's acne, Johnny. Oh, you poor boy! It's such a shame that this so often happens at a time when young people are self-conscious enough without being given something extra to cope with. Such a shame. Oh, Johnny, you poor, poor boy! But don't worry. We'll let Dr McDonald have a look at you. I'm sure there'll be something he can do.'

Uncle George had said that one of my pustules, '. . . the third one to the left, on the right of your nose', reminded him of a photo he'd once seen of an erupting volcano called Mount Etna. But Auntie Pat told him to 'Shut up!' and that his '. . . humour isn't appreciated'.

I had, of course, ascribed my sudden outbreak of

rampant, reddened facial pimples, each bearing its own yellow proclamation of erupting pus, to the old witch punishing me for something. But I had only masturbated that once, many months before, and I knew witches were definitely not dilatory in dispensing their justice so I didn't think it could have been for that. Quite frankly, I was at a loss to know what I had done to deserve Her malediction. But, that was the trouble with witches; sometimes their justice seemed not only unfair, but unfathomable.

Dr McDonald obviously didn't know about the retribution of the wicked old witch; the ways of Her kind, as I suspected, were beyond his understanding and perception. He attributed my unfortunate condition to there being '. . . too many hormones rushing around doing ineffable things to inauspicious parts of the anatomy'. I don't think Auntie Pat understood his diagnosis any more than I did because, when I looked at her with an expression which sought enlightenment, she simply screwed up her face into a kind of bewildered smile and shrugged her shoulders.

I knew the medicated cream Dr McDonald prescribed would not provide an antidote to the witch's spell. It was as much an attempt to soothe the anxiousness of Auntie Pat as the tender inflammations of my boils that made me religiously apply the cream twice a day, according to the doctor's instructions. But all that was achieved was an acceleration of the cyclic succession of pustules, pus and more pustules and, after a week, my face was a seething pit of bacterial iniquity.

In desperation, Auntie Pat sought the advice of Mrs Jessop who, it would seem, assumed the role of alternative medical advisor in addition to her responsibilities as a one-woman neighbourhood watch.

I had always had suspicions about Mrs Jessop being in league with that sisterhood of old crones but, when she suggested that I take essence of something or other to 'purify my blood' and apply evil-smelling coal tar to my face which Uncle George said made me look like the Robertson's golliwog, any benefit of doubt I may have given her was removed from my mind. But then, I reasoned, who would be better to contest a witch's malediction than another old witch? So I went along with Mrs Jessop's remedies and suffered the daily ministering of her acrid 'essence' and the painful application of her face packs. Two weeks later, my red pustules with their glowing yellow heads were still as profuse and profligate as ever and even Mrs Jessop admitted defeat. When Mrs Jessop's potions failed, Auntie Pat marched me back to Dr McDonald's surgery.

The doctor peered into my raw and tender face. 'Och! They are persistent little blighters, aren't they, laddie?'

He thoughtfully considered my predicament. 'Think we'll send you to the hospital for some ultra-violet treatment. That should do the trick.' He turned to Auntie Pat. 'I'll make the arrangements for his treatment but, in the meantime, let's cut out all fat from his diet.' He turned back to me. 'No more chips, Johnny. And no more chocolate bars either. We've got to make sacrifices if we're going to lick these little so-and-so's!'

I didn't mind my abstinence from chips and chocolate but the ultra-violet treatment made my face look like a beetroot. I suppose it might be true to say that it did appear to alleviate the condition; if only because it camouflaged the rest of my face to look as red as the pustules themselves. But still, the yellow heads they bore shone out like glowing canary beacons. At school, I noticed other boys with bright beetroot faces. We acknowledged each other with knowing glances.

I then made a momentous decision. If the wicked old witch was going to continue punishing me for something I hadn't done, I might just as well do something deserving of Her retribution. I had already made up my mind what form that naughtiness was going to take. There was a boy at school named Vivien Spivy – affectionately known as 'Viv the Spiv' – who did a roaring black-market trade in the supply of girlie magazines. If acne was going to commit me to the life of a social pariah, I would buy some of the Spiv's magazines to enliven my nights of loneliness.

When I think of the blatant pornography available nowadays over the counter of any corner newsagent, those magazines were, by comparison, totally innocuous. But, in the days of my first risings of sap, those photos of scantily clad lovelies in their high-heeled shoes and suspender belts were the very ambrosia of fascination and delight. Since I had first made the decision to sample their enchantments with my torch under the bedclothes, I had thought of nothing else.

Some of the boys had said doing that made you blind but, after two weeks, my eyesight, even in torchlight under the darkness of my quilt, was as keen as ever, if not keener. I had concluded that the theory was nothing more than a vicious plot, conjured up by long-suffering mothers, to deter their male offspring from this particularly disgusting form of naughtiness.

By this time, I had completely given up my quest to rationalise the perturbing problem of feminine behaviour. It would seem that not all females, despite my mother's contestations, were made of the wholesomeness of 'sugar and spice and all things nice'. Some, like those who posed for the photographs and the girls I had seen with the boys behind the bike sheds and in the park, obviously had a propensity for naughtiness which I found both enticing and stimulating. And they didn't have even one pimple on their face, or on any other part of their anatomy that I could see, as payment for their rude impropriety. I wanted one of that 'unwholesome' kind for myself but, until the opportunity came along, I knew I would have to be content, alone with my magazines, to unveil only in my vivid imagination the scant lacy lingerie which kept their real charms from my judicious eye.

In August, Auntie Pat and Uncle George took me on holiday to the seaside. It was hot on the beach and I had to wear a sunhat to prevent my already inflamed and sensitive face becoming even sorer from the effects of sunburn. It was a miserable time for me. Acne had transformed my ordinary, unremarkable face into a hideous one and I could only gaze in amazement at the preponderance of bikini-clad flesh; young females I was sure belonged to the 'unwholesome' kind, whilst feeling too self-conscious to even go and talk to one of them. I remember thinking that this was what it must be like dying of thirst on a desert island – seeing water all around you but not being able to drink any of it.

I was fourteen years old, it was the awakening of my sexual awareness but the inequity of my life had turned me into a shy, retiring boy unparalleled in his ordinariness. And acne was the one occurrence which had cloaked my face with any kind of distinction. I was glad I was forced to wear my gigantic sunhat, not only to hide my grotesque countenance but also so I would not be noticed wallowing in my lamentable mood of self-pity.

One day on the beach, Auntie Pat observed I was

looking particularly forlorn. I think she knew why I was feeling so miserable because she came over and sat with me and gave me another cuddle.

'You know, Johnny,' she began, 'sometimes life seems to give you a real kick in the teeth, doesn't it?'

I just looked at her, wondering what was coming, knowing in my heart of hearts that no pearls of wisdom could drag me up from the abyss of my doldrums.

She recognised my hopelessness and smiled sweetly. 'There was a time, a few years ago, when I felt miserable like you do now. I didn't have acne, that's true, but life seemed so depressing I thought I couldn't go on with it. Then one day, do you know what happened?'

I shook my head.

'Well, just when things got so bad I was thinking of ending it all—' I must have looked surprised because she smiled and added, 'Yes, you wouldn't have believed that happy, bubbly old Auntie Pat could ever have felt like that, would you?' I shook my head again. 'Well – the very next day I met your Uncle George and, do you know something, Johnny? Since then I've never been so happy in my whole life.

'So you see, nothing stays bad for ever, Johnny. No matter how bad it seems right now. You'll wake up one morning and, although you won't know it then, that'll be your day, Johnny. The very day when things will change for you.'

Of course, I attached no credibility to her remarks whatsoever. She was only trying to cheer me up but I could not have been cheered by all the clowns in all the world giving me an individual performance. There was only one cloud in those otherwise bright and sunny skies – the cloud of woe, which positioned itself over my head from the moment we left the hotel in the morning to the moment we returned to it at night.

But the time finally passed and, on the train journey back to London, Auntie Pat was full of regret that the holiday had to come to an end. She kept saying, 'Wouldn't it have been just wonderful, Johnny, if we could have stayed there for ever and ever?' Then she would hug me again, making my sunburned arms and shoulders, thickly covered in calamine lotion, scream out with indescribable pain. I was just glad my ordeal was finally over.

Two weeks later, on the day I was to return to school, I had good reason to remember Auntie Pat's fine counsel. The morning started inauspiciously enough. It was murky and cold and a fine drizzle was falling. I looked into the mirror to find that no new pustules had emerged on my face overnight. I knew that, in itself, was not enough to mark this day as the one which would change my life but it was, at least, a start in the right direction.

But all the optimism in the world could not have prepared me for what was to come. A new girl had started school that day. I suppose, on reflection, she was just a plain, ordinary looking and totally unremarkable girl who probably wouldn't have received a second glance from boys blessed with less ordinariness than myself. But what made Dorothy Thatcher so special and appealing was her beetroot red face bearing its own beacons of bright canary yellow.

My mind buzzed with conjecture as to what wonderful, delightful 'unwholesomeness' she could be guilty of to warrant the wicked old witch's curse. It was inconceivable; such retribution was simply unheard of amongst the entire feminine gender. Surely, this one was capable of naughtiness in the extreme. I had to get to know her. I had to possess her before any of the other boys realised her lascivious wantonness.

She quickly became known as 'Spotty Dotty', a nick-name she didn't seem to appreciate. I could see that the telltale signs of the witch's castigation had made her a shy, retiring wallflower like myself because at break times she would stand alone in the playground with her head buried in a book. This gave me ample opportunity to get to know her but it wasn't till the third day that I finally plucked up the courage to introduce myself.

'Hi! My name's John!' I had practised saying that over and over in front of my mirror the night before. During my practice runs, it had sounded like a pretty good imper-sonation of John Wayne nonchalance. But, on the occasion of its performance, it came out sounding any-thing but the deep resonant tenor of manliness. It was more like a high-pitched squeal.

She looked up at me nervously. It wasn't until she had deeply scrutinised my profuse growth of red and yellow pimples that she offered the coy, embarrassed smile of an associate in anguish.

'Hi! I'm Dorothy!'

It was my turn to speak but I had forgotten to rehearse beyond my opening gambit. I felt stupid. It was fortunate that my bright beetroot face did not reveal the humilia-tion of my blush. There was a silence that seemed eternal. I had to say something; anything to relieve my embar-rassment.

'Do you fancy going behind the bike sheds with me?'

But not that! Why on earth did I say that? Even now, thinking about that moment, I am filled with humiliation and shame. I knew you had to build up to these things gradually, even with a girl of singular unwholesomeness like Dorothy Thatcher, not blurt it out like a deranged lunatic after only ten seconds. I suppose I said it because, when you don't know what else to say, you spout out the first thing that comes into your mind. And going behind the bike sheds with Dorothy was the *only* thing I'd had on my mind since first meeting her.

I remember she looked deep into my eyes and her smile faded into a look of painful scorn. I was next aware of a sharp stinging pain in my already inflamed and tender face, and seeing Dorothy Thatcher storming off towards the classroom.

I didn't sleep at all that night. My mind was in turmoil trying to fathom the unfathomable mysteries of females. I could tell from her smile that she liked me and, even though my invitation was perhaps untimely and premature, there was surely no need to slap my face. I chose to decide she was just playing hard to get. It was the only explanation which wouldn't irrevocably damage my already damaged ego. That decision made me feel a little better and allowed my mind to recast that painful experience into a meritorious one. Dorothy Thatcher, I decided, was a wildcat when roused and I was more determined than ever that I would be the one to arouse her.

The next day, I positioned myself along the opposing wall of the playground, my own head buried in a book, pretending to read. I noticed that, whenever I glanced in her direction, Dorothy seemed to be looking in mine. I suppose I must have actually become engrossed in the book because I didn't see her approach me.

'I'm sorry I did that to you yesterday.'

Her voice sounded subdued and culpable. We were staring into each other's eyes and my heart skipped a couple of beats.

Then her gaze drifted downwards. 'If you still want to – go behind the bike sheds with me, I mean – well, I guess that's okay.'

She told me some time later that she only relented because she was the only girl in her class who didn't have a boyfriend and she didn't want to be ostracised because of it. I, of course, didn't believe that was the true caprice behind the motives of the one female I had ever seen who bore the visible manifestation of 'unwholesomeness' but, as I concluded then and still conclude to this day, females are unfathomable. If that was what she wanted me to believe, it was all right with me.

At the time, I remember I was mindful only of my own transportation to the dizzy heights of euphoria. The reasons for her reformation were immaterial, my senses were totally consumed with feelings of blissful expectation. I wasn't capable of any lucid thought. The unhygienic consequences of our contact, like the possible propagation of our acne, didn't enter my head. And, even if that thought had occurred to me, I'm sure I would have disregarded it. Propinquity with Dorothy's wantonness was my all-devouring passion. I would have suffered purgatory for just one moment with her.

Chapter 10

I have not recounted these happenings merely as a gratifying interlude to an otherwise ordinary and unremarkable tale. Those heady days during the onset of my sexual awareness were portentous in the stamping of my destiny and have even more relevance in the fact that Dorothy Thatcher ultimately became my wife. It was a disastrous marriage which remained unconsummated. But that belongs to another chapter of my story.

By the time I reached sixteen, my experiences with Dorothy and my keen examination of womankind in general had taught me that the breed of female inspired by my mother's teachings – superior, wholesome, blameless, pure in thought, word and deed, and sullied only through unpropitious contact with disgusting and inferior males – must be too elusive to exist. She was simply the woman of my early perception, the woman conjured up by constant and undeviating brainwashing during my impressionable years and who, like the fabled unicorn, was too perfect to endure in an imperfect world.

Instead, my observations classified females into three basic types. There were the gentle, sympathetic ones like my Auntie Pat and most of the mums of the other kids I met who, I supposed, might be of the 'wholesome' variety but who definitely didn't seem superior and gave no impression that they wanted to be. They seemed happy and content enough to apply their wholesomeness to the gentle and compassionate role of wife and mother.

Then there was the attested 'unwholesome' type. Most of my female peers fell into this category. Not only did they seem to enjoy being sullied by contact with disgusting inferior males but they often actually initiated it. When I first realised they existed, and in such abundance, you can imagine my astonishment.

Finally, there were those who treated all men with disdainful contempt; the viragos who seemed to have the power to cast a spell over even the strongest male and reduce him to nothing more than an obedient henpecked wimp. Females like my mother who reigned over the lives of my father and me with the clench of a vile and cruel oppressor. And Mrs Jessop, who many say drove poor Mr Jessop into a sad and early grave. You know the type I mean, don't you? Imperious, superior and meddling; the type of woman who looks at you as if you were something the cat has just dragged in – something odious and contemptible. The type of woman you daren't look straight in the eye in case she ensnares you in some kind of evil spell. The type of woman who lives among us all but who serves the One that dwells in that deep, dark and secret forest.

I began to think, or perhaps I simply dared hope, that I had become forgotten by their mistress – the wicked old witch Herself – because Dorothy and I continually practised naughtiness, without ever going all the way, of course. And why didn't we go all the way? Only because I could never think of a way of manufacturing an opportunity. I was too young then to hold a driving licence so, even in my wildest dreams, I would never have dared whisk Dorothy off to some dark and leafy lovers' lane where the consummate deed could have been done, even if I had known someone stupid enough to lend me a car. I've heard that joy-riding is a popular craze even with pint-sized kids these days. But do you know, I'd never have thought of stealing a car – even if I did know how to hot-wire one – either for the sheer hell of it, or for the pleasurable pursuit of having my wicked way with Dorothy Thatcher. Neither would any other kid I knew. Such a thing was unheard of in those days.

And Dorothy and I wouldn't have considered turning up at a hotel pretending to be married either, and not just because we would have been seen for what we were – two spotty adolescent kids bumbling and stuttering their way to nothing but acute, red-faced embarrassment. It may have been 1966, the very midpoint of the 'swinging Sixties', but that didn't mean those times were unscrupulous. Kids then still understood that adults hadn't completely given up the battle of upholding what they believed to be decent moral values. We didn't consider something like that because we knew we'd achieve nothing but being sent away again with a flea in our ear. No, the only place we could find to be alone together was the kind of place teenage lovers where we lived had used for years: behind a bush in a busy park where the gates were locked every evening when the sun went down. But we made the most of what we had. And we went as far as our scant concealment would allow. We fondled and we groped, and we enjoyed the enquiring search of each other at every possible opportunity.

But not only were my actions never punished but my

acne, one of the supreme injustices of my life, actually got better almost as suddenly as it had materialised. I was totally bewildered. In trying to ponder this imponderable, the only conclusion I could come to was that witches may be witches but they were still of the feminine gender and, consequently, an even more baffling version of the already incomprehensible.

But I'm meandering. Let me return to my story before I lose the thread of it entirely . . . It is time to tell you more about another of the kind of woman I have just described: one of the overbearing, imperious kind who, I readily confess, has always struck terror into my very heart and soul. It was two weeks after my sixteenth birthday and Auntie Pat called me down from my room.

'Johnny, Miss Ramsbottom's here. She wants to talk to you!'

We went into the living room where the social worker, who I would guess was my senior only by some seven or eight years, was seated in an armchair drinking a cup of tea. She looked up as we entered, and smiled. I say smiled, but I didn't think then that Miss Ramsbottom was capable of a genuine smile; the kind which radiates a warm sincerity. Miss Ramsbottom's smile was merely a lifting of her thin, shapeless lips at their corners and a slight puffing of her already podgy cheeks. It was a gesture of acknowledgement rather than pleasure. A gesture which lasted just long enough to be recognised before reverting back to its former display of sternness and austerity.

She looked at me with her penetrating, beady eyes which seemed to permeate my innermost thoughts. Then she gave her lip-lifting half-smile to Auntie Pat.

'Mrs Wilkinson, would you mind very much if I had a little chat with Johnny alone for a while?'

I remember Auntie Pat first looking a little bemused at her out-of-the-ordinary request. Then she smiled benignly and asked Miss Ramsbottom if she would like another cup of tea. When her offer was declined, she took Miss Ramsbottom's empty cup and disappeared into the kitchen.

When the door clicked shut, Miss Ramsbottom glared at me again and her lips momentarily rose at the corners. She looked strangely preoccupied on that visit, lacking in her normal self-assuredness. No, on reflection, she seemed more than preoccupied, she appeared anxious, almost nervous.

'I wanted to have this little chat with you, Johnny,' she began, a little agitatedly, 'you know, to talk about your future – look, why don't you sit down over here, dear?' With the giving of that directive, she sounded a little more like her normal self, her voice becoming superior and patronising. I remember, she patted the seat of the armchair next to hers and I meekly obeyed her instruction to sit. I stared into her face and noticed that she graced me with another thin-lipped smile of fraudulence.

'Johnny—' she began again, with an inflection which reminded me so much of the ones that preceded my mother's warnings. Miss Ramsbottom paused and her beady little eyes glared in examination of whatever little clandestine musings they were probing. I was certain that even my innermost thoughts were an open book to her. I looked away.

'—we've known each other for – what? Five years, isn't it? I hope you now look upon me as more than just your social worker – more as a friend, someone you can trust. Do you, Johnny?'

She paused for my response. I didn't give her one.

Miss Ramsbottom continued. 'Only, sometimes, Johnny,

I feel – oh, how can I put this? – that you're not always open with me, and friends should always be open with one another, shouldn't they, Johnny?'

Her voice was now oozing contempt. She gave another lip-lifting half-smile before her trickle of words continued their sickly flow.

'I wanted to speak to you about this before but now you're sixteen – well, you're grown up enough for us to be able to speak together as grown-ups. Johnny, is there something you haven't told me about your mother? I don't know what it is exactly, but I've had the feeling for some time that you know more about her disappearance than you've actually said. I mean – if there is something, Johnny, like a favourite place she went to or even somewhere she said she'd like to go to or, perhaps, someone she knew and was fond of, I'd like you to tell me. I know the police have asked you questions like this before – but is there anything you'd like to tell me now? Now we're having our little adult chat?'

I was maddened by her patronising tone.

'Why are you asking me? You should know! You're one of her—' I managed to stop myself completing the sentence. Adding the word 'kind' would have acknowledged the fact that I recognised them both as the witch's crones. And that would have been disastrous for me.

Her beady eyes examined the corridors of my mind for the missing word. 'One of her what, Johnny? I never ever met your mother.'

I had to think fast. 'Er – you're one of her gender! I mean, you're both women. To be honest with you, Miss Ramsbottom, I've never had much success in understanding the intricacies of the female mind. It's quite a problem for us mere males, you know.'

It was a brainwave. It was sheer genius. It was a statement of poetic virtuosity; a piteous submission to the intellectual supremacy of womankind. It actually made Miss Ramsbottom smile; a genuine, sincere smile. Something I had always thought her incapable of.

'My, my! You do have a way with words, Johnny. But – we're not really that hard to understand surely, are we?'

That moment of lightheartedness seemed to make her lose all sense of propriety. She laid her hand on the inside of my thigh, abruptly yet gently, and left it there, stroking my leg almost involuntarily with a delicate rubbing of her forefinger, just long enough to send cold little shivers of excitement up into my groin. I shrieked with surprise at the sudden unexpectedness of it all. Then, seemliness appeared to return to Miss Ramsbottom very quickly. Her podgy cheeks glowed and she removed her hand as swiftly as if she'd grabbed the end of a red-hot poker. She looked at me and smiled again, but not one of her normal fraudulent kind. This time, her eyes seemed to sparkle though they didn't hold my gaze. They looked down and her face blushed to a bright crimson. Miss Ramsbottom was clearly embarrassed. She looked flustered, highly agitated, and sat with her hands clasped tightly to the arms of her chair as if to keep them in check, staring in reddened disbelief at the back of the hand that had fondled me.

Had I known then what I know now, that incident might have made the whole of the rest of my life turn out so very differently. But, even in my wildest fantasies, I could never have interpreted Miss Ramsbottom's little display as anything other than a gesture of simulated friendliness; something designed to win me over, to gain my confidence. I didn't recognise it as an act of spontaneous wantonness. She wasn't one of that 'unwholesome' kind of female, I was sure of that. Miss Ramsbottom had always seemed like a younger facsimile of my superior puritanical mother, incapable of having murky, sullied thoughts or cravings of salaciousness, especially with a lowly and detestable boy like myself. There followed an awkward silence. It was some little while before her embarrassment receded and Miss Ramsbottom felt able to look at me again and continue with her colloquy.

'There is a reason why—' Her voice sounded awkward, her face was still a little flushed. She gave a little cough and tried hard to regain her composure. 'There is a reason why,' she began again, 'I want to be sure you can't give us any clues to the whereabouts of your mother, Johnny. And it really does concern your future. I know it has already been explained to you that if she remains untraced for seven years she can legally be presumed dead and you'll inherit everything that is hers. Not immediately, of course. The estate – that's things like the house and her other assets – is now in the hands of the authorities and, if your mother doesn't come back, it'll be held in trust until you become of age when you can do with it as you will.

'So we must give some thought to these things. You see why it's even more important than ever for us to locate your mother soon, if that's at all possible, so we can clarify your position in all this.'

'She just went away. That's all I know. She didn't tell me where.'

There was something in the way she looked at me then which made me perceive she had discerned my falsehood. She gave her curious half-smile once more. But the look in her eyes somehow seemed to shout out her unspoken words; clear, unmistakable expressions of truth: 'I *know*,

Johnny Smith. I know what it was you did five years ago! I know you sent your mother away to the deep, dark forest of her mistress.'

I looked into her smile – a smile of knowledge somehow fashioned with a scowl of sadness; a cold, callous smile somehow graced with a warm entreaty. 'But She's also *my* mistress,' it seemed to say. 'Show me, Johnny. Please, please show *me* the way to Her too!' I noticed a certain sadness in that smile – it became more a smile of desperation and pity – a smile that begged my help.

Right there and then, I closed my eyes and petitioned the Mistress. I asked that I might know what it was She wanted me to do. And, in an instant, my plea was answered with the conception of a plan which could only have come to me through the power of the wicked old witch Herself.

'It was – it was all so long ago. Perhaps, if I could go back to the house, it might jog my memory. You know, help me to remember exactly what it was my mother said.'

Miss Ramsbottom's eyes lifted in an expression of thoughtful consideration. She smiled again. It was the same fraudulent smile but the look in her eyes was now one of warmth, almost of thankfulness. She whispered, quite breathily, 'Mmm. All right, Johnny. Why not?' She blushed again and leant towards me till her face was very close indeed. I could smell garlic on her breath. 'Look, why don't you call me Joyce? I mean, now we're acting like adults you might as well call me by my first name, eh?' Her lips smiled at me again, the corners of her mouth lifting up higher than I'd ever seen them do before. Then she seemed to stretch out a hand but stopped it short of touching the side of my face. 'Oh, Johnny, this is really quite thrilling. You are a naughty boy, aren't you? Are you excited too?' Then she giggled. She actually giggled just like the girls used to giggle at school in Mr Hacker's assemblies. 'You know I shouldn't do it really, don't you? So you must promise me you won't tell anyone. But I'll see if I can get the keys for tomorrow. Let's say I meet you outside the house around – four-thirty. Is that all right with you, Johnny? You will be there, won't you? You promise?'

Miss Ramsbottom winked at me and I nodded. 'Yes, Miss Rams – er, Joyce! I'll be there. And it'll be our little secret. You can bank on it.'

She had asked me if I was excited. Yes, for some reason I couldn't explain, I was excited; so much so that I just stood there after Miss Ramsbottom left and shook in a delirious frenzy. It was some little while before I could face Auntie Pat again. She, of course, was curious about why the social worker had come to see me and why she wanted to talk to me alone. I told her everything; well, not quite everything. I certainly didn't divulge my arrangement to meet Miss Ramsbottom at my old family home the next day.

Auntie Pat viewed the confirmation of my inheritance with her usual sympathetic consideration. She cuddled me and she smiled. But her smile was somehow cast with a curious sadness. I remember she stared at me then and sighed. There was a long pause before she finally said something I wasn't expecting; something which echoed her true feelings and fears for the first time in the five years I'd lived there.

'Johnny, when your Uncle George and I gave you a home, we did it because we really wanted to. It was done out of love, Johnny, not out of any sense of duty to my brother Harry, even though I loved him dearly. Of course we knew that one day you'd want to leave here and start a life of your own. It's no more than you deserve, to inherit what is rightfully yours. Heaven knows, that mother of yours wasn't very kind to you while she was living there, it's only right and proper she should make it up to you in this way now she's not. After all, she doesn't want the house any more, does she? Maybe, one day, you'll settle down in that house with your young lady – what's her name? Dorothy, isn't it? She's a nice girl, Johnny. Or, maybe, when the time comes, you'll decide to sell it, invest the money, and stay with us for a while longer.

'What I'm trying to say is, whatever you decide, it's all right, Johnny. Just look on your home here as a kind of halfway house. A home where I hope you've been happy. A home where you can stay for as long as you want. Just promise me you won't forget us. Promise me you'll stay in touch.'

There were tears in her eyes. I returned her cuddle and she placed her hand on the one I'd placed on her shoulder.

'Yes, I know, Johnny – Auntie Pat's being very silly and emotional, isn't she? Women get like that sometimes. If you haven't found that out already, you soon will. It's not as though anything's going to happen for a long while yet, is it? Oh, Johnny! Why am I crying like this? It's stupid!'

I remember feeling bewildered. I doubted I would ever really understand women. True, I had learnt they weren't all like my tyrant of a mother but I had never really felt comfortable in any woman's presence – apart from my Auntie Pat's, of course. But tomorrow I had voluntarily arranged to spend some time alone with one of the superior kind. Miss Ramsbottom made me feel more than just uncomfortable; she terrified me. Yet, strangely, the thought of being alone with her in my childhood home also excited me beyond belief.

As my social worker, Miss Ramsbottom had been a periodic visitor to my halfway house. Her visits were quite frequent when I first went to live there though I had seen her less during recent years. In the beginning, apart from her beady little eyes and my knowledge of what she was and who had sent her to spy on me, there was nothing more explicit to explain my immediate loathing of her. She played her role of deception well and I suppose it could be said she even appeared quite kindly, asking me if I was happy living with Auntie Pat, if I had everything I needed, and did I want anything else brought back from the old house?

But, as time went on, those eyes of hers seemed to grow more sinister and piercing and I began to discern her perception; a tacit knowledge of something about me which I recognised as threatening. And now, I needed to be rid of that fear.

I leant back against the gatepost of that old house and looked at its downstairs boarded windows and overgrown front garden. It was once my home but now it was just a shell made of old bricks; a sad and unremarkable memorial to my unremarkable childhood.

I had made many pilgrimages back there before – more so, I suppose, in the beginning when I first went to stay with Auntie Pat and Uncle George. I would just stand in front of that house and stare at its facade, letting my mind replay the events of my formative years.

I don't know why I did it, the memories it bequeathed were hardly pleasurable. They always culminated in the happenings of that last, long, hot summer when an existence that was unremarkable yet bearable became unendurable agony.

Being there evoked both sadness and anger. I would remember Ben and the dear man I still called my father. I would remember the mother I hated and her callous reign of oppressive terror and malicious silence. Yet, that old house still held a morbid fascination; it somehow still bewitched me. But it all seemed so very different now. The fear of it was gone. I felt liberated from the horrors it once contained. They were more like ghosts locked in the closets of its sad brick shell. Standing outside, at least, it felt safe for me to release my remembrances.

But I knew that some things could never remain secured behind its dim and murky fabric. I remember one night, when it was just getting dark, I went down the back alley and peered over the fence into the garden. I saw that big old yew tree bathed in the jaundiced glow of the spooky moonlight and, in the shadowed recesses of its depths, on the very boughs where my tree house once stood, reclined the hideous figure of the wicked old witch. I saw Her clearly. I really did. I knew She was waiting for me. It was confirmation, as if I really needed it, of Her immortality and eternalness. She was still free. She could not be incarcerated. I ran from that alley and have not been back there since.

I was conscious of the net curtains twitching in an upstairs window of a house across the street. It was Mrs Jessop's window. She was watching me. She had seen me outside the house before. Sometimes, she had made a point of coming over to me. 'A little trip down memory lane, is it, Johnny?' she would say in her obnoxious, supercilious way . .

'Gracious, it's so hot today! I thought it would be nice

for me to leave the car at the office and walk here, but now I'm not so sure it was such a good idea. Johnny? Are you all right, Johnny?'

I was so deeply in thought I was completely oblivious of Miss Ramsbottom walking up the front path.

'Er – oh, Miss Rams – er, Joyce! Sorry – must have been miles away.'

Her lips were curling at the corners in their usual insidious excuse for a smile. I blinked my eyes. She looked so different. I had never seen her dressed like that before. Normally she wore sober-looking business suits with a skirt cut well below the knee. But today, she wore a low-cut, loose-fitting blue satin camisole top held to her shoulders with string-like ties and a white pleated miniskirt over her well-rounded backside, so short I could see the tops of her thick-set thighs and the lacy edges of her white cotton knickers as she bent away from me to fumble in her bag. I remember noticing that the sun was turning her exposed shoulders and arms a delicate shade of pink, an uncharacteristic contrast to the shadowy whiteness of the more intimate areas of her she normally kept well-hidden but that today, for some reason, were being flashed in front of my naive and unsuspecting eyes.

'I've got the keys in here somewhere, I know – ah yes. Here they are.'

Miss Ramsbottom spun around and faced me. She was still bending over, peering into the opened handbag clutched to her midriff. I looked into the swell of her cleavage. I really couldn't help myself. Her blouse was so revealing and, bending as she was, there was precious little of her breasts which remained concealed. I had not appreciated Miss Ramsbottom in this light before. She was a very buxom girl indeed and, for a fleeting moment, my mind involuntarily recast her as one of the 'unwholesome' kind of female depicted in the magazines supplied by Viv the Spiv. I shut my eyes and shook my head to purge my unclean thoughts. I knew such notions were debased, especially with a woman of the imperious kind.

When I opened my eyes again she was staring directly into my face, holding up three keys tied with wire and attached to a large white tag endorsed 'Smith 122 Melrose Rise' in a hand that seemed peculiarly detached from her body. Her face was flushed and she looked away from me sheepishly and coyly, pressing the front door key firmly into its lock.

'Why, you are a very naughty boy, aren't you, Johnny Smith? I saw you looking at me just then. Did what you see excite you? Yes, I can tell it did. Why, you naughty, naughty boy!' She giggled once again, sounding just like those girls sniggering at Mr Hacker's attempts to restore some decorum back at school.

I felt a sudden anxiety. Her constant allusion to my naughtiness made me think of her mistress's words to me all those years ago in Her courtroom of my dreams. I suddenly wondered if She had sent Miss Ramsbottom to me as a temptation – to see if I would dare succumb to the heinous crime of naughtiness with a woman of her calling. That one thought instantly dismissed any previous feelings of arousal in one overriding cold sweat of dread.

'Let's get inside quickly, shall we?' Miss Ramsbottom continued excitedly. 'You know, before anyone sees us? Gosh, Johnny, you've made me go all hot and bothered!' And I could see that was true. Her face was so red, it was positively glowing. Her voice sounded strangely urgent, eager and quite breathless.

Despite years of idleness, the key turned effortlessly. She pushed the door ajar, then stopped and turned to face me. 'Now, remember what I said, Johnny. I shouldn't be doing this. You know what I mean, don't you? It will be our little secret. All right?'

I smiled at her. 'I understand, Joyce. Rest assured. I won't tell a living soul!'

I tried to make my remark sound sincere and friendly but she seemed to pick up on some inflection in my voice that momentarily absorbed her. I don't know exactly what it was she discerned but Miss Ramsbottom visibly shuddered, just like, as the expression goes, someone had walked over her grave, and her feigned smile instantly evaporated. For a while, she seemed in a torpor, like a motionless rabbit staring into the headlights of an approaching car.

'Joyce? Miss Ramsbottom? Shall we go in?'

All of a sudden, the curled-up lips returned and she silently pushed open the door and motioned for me to enter. But she didn't stand back. She made me squeeze past her body, already occupying much of the doorstep, seeming to thrust herself onto me as I tried to slither through the narrow gap between her voluptuousness and the doorframe.

'Oh, Johnny! You are an impatient young man, aren't you? A naughty, impatient young man,' she whispered hoarsely as I momentarily became firmly wedged between the two immovable objects.

She giggled again, almost bulldozed me inside, then closed the door behind us with a strange sort of urgency. As I stood in that hallway, the house's closets were instantly unlocked and the ghosts of the past revisited. I thought I felt Miss Ramsbottom's body press up against my own and her hands undo the buttons of my shirt and explore the nakedness of my chest but I can't be sure about that now. My mind was obsessed with so many other things. It was like stepping back through time. I almost expected to see my mother come out of the kitchen. I felt a sudden and consummate terror.

I seem to remember that I pushed Miss Ramsbottom aside and was suddenly enveloped by an atmosphere of dank stuffiness; the stifling oppression of enclosed and unventilated air. With the hall's lower window boarded, it was dull and dingy, being lit only from a small skylight above the stairwell. As my eyes adjusted, I began to notice the little intimate things that had once made this place a home. The alabaster lady – once prized by my mother – still taking pride of place on the occasional table by the living room door, and the miniature glass lighthouse beside it, filled with different coloured sands and with the words 'A souvenir from the Isle of Wight' etched into its seashell base. Memories swept over me in great tidal waves of nostalgia. I felt I was going to drown in them.

I stumbled into the living room. Here fingers of intense golden light from the direct sun outside infiltrated the gaps in the ill-fitting slats that boarded the windows, and motionless clouds of dust hung in the shafts, glittering like miniature diamonds.

In the dismal gloom, the dreary alcoves each side of the fireplace, dressed in their shabby red flock wallpaper, looked even more sombre than I remembered. But, as I stared at these things I had once regarded with contemptuous familiarity, forgotten during the misty haze of absent years, they were suddenly lit with a new flickering brilliance.

The grate! There was a roaring fire in the grate! My

eyes were drawn to the redness of its coals and its dancing yellow flames. I felt its heat and heard the splintering crackle of its red-hot embers. And there, in the very centre of its ferocity, the flames were licking the words 'Merry Xmas Mummy' as a canapé. Then I saw the blackness of my mother's woollen gloves become swallowed by their all-consuming appetite.

My eyes filled with tears. I ran into the dining room and out into the kitchen to the backyard door. I frantically turned the handle and pulled, kicking the door repeatedly and violently. It rattled and vibrated as I manhandled it.

My recollection of that hateful Christmas day had completely disoriented me. I forgot Miss Ramsbottom was there at all until a hand on my shoulder reminded me of her presence.

'Johnny! What on earth . . .'

I turned.

'It's okay, Miss Ramsbottom. I was – I was reminded of something a little upsetting. It – it happened a long time ago. But I'm okay now. Okay now.'

'Do you want to talk about it, Johnny? You seem very distressed. Remember, I am your friend, you know, and sometimes it helps to—'

'No!'

Miss Ramsbottom looked shocked at the strength of my response. She opened her mouth to speak then closed it again without articulating a word. I might have felt pity for her helplessness if I hadn't loathed her so much.

There was a long silence before Miss Ramsbottom finally found her voice again. 'Johnny, I'm only trying to help, you know.'

She looked at me, as if gauging my reaction, but I remained silent and she decided to continue.

'Will you just tell me one thing? Was it there – in the living room – your mother told you she was going away?'

I shook my head.

'Was it here then, in the kitchen?'

I shook my head again.

Miss Ramsbottom looked around the room. My silence gave her the confidence to carry on.

'I always feel a house that hasn't been lived in for a while has a peculiar coldness to it. I don't mean temperature exactly. It's more like – it's lost its soul. Like it's given up its warmth because no one cares for it any more. Am I being silly, do you think, Johnny, or do you know what I mean?'

I shrugged my shoulders.

Miss Ramsbottom stared me straight in the eyes.

'Is that why you wanted to get out of the house, because you sensed its coldness? Because you remembered the coldness of the mother who never cared for you? It's all right, Johnny. Your Auntie Pat has told me your mother treated you badly. This wasn't a very happy house for you, was it?'

Still staring at me, she raised her arm as if to put a consoling hand on my shoulder. Then she seemed to think better of it and withdrew her hand again, almost immediately.

I held her stare for a while but her beady little eyes pervaded the privacy of my mind again like searing red-hot pokers and I was finally forced to look out of the window, squinting at the brightness outside in the garden.

'Was it out there perhaps – in the garden – your mother said she was going away?'

I nodded. 'Yes! In the garden. She said – she said—'

'Do you want to go out there, Johnny? Would it help you to remember what she said?'

I could only nod my head again.

Miss Ramsbottom was still clutching the keys. She opened her palm and picked out the one to the back-yard door. The lock turned easily enough but years of neglect had warped the door and firmly wedged it in its frame. I remember that Miss Ramsbottom had to yank at it furiously before it finally yielded.

It opened with a shuddering groan of reluctance onto the small patio my father had built against the shadowed wall of our neighbour's garage. A profuse variety of weeds had resolutely established themselves in the cracks between the big stone slabs.

I went out and peered into the brilliance of the garden beyond the shadow of the house, and saw the charred skeleton of the big old yew tree, now completely lifeless, soaring like a mournful obelisk. It served as a faithful memorial to the ones who were taken, and reminded me – the one left as a living testimony to those inequitable judgements – of the oath I swore in their remembrance.

I felt intense anger rise up as I ran down the garden, cutting a swath through the knee-high grass interspersed with entwining vetch that linked its tendrils to bridge the hidden pathway. I lashed out at the undergrowth in my fury and grief, fleetingly conscious of the flower beds on either side, once nurtured with loving patient care by my father and now suffused with asphyxiating convolvulus.

It was a sad testimony to the changing nature of things; evidence that nothing remains constant. Just as my father had been so cruelly robbed of his pleasure in this place, his garden itself, the very manifestation of his joy and his peace, had been plundered by the ravages of time.

I reached the yew tree and pounded its charred bark

with my fists, enraged that the beautiful garden he had created with his precious toil and sweat should now be transformed by nature's whim into a thing of such ugliness.

'Johnny! Johnny!' Miss Ramsbottom was chasing me up the garden. She reached the yew and I turned to face her. The left tie of her camisole had slipped off her shoulder, exposing a barely covered breast which heaved in and out as she breathed deeply, brimming over the soft, silky gossamer of a brassiere cup much too small and delicate for her. I could see a large nipple, like an overripe cherry, peering pertly up at me from underneath its dainty lacework. Miss Ramsbottom was so flustered, I don't think she even realised her state of undress. Or, if she did, she made no attempt to cover herself up.

'I've never seen you like this!' she stuttered breathlessly. 'Perhaps it wasn't such a good idea to come here after all. It's distressing you, Johnny. Distressing you so very much.' She appeared to hold out her arms like a siren enticing me onto the alluring rocks of her mistress's retribution. 'Come here, Johnny. I'll make you feel better. I'll make your hurt go away.'

Miss Ramsbottom's beady little eyes were permeating my thoughts again as if, through her very perception, her mistress was observing the testing of my allegiance and devotion. And I would not be swayed in my constancy and faithfulness to Her. I was determined I would pass the test, to be adjudged worthy, no matter how pleasurable the distraction. I looked away from Miss Ramsbottom's obvious charms.

'But you want me, Johnny! I know you do – I've seen the way you look at me sometimes. I've seen that look in your eyes. Well, maybe I shouldn't feel the way I do. I know it's wrong. But I want you, Johnny. Why do you think I took this chance to get the keys so we could be alone together? Come to me. Let me prove how much I want you.'

She wanted me? Yes, I know she did – as a Venus flytrap wants a fly. Seducing it into her inescapable lure of deceit so I could finally be adjudged naughty enough to be taken away by her mistress and gobbled up. She looked at me strangely, at the same time, reaching down for the loose tie of her camisole top, tugging it back up over her shoulder, and withdrawing her alluring bosom from my sight.

'Johnny,' she questioned me, 'why are you so distressed? Why? You know where your mother is, don't you? Where is she, Johnny? Where is she? Tell me! It'll just be between you and me, Johnny. I'll tell no one else. I promise. It'll be all right. I'll look after you now.'

She had discerned my secret. Her persistence and insight had perceived the truth. It was useless to equivocate.

I pointed to the forest. 'She's there! Over there!' I screamed at her. Globules of my spit sprayed her face; a face that was suddenly bleached of colour. Her slender little lips puckered to form a perfect letter 'O' and her beady eyes dilated and moved rapidly from side to side within their sockets. It looked like the face of a big white cod on a fishmonger's slab; a face paralysed in an instant of terror. It reminded me of Ben's face, frozen in his tomb of petrified whiteness.

At that time, I couldn't really understand why she was so afraid. I was only showing her the way, after all; the way to that dense, dark place of witches so she could be with her mistress. In fact, it was She who had told me to send her there, wasn't it? It was somewhere Miss Ramsbottom would be deliriously happy. It was my duty to do it, my obligation, and that thought made me even more determined. Suddenly, I could smell that smell. The same loathsome smell that I'd first smelt that night in the tree house when Ben was taken. It was entrenched in my nostrils.

It was hard for me to discern now where the forest ended and the true garden began. But the butterflies knew. They were faithful to the tract; motivated, I supposed, by the same kind of instinct which makes salmon return loyally to their breeding grounds to spawn offspring of their own. I had never seen so many little coloured wings fluttering around the forest before. They showed me the way.

I have already spoken of Miss Ramsbottom's fear and, on reflection now, perhaps I can identify with it. I'm sure it was an excited fear, a mixture of nervousness and exhilaration. After all, she was going on to a new incarnation, something previously unknown to her. No wonder she felt a certain trepidation.

I, myself, felt fear. I remember that clearly. But my fear was more the fear of failure, the fear of falling short, of being found wanting in my service of the Mistress. Not that I needed to have worried about that. For She was constant to me. She turned my fear into exuberance. I remember being fired with a strength that was almost superhuman, like the strength granted to Samson by the One he served. As I ran to the shed to fetch my father's rusty old spade – so the secret way could be opened up and then concealed again from the prying eyes of others – I felt my energy was infinite. I almost ripped the door from its hinges and, once inside, I had to press myself tightly up against the wooden wall, my eyes closed, my heart pounding, feeling the power She had implanted in me surge through my body and gush round every muscle and sinew like a torrent.

I breathed deeply, trying to check the force of that power, trying to control it, feeling that my heart might soon explode unless it could be contained. And slowly, its flow subsided, at least enough for me to feel I could restrain it within my human frailty. And, when I sensed I was in control of myself again, I picked up my father's spade and rushed back into the garden.

I have this vision in my mind of the events that happened next; a last recollection of Miss Ramsbottom as she slithered her way through the earthy portals of the secret way into the mysterious deep, dark and secret forest of her mistress. An arm. Just one arm. It seemed to remain suspended, detached, disconnected from the rest of her by a brown clumpy sea, a limp hand hanging from the end of it, fingernails split and caked with dirt, and two digits still clamped firmly together from which dangled the house keys, the large white tag now streaked with black, filthy smudges.

It was nice of Miss Ramsbottom to draw my attention to the keys. But then, she had no further use for them, I suppose, did she? I expect she realised I wanted those keys because I needed to expunge from the house's closets its painful spectres, to purge them from my mind, to finally put them to rest. And I guess she knew, even then, that if I took them, others could soon follow my mother and her to that deep, dark and secret abode of witches.

Two days later, in the early evening, I revisited the house. I had only been there a few minutes and was standing in the hall waiting for the first grip of terror to abate when I heard a knock on the front door. My dread increased. Not so much because a visitor to an uninhabited house in which I was a trespasser was a portent to disaster but because I was suddenly transported back to a time when a knock on the door would have been natural and commonplace; a time when the house, and everything in it, was ruled by a callous female dictator. I even thought I heard her footsteps descending the stairs and it wasn't till the knock sounded again, and still my mother hadn't appeared, that I realised my fears were nothing more than a self-induced imagining.

For a third time the knock sounded. Whoever it was, my visitor was certainly persistent. I debated with myself the wisdom of opening the door. Perhaps, I reasoned, if I remained quiet, he or she might simply go away. But then, everyone in the neighbourhood knew the house was empty so who would bother to knock with such resoluteness unless they saw me come in here? With that thought came the instant realisation of who my mysterious visitor must be. I opened the door.

'Hello, Mrs Jessop! What brings you to my old abode?'

She stared at me with her pompous air of self-importance.

'Oh, Johnny! So it was you I saw go in. You can't be too careful these days, can you? Er, is that lady with you? That one you came with a couple of days ago? Miss – Miss—?'

'Ramsbottom.' I put her out of her misery; the misery of ignorance which, to Mrs Jessop, was unendurable.

Her eyes were not small and beady like Miss Ramsbottom's but they had, nonetheless, that same talent of searing into the mind and roving about in search of minutiae; relevant or trivial, it was of no consequence to Mrs Jessop. Her senses would latch onto every detail just the same and file it away for future reference. Finished with her sortie into the corridors of my mind, she craned her stubby neck to peer behind me into the hallway.

'Would you like to come in, Mrs Jessop? I'll introduce you to Miss Ramsbottom.'

I knew Mrs Jessop would never refuse an invitation like that!

CHAPTER 11

I thought it terribly amusing that the main preoccupation of the nosey Mrs Jessop was the notion that Miss Ramsbottom and I had used the house to have sex. I put her right on that one. I told her the truth. There was no reason not to; after all, I knew she'd be going away herself soon, and to the very same place Miss Ramsbottom had gone. The Mistress had told me to send her as well, you see. So the truth would have been made known to her eventually.

I began to feel that same strength and power surge through my body. The exhilaration of that wonderful fear She inculcated in me. I knew I would need all of that power to send the corpulence of Mrs Jessop through the secret way. She was a very powerful woman indeed.

'I am pleased to learn that you and that Miss Ramsbottom were not using this house for immoral purposes, Johnny. That would have given the neighbourhood a very bad reputation indeed, wouldn't it?' She looked at me through her deep-set eyes which seemed to give out shimmering little glints of scorn. 'But even though the reason for your visit here was – how shall we put it? – inoffensive? –

you must be more discreet. Some people put two and two together and make five, you know, and we don't want to start tongues wagging unnecessarily, do we now? There are a lot of meddling, interfering people out there who have nothing better to do than poke their noses into other people's business. Tut! Tut!'

I thought it funny that most old witches' crones seem to do a lot of campaigning in the cause of one moral issue or another. Before she went away I appeased her by saying that her motive was a very fine and principled one, though I thought she was fighting a losing battle. Her last words before she departed were, 'I know. It's such a sad, degenerate world we live in now, isn't it? Young boys nowadays seem to have nothing else on their minds but sex, sex, sex. Present company excepted, of course. Wouldn't you agree?'

The delicious irony of Mrs Jessop's assumption was that, certainly during the occupation of the Smith family, as I had learnt from Auntie Pat – although I obviously cannot speak for the goings-on before that – the poor old house where I once lived had never witnessed one single act of copulation. And in fact, from that day on, at least while I still owned the place, it never would. It was as if sex were an interdiction there, something neither to be practised nor spoken of.

Perhaps I was an unusually incurious child, but I never once questioned where babies came from or what Mummy and Daddy did in the privacy of the room they shared. But, if I had asked my mother about these things, I don't think she would have fobbed me off with stories about babies being found under gooseberry bushes or being brought by storks. No. I am sure I know what she would have said. It would have been a factual and truthful, if somewhat coloured, account of precisely how babies are made. I can even hear in my mind the exact words she probably would have used.

'Slugs and snails and puppy dogs' tails, Johnny! All little boys have a puppy dog's tail, don't they, Johnny? That puppy dog's tail controls them. It rules their lives. It's the revolting things they do with that disgusting and loathsome puppy dog's tail, Johnny! That's why babies happen!'

You may wonder how I can be so sure that, had I asked her, my mother would have explained the delicate subject of the birds and the bees in such an indelicate way. I have said that sex was never mentioned under our roof. Well, that is indeed true, but there were many occasions it was alluded to; or rather, that revolting male instrument of sexual invasion was alluded to – and mine in particular.

Every Friday evening at seven o'clock, I was routinely directed to take my bath. My mother would order me to '. . . cleanse every inch of your body of its disgusting filth.' I often wondered how she knew the precise moment to enter the bathroom to observe me, but that was before I knew about the canny insight given her by her mistress.

She would stand silently at the bathroom door and stare at me kneeling in the tub washing my privates. 'Scrub it, Johnny!' she would say. 'Cleanse it of its foulness. But remember, Johnny—' That inflection would be back in her voice. I knew a warning was imminent. '—the wicked old witch knows the difference between little boys scrubbing their puppy dog's tail and playing with it! Scrubbing it is an act of purging and refinement – a good thing to do, a demonstration of the desire for redemption. Playing with it, however, is an act of filthy self-abuse. She will punish you for that – take you away and gobble you up. Remember that, Johnny. And remember it well.'

You can probably understand now why, in the beginning, I was so fearful of experiencing the perfectly natural feelings of sexual arousal, why I tried so hard to keep them under control, and why my conscious decision to actively engage in masturbation was such a momentous one. It was an act of extreme defiance against the witch's authority and a testing of Her power and discernment, which I had been led to believe were absolute. I was sure I would receive nothing less than Her total retribution for such deeds of overt disobedience.

But many years had elapsed since then and, as time went on, not only did my dread begin to fade but life actually seemed to improve for me despite my continual practice of naughtiness, first within the fantasies conceived under my quilt and later in the flesh with Dorothy.

Ah, Dorothy! It is perhaps timely to tell you more of my relationship with her. She was a sweet girl. I say 'was'; she probably still is though I haven't spoken to her in a long while now. There is one event I can recount which I think will illustrate how our friendship had developed by this time. Strangely enough, it happened the day after Mrs Jessop went away.

It was a Sunday and Dorothy and I went behind our favourite bush by the playground in the park. She had been moody all day but I had become used to her fickle ways; such moods, I thought, were just another of the totally inexplicable facets of woman.

We began to caress but I could tell her heart wasn't in it. Suddenly, she started to sob; actually, the sobs were more like soft whimpering moans. Despite my reluctance to enquire about the cause of her distress, due to a strong premonition I always had on occasions like this that I'd be opening up a can of worms or maybe even something much, much worse, I didn't see I had any alternative. I asked her what was wrong.

'You don't love me any more!' she cried.

I was bewildered. I had spent the last fifteen minutes trying to prove that I did. I told her this.

'That's just the point!' she answered. 'That's all you want to do. All I am to you is a quick grope in the bushes. If you loved me – really loved me – you'd want to *make* love to me, wouldn't you?'

I couldn't think of any suitable rejoinder except to define the practical problems involved. 'We can hardly do that here, can we?'

'Of course not!' she snapped. 'But the boyfriends of the other girls find somewhere they can go to be – alone together.' She looked and sounded embarrassed. 'And anyway – I'm fed up with being the only virgin in my class. The other girls are taking the mickey out of me.'

Dorothy was lying, of course. After all, how could the only female I had ever known to bear the visible scars of the wicked old witch's punishment for wantonness still be pure and chaste? I knew it was all just a ruse to get me to succumb to her feminine wiles. But I didn't challenge her. Why would I? This was the very opportunity I'd awaited for so long. I was beside myself with blissful expectation. And, for the first time, I realised we did have somewhere now where we could go. I remember asking myself why I'd never thought of taking Dorothy back to the old house before and, to be truthful, I couldn't come up with any logical reason; except to say that something beyond rational explanation, something synonymous with the spirit of that old house, had kept thoughts of its use for such salacious deeds firmly locked away in an unreachable part of me. But Dorothy's words had released them. Oh yes, they had very definitely released them.

'I know a place we can go, but you must promise me you'll never tell anyone I took you there!' I blurted out.

She looked deep into my eyes, nodded, then she started sobbing again. It was the first real occasion that gave me cause to remember Auntie Pat's profound words. And she was right, women do get emotional sometimes.

I arranged to meet Dorothy at the top of the road at eight-thirty but it was nine o'clock, and just getting dark, when she finally arrived. I knew her father had said she had to be home by ten and I calculated that, allowing for walking her home afterwards, it left us with a little less than half an hour. I didn't know exactly how long making love would take but I figured that would probably be enough time.

Her mood then could only be described as subdued and we walked to the house without saying a word to one another. I think I was more nervous on that visit than I had been on either of the other two recent occasions I had been inside. I remember, I even looked up anxiously at Mrs Jessop's window, expecting to see her net curtains twitch, before realising she didn't live there any more.

I opened the front door. Dorothy knew it was my old house, the place I lived in with my mother before she went away, but she didn't say a word to me; she didn't question where I got the keys, she didn't ask if we were allowed to go in there, she said absolutely nothing. All I remember about that moment, is Dorothy's sad, doleful eyes – not enquiring, not challenging – staring up at me in the half-light, as I quickly ushered her inside. Then I took hold of her hand and almost pulled her up the stairs.

This was now my third visit to the house and I began to believe that, finally, the phobias it inspired in me were starting to subside. I thought I might put that to the test and considered using my parents' room but then revoked the idea. I suppose I still didn't feel strong enough to exploit my mother's private place for such a disgusting endeavour. So we went into my bedroom.

I lowered Dorothy onto the bed and she complied without offering resistance. But I could tell her heart still wasn't in it. And to be truthful, neither was mine.

It is a funny thing about indoctrination; you succeed in subduing it for a while and then a situation arises which causes all those old disciplines inbred in you during your early years to rise up again like a freak flash flood. All I could hear were my mother's insidious words: '*Sugar and spice and all things nice, Johnny! That's what little girls are made of!*'

Then I saw her invading the privacy of my ablutions and her callous instructions for me to cleanse my phallus of its foulness. In my mind I pictured her screaming out that I was attempting an act of desecration. I was planning a violation of the holy of holies and suddenly I was filled with a sense of intense self-disgust. The feeling was so strong, I thought I would vomit. I jumped up from beside Dorothy on the bed.

She looked up at me. Her expression was so pitiable I felt sure she was going to cry again.

'What's wrong? Is it me? Don't you fancy me?' she whimpered.

I knew my answer would be crucial. One wrong word would topple Dorothy into the depths of that feminine caprice to be avoided at all costs: emotional hysteria.

I summoned up all the tenderness and gentleness I

could. 'No, Dorothy! Of course it's not you. You're wonderful and I love you. This just doesn't seem right somehow. I guess I respect you too much. Maybe we should wait till we're married. It'll be okay then.'

Then Dorothy did cry. She jumped up suddenly, threw her arms about my neck, pulled me down towards her and wouldn't let go. My shoulders became soaked with her tears. For one terrible moment, I thought I had failed in my objective; that I had, despite all my good intentions, said something to upset her. Then I realised they were tears of joy. Her mood had changed again within the twinkling of an eye.

We left and I carefully relocked the old house and slunk away with her into the darkness. On the way home, she told me of her happiness; how she could now truthfully tell the others girls she had been somewhere alone with me and how fabulous I had been to say the one thing she had wanted to hear above all else. She babbled on about how caring and romantic I was and that I was right to want to wait till we were married.

'After all,' she said, 'supposing I had become pregnant! I want you to marry me because you want to, not because you feel forced into it. I would hate that, Johnny. I would really hate that.'

In fact, I couldn't stop her talking. At the corner of her road, she pulled me to her and kissed me.

'You are wonderful, Johnny. I do love you, you know.' Her words sounded soft and delicate, as if spun on threads of gossamer. I watched her skip up to her front door which she opened. And, from the back-lit glow of the lighted hallway, her silhouetted figure blew me a kiss.

Women were still a profound mystery to me but at last I thought I was – just perhaps – beginning to understand how to handle them. Or was it, as the nagging fear at the back of my mind suggested, that this superior and imperious gender known as womankind, was possibly handling me, manipulating me, exploiting me, and orchestrating situations to their own advantage?

CHAPTER 12

'When was the last time you saw Miss Ramsbottom, John?' Sergeant Dixon's voice boomed out around the living room.

Auntie Pat felt obliged to intercede on my behalf. 'That would be last Wednesday, wouldn't it, Johnny? About fivish! Do you remember, you had just come home from school and I called you down from your room to tell you Miss Ramsbottom wanted a word with you.'

Sergeant Dixon stared at Auntie Pat, then briefly at me. Somehow, without uttering a single word, his look managed to convey the statement, 'I was asking John the question, Mrs Wilkinson. Not you!' Auntie Pat looked sheepish.

The sun was streaming in the window, seeming to be focusing its rays on the sergeant's armchair and highlighting his face in its radiance. I remember thinking the five years since I last saw him hadn't really changed him that much. His hair was a little greyer, perhaps it was even a little thinner. But his moustache was just as black. And if anything it was bushier, longer, being grown to turn up at the corners like an indecisive handlebar.

'So – it was about five o'clock.' He wrote in his notebook. 'And, what did she want to talk to you about?' The ends of his moustache quivered as he spoke. It was the first time I'd ever noticed them do that.

Auntie Pat opened her mouth to speak, then thought better of it.

I held the sergeant's stare. 'She said she wanted to discuss my future, sir.'

'Your future?' echoed the policeman. 'What did she mean by that?'

'I think she just wanted to make sure there wasn't anything else I could tell her about my mother – and where she might have gone, I suppose. She explained to me again the legal situation about missing persons and that, after seven years, they could be presumed dead. She said that meant my mother's estate would pass to me – held in trust were the words I think she used to explain what was happening to it at present, sir.'

There was a moment's pause while Sergeant Dixon scribbled something into his notebook again.

'And, could you? Tell her anything about your mother we don't already know, that is?'

'Really, Sergeant!' Auntie Pat could not be restrained. 'Poor Johnny's suffered enough over that! It was five years ago now. He was only eleven when it happened. He's told you everything—'

'Please, Mrs Wilkinson!' Sergeant Dixon's voice boomed out even louder. 'We are conducting important enquiries here. Let John answer for himself.'

Both faces turned to me in unison. They were staring vacantly, waiting with eager expectation.

'Er – no. I could only tell her what you already know. My mother didn't say anything, sir. Only that she was going away.'

Auntie Pat would not be silenced. Her role as my protector, *in loco parentis*, was a joy to behold. 'What's this all about anyway, Sergeant? Why is Johnny being hounded like this?'

Sergeant Dixon inhaled a deep breath of exasperation. 'Mrs Wilkinson! I think that's a bit of an overstatement, don't you? John is not being hounded. I am merely asking him some questions in connection with Miss Ramsbottom's disappearance. We are following up all her diary appointments prior to when she was last seen.' He referred to his notebook. 'That would be last Thursday, the seventeenth. It is standard procedure in this kind of enquiry.'

'Miss Ramsbottom? Disappeared? Oh!' And those words having been said, Auntie Pat could find no more. But Sergeant Dixon obviously felt the situation required a little more explanation.

'We know she kept her last appointment at—' He lowered his eyes to consult his book, '—three-thirty last Thursday, then nothing. She hasn't been seen since. Didn't even return to the office to collect her car. Just disappeared without a trace. So you see, Mrs Wilkinson, how important it is for me to speak to anyone who had contact with her over those last couple of days. We have to build up a picture of her movements, find out if she kept all her appointments, whether she said anything unusual, appeared different, acted out of character – that kind of thing.'

While this was being said, Auntie Pat just uttered an occasional, acquiescent 'Oh!' and Sergeant Dixon, confident that she had now been pacified, focused his attentions totally on me.

'So, John, can you remember if there was anything else she said – anything at all, no matter how irrelevant it may seem to you?'

I paused, to appear to give the matter the thoughtfulness it deserved and, in truth, it was receiving my most serious consideration.

'Er – yes, Sergeant. Come to think of it, there was something. I didn't pay it much notice at the time. Not really any of my business. But she said she wouldn't be seeing me again for a while because she was going away.'

The policeman stared at me.

'Going away!' The echo boomed. 'Did she say where? Or give any indication whether it was on business, perhaps, or if she intended taking leave?'

'No, sir. And I didn't ask either. As I said, it wasn't really any of my business, was it?'

Sergeant Dixon still held me in that fixed stare of his. 'And how did she seem, John? In herself, I mean. Did she seem anxious or excited or worried, perhaps?'

'Can't say I noticed any real difference in her, sir. Miss Ramsbottom always seemed the same to me – very businesslike is the only way I can describe her. Sensible. Serious. Just like those business suits she used to wear.'

'Used to wear?' The sergeant looked at me from beneath a raised eyebrow.

'Er – still does, I expect. Just a figure of speech. I didn't mean anything by it—' I stopped. I had said too much already.

The sergeant continued to observe me for a while. I tried not to look away. Then he slowly lowered his gaze and wrote something else in his notebook. Suddenly, he stopped and looked up at me again. There was a quizzical expression on his face.

'Your aunt tells me Miss Ramsbottom asked to speak to you alone. But there doesn't seem anything in what you've told me she said which couldn't have been mentioned in front of your aunt, does there? Nothing of a personal nature, I mean. The legal situation had already been explained, hadn't it?'

He looked to Auntie Pat who nodded confirmation, then he looked back at me. 'Tell me, John, do you have any idea at all why Miss Ramsbottom should have regarded those things as so confidential?' His stare intensified. 'Are you sure – absolutely sure – there was nothing else she said that you may have forgotten to mention?'

I thought for a while then shook my head. 'No. As I said, only that she'd be going away for a while.'

The policeman looked down at his left hand and played with the ring on his little finger. Then his face slowly lifted.

'You know, it's funny that, John. She tells you she's going away for a while but she doesn't mention it to any of her other cases. Don't you think that just a little odd? Why do you think she singled out you alone to be privy to this information?'

This new line of questioning made Auntie Pat stand up again in my defence. 'Really, Sergeant! This is going too far. How can the boy possibly know the answer to that?'

There was an even longer intake of 'exasperated' air before the voice boomed out again.

'*Please,* Mrs Wilkinson. Let John answer my question. You see – what I really find strange is that John is no longer one of Miss Ramsbottom's official cases. He was taken off her case list after Mr Wilkinson and you fostered him. You've given John a nice home here and he is obviously well cared for. So why, I ask myself, would an overworked social worker continue to take an interest which can only be described as personal rather than professional?'

Their heads turned again to face me, awaiting my response.

'I – I really don't know, sir. I've known Miss Ramsbottom for five years. She did say she wanted me to think of her as more than just a social worker – "I want you to look upon me more as your friend," she once told me. And she was very nice to me. I think maybe I did regard her more as a friend. I respected her, as I've said, she was very nice to me.'

Sergeant Dixon stared into my eyes, expecting me to add more. I did.

'But – I don't know why she kept coming here – if she didn't have to, I mean. She certainly didn't tell me why, anyway.'

There was a long silence then which Auntie Pat, probably out of embarrassment, felt obliged to break.

'Perhaps she had a soft spot for Johnny, Sergeant. Oh, I don't know – Johnny's growing up now and, well, it does happen, you know, older women interested in young boys.'

The policeman breathed deeply. 'No, Mrs Wilkinson! I agree it does sometimes happen but I don't think so, not in this case. You see, Miss Ramsbottom is – how shall we say? – of a different sexual persuasion.'

'You mean—oh!' Auntie Pat was mortified.

'She lived with another young lady. And, yes, we have contacted her. Contrary to popular opinion, the police do follow up the obvious lines of enquiry, Mrs Wilkinson.'

Strangely, I was not at all shocked by this revelation. The enlightenment of the swinging Sixties had made such things much more acceptable. And hadn't Auntie Pat said that my mother only tolerated my father because he provided for her? Well, Miss Ramsbottom was one of her kind, wasn't she? No, I wasn't surprised at all to learn that Miss Ramsbottom didn't live with a repulsive and disgusting male. On the contrary, living with another old witch was what I would have expected of her. This news only proved my suspicions that Miss Ramsbottom was interested in a lowly detestable boy merely to tempt him, to try and discredit him, and to test his devotion to her mistress.

'So, John, apart from telling me Miss Ramsbottom just said—' He consulted his notebook again, '—that "she was going away for a while", there's nothing else you can tell me?'

'No, sir.'

'You mean she just told you like that. In the same way your mother told you she was going away?'

His reference to my mother irritated me. It was disquieting. And, what was more, I was on my own. Auntie Pat had at last been subdued into silence.

'No! It wasn't the same!' I blurted out. 'She didn't make an issue of it. She simply brought it into the conversation – a by-the-by kind of thing – it was no big deal.' I tried to remain calm; I tried so very hard but I couldn't help raising my voice a little.

Sergeant Dixon smiled; a wry sort of smile. 'Are you saying, John, your mother did make an issue of it?'

'No! Yes! Oh, I don't know. It was all so long ago.' I was almost shouting now. Auntie Pat looked concerned.

The sergeant stared at me for a while with that enquiring smile etched on his face. Then he got up suddenly. 'Well, thank you, John, Mrs Wilkinson. I won't trouble you further today. You've both been very helpful.'

I could see Auntie Pat was troubled. She got up as well to show the policeman out.

Sergeant Dixon reached the door, then he stopped and turned to face me again. 'Oh, by the way, John. Have you seen Mrs Jessop recently?'

He scrutinised me. I shook my head.

'Yes. Strange that. No one's seen her for a good few days now. As you know, Mrs Jessop wasn't the kind of person to keep herself to herself. We know she bought a return ticket to Liverpool last Friday. Got a sister up there apparently. Probably nothing to it. Gone to catch up on all the gossip there, I 'spect. Odd though, she didn't tell anyone. Still, the Liverpool police will let us have the answer soon. See you, John.'

He disappeared through the door and Auntie Pat followed him.

I thought about my predicament. Sergeant Dixon was shrewd and clever but there was nothing he could know for sure; probably just following up on a hunch. But what had I to worry about anyway? I had simply showed two witches the way to the dark secret forest of their mistress. I had helped them find their happiness. And the wicked old witch Herself had told me to do it. I had done nothing wrong. But, at the back of my mind, there was a nagging feeling that Sergeant Dixon might not see it quite that way. Suddenly, my head began to throb with words remembered long ago from the callous utterings of a hated wicked mother. '*You mark my words, Johnny Smith, and you mark 'em well. If the wicked old witch doesn't get you, then one day, that policeman will. One day, and I don't think it is too far away now, you'll be naughty enough for one of 'em to get you! It's what you deserve, Johnny Smith! It's what you deserve!*'

Auntie Pat was furious at the way Sergeant Dixon had conducted the interview; so furious, in fact, that she wrote a letter to his Superintendent asking for an enquiry into his 'harassment of a minor' and, despite my protestations, the letter was still posted. I don't think it was viewed with any seriousness by Sergeant Dixon's superiors although, some two weeks later, she did receive an acknowledgement to say the matter was being looked into. But, as far as I know, the complaint was never officially investigated.

Sergeant Dixon didn't bother me again for a long while and, gradually, I began to relax a little. But I wasn't allowed to forget about the two women I had sent away. Mrs Jessop was so well known in the neighbourhood, her disappearance was a constant talking point and many rumours abounded. By this time, of course, it was common knowledge that she had never arrived at her sister's house in Liverpool.

The local paper, the *Comet*, picked up on the story and featured it for several weeks; the obscure disappearance of two local women 'in very mysterious circumstances' being the most newsworthy happening in the locality for many a year. They came to be known in the *Comet*'s journalese as the 'Where-Are-They Women' and the intrigue surrounding their disappearance commanded more attention locally than the nationally renowned case of Lord Lucan a decade or so later.

The *Comet* reported, 'Police are baffled by the mysterious disappearances of the two women who, like those aboard the *Marie Celeste*, made no preparation for their departure. An official statement says, "There is nothing to link the two disappearances but we are keeping an open mind on whether or not the incidents might be related." However, investigations by the *Comet* have revealed that,

I have already mentioned her ordinariness and it is not my intention now to display even more unkindness – not that unkindness to her was ever my design – after all, as I have already said, there is nothing about me which can be described as anything other than ordinary and unremarkable. In that respect we were totally compatible. But I still behold that vision of Dorothy the Seductress in my mind's eye and, even now, I can't control a bemused smile. Compared to the similarly clad lovelies in the Spiv's magazines, Dorothy bore about as much resemblance to a femme fatale as a trussed-up chicken ready for the oven.

I just looked at her, my mouth agape; an expression she mistook for lustful craving. She sat down beside me on the couch and guided my hand to the delicate sheer lace that veiled her small breasts. I remember her pert nipples moulding taut impressions in their diaphanous mantle.

'I'll take it off for you,' she whispered. And, before I had time to reply, my hand was cupping her nakedness.

That seemed to incite Dorothy into a fervour. Her tongue began to search out my tonsils and her hand wandered to my crotch where she started to knead my manhood and grope with my zip. It was an intensity of eagerness unimagined even in my wildest fantasies of feminine unwholesomeness. I was terrified by its potency. My head ached from its unyielding nature. I was restrained only by the sudden recollection of my mother's venomous words.

'*Sugar and spice and all things nice, Johnny, that's what little girls are made of . . . It's the revolting things men do with that disgusting and loathsome puppy dog's tail, Johnny . . . Cleanse it of its foulness!*'

Its foulness! I could never subject Dorothy to that, even though she didn't seem to mind. On the contrary, she was so aroused, it was difficult to stop her. I disentangled myself from her amorous advances and jumped up. It was not an act of honour, just the stupid behaviour of a pathetic fool who still allowed himself to be controlled by a lost mother's hateful tauntings.

I will never forget poor Dorothy's face. It was a picture of total astonishment. She suddenly looked down and observed her uncovered breasts and, letting out a little squeal of disquiet, flung up her hands to cup the cause of her embarrassment. It was more the act of someone whose privacy had been rudely interrupted behind a locked bathroom door than one who, a few seconds earlier, had been a willing partner to the naked deed of intercourse.

Dear Dorothy. My dear, dear Dorothy. Even then you blamed yourself for my inadequacies. Even then you berated yourself for your lack of self-control whilst commending me as the champion of the principles we had agreed; to wait till our wedding night to consummate our oneness.

Dear Dorothy. If only I could have told you the truth. Maybe you could have helped me overcome my torment and the future might then have followed a very different course. But the world is full of those uttering the poignant words *if only*.

I really wanted Dorothy that night, and she had aroused me even though her wantonness made her act more like a voracious alley-cat than the purring sex-kitten of my fantasies. I told myself it was only my mother's indoctrinations which had held me back; a discipline that reached far beyond the hated memories of that old house. It was a discipline ingrained within the very fabric of me.

I agonised over my impotence. There was a popular song of the time, from one of the current West End shows, I think, which began with the words 'Pardon me, miss, but I've never done this with a real live girl.' It was a wonderfully apt signature tune and one I would sing for the rest of my life unless, of course, I could somehow exorcise myself of my mother's influence.

Like the subject of that song, I'd seen photographs and facsimiles, and had frequently used these to fan the embers of my fantasies into the searing fulfilment of sexual release. I knew the girls in those photographs were defiled. I supposed that was why it had been so easy to fantasise over doing it with them.

But there was something else. I remembered the two women I had sent away. They had gone to a place of defilement, to a mistress whose very justice was vile and iniquitous. I had felt a tremendous excitement as I showed them the way; an excitement which drove me to heights of ecstasy I had never thought possible. I remember afterwards, rushing back to the halfway house, straight up to my bedroom, my loins throbbing painfully with an inglorious rapture.

It was Miss Ramsbottom and Mrs Jessop who appeared in my fantasies then. I heard them scream out in pain at the frightening strength of my virility. It was the consummate union, not an act of love but an act of degradation. I was violating them with my own stamp of foulness.

Suddenly, it all became clear. I knew how to exorcise myself. I knew how to purge my mind and drive out the cancerous spirit of my mother's hatred. She had defiled me. And even though I could not now defile her, I could defile another of her kind; an eye for an eye, a tooth for a tooth, a defilement for a defilement.

Yes, that was the way to avenge the taking of Ben and my father. That was the way to avenge myself of my mother's heartlessness. And, in doing so, I would be a champion in the cause of lowly downtrodden males everywhere who were languishing under the reign of a ruthless woman's scorn. I would defile one of their kind. I would violate her. And only afterwards would I show her the way. I felt strong. I felt invincible. Even fears of the retribution of an omnipotent mistress paled into insignificance. After all, it would be nothing more than justice; an all-consuming justice which would both vindicate and heal. A justifiable justice; right, fair and defendable. That very justice itself would protect me. It would give me power. And, something I couldn't explain – something deep within me, a curious insight closeted away inside an untenable part of my mind – told me it was a justice even She might understand.

Chapter 13

I remember the teacher at school who took us for Religious Instruction once read out the Bible account of Genesis. He told us it was Eve who first gave in to disobedience in the Garden of Eden by eating the forbidden fruit. Apparently, it was that deed which is supposed to have fashioned mankind, from that day to this, with a knowledge of both good and evil.

It's a nice story, I suppose, but that's all it is – I mean, have you ever heard of a talking snake? And Eve must have been a woman of the superior kind to have dominated Adam the way she did; it was she who persuaded him to go against his conscience and eat the apple in the first place, wasn't it? So I'm sure she wouldn't have listened to a stupid old serpent. I know my mother wouldn't have. She didn't even allow my father to tell her what to do. But I do know what our teacher meant when he said that forbidden fruit always seems more exciting. That did make sense. It was strange how the apples in Mrs Jessop's garden always looked more rosy and succulent than those we had in our fruit bowl back home. And, looking back on my childhood now, I remember many other things we wanted to experience before their due time, like Ben and me sneaking in to see X-rated movies and coughing and spluttering through our first cigarettes.

It was that same craving to sample forbidden fruits that made me, and a group of guys I hung around with, first visit the Blue Parrot, a notoriously seedy nightclub which didn't seem to be too discriminating in who it allowed through its shady doors.

The reputation of the Blue Parrot was well known both to local residents and the police. The *Comet* regularly reported police raids to investigate rumours of marijuana peddling and after-hours drinking, and there had been numerous attempts to shut it down. Those attempts were finally successful some years later and I understand that a supermarket now stands on the site where the ignoble Blue Parrot once stood.

I remember now with some amusement the lengths to which some of us went to make ourselves look older than our seventeen years. Tommy Callaghan partially made up for his lack of height by wearing the 'elevated' shoes he bought after seeing an advertisement in one of the Sunday papers. And, long before the days when designer stubble became fashionable, Tony Gallini, a swarthy boy of Italian descent, would attempt to change his angelic features by not shaving for a week or so. But Tony still looked like a cherub; he merely became the incongruous sight of an untidy, dishevelled one.

With the hindsight of years, it now seems the height of stupidity to venture willingly into a den of such iniquity, especially in our adolescent innocence. Anything could have happened to us, and I suppose we were lucky nothing ever did. The place was frequented by known criminals and drugs were openly traded in its murky gloom. There was also a rumour that the Kray twins, Ronnie and Reggie, sometimes graced the Blue Parrot with their patronage, though I don't think we ever saw them there; not that we could have picked them out anyway in the nebulous sea of perfidious faces peering from those tables. But I guess, like the fabled Eve, it was the desire to be emancipated from the dictates of what seemed like petty and unnecessary rules and regulations that made the Blue Parrot's lure so exciting. I suppose in that sense we were really no different from most other youths.

Not that we need have bothered with our attempted masquerade. The Blue Parrot's only rule for admission was the ability to pay its exorbitant prices. On our meagre pocket money, a single drink had to last us all night, so one of our desired objectives – to experience the dubious delights of becoming stoned out of our minds – was never once achieved. But the Blue Parrot did put on a raunchy, if amateurish, floor show and had a group which gave a passable impression of the Rolling Stones.

Though these debatable attractions certainly lured us to the Blue Parrot in the first place, I found new delights within its dimly lit seediness which made all its other enchantments pale into total insignificance. You see, it was a meeting ground for the very kind of woman I was seeking. The Blue Parrot Club was full of them. They would sit by the bar or at tables in the dingy corners by the men's toilets and scour the gloom with expressions of disdain on their faces.

Often, they would approach men and sit with them for a while with an air of contemptuous arrogance. The men would buy them drinks before disappearing with them into the obscurity of the shadows. I knew what kind of women they were. Two hundred years ago they would have been tied to a stake and burnt alive. But so-called twentieth-century enlightenment allowed them to exist in the dingy havens of places like the Blue Parrot to wage their war on the offensiveness of insufferable males. Tony Gallini said they were prostitutes and, of course, he was right. But that was their livelihood, like Miss Ramsbottom was a social worker. I knew the real truth. I knew the conviction of their calling.

I went back to the club one night without my friends. I wanted no witnesses to what I had to do. And I knew none of its regular inhabitants would notice me. It was much too dark and, anyway, most of the Blue Parrot's clientele were more concerned with preserving their own anonymity.

The women were there as usual, their eyes roving about in search of recalcitrant mankind. I noticed that one in particular was glancing at me so, when our eyes met, I held her stare. Her look was cold, haughty and scornful. I felt its frigidness. She whispered to another of her kind and they both looked in my direction with that same derisive stare.

She got up and sauntered over to my table, holding me in a protracted glance before sitting down in the chair opposite mine.

'Something I can do for you, luv?'

Her voice oozed condescension. She took a pack of cigarettes from her bag, placed one in her painted mouth and leant forward, expecting me to give her a light.

I disregarded her.

'Maybe,' I answered. I was noncommittal. Frankly, I had no idea how one was supposed to act on these occasions. I was playing it completely by ear.

She lit her own cigarette and contemptuously puffed a billowy cloud of blueness into my face.

'You're young, ain't yer? You got money?'

I nodded. To be truthful, she didn't seem much older than me. She was certainly younger than Miss Ramsbottom and the aged Mrs Jessop. I remember thinking the Mistress must have recruited her at an exceptionally early age.

'Yes! I've got money.'

'How much?'

I had thought very hard about the expense of my deliverance and had taken twenty pounds from my savings. Thirty years ago, twenty pounds was a lot of money but I decided that you can't put a price on justice. I figured I had enough and spoke that thought.

'Enough!'

I wondered what concoction she would want to drink. I had heard that some of the cocktails at the Blue Parrot cost an arm and a leg.

'Ain't you gonna buy a girl a drink?' She stared at me vacantly through a screen of cigarette smoke. 'I'll have a G an' T.'

I was relieved. I ordered her drink, and a beer for myself, from one of the scantily clad hostesses who, I distinctly remember, tried to get me to buy a bottle of the house champagne instead. I offered a five pound note as payment and noticed that only two pounds ten shillings was deposited as change on the tray. I think the hostess expected me to leave it all for her as a tip but I picked the money up and put it into my pocket. My disdainful companion didn't thank me for buying her that drink but I've never met a female of her kind yet who thinks she has to thank downtrodden males for anything. They think men were only put on this earth to use and abuse, then to condemn for their offensiveness.

She looked at me from over the top of her glass, savouring her tipple as though it was provided as her rightful entitlement. 'You got somewhere to go?'

I nodded. 'Yes! I've got somewhere!'

The stare continued. 'Don't say much, do yer?'

'I don't want to talk to you!'

I don't know why but that remark made her smile. There was something in that smile which reminded me of Miss Ramsbottom. It wasn't a genuine smile. It was cold, it was distant and it soon disappeared.

'You're a cool one, ain't yer?'

She gulped down the rest of her gin and tonic, looked at me and said, 'You wanna go, or what?'

I took a sip of my beer, got up from my seat, and she followed me into the vagueness of the shadows, up the large iron staircase which led up from the club's basement gloom into the dingy street outside.

We took a cab to the top of Melrose Rise and walked the two hundred yards to the house. It was a cold night and she pulled up the collar of her cheap, short, simulated fox-fur coat as protection from the biting wind.

As we turned into the front path of number 122, I noticed her glance at the boarded, ground-floor windows.

'Christ! What is this place yer takin' me to?'

'It's all right,' I answered. 'It used to belong to my mother. It'll be mine soon.'

She gave me a brief indignant stare, made some comment about supposing she had been taken to worse places than this in her miserable and contemptible life (oh, how very kind of her!), and shrugged it all off with a hoarse cackle and the ungracious remark, 'Ah well, let's get it over wiv, shall we luv?'

I opened the door and we stepped inside. She followed

me into the living room where I lit a candle I had placed there for the purpose.

She shivered. 'It's friggin' freezin' in 'ere. Can't you light the fire?'

I looked into the fireplace. There were no glowing embers or dancing yellow flames. Just the sooty blackness of a cold unlit grate.

I shook my head.

She shivered again. 'Okay! But you'll 'ave to be quick! It's too cold to 'ang around in this place – and, I'm keeping me coat on!'

I can't remember now my exact words but I told her I didn't care about that. I said the business I had in mind wouldn't take long. But I do remember her reply very vividly.

'Bus'ness?' she said. 'An' exactly what kind of bus'ness *do* yer 'ave in mind? 'Ere, before we start any kind o'bus'ness, mister, I wanna see the colour of yer money!'

Her preoccupation with money irritated me greatly but, to keep her agreeable, I withdrew three crisp five-pound notes from my wallet and laid them on the coffee table.

She seemed cheered by their pristine blueness. I thought I saw that weak smile momentarily grace her lips again, then it was gone.

'So, what yer want me to do? I'll take me skirt and drawers orf but, like I said, mister, I'm keeping me coat on!'

She removed her skirt and knickers without ceremony and flung them over the back of the couch. Then she just stood there, facing me, the whiteness of her skin framed by the coat's hem and her black stocking tops. My eyes were drawn to the darkness of her pubic hair which stood out so clearly against her ivory skin, even in the flickering half-light.

It was the first time I had ever seen the hair between a woman's legs; none of the Spiv's photographs had revealed such intimacy. I thought it looked ugly and sinister, like the profuse and stubbly black hairs growing out of a witch's warts. I didn't want to look at it.

I went round the back of her, placed my hands about her shoulders and guided her to the side of the couch where I pushed her shoulders down, reclining her forward over the arm.

'So you want it like a dog, do yer! Well, be quick, mister! It's friggin' freezin' in 'ere. And it's creepy! Gives me the creeps, anyway!' Her head was turned round, looking at me from over her left shoulder.

I gazed at the rounded fullness of her buttocks. She was already tarnished. She was going to that place of defilement. Even her posture was one of degradation. I knew I wouldn't hear the hateful mutterings of a malicious mother this time, despite my salacious intentions, because she was awaiting her; my guest was expected in that deep, dark, dense, defiled place of witches, very soon.

I felt incredibly aroused and unleashed my manhood. Then, as I stared into the fissured whiteness of her bottom, I seemed to sense a superimposed vision of terror.

Ben's face! Ben's petrified face! It was there I saw it; engraved upon her skin as though her very buttocks were a shrine to his remembrance. I couldn't violate her. That would have seemed an act of profanity against Ben himself. I felt anger, intense anger. And my erection instantly relaxed into a flaccid apology that couldn't even have violated a paper bag.

'Friggin' 'ell! What's keepin' yer, mister? For Christ's sakes be quick! I'm catchin' me death 'ere!'

And I was quick. I smelt that smell, that same odious smell entrenched in my nostrils. I felt the power the mistress instilled in me just as before, and that contemptuous tart was sent to that secret place of witches before she knew it. But I made her scream out first. She screamed and screamed with the anguish of her pain.

Back at the halfway house, I relieved myself that night. That girl with the pretty face and painted lips was the subject of my fantasy. I heard her scream out again; long, loud shrieks of agony. My ecstasy was divine.

The following week, I returned alone to the Blue Parrot Club again. I had to. Justice was not yet done. A woman of my mother's kind had not yet been defiled and my mind was still uncleansed.

The next one was older. She was even more contemptuous and she was ugly. Her flesh sagged in great big rolls of unsightly corpulence. We went up to my mother's bedroom this time. I didn't take the candle. I didn't have to. Even the feeble moonlight shining through the window was enough to reveal her ugliness.

I told this one to lie on her back on the bed. She watched me expose my manhood. She laughed, a laugh of scornful derision. She shouldn't have done that. It was a terrible thing to have done. She wasn't even worthy enough to suffer the dishonour of my foulness. But I made her scream out before I showed her the way. She screamed so loudly I had to stuff her own knickers in her mouth to deaden the noise.

*

At least the *Comet* appreciated my efforts. They were able to resurrect the saga of the 'Where-Are-They Women'. They became the 'Where-Are-They Three' and then the 'Where-Are-They Four'. In the best traditions of investigative journalism, the *Comet* desperately tried to establish the link between them. But they couldn't really see it.

A couple of months later, with its headline 'It's now the Where-Are-They Six!', the paper reported, 'A police spokesman said last night, "There is obviously a very clear connection between the last four disappearances. The women were all prostitutes who operated from a nightclub called the Blue Parrot. However, we have uncovered no obvious link between these more recent incidents and the disappearance more than a year ago of a social worker, in the employ of the local council, and a local resident."'

But the police had uncovered the link with the Blue Parrot. After that, of course, I couldn't use the club again but that didn't really matter. It was easy to find contemptuous witches. The streets and bars were full of them.

If you think my story from here on in will be nothing more than a repetitive cataloguing of each and every time I sent a woman through the secret way, please don't get concerned. I have much more interesting things to recount than my brief encounters with those women. You already know the outcome of my little exploits anyway – I was convicted of despatching twenty-six of them – although I swear now, just as I swore at my trial over twenty-four years ago, that verdict was unfair. But I feel no bitterness over that injustice and, as for the women – well, they've forsaken their miserable existences here in this miserable little world for better things – significant things – in the service of their mistress. So there is really no need to feel dismay for any of us. We are all living happily ever after, aren't we?

But one question you might be asking is why did I have to keep on finding them? After all, wasn't my original motive simply to consummate one act of carnal defilement to avenge myself and finally exorcise my mind of my mother's defilement of me? Well, yes it was! But, you see, I never did fulfil that aim.

I have told you of the first two incidents and I won't bore you with the intimate details of any more. I don't know why I could never achieve my objective. Perhaps my mother's discipline was so inbred, I could not allow my foulness to defile even those already defiled. One, I remember, was even more defiled than all the rest. She was only a slight girl but she was strong. She put up a hell of a fight when I tried to show her the glory of the secret way. It's funny how superior females sometimes don't know what's best for them. Yes, I remember her vividly. Her name was Patsy. I know because she told me. In our struggle she scratched my face rather badly. I told my Auntie Pat it was done by our neighbour's dog, whose name was Rusty, as I recall – a big lumbering but friendly golden retriever mutt – who was always jumping our fence to greet us whenever we came out into our backyard. He would bound over to us and jump up, pawing the air in his jubilance. Fortunately Auntie Pat accepted my explanation without question. Rusty had once clawed her arm, producing similar-looking scratches to the ones Patsy's long fingernails had given me.

I remember I nearly did it with Patsy. Justice was so nearly dispensed. It would have been but for that tattoo on her right thigh. It was only small but I saw it nonetheless – a purple heart with an arrow through it, encircling the name *Ben.* She told me Ben was the name of a former boyfriend of hers but, whether that was true or not, it fired my remembrance of my dear childhood pal, inequitably taken that night in the tree house. Then I saw his face in the whiteness of her skin. I covered it with her skirt but it was too late. His image was already etched in my mind and my arousal was lost to it.

But, as time went on, I found myself seeking out those women because a secondary mission superseded the first. More and more it became a personal crusade to redress the cause of suppressed males everywhere; men like my dear father, whose life, I could never forget, was made intolerably wretched and miserable – a poor man never to be granted the peace he so justly deserves because he is now condemned to suffer eternally in the wicked old witch's service. And I remembered my vow, my promise made in Ben's memory; the promise which fuelled my hatred of women like my mother and my detestation of their power. I needed to prove I had power over them.

It became a contest where each confrontation was just a battle won in an interminable war. And whatever you may think, I swear I was not the bringer of inglorious vanquishment. I did not send those women to a place of unconsciousness and obscurity. On the contrary, I know they are alive in the abode of their mistress and, what is more, they are happy with Her. And how can I be sure of these things? Because I have seen them with my own eyes, living in Her mystical world in that deep, dark place of witches. I have been given my own exclusive insight into that world, you see – a privilege granted me by the power of the Mistress Herself. It is of these deep clandestine things I really want to tell. They will be revealed as my story unfolds, and it is in these things especially I want you to believe. For they are true and I will swear that till my dying day.

Chapter 14

We all have our fears, don't we? Those little foibles and insecurities that sometimes stop us dead in our tracks before we even begin something. I have already told you of my fear of failure, the fear of falling short, of not attaining what is expected of me. Well, it was precisely that fear which decided me to leave school three weeks before I was due to sit the exams which would have determined whether or not I could have gone on to university. Though my teachers had faith that I would pass, I suppose I felt the fear of exposing my inadequacies too greatly to take that chance.

Auntie Pat was devastated by my decision, she tried so very hard to dissuade me but I would not be moved, though I think, in the end, I managed to reassure her by saying I was bound to get a good job anyway. I'd decided to pursue a career in journalism and had applied to all the national newspapers, sending them examples of my penmanship. But, one by one, I received kindly letters of rejection; messages of 'Thanks but no thanks!' disguised in platitudes like '. . . nothing at the moment but we are keeping your application on file should an opportunity arise in the future'. I was beginning to believe the *Comet*'s earlier offer would be the only one I would receive.

Two months or so before my eighteenth birthday, I accepted the inevitable and wrote to the *Comet*, reminding them of their promise and that I would like to avail myself of their offer should they still consider me a potential candidate for employment.

It was a delicious irony that I received their reply, suggesting I attend an interview, on the very same day their huge headline 'Now it's the 'Where-Are-They Nine!' covered the front page. Yes, nine! Exactly ten months had passed since that night I first went to the Blue Parrot on my own and invited that first witch's crone back to the house of my mother. It had been a busy period in my life, in fact busier than you might expect, because the *Comet*'s investigations were running way behind the truth. By this time, with my mother – a disappearance now so long ago it was not linked to the current spate – I had sent thirteen women to the dark secret place of the witch's abode.

I was sitting in the living room of the halfway house, idly reflecting on these things. I remember the television was on, showing a cartoon of Tom and Jerry, when the doorbell rang. I didn't take any notice of it because I knew Auntie Pat was in the kitchen baking another chocolate cake.

After a short while, the door opened and Auntie Pat came in. She didn't say anything immediately but glanced at me with a look of concern and went over to the television set and switched it off.

'Johnny! Sergeant Dixon's here to see you,' she whispered, her face a picture of anxiety. Then she turned her head towards the door and in a louder voice she said, 'Won't you please come in, Sergeant.'

I watched Sergeant Dixon enter the room. He nodded to me and was shown by my foster mother to an armchair. He sat down and declined Auntie Pat's offer of a cup of tea. Auntie Pat positioned herself in the armchair opposite, in readiness as my guardian protector.

As Sergeant Dixon settled in his chair, I noticed that the couple of years since his last visit had definitely aged him. His hair was certainly thinner now, still pushed back at the temples but now shaped into a definite salt-and-pepper widow's peak. Even his moustache was streaked with grey but now it was trimmed, the blossoming handlebar had become a more subdued ornament that sat perched on his upper lip like a fat, ageing slug.

'Our paths seem to cross every few years, don't they, John?' Sergeant Dixon was obviously in a satirical mood.

I remember a folded copy of the *Comet* was lying on the coffee table, its emboldened headline blazing out the message of the 'Where-Are-They Women' for all the world to see. I wanted to go and cover it up but, of course, I didn't.

'Hello, Sergeant Dixon. What brings you here again?' It was all I could think of to say.

He looked at me with that knowing stare of his.

'Something interesting has come to light, John. I was wondering if you could help me clear it up.'

'Er – I'll try, sir.'

He paused to take his famous notebook from his inside breast pocket.

'The keys to your mother's house – er—' He consulted his notes, '—122 Melrose Rise, that's right, isn't it? Two sets were kept in the safe at the Properties Division of the Civic Offices. One set appears to be missing.'

He paused to gauge my reaction before carrying on.

'Only came to light because of routine checks. Houses held under the protection of the local authorities are inspected every so often. Just to make sure everything is all right. The keys themselves should be regularly checked as well, of course, to ensure all the sets are still there. But, like most routine procedures, I suppose, it sometimes gets overlooked. Otherwise we might have got to know about it sooner.'

'Really, Sergeant! You're surely not suggesting Johnny had anything to do with—' Auntie Pat was jumping to my rescue again.

'No, Mrs Wilkinson, I am not!' The sergeant's voice boomed out loudly. He inhaled a gasp of air, then continued, 'Mrs Wilkinson, I am mindful of the complaint you raised when I last interviewed John. So let me make my intentions perfectly plain before I go any further. I was not harassing John then. I do not intend to harass him now. Neither am I accusing him of anything whatsoever. I merely want to ask him a few questions which may help us in our enquiries. Now Mrs Wilkinson, may I please continue with what I came here to say?'

The sergeant transferred his stare from Auntie Pat to me.

'Look, John, I'm not accusing you of taking the keys. That would be ridiculous. I know you couldn't have had any access to them. But the register was last monitored over two years ago. That would be just before Miss Ramsbottom disappeared. No one has officially signed them out – could have been an oversight, I suppose, except they have a strict hand-over procedure regarding keys of properties under protection. No. I think it seems more likely that the keys were taken unofficially, probably by this person, whoever he or she was, acquiring the keys to the safe, taking out one set of house keys, and returning the safe keys before they were missed.

'Now, I have no proof of this. It's only what you'd call a hunch. But the thought occurred to me that maybe – just maybe – Miss Ramsbottom took those keys and, if she did, it would have to have been unofficially because, as I've already told you, you weren't on her formal case list and she had no authorised access to them. And if she did take them, John, then I ask myself why?'

He paused. 'I suppose what I'm asking you to do is think back. Can you remember wanting her to bring you anything back from the old house? Or was there something, perhaps, you asked her to check out there for you? It might be a vital clue to her disappearance.'

I thought hard and long. 'No, Sergeant. I really can't remember anything like that.'

'I take it you've checked inside the house, Sergeant?' Thank God Auntie Pat asked that question on my behalf.

'Yes, Mrs Wilkinson. Nothing out of the ordinary. Everything seems exactly as it should. A full inventory taken. Nothing missing.'

I breathed an inward sigh of relief.

The sergeant scrutinised me again. 'Are you sure, John? Absolutely sure there's nothing you can tell me?'

There was almost a sense of despair in his voice, the exasperated tone of an investigation going nowhere. For the first time, I felt quite sorry for him.

I shook my head. 'I wish I could help you.'

Sergeant Dixon got up.

'Ah well. It was worth a try, I suppose. I guess if Miss Ramsbottom did take those keys they've disappeared with her. We'll probably never find them now, will we?'

Auntie Pat, always the perfect hostess, rose as well, to show him out.

The sergeant got to the living-room door, then turned.

'Oh, by the way, John. You ever been to the Blue Parrot?'

I shook my head. 'I'm not old enough to be allowed into a place like that, Sergeant.'

The policeman smiled. 'At the Blue Parrot they're not at all fussy about that kind of thing, John. So – you haven't been there, is that what you're telling me?'

'I've never been inside, if that's what you mean.'

'But you do know the club, I take it?'

'I think everyone round here knows the Blue Parrot, Sergeant. It's got quite a reputation!'

The sergeant's smile grew wider. 'Yes, John, indeed it has! Guess you know that some of those women who disappeared visited the Blue Parrot. That was reported at great length in the *Comet*. By the way, talking about the *Comet*, I enjoyed your little piece about Miss Ramsbottom and Mrs Jessop a couple of years ago. "Personal Recollections of a Friend", wasn't it? When I read that, I recall thinking to myself, the next time I see John I must commend him. Must have made an impression for me to remember it after all this time. Yes, nice bit of writing that – full of warmth and emotion!'

Auntie Pat joined in, her voice full of foster-motherly pride. 'Yes, Sergeant. And you may be reading a lot more of Johnny's pieces in the *Comet* soon. He has an interview for a job with them next Friday.'

The sergeant looked at me. 'Is that so. Well, John, let me wish you the very best of luck.'

He smiled again. 'Thanks for your time, John, Mrs

Wilkinson. Maybe I'll see you in another couple of years, eh?'

But I didn't have to wait another two years for the dubious pleasure of Sergeant Dixon's next visit to the halfway house. In fact, he paid me another call just two months later. It was the day before my eighteenth birthday. I remember because Auntie Pat was baking me a birthday cake when he arrived. My dear aunt was always baking. When I think of the hundreds of chocolate cakes I swallowed during my years at the halfway house, it's a wonder I didn't turn out like the Michelin Man . . But, before I allow myself to digress, let me recount the happening I observed on the way to my interview at the *Comet.* By a fortuitous coincidence, my walk to their offices took me down Melrose Rise where I saw council workers changing the lock on the front door of number 122. On the way back, I passed by the old house again and they had gone.

At first, I felt enraged that access to the house had been barred to me but, as my anger subsided and logical reasoning returned, I realised it was something I should have foreseen following the disclosure of the missing keys. I then began to understand how fortunate it was that fate had directed me to the right place at the right time to witness the event taking place. But I knew it was more than fate. It was a sign of the justice of my cause. It was sublime guidance, curbing my natural impetuousness by instructing me in the value and virtue of patience. I threw the old keys away down a drain grating in the road. I knew that, in the fullness of time, the very righteousness of my campaign would ensure that I would find a way to continue it. Until then, I had to learn the discipline of the patience I was being guided towards.

I was offered the job at the *Comet* and began work the following Monday. My weekly wage was the estimable sum of fifteen pounds seventeen shillings and sixpence – an unremarkable income for an unremarkable job. Any delusions I may have had were shattered the very first morning when I found out I was only a glorified office boy, making the tea, running errands and pasting copy; in short, I was nothing more than the *Comet*'s dogsbody.

That Friday, my very first pay day, I had the opportunity of discussing my lack of job satisfaction with Mr Garside, the assistant editor, when he called me into his office for a how-are-things-going kind of chat. I respectfully told him that I thought I had been given the job because of my writing 'style and flair' – and that they were his words not mine – but, so far, my fingers hadn't been anywhere near the hallowed keys of a typewriter.

He smiled; a warm, kindly, gentle smile. 'The impetuousness of youth!' he replied. 'John, you've so much time left to you to learn the tricks of the trade and you have the makings of becoming a very fine journalist. But do y'know the first quality a reporter must have?'

I shook my head.

'Patience, John. Above all else, a journalist must learn the gentle art of patience. Many a time you'll find yourself digging around in the wrong backyard and, unless you master the noble quality of endurance, you'll never make it in your chosen profession. Develop that virtue, John. Use these menial beginnings to conquer your impulsiveness and learn. Learn to do everything well, from making the tea to editing the front-page story. A good journalist must be a Jack-of-all-trades, John, and a master of them all too.'

Mr Garside was a wonderful mediator. He could dispel

any grievance by his well-chosen pearls of wisdom. He had developed the enviable knack of making even the meaningless sound profound, significant and believable. It seemed that everything was instructing me in the laudable virtue of patience and I could not allow myself any other course than comply with it.

The eve of my birthday fell on a Saturday. When Sergeant Dixon rang the doorbell, I was in the kitchen cleaning my shoes in readiness for a date with Dorothy that night. We had arranged to go to the cinema. Our relationship had hit a bad patch but I will come to that later.

With a 'Who can that be?' Auntie Pat left the wooden spoon suspended in the cake mixture and went to answer the door. She showed the sergeant into the living room, then came back to the kitchen to fetch me.

'Oh, Johnny! Sergeant Dixon's here again. He looks – well, grim is the only word I can use to describe him. Didn't want to tell me anything. Just asked me to go and get you. What's this all about, Johnny? You haven't done anything wrong, have you?'

I tried to allay Auntie Pat's fears with a sweet smile but I knew it wasn't convincing. It certainly did nothing to reassure me.

The sergeant glanced up as we entered the room.

'Hello again, John!' his voice boomed. Auntie Pat was right, he did look grim. And sombreness made his face look much older.

Auntie Pat and I sat on the couch opposite him. His gloomy, almost melancholy, stare was fixed firmly on my expression of very obvious anxiety.

'You told me a lie, John. I don't like that. It makes me wonder how many more lies you've told me.'

'I – I—'

The sergeant interrupted my stuttering. 'The Blue Parrot! You told me you'd never been in there. But I know that was a lie, John. We were called to a little ruckus at the club last night. Found a couple of your friends in there.' He reached inside his breast pocket and pulled out his notebook, turning pages until he found the appropriate one. 'Antonio Gallini and Thomas Callaghan. They are friends of yours, aren't they?'

I lowered my head in a gesture of shame and nodded in acknowledgement.

The policeman continued. 'When questioned, these two friends of yours admitted they'd visited the club before on several occasions, along with—' He consulted his book again, '—Robert Russell, Vivien Spivy—' Then he paused and looked me straight in the eyes, '—and one John Smith! Do you deny that person is you, John?'

Still looking at the floor, I shook my head.

'So, why, John? Why did you tell me you'd never been there when I asked you before?'

'Really, Sergeant!' Auntie Pat interjected. 'Even if it is true that Johnny's been to that club, is it really such an issue – I mean, I know he did wrong but why are you making such a thing about it? Boys will be boys, as they say.'

Sergeant Dixon shifted his gaze to my aunt. 'Mrs Wilkinson, I am investigating the disappearances of a number of women, some going back several years. We thought at first there was nothing to link the disappearances of Miss Ramsbottom and Mrs Jessop with these later ones, but now it appears we may have uncovered one possible connection with at least six, if not all of them—'

Auntie Pat understood the sergeant's inference. She

rose stoically to my defence. 'And I sincerely hope you're not daring to suggest that connection is Johnny, Sergeant? Just because he went to that club, it doesn't mean to say he met those poor women, or had anything to do with their disappearance. Such a suggestion is ridiculous. Totally ridiculous! Johnny and his friends are just a group of silly boys being too big for their boots. It's not their fault. If you're looking for someone to blame, blame the people who run the Blue Parrot. They're the ones who let them in—'

'Mrs Wilkinson, please!' Sergeant Dixon's boom was almost a roar. It had the effect of silencing Auntie Pat in mid flow, her mouth still open with the formation of its last spoken word. The policeman sucked in a huge gasp of air. 'If it is any consolation to you, Mrs Wilkinson, an application is in hand for the revoking of the Blue Parrot's licence and, this time, I think it can be enforced. But that is not really the point we're discussing, is it? I'll tell you what the facts are, Mrs Wilkinson. John knew Miss Ramsbottom – and she disappeared. He knew Mrs Jessop – and she disappeared. He had a mother who disappeared, suddenly and without warning. She's now been missing for nearly seven years. Now I've found out he frequented a place where he could have met other women who have since disappeared. Wouldn't you say that's quite a coincidence? Perhaps just too much of a coincidence?

'I'll tell you something, Mrs Wilkinson. It's enough of a coincidence for me to conduct this interview down at the police station if I cannot be allowed to ask the questions I need to ask here. The choice is yours, Mrs Wilkinson. Now, may I please continue – uninterrupted?'

Auntie Pat, her mouth still agape, was reduced to nodding sheepishly. She could find no more words to say.

The sergeant centred his searing stare on me again. He began to speak but I was only vaguely conscious of what he was saying.

'So, John, what did you get up to at the Blue Parrot?'

Instead, my head echoed other words, words remembered from a distant time but recalled with the clarity of yesterday. '*If the wicked old witch doesn't get you, then one day, that policeman will . . . If the wicked old witch doesn't get you, then one day, that policeman will . . .*'

Those words reverberated through my head. I became dizzy. I thought I was going to pass out.

'What did you get up to at the Blue Parrot, John? The Blue Parrot, John? – John?'

'Er . . . *Take a deep breath, Johnny! Take a deep, deep breath. Concentrate. Shut out her obnoxious utterings. Shut her out of your head.*

'We—' *Yes, that's a good start . . . plural, 'We', make him think you only went there with the others.* 'We had a drink – you can only afford one at the prices they charge – and we watched the floor show and listened to the group – they're not bad actually. The lead singer does a pretty good impression of Mick Jagger.'

'Did you speak to anyone else while you were there?'

'No. We sat at a table on our own. The only time any of us spoke to anyone else was when we went to the bar to buy a drink. Only to the barman, that's all. And sometimes the hostesses, when they came to our table, trying to flog us champagne and packs of cigarettes.'

'Did any of the other women there come up to you – say anything at all to you?'

'No.'

'Some of the women we've questioned said they remembered a boy of about eighteen or so, who was in there alone. They said they saw him speak to a couple of the other girls. They said he went off with them. Have you ever been to the Blue Parrot on your own, John?'

'No!'

'I'll ask you again: have you ever been there alone? Think carefully before you answer, John.'

'No!'

'You've lied to me before, John, why should I believe you now?'

'Because it's true! It's true!' I was near shouting now.

There was then a pause, a long hesitant pause which I think was part of Sergeant Dixon's design to induce me to say more. I didn't rise to the bait. I just sat there, holding his cold grim stare.

'So, how many times would you say you and your pals went to the Blue Parrot, John?'

I thought for a while. 'About four or five times, maybe. No more than half a dozen at the most. At their prices, we couldn't have afforded to go more often even if we'd wanted to.'

'Over what period of time?'

'Six months. Eight months. Maybe a year. I don't know!'

'And – when was the last time you went there, John?'

When was the last time we were there together? I couldn't remember. Tony Gallini would have remembered. Sergeant Dixon would have asked him and Tony would have remembered.

'I – I honestly don't know but I suspect Tony told you when it was.'

'He said the last time you were there with him was three months ago.'

'Well – that's when it was then.'

The sergeant suddenly tried another tack. 'Do you have a girlfriend, John?'

Why did he ask me that? Had he been talking to Dorothy? Had she told him she had gone to the house with me?

Auntie Pat saw this new line of questioning as her cue to get involved again, probably in an attempt to mould the conversation round to a more congenial topic.

'Yes, Sergeant. Her name's Dorothy. She's a lovely girl. Johnny's seeing her tonight and she'll be coming to his party tomorrow night. Johnny will be eighteen tomorrow.'

But Sergeant Dixon could not be swayed from the subject of his former questioning. 'Did you ever take her to the Blue Parrot, John?'

'No!'

'You just went with your other friends, eh?'

'No! Yes! I mean, Bob – er, Bob Russell, didn't always come with us.'

'But you never went there on your own?'

'Really, Sergeant!' God bless Auntie Pat. 'Johnny's already told you he's never been there alone! Why do you keep hounding him like this?'

This time his booming voice did not display its usual exasperation. It was calm, dispassionate and impassive. He turned slowly to face my aunt. 'I'll level with you, Mrs Wilkinson. I'm a worried man. I'm currently investigating ten missing-person enquiries which I think are all connected.'

No, Sergeant! You're way behind the times there; it's thirteen now. I've shown thirteen of them to that deep, dark, secret place.

'And we have a pretty good description of someone we feel may be able to help with our enquiries. A young man, in his late teens – and from the description we have, a perfect ringer for John – was seen leaving the club with two of the missing girls.'

'Look, Sergeant, why can't we clear this up once and for all? I know Johnny and I trust him when he says he's never been to that club alone. Why can't you arrange one of those identity line-ups, or whatever you call them, so that Johnny can be eliminated? Then perhaps you'll go away and leave him in peace!'

Sergeant Dixon glared at my foster mother, a droll smile momentarily consuming the grimness written on his face. 'I would like to eliminate John from our inquiries too, Mrs Wilkinson, but I'm afraid that just isn't possible. Unfortunately for us, and I hope for John too as I'm still willing to give him the benefit of the doubt, those two women who gave us the description of this young man have since gone missing themselves.'

I couldn't control an expression of smugness at hearing this news. I thought, however, for the very briefest of instants, that the policeman's eyes shifted from Auntie Pat to me, at the very moment I displayed my self-righteousness. But there was nothing he could do. The virtue of my cause was preserving me, officiating as my shield and protection. It had directed me to the very ones who could have terminated my endeavours. Then, more than ever before, I felt it was also guiding me in the meritorious path of forbearance. 'Patience, Johnny, patience.' I repeated that thought over and over in the stilled tranquillity of my untroubled mind.

'So, Mrs Wilkinson, John cannot be eliminated from our inquiries. In fact, at the moment, he features very strongly in them.'

I was only vaguely conscious of his further words. I felt

myself to be completely absolved from all blame with the knowledge that I was the avenger of an injustice and my actions were sanctioned by a greater and more righteous authority than the one Sergeant Dixon represented. I knew it was a superior authority, it had suppressed the insufferable utterings of a scornful, mocking mother whose words used to be able to reach me even from the deep, dark depths of the place I had sent her. '*You mark my words, Johnny Smith, and you mark 'em well. If the wicked old witch doesn't get you, then one day, that policeman will. One day, and I don't think it is too far away now, you'll be naughty enough for one of 'em to get you! It's what you deserve, Johnny Smith! It's what you deserve!*' But now her voice was silenced.

'I don't like people disappearing on my patch, John. It bothers me and it gives me a great deal of unnecessary work.'

Sergeant Dixon was speaking to me again. I tried hard to concentrate on what he was saying.

'I'll get to the bottom of this, John. I promise you that. Whatever's going on here, I'll get to the bottom of it, if it's the last thing I do!'

Sergeant Dixon got up to leave. 'John, Mrs Wilkinson.' He reached the living-room door, then turned. 'By the way, John, Happy Birthday for tomorrow. Just think – from tomorrow on you can have a drink in the Blue Parrot quite legally. No longer a juvenile, John. You can be treated like an adult, eh? Have fun at your party. See you again soon, I expect.'

When Auntie Pat returned from showing Sergeant Dixon out, she was greatly troubled.

'What's going on, Johnny?' she said. 'I think we should all sit down and talk about this when your Uncle George gets home.'

I think I managed to persuade her there was really nothing to be concerned about. 'It's a case of mistaken identity, Auntie Pat. That's all it is. Don't worry, justice will prevail.'

And I knew that to be true. The justice of my cause would indeed prevail. Auntie Pat didn't seem so convinced. But, then she couldn't perceive things with the same enlightenment as me, could she?

I slept soundly that night. Even an argument with Dorothy didn't interfere with the soundness of my slumbers. I slept the sleep of the just.

I have already told you that things with Dorothy had, by this time, hit a bad patch. For some time she had been getting increasingly amorous and eager to consummate our relationship, so much so that the old subterfuge of holding fast to our old-fashioned values of no sex before marriage, didn't seem to sway her any more. She accused me of not loving her, of not fancying her and of wanting only 'to continue a relationship of pretence'. And, what was more, if I didn't want to love her in a proper physical way, she would find someone who did.

The only thought I allowed myself about all this was to conclude that if that was what she wanted to do, it was probably for the best. I didn't love Dorothy anyway. Perhaps I never really had. I was old enough now to appreciate the truth – I was infatuated with her simply because she once bore the witch's manifestation of unwholesomeness. And as far as I was concerned, if she chose to take matters into her own hands, it would save me the trouble of having to tell her so. There was no room in my mind to worry over such irrelevances anyhow. It was too fired with its one overriding mission – the mission of redressing injustice. Dorothy was no longer part of my obsession or desire.

She still came to my party though. She came with the obvious intent of flirting with every available boy she could find and of flaunting her philanderings right under my very nose. But what did I care about that? Dorothy Thatcher was only demonstrating what I had always known; that she was a girl of singular unwholesomeness. It's strange how the qualities that first attract you to someone sometimes become the very ones you later find abhorrent.

I had more important business to conduct anyway. I gathered Tony Gallini, Tommy Callaghan, Viv the Spiv and Bob Russell into the kitchen.

'What did that copper say to you when he caught you at the Blue Parrot?' I asked.

Tony and Tommy looked at each other, then at me.

Tony replied, 'He asked a lot of questions about you, Johnny.'

'Like what?'

'Like how many times you'd been there, did we know if you'd ever been there alone, that kind of thing.'

'And had you ever bragged about picking up any girls from the Blue Parrot,' added Tommy.

'And, what did you say?'

They looked at each other again and shrugged their shoulders.

'Dunno. Just that you'd only ever been there with us, as far as we knew. Said you'd never mentioned going there on your own, anyway.'

I thought for a while. 'Look – we've got to get our stories together on this.'

'But what's the big deal, John?' Tommy asked. 'We were let off with a warning. He's not going to do anything else about it now, is he?'

'Listen, you dummies! Some of those tarts who disappeared worked from the Blue Parrot. And I've found out that a boy about our age was seen walking off with a couple of them. Do you want us to be hauled in for further questioning just because he now knows we've all been in there? I know I don't! As long as we get our stories right we can't drop ourselves in the shit.'

'But we didn't do nothing anyway. We ain't got anything to worry about, have we?' interrupted Bob; grammar was never his strong point.

'That,' I said, 'is a chance I don't want to take, do you?'

They all agreed they didn't. So we spent the next three hours remembering dates, remembering everything about our collective visits to the Blue Parrot Club. We got our stories together, down to the minutest detail, even recounting the songs played by the Rolling Stones impersonators and the number of feathers discarded by the 'Delectable Fifi' in her floor shows. And, when we couldn't recall the truth of this trivia, we invented it. In the end, we were able to recount every second of each of the times we went to the Blue Parrot Club, with one like mind.

When we rejoined the party, I remember Gerry and his Pacemakers were wailing out 'Ferry 'cross the Mersey' and Dorothy was smooching with a runtish nerd called Kevin Blowser. When she saw me, Dorothy deliberately lowered her hands and began to grope Kevin's bottom as they danced. I remember that Kevin looked embarrassed but he needn't have worried. I treated Dorothy's blatant demonstration of wantonness with the contempt it deserved. 'Is he the best you can do?' was the only remark I made to her all evening.

Auntie Pat had allowed the party on the strict understanding that no alcohol be consumed but I knew that beer and wine had been smuggled in and, already, many were displaying the effects of intoxication. I knew, as well, that was not the only house rule destined to be broken that night.

As Auntie Pat and Uncle George left the house to, in Uncle George's own words, 'leave us young'uns to it', Auntie Pat had admonished, 'Now, Johnny, be on your best behaviour tonight. I want no trouble. Keep the noise down – and no hanky-panky in the bedrooms! You're already in enough trouble with the police, I don't want you adding to it.'

But, as the lateness of the hour increased, so did the volume of the music despite my continual efforts to adjust it downwards. By eleven-thirty, Dave Clark was screaming out how he felt 'Glad all Over', and I had conceded defeat.

The alcohol was also breaking down the inhibitions of the groping couples and hanky-panky in the bedrooms was, I feared, yet another inevitable consequence – as was my having to clear away the disgusting piles of vomit which overshot the toilet bowl.

The Spiv and a girl called Gloria Stubbs were the first to disappear upstairs and, from the looks of things, three more couples were in the throes of swiftly following; among them Dorothy Thatcher and Kevin Blowser.

At two-thirty the following morning, I had had enough and Tony, Tommy and I began the process of chucking out and clearing up. I must admit I enjoyed bursting in on Dorothy and her nerdish lover and illuminating their embarrassment. Dorothy glared at me with a look of malice as she left with Kevin that night. I thought that was the end of our relationship but I was wrong. Yes, I was so very wrong.

Fortunately no one complained about the noise. Even

more fortunately, by eight o'clock on Monday morning when Auntie Pat and Uncle George arrived back after spending the night with friends of theirs, the house was cleared of debris and was shining like a new pin. The only casualties were two ashtrays and four glasses which, along with the empty evidence of our illicit inebriants, were disposed of far away from the perspicacious eye of Auntie Pat. I remember going into work that morning feeling like the walking dead and vowing only ever to go to parties in future thrown by someone else, so they could have the dubious privilege of clearing up the mess.

The next eighteen months were a very monotonous and wearisome period in my life. I existed even more within the obscurity of ordinariness, my days marked with little I can think of to write about. I would still socialise with Tony and Tommy, no longer at the Blue Parrot which suffered its final demise after its licence was successfully revoked, but somehow, the excitement of going to bars and clubs was lessened now we could all do it legally. The only joy for me was knowing that women of the witch's kind still abounded in havens such as these. I would return their contemptuous, arrogant stares and long for the time when the route to the secret way would be opened up to me again. The fetter of patience was becoming a severe and wearisome impediment.

I heard that Dorothy had left school and had got a job in a bank. The only time our paths ever crossed was when I was late for work. I would then sometimes see her scurrying down the road, rushing to catch her bus. But we never spoke.

During this time, which can best be described as a period of enforced restraint, I can remember but three highlights. The first occurred some two months after his last appearance at the halfway house when Sergeant Dixon paid me another visit, this time accompanied by a detective constable armed with a search warrant.

He never did tell me what he expected to find. I wondered if he might be looking for the stolen keys to my mother's house but he found nothing in my room which seemed to interest him, except the assortment of girlie magazines hidden under a pile of old and unremembered books at the bottom of my wardrobe. I was extremely irritated that he left them strewn all over my bed after he'd finished ogling them. When they were discovered by Auntie Pat, these once venerated facsimiles of female loveliness ended their ignominious existence in the rubbish bin along with the rest of the household refuse.

The second highlight happened on July 20th, 1969, when Auntie Pat, Uncle George and I stayed up into the early hours to watch the fuzzy black and white television pictures of Neil Armstrong descending from Apollo 11 to take the first faltering human steps to the surface of the moon with his now famous words, '. . . one small step for a man, one giant leap for mankind.'

And, at work, my days as the office gofer finally ended when a lovesick junior reporter was fired after it was discovered he'd been using the office telephone for many a happy hour to whisper sweet nothings into the ear of his girlfriend visiting a relative in Australia. I remember my very first journalistic assignment, covering a baby show organised by the Women's Institute. I remember, too, Mr Garside defacing my pristine copy with his celebrated red pencil.

'It's a beautiful baby contest, Smith!' he had said without even looking up at me, handing back a piece of paper displaying more red than black. 'A baby show may seem as boring to you as watching paint dry but that doesn't mean you have to make it sound like a commentary on the three-thirty at Newmarket. The mothers of those cute little darlings are going to cut out your words of literary intent, and put them in scrapbooks to remind their little darlings what wonderful little darlings they were when they have little darlings of their own. Do you remember what I said about patience, Smith? You'll get to the more interesting stuff soon. This tedious interval will one day come to an end . . .'

But just as my ordinary and unremarkable life continued, I was greatly saddened to hear of an extraordinary life which had come to an end. Dr McDonald died after a long illness and the Wilkinson family and their foster son, John Smith, sent a floral tribute. His practice was taken over by a dark-skinned man with a white bushy beard, called Dr Singh. Uncle George said he must have had a bad accident because he always wore a big white bandage round his head. Auntie Pat was more worried about practicalities, reckoning she couldn't '. . . understand one single word he says. I only hope the chemist can understand what he writes in his prescriptions!'

There were many times when I examined the changing paradigms of my own unremarkable life in an attempt to reconcile the worth of my ordinariness against the calibre of someone like Dr McDonald who left an entire community feeling a tremendous sense of loss. I longed for just one distinction; one achievement that could be chiselled on my tombstone after my death as a pronouncement of accomplishment. I think I saw my mission – or my crusade if you prefer to call it that – as my one and only chance of achieving this.

For months and months on end, that one thought occupied my mind. It became an obsession; a fixation. I endured Uncle George trying to cheer me up with his constant attempts at humour and Auntie Pat administering her usual brand of sympathetic understanding until they nearly drove me mad with it. But, of course, I couldn't tell them why I was feeling so miserable. I found it almost impossible to control my impatience. I remember I was grateful for Mr Garside's remark 'This tedious interval will one day come to an end', which, for some reason, I found myself repeating over and over again. I had to concentrate hard on that thought because, such was my obsession, there were so many times I nearly succumbed to the irrationality of foolishness. The secret way was still there, locked in its same deep, dark furtiveness; so near, yet it might just as well have been on the far side of the moon. I think it was only Mr Garside's words of encouragement that both reassured me and acted as a bridle of restraint.

And he was right. That tedious interval did indeed come to an end one cold and frosty February morning in the twentieth year of my life when the legalities of my mother's estate were finally settled. She was lawfully presumed dead and the house and the funds which, with the interest they had accrued, amounted to more than two thousand five hundred pounds, passed to me as her only child, to be held in trust till my coming of age. Auntie Pat became the estate's trustee and administrator. But the glory of that day was not made manifest in my newfound wealth but in my regained access to the secret way. The keys to the house now hung in a closet in Auntie Pat's kitchen. I had duplicates cut at the first opportunity.

Chapter 15

My work could begin again but I was warned of the necessity of prudence by the very One who once filled me with consummate dread and horror, and condemned me as guilty in my childhood nightmares.

I was on trial in that same old oak-panelled courtroom. The figure of the wicked old witch was again the judge but, this time, there were thirteen jurors. I could clearly see the forms of my mother, Miss Ramsbottom, Mrs Jessop, the girl known as Patsy and the recognised but unnamed faces of the other nine contemptuous females I had sent to that deep, dark and secret place.

The wicked witch banged Her stuffed cat down on the desk.

'This court is now in session, Johnny Smith, you have passed the age where your slugs and snails and puppy dogs' tails are tender enough for gobbling. You are not scrummy enough now! No, indeed. But you have been accused yet again of being a very naughty boy!'

There was a rustling whisper around the courtroom then the hairy, warty voice of the wicked old witch continued.

'Who is the one bringing the charge against Johnny Smith?'

'Me!'

A loud voice boomed out. I looked down at the rising figure of Sergeant Dixon. He raised his arm and pointed at me standing in the dock.

There was an audible gasp. I remember the policeman's index finger on the end of his extended arm waggling at me accusingly.

'I know, John Smith, that you have committed a heinous crime!'

Again, a discernible intake of breath filled the courtroom.

'And – of what, exactly, is the naughty Johnny Smith accused?'

I looked down at Sergeant Dixon's waggling finger.

'He keeps making women disappear, your honour.'

The witch laughed; a sinister, inhuman snigger. *'You mean – he's some kind of magician? Does he put them into a magic disappearing cabinet and when he opens the door – hey presto! – they are gone?'*

A roar of laughter echoed round the room.

The policeman glared at the judge, then at me. I could feel the heat of his scrutiny.

'I don't know how he does it, your honour, but I know it's him. I know it!'

'And who, tell me, has he made disappear?'

Sergeant Dixon shifted his gaze to the jury. Once more he raised his arm and pointed. 'Them!'

'Them! But how could he have made them disappear when you see them sitting before you in this very courtroom? Let me see, should we perhaps put your ridiculous supposition to the test and ask the naughty Johnny Smith to try and make them vanish now, in a puff of blue smoke?'

An eruption of hilarity filled the room. The policeman was silenced.

'Of course they have not disappeared. They live with me in my dark, dense and secret place. It is where they've always wanted to live.'

The jury nodded in agreement.

The wicked old witch, Her worshipful honour, pointed Her stuffed black cat at Sergeant Dixon. *'Remove this object of derision from my courtroom!'* she howled.

Amid bellows of raucous laughter, the policeman was hustled from the room by two attendants. His face strained round to stare at me from over his left shoulder, his mouth shouting the words, 'I don't like people disappearing on my patch, John. It bothers me and it gives me a great deal of work to do. I'll get to the bottom of this, John, I promise you that! Whatever's going on, I'll get to the bottom of it, if it's the last thing I ever do!'

He was ushered out, the doors were closed behind him and his shouts were lost to my ears. Her honour lifted Her stuffed black cat, banging its head down on the desk three times. The caterwaul of laughter ceased abruptly as if the stop button were suddenly pressed on a tape machine.

There was silence; a stillness which was daunting. Then the wicked old witch slowly turned Her head and gawked at me with Her beady red eyes.

'You have appeared in my court many times before, Johnny Smith, and always the charge laid before you was that you were a very naughty and very ordinary little boy. Often, I so very nearly sentenced you to be taken away and gobbled up because your slugs and snails and puppy dogs' tails were almost tender enough for gobbling. Like your wonderful mother who cared for you and nurtured you and tried to educate you in the wisdom of

discipline, I thought you would grow up to be a layabout and a waster, destined always to be made of unwholesome things.

'But it appears you have redeemed yourself by attempting, at long last, to make something of your life. You have shown many worthy women to the deep and dark way where I can reveal to them the secret and furtive practices of my mysticism.

'Because of this, I will overlook those other misdemeanours of yours you thought were unseen. Your filthy self-abuse, your attempts to deflower the sugar and spice of Dorothy Thatcher with your foulness and all your other lewd and lascivious pursuits, for which you have remained unpunished, I will overlook. But that does not mean you have been pardoned.

'Johnny Smith, you are free to go! Free to continue with the fine and illustrious labours you began of your own free will. But do not be misled, Johnny Smith, do not be misled! I know your motives in doing these things are not pure. You think you are carrying out a crusade and striking a blow for the repressed and lowly male but, true to the inferior intelligence of your gender, it has never occurred to you that your work is benefiting my service by recruiting more and more like me to the worthy cause of punishing other little boys who pursue a life of naughtiness. You have always been selfish, Johnny Smith! You never did spare a thought for those "other little boys", did you? Just as long as you weren't one of them.

'Still – never mind, despite your fallacious reasoning you are serving me now. That's all that really matters. I'll have lots and lots of naughty little boys to gobble up. They're scrummy! Ver-ry scrum-my indeed! But let me give you two little morsels of advice you will do well to heed.

'Never – never again, Johnny Smith – aspire to gain carnal knowledge of any woman you discern is of my calling. I will permit none to be contaminated even with thoughts of your odiousness.

'And, pay attention, Johnny Smith – it will be good for you to listen intently to this. Temper your diligence with caution and circumspection. I do not suffer fools gladly! I cannot continue to protect you. Be wise, Johnny Smith! Be careful. Be wary. Be conscientious. That Sergeant Dixon is like a bloodhound with your sniff about him!'

She then brought down Her stuffed black cat, bang, bang, bang, three times on the desk. *'This court is now adjourned!'*

A month or so later, I remember sitting at my desk at the *Comet*, bashing my typewriter, working on a report of the local football team's five-nil drubbing by Addlestone Rovers. I could see into the goldfish bowl of Mr Garside's office. He was talking on the telephone, gesticulating with great excitement, sometimes sitting and waving his free arm about all over the place, and sometimes pacing wildly up and down as far as the cord would allow. I watched him slam down the phone and rush out into the general office.

'Hold the front page! What number did we get up to on the Where-Are-They-Women story? Whatever it was, add two more. Would you believe it? After eighteen bloody months, it's all started up again! Johnson, in my office; Appleyard, get in touch with the police for an official statement. See what you can find out about these new ones. Names? Were they whores? Ages? And whatever else you can dig up. I want to know everything there is to know. Even their bloody vital statistics!'

The lead story the following day was headlined 'A Baker's Dozen! The Where-Are-They-Women tally now hits thirteen.' The report continued: 'Two more local women have disappeared. Thirteen women living in the area have now mysteriously disappeared over the past five years.

'The *Comet* began its reports with the sudden and unexplained disappearance in 1966 of a social worker, Joyce Ramsbottom, aged 23, and a well-known and respected resident of Melrose Rise, Gertrude Jessop, aged 72. Fifteen months later came a spate of disappearances of women who were all known prostitutes. The women, many of whom were using the now closed-down Blue Parrot Club, went missing on a regular basis over the next ten months.

'Now, after a further eighteen-month lull, two more women have gone missing. An official police statement says, "The two latest women are thought to be prostitutes but, at this early stage of our inquiries, I'm afraid we cannot divulge any further details."

'The *Comet*, however, can report yet another disappearance, previously unconnected to the more recent ones, which occurred as far back as 1962. In this year a previous resident of Melrose Rise, Mrs Helen Smith, then aged 29, disappeared without trace. Mrs Smith once lived in the house opposite Mrs Jessop's. She has now been presumed dead. (Full story on page 3.)'

On page 3, the whole story was set out in detail.

'Are the strange disappearances of the Where-Are-They-Women part of a nine-year-old intrigue? That is the question posed by the *Comet* as two more local women go missing.

'On March 15th, 1962, an eleven-year-old boy named John Smith, who by coincidence now works as a junior reporter for this paper, was found living alone at his home in Melrose Rise. His mother had simply told him she was 'going away' though she didn't say where. The mother,

Mrs Helen Smith, has now legally been presumed dead after being missing more than seven years.

'She was not numbered among the count of the mysterious Where-Are-They-Women at first, since her disappearance happened five years before Miss Ramsbottom and Mrs Jessop went missing in 1967. Mrs Smith was originally thought to be just one of the many thousands of missing persons reported throughout the UK every day.

'But now we can expose some startling revelations surrounding the disappearance of Helen Smith and the later disappearances of Joyce Ramsbottom and Gertrude Jessop. Mrs Jessop was a very close friend and confidante of Mrs Smith and it was Gertrude Jessop who first discovered John living alone after his mother went missing. Mrs Jessop's later disappearance therefore does beg the question, did Helen Smith perhaps impart some confidential information to her very close friend and neighbour about her intent to go missing? Or perhaps, did Mrs Jessop later discover something about Mrs Smith's disappearance which might, in some way, have been responsible for her own?

'The strange intrigue continues following the disclosure that Joyce Ramsbottom was the social worker assigned to John Smith's case. She kept in contact with the boy long after he was removed from her case list. A police spokesman has admitted her continued interest may have been as a self-styled "private detective" intent on solving the strange case of Helen Smith's disappearance. Did she uncover the same vital clue, perhaps, as Mrs Jessop? A critical discovery which might eventually have led to her own mysterious disappearance?

'These questions are as yet unanswered but the police

have given their permission for these details to be made known in the hope that our readers might be able to give them more information which will aid their inquiries.

'Detective Sergeant Dixon, one of the police inquiry team, disclosed yesterday, "These are very curious cases and, as time goes on, they grow even more perplexing." When asked if the cases could turn into murder inquiries, he added, "I can only comment on that if and when we discover a body or bodies. But, through your paper, I'd like to appeal to anyone who knows any of the women who have been reported as missing and who hasn't yet contacted us, to come forward. We need to hear from anyone who feels they can help us build a personal profile of any of those who have disappeared in order to establish if a definite link exists between them." (A full list of the missing women appears on Page 6.)

'An incident room has been set up for all enquiries. Alternatively, you can contact the *Comet*'s editorial desk and we will put you in touch with an officer in the police investigations team.

'In the meantime, the intrigue surrounding the curious and bizarre case of the Where-Are-They-Women continues to unfold.

'The *Comet* will keep you informed of any further developments as and when they happen.'

The full story on the *Comet*'s inside page was written by yours truly – the first journalistic assignment of any merit I was given to do. At last, I was presented with the opportunity to demonstrate my writing skills. And on a subject of which I had inside knowledge. The words came easily.

You may think, just as I did at the time, that the *Comet* didn't have a clue about connecting my mother's disappearance with the missing 'Where-Are-They-Women', her demise being hidden in the mists of too many distant years. I certainly didn't volunteer the information about her to the paper, I can assure you of that. Perhaps I should explain exactly how it happened. That day is etched on my memory as clearly as if it were yesterday.

Soon after rushing in to tell us about the two new missing women, Mr Garside went out for a couple of hours. When he returned, he closeted himself in his office, speaking constantly on the telephone and referring to the journals he'd brought back with him, which now completely covered his desk. Then, early in the afternoon, his roar of 'Smith! Get in here!' rose above the customary clatter of the general office.

He looked up at me as I entered his inner sanctum, an incredulous expression on his face. 'I've just been reading a report from our High Court correspondent on a case in the family division a few months back. I've done a bit of checking. A Helen Smith who disappeared over eight years ago just happens to be your mother! Do you want to know what else I've found out?'

No, I did not want to know. I remember standing there feeling very uneasy, wondering exactly what other bit of information his investigative delving might have uncovered. I just looked at him, sensing the colour instantly ebb from my face. 'Er – yes – of course, Mr Garside,' I lied.

I don't think he noticed my apprehension because he carried on as if I wasn't there. 'Miss Ramsbottom; Mrs Jessop! You knew them too, Smith, didn't you?' He sounded surprised.

Yes, of course I knew them! Had he forgotten it was my testimony of knowing those two women – my 'Personal Recollections of a Friend' – that got me this crappy job in the first place? I felt a little easier, my peace of mind restored by the realisation that his brand-new disclosure was probably nothing more than the recent placing of an unremembered bit of trivia.

'Yes, I went out to see old Bob Miller earlier,' he continued.

'Who?' I questioned.

'Bob Miller! Retired before you came here. Used to be a reporter back in '66 when the "Where-Are-They-Women" story first broke with Miss Ramsbottom and Mrs Jessop. Except they weren't the first, were they, Smith? It now seems your mother was! Anyhow, Bob remembers hearing a rumour that you knew them both. Said he even interviewed you but he didn't get anything he could use. Then it came back to me. "The Where-Are-They-Women – Personal Recollections of a Friend"!' He pointed to a page of an old copy of the *Comet* spread out on his desk, his red pencil having highlighted my essay inside a lopsided circle. 'See there! By John Smith, aged sixteen.'

'But, Mr Garside, I thought you knew! I mean, I thought you realised. Wasn't it that article which made you offer me the job in the first place?' I uttered, mystified.

Mr Garside first looked nonplussed, then a little embarrassed. 'Er, not exactly.' He looked at me and smiled, his face softening with a strange expression of entreaty. 'Look, John, do you have any idea how many letters we get every month from readers hoping against hope that we'll publish them in our humble little rag? Hundreds, literally hundreds. Of course I remember your article now. But the old brainbox is not what it used to be. I didn't place the connection – not until today anyway. I must confess, I didn't even remember it when you came for your interview and you showed me the letter I sent promising you a job here. Goodness, I even have trouble these days remembering what happened yesterday. When I took you on, all I knew was that we needed a junior and, if I'd promised you a job all those years ago, well, there must have been a damned good reason, mustn't there? Now, of course, I remember what that reason was.' His eyes lowered and he pointed to the words encased within his thick red pencil mark. 'This shows – this shows—'

'Style and flair?' I answered sarcastically.

'Yes—'

I remember he looked up at me then, long and hard, the enthusiasm that had previously shone in his face draining away to a look of bleak contemplation. He instantly dismissed any further praise for my article of yesteryear as he focused his mind on another, less agreeable, thought.

'So – you knew Miss Ramsbottom; you knew Mrs Jessop; you obviously knew your mother. Tell me, Smith, did you by any chance know those prostitutes as well?'

He surveyed me quizzically and he had called me Smith again. I realised we had now returned to professional issues rather than personal ones. I felt that same apprehension capture me and swallow me whole. It was difficult to think, but I had to. And fast. Mr Garside was no fool.

'Prostitutes? Mr Garside, you are joking, aren't you? I served my misspent youth in the Sixties. You know, miniskirts, promiscuousness and birth-control pills? I'm surprised prostitutes can still make a living. I mean, does *anyone* really have to pay for it any more?'

His sullen stare continued for a while then, quite suddenly and unexpectedly, he threw back his head and laughed. It took me by complete surprise because I'd never heard Mr Garside laugh before. 'I'm afraid we're not all blessed with still being in our prime, John,' he said when he was in control of himself again. 'I doubt the new breed of enlightened, miniskirted young lady you hang around with would be quite so willing to open up her charms to battered old farts like me, no matter how promiscuous she is. No, John, while there are still middle-aged men around, the world's oldest profession will survive, even in these so-called liberal times.' He thought for a moment in silence, then added, 'I'm willing to bet that's who our abductor is, John – a lonely, middle-aged bloke with a chip on his shoulder, probably someone who's had a bad experience at the hands of some calculating female at some time in his life. Yes, that's the kind of bloke who's doing it. You mark my words! But what's he doing with them, John, that's the real poser, isn't it? They seem to be disappearing off the face of the earth.'

He had called me John again, so I thought the moment might be right to try and use my obvious personal interest to my own advantage. 'Mr Garside,' I said sheepishly, 'what about giving me a crack at writing this story? After all, by some strange coincidence, I actually knew several of the women involved so I can probably give it that warm, personal touch. You know – that little bit of extra *je ne sais quoi*, that bit of style and flair.'

I remember he put his hands behind his head and leant back on his swivel chair, his eyes raised to the ceiling. There was a pause; an interminable pause.

'Okay, Smith!' he said. 'But be prepared for your beautiful work to suffer the consequence of my infamous red pencil! Have it on my desk no later than three-thirty.'

I just stared at him in disbelief.

'Well, Smith! What are you waiting for?'

And so, founded only on Mr Garside's reacquaintance with a long-forgotten piece of written nonsense, and a moment of lightheartedness that seemed to promote a theory in his mind which removed me from the frame of implication, I was given my big opportunity to prove myself. I rushed from his room straight over to my desk and typewriter and within the hour he was reading my copy. He returned it without appending a single red pencil mark.

'Well, Smith! Seems as if the tedious interval may have passed sooner than either of us expected.'

I knew that was the nearest I would ever get to a commendation from Mr Garside.

'Yes, Mr Garside,' I replied, 'perhaps it does!'

I still remember riding high on that wave of euphoria. Even Ted Clark, the *Comet*'s bad-tempered office chief, known satirically as 'mild-mannered Clark', complimented me on the article. But I really wanted to publish the truth; I knew it should have been the 'Where-Are-They-*Fifteen*' and I wondered about the sad lives of the undisclosed two whom I had sent to that deep, dark secret place years before, yet their disappearances still hadn't been reported. I thought it was sad that nobody seemed to care enough to miss them. But at least they were happy now.

That night, I wanted to demonstrate my appreciation of these things by showing another one the way to her happiness. But I was restrained by the counsel of the wicked old witch Herself; Her words of prudence were recited in the silence of my mind.

'And, pay attention, Johnny Smith, it will be good for you to

listen intently to this. Temper your diligence with caution and circumspection. I do not suffer fools gladly. I cannot continue to protect you. Be wise, Johnny Smith! Be careful. Be wary. Be conscientious. That Sergeant Dixon is like a bloodhound with your sniff about him!'

Chapter 16

So the cause continued to proceed; slowly, with diligence, with care and with wisdom, aided by inside information on the progress and direction of the police inquiries afforded me by my job at the *Comet.* Because of the good work I had done on the 'Where-Are-They-Women' story, from that day on I became one of the paper's fully-fledged reporters so I had access to all the information the police released on the case and was always able to keep one jump ahead of the 'sniffing bloodhound'. And, talking of Sergeant Dixon, he didn't bother me again while I continued to live at the halfway house. I guess his fruitless search of my bedroom satisfied his curiosity, for a while at least.

Perhaps I should explain that I was born of a time when most youngsters were conditioned into believing that adulthood begins at twenty-one. Although my teenage years saw the advent of lobbying against the legislative nonsense which permitted youths of eighteen to die fighting for their country yet gave them no voice in voting for the government that might send them off to war, and led to the age of majority being reduced to eighteen in 1969, I don't believe my mind will ever release the concept that adult life begins at twenty-one. And now I would soon be that age; the mystical age of old universal suffrage when my conditioning dictated I would be legally accountable for my actions as an adult. I suppose it could be said I began to feel that I was finally making something of my life and could embark on this new era with confidence. Things definitely seemed to be improving and I even began to think I might haul myself up from the rut of ordinariness. But, if I were ruthlessly honest with myself, I suppose the underlying reason for my newfound self-esteem was the thought that I was finally achieving something worthwhile to make my mother proud of me.

Yet, as so often seems to happen in life, at the very moment you begin to feel in control again, fate decides to take a hand in the reshaping of your destiny by initiating a brand new set of circumstances. It wasn't that the new player in the game of my life was unknown to me, but her predicament certainly was.

I remember I had worked late that night on the latest milestone in the continuing saga of the 'Where-Are-They-Women'. The paper's tally had then hit nineteen with the inclusion of my mother, accepted from that day on by the *Comet* – for the sake of sensationalism, if nothing else – as the first to do a vanishing act. However, my diary recorded the actual number as twenty-two. It seemed I had been directed to yet another poor cow who had no one in her miserable life to report her as missing. But, thankfully, I was able to redeem her sadness by showing her the way to the salvation of the sisterhood.

The mysterious case of the missing women had long since commanded national coverage and the local police, frustrated by the adverse publicity of drawing blanks, had enlisted the help of Scotland Yard in solving the ongoing and baffling enigma. The view still held by Detective Sergeant Dixon was that all the disappearances were somehow related whereas the current theory proposed by Detective Inspector Ribble – the new chief of the investigations team – was, it seemed, to dismiss any connection between the disappearances of my mother, Miss Ramsbottom and Mrs Jessop and the disappearances of the prostitutes as nothing more than a red herring. He had said, 'We now believe there is no link between the two groups of disappearances. We are dealing with two separate and distinct sets of incidents and are concentrating our immediate efforts on the later ones because the disappearance of these girls seems to be an ongoing situation.'

I remember, too, that Jimmy Appleyard – a fellow *Comet* drone, assigned to cover the 'Where-Are-They-Women' story with me – had asked Ribble if the police had any clues on the likely abductor of these girls. He answered immediately, almost smugly, 'Yes, we've carried out an exhaustive psychological profile on the type of person who might be involved in some way with these disappearances. We think he's probably a middle-aged man, a loner, almost certainly without any regular girlfriends or even female companions, someone who keeps himself pretty much to himself, more likely than not in his mid-forties to early fifties.' It seemed a case of the blind leading the blind. I learnt later that Ribble and Mr Garside had become bosom golfing buddies and the 'psychological profile' was probably nothing more than an amalgam of the theories they had discussed at the nineteenth.

I had had a long day unravelling all these confused and muddled theories into a concise and intelligible report for the next morning's edition of the paper and was looking forward to unwinding – perhaps reading, perhaps dozing, against the backdrop of mindless television – when the doorbell rang. Auntie Pat and Uncle George had gone out for the evening so I decided I could, and would, ignore the intrusion. But the doorbell rang again. Then again. Its persistence was driving me to distraction. The fifth ring was determined and unending. It was still sounding when I angrily opened the door. I looked at the pathetic figure on the doorstep.

'Dorothy!' My anger quickly subsided.

I could see she had been crying. Her eyes were puffy and red and her mascara had run down her cheeks in black powdery rivulets.

'I knew you were in, Johnny. I had to speak to you!' Her words were almost inaudible through her persistent whimpers.

'Dorothy, what on earth is wrong with you?'

She just looked up at me with sad, doleful eyes.

'You'd better come in,' I said.

I showed her into the living room and offered her a cup of tea. Then I remember suggesting she might like something stronger, knowing Uncle George kept some brandy in the sideboard, '. . . for medicinal purposes only, of course!' Her silence declined my suggestion.

I sat beside her on the couch. 'Now, tell me what's wrong.'

She flung her arms around me in one involuntary action, buried her head in my chest and howled. Her tears came in floods and I began to think they would never stop.

I remember feeling irritated at this woman who, by her own choice and not my own, had entered my life again for the first time in nearly three years only to use my shirt as a handkerchief. And what was more, I liked that shirt and she was ruining it with her mascara-laden tears. I pushed her away from me and held her face between my hands, forcing her to look me in the eyes. She fought against my grip, seemingly intent on nestling into my chest again to continue soiling my shirt.

'Dorothy, for God's sake tell me what's wrong!'

She just went on whimpering.

'Dorothy!' I shouted. 'What is it?'

She stopped crying. It was almost an act of defiance. 'Sometimes I hate you Johnny Smith! I'm pregnant!' she screamed at me. There was anger in her voice; extreme anger.

Two things occurred to me on hearing her news. Why did she hate me? I wasn't the one responsible for her condition. And, why was she telling me anyway and not the one who *was* responsible? I wondered which of these enquiries I should submit to her first.

I decided on the former.

'So why do you hate me? I didn't do it to you.'

She stared into my eyes again. 'That's another thing I hate about you, Johnny. You're stupid sometimes!'

Not getting any sense from my first line of questioning, I presented my second. 'Why are you telling me and not the bloke who made you pregnant?' I then added as an afterthought, 'Was it that nerd, Kevin Blowser?'

Her eyes blazed with hatred. 'He raped me! That bastard raped me!'

She screamed and burst into uncontrollable tears again.

This time I let her nestle into my chest. I had resigned myself by now to the fact that my shirt would be irrevocably ruined.

I remember looking down at the back of her head, gently rocking from side to side as she sobbed into the sanctuary of my shirt-front. Her chestnut hair still glistened and smelt of the same fragrant shampoo it always had. I softly stroked it, letting its silky strands cascade gently through my fingers.

Slowly, her sobbing stopped. Her anger had passed and her words were softer, more subdued. 'Kevin raped me, Johnny! I'm going to have his baby.'

She lifted her face and her eyes looked into mine as if to gauge my reaction. To be honest, I don't know how I felt at that moment. I think I was still too nonplussed by her sudden reappearance into my life to be able to give her new predicament much consideration. On reflection, I suppose my next remark was not the most sympathetic or compassionate of responses I could have made.

'You didn't seem to be putting up much of a fight the last time I saw you with that nerdy Blowser. Remember? My party, three years ago?'

She released herself from my arms and jumped to her feet, standing with her back towards me. I thought she would get angry again but, instead, there was a long silence while she struggled to regain her self-control. Suddenly she turned.

'Like I said, Johnny, you're so stupid at times and you don't know much about women! Don't you understand I only did that to hurt you? I never really fancied Kevin. I wanted to pay you back for – for—'

'For what?'

The whimpering came again, her words only forming

on the crest of each breath. 'I – only –ever – loved – you –Johnny – but – you – never – wanted – me!'

Her sobbing was uncontrollable again. She collapsed back onto the couch, her head cupped in her hands.

Of all the things I have ever had to face in life, I think that moment with Dorothy was the most upsetting. She looked so pitiful, so forlorn, I knew I would have done anything to ease her pain. I would have done it without thinking, without regard to any consequence of that action. I believe I would have cut off my right arm there and then if I thought it would have turned her tears into laughter. I would have performed three back flips or attempted to walk across the ceiling. Perhaps it would have been preferable if I had striven to accomplish any of these things because, instead, I did something even more foolish; something a nagging voice in the back of my head told me would have repercussions much more serious than I could ever imagine. But I didn't listen to that voice. It became lost beneath the sounds of Dorothy's incorrigible snivels.

I put my arms around her. 'Marry me, Dorothy. Please marry me. I'll look after you. You and the baby. We'll say the baby's mine!'

As I was saying those words, I thought of the moment fate had directed Harry Smith to that home for unmarried mothers in Addlestone. I thought of my father's altruism in sacrificing his life in a loveless marriage for my sake. I knew that was why I had given that pledge. I owed it to my father's memory to sacrifice my own happiness for the life of someone else's bastard just as he had done for me. He was a wonderful man and I will always love him. It was my way of proving that adoration.

Dorothy's sobs turned to little sniffles, she threw her

arms around my neck and found my mouth with hers.

'You – you really love me that much? Enough to tell the world the baby's yours? Oh, Johnny, my darling Johnny!'

She held me again and would not let me go.

And so it happened that my fate was sealed; sealed in a brief and blind moment of foolishness inspired by the memory of eleven cherished years of devotion shown me by a truly wonderful and remarkable man.

It wasn't till I walked Dorothy home that I began to perceive the significance of my reckless oath as my mind gradually cleared. As I half listened to her ceaseless babble about the wonderful future we were bound to have together, my own unspoken thoughts brought up a multitude of obstacles, not the least of which was my evident impotence.

Dear Dorothy! Why did you have to reinvade my life and remind me of my inadequacies? Why did you have to force me to make a promise that should never have been made? But my vow had been sworn and my father, in whose dear remembrance I had sworn it, always impressed upon me the seriousness of a spoken oath. 'Always keep your word, Johnny,' he had said. 'Never break a promise you have made.' And, with the same misguided allegiance to his honour which first caused that vow to be uttered, I knew the promise it carried would remain with me for ever; always for worse rather than better, always done out of a burdensome obligation, never out of love.

That night I waited for Auntie Pat and Uncle George to come home and made them sit down in the living room without even giving Auntie Pat the chance to make their nightly cup of cocoa.

'I've got something to tell you both.'

I should have sounded happy but, of course, I didn't. I remember they looked at each other with expectations of a pronouncement of doom rather than the announcement of my engagement.

'Dorothy and I are getting married.'

'But – but—' stuttered Auntie Pat, 'I didn't even know you were seeing her again. How long have you been—'

'I wanted to make sure about things this time,' I interrupted, 'before telling you we were really serious about one another.'

Auntie Pat stared at me with that look of wise perception which usually meant she had discerned something contradictory in my words.

'Johnny!' she almost bellowed, 'you don't have to, do you? Get married, I mean?'

I didn't want to lie to them but neither could I commit Dorothy's disgrace to the villainy of someone else, especially a nerd like Kevin Blowser. In the circumstances, I thought it best for Auntie Pat to draw her own conclusions from my silence. I just stared at the floor with a feigned expression of shame. It had the desired effect.

'Johnny! How could you! And I'm surprised at Dorothy! I always thought she was a more sensible girl than . . . Oh, Johnny, don't get me wrong. I like Dorothy and I know she'll make you a lovely wife. I just wish it didn't have to be like this for you both.'

I wanted to explain to her we'd only just come out of the swinging Sixties, the age of so-called sexual enlightenment. Sex before marriage – and conception out of wedlock, for that matter – were no longer regarded with the same disgrace they used to be. But, of course, I didn't say these things. Apart from Dorothy herself, Auntie Pat was the only woman who had ever shown me love. I couldn't debase that love by deriding her highly principled values.

She looked at me, then she smiled. 'Ah well! What's done is done, I suppose. Can't be undone now, can it?'

With that, she rushed over to me and gave me a big hug. 'Be happy, Johnny! Be happy.' Her words came tearfully.

Uncle George then came and shook my hand, at the same time giving me a knowing wink. 'Congratulations, lad! 'Least it shows you've got lead in your pencil.'

'Shut up, George!' Auntie Pat didn't appreciate his humour and, for the first time I can really remember, neither did I.

'How far gone is she, Johnny?' Auntie Pat left no time for me to answer which was just as well since I didn't have an answer to give. 'We've got to make the wedding arrangements quickly. I'll speak to Dorothy tomorrow – and her mother. Us girls will take over now; make all the arrangements. You just leave everything to us.'

And that was a matter in which I knew I had no choice.

On the occasion of my twenty-first birthday a week or so later, there was no rowdy party such as marked my eighteenth. The evening was a quiet affair spent at a local restaurant where Dorothy and I nervously entertained Mr and Mrs Thatcher, Auntie Pat and Uncle George. It was part of the arrangements made by 'the girls' so we could all get to know one another better and make an event of the official engagement of Dorothy and myself. The moment of putting the ring on her finger was toasted with champagne and accompanied by oohs and aaghs, and a blush from my fiancée.

The wedding date had already been arranged. I was to be a bachelor boy for only two more months. 'The girls' had decided Dorothy would be a late autumn bride. It was simply assumed, or probably it's more accurate to say it was yet another decision made by 'the girls', that we would set up home in the old house. No one bothered to ask me how I felt about that but I suppose, since every other arrangement had been reached without consulting Uncle George or me, who were we to question this one? But, actually, I didn't really think it was such a bad idea. At least I could remain the vigilant caretaker of the secret way.

Auntie Pat had agreed that five hundred pounds of my inheritance could be used to fix up the house after more than ten years of neglect, and a firm of building contractors was hired to do the work. But, by a unanimous decision of 'the girls' under Auntie Pat's chairmanship, the labours of Uncle George and myself were donated completely free of charge, to work on the house at weekends to render that 'personal touch' under the committee's supervision.

So Uncle George and I began our toil, most of the time under the direction of at least one of the committee who would be there with books of wallpaper samples or swatches of fabric or with a tape measure assessing the amount of curtain material or carpeting required. We were packed off in the morning with sandwiches and a flask of tea so none of our precious time would be wasted in taking pub lunches. As Auntie Pat had said, 'Us girls will take over now!' And so, indeed, they had.

I remember one particular Saturday. It was just one beautiful day in a glorious Indian summer. Uncle George and I were eating our sandwiches sitting on the back patio by the kitchen door.

He looked at me with a typical expression of the resigned forbearance of the downtrodden male.

''Spose we'll have to think about doing something with this garden soon, Johnny. It's looking like a forest out here – God, it's gonna be one helluva job!'

Our eyes met, he shrugged his shoulders and appeared to lift his gaze skywards as if to seek divine inspiration. Then he carried on munching in silence.

It was certainly true. There was no demarkation of the forest at all now. My mother's special patch had gradually slithered its borders all the way down to the backyard door. Brambles, nettles and clambering convolvulus had strangled out the beauty of my father's rose and fuchsia beds and those pretty little border flowers which, in the distant recesses of my memory, I remembered by sight if not by name. For an instant, I again felt sadness and anger at this good man's wasted labour.

'And that dead tree! I 'spose that'll have to come down.' Uncle George was still contemplating the 'helluva job'.

He looked at me apprehensively, wondering, I suppose, if his comment had evoked any remembrances of that terrible tragedy in the tree house which once nestled in that sad dead yew. I smiled at him to convey the thought that all those horrors had now passed. But there was one overriding apprehension his remark had raised.

The forest. The whole garden had now been swallowed up in its denseness. Sooner or later, Dorothy, or one or other of the committee, would demand its clearance. But I needed it to stay intact and undisturbed. It hid the secret way and had to remain, just as nature had embellished it.

Uncle George stopped munching again.

'I see you've already made a start at clearing it. Isn't that a freshly dug patch over there?'

His finger was pointing at a plot of newly dug sods

which, although growing a profusion of tender green sprouts, had obviously been cleared of the dense bramble growing either side of it.

'Er – yes!' I stuttered. 'I had a go at that a couple of weeks ago. Too much like hard work though. That's all I did. Gave up after that bit! Growing again already, I see! Doesn't take long, does it?'

Uncle George gave that look of despair again.

'Look, Uncle George! I think we've got enough to do inside the house. That's the most important thing, isn't it? Let's go in and shut the door. Forget anything out here exists – at least for a while.'

He turned his head and gave me a long hard stare. 'I'm with you on that one, Johnny boy. If we'll be allowed to get away with it, that is!'

We went inside, Uncle George still muttering, 'A helluva job! A helluva job!'

Six weeks later, the redecoration of the house was complete and its refurbishment, apart from a few pieces – presents from Dorothy's parents still to be delivered – was finished. Also, three more patches of freshly dug earth had appeared in the forest, unnoticed amid the debris of building waste temporarily cast into the garden. And, mercifully, not one of the committee had made an issue of restoring the garden to any semblance of its former glory. It was a unanimous decision that not enough time remained to undertake the task before the wedding but I had to give a promise that I would give the chore my attention in the not too distant future.

It was a busy time for me but, despite everything else which had to be done, the three newly dug plots confirmed my continuing conviction to the cause.

In case it is difficult for you to keep abreast of the number of witches I had shown to that deep, dark and secret place, the real tally by then stood at twenty-five. It had become more difficult to find them; the national publicity given to the case had made them too fearful to ply their trade in the local haunts and I had to go further afield in my quest. This confounded the police enquiries even more and the official count had only reached twenty-one. I remember my headline for the *Comet*, 'Where-Are-They-Women Come of Age! Twenty-one now centre in missing persons hunt'. I was proud of that. It appealed to my droll sense of humour that we had both come of age together.

I say it had become more difficult to find them and that is indeed true. But once I had found one, sending her through the secret way was not an onerous job at all. It was easy to get them to come back to the house with me. They were led by their very arrogance; by their very despising of the lowly detestable men on whom they preyed. They believed they were servicing a need. And indeed they were. But, in my case, it was a different need. I wasn't like a normal client, one of the weak submissive kind of man who allows a little puppy dog's tail to control his life. I was strong. I had power over them. And, believe me, those women soon found that out.

'Yes, but twenty-five?' I almost hear you say. 'That's almost unthinkable. How come you managed to despatch that number without once being observed in the act? And you must have had a very large garden as well.' Well, yes, I had. Though that 1930s terraced house was small, the garden was relatively large. And anyway, it's surprising just how small a forest you actually need to despatch twenty-five women if you plan it well enough! And I was also fortunate that our garden was screened on either side by a row of poplars that had grown to a height above the level of our neighbours' bedroom windows. My showing those women the secret way was never observed. Anyway, as I have already said, the righteousness of my cause was protecting me.

Yes, I had sent twenty-five contemptuous women to the service of their mistress. But I knew it had to stop there. Yet I thought at first it would just be a temporary lull, a respite. Although I hadn't really considered how I would continue my work after Dorothy and I were living under that one roof, playing at the charade of being husband and wife, I had figured I would be shown a way. Little did I know then that was where it would stop, for ever, thwarted by the consequences of a ridiculous and disastrous marriage. But I was close – so damned close to completing an assignment which would have absolved me. It was on the night before my wedding when the mistress told me just how close I was.

The court was in session. I was again charged with the naughtiness and ordinariness of which I had so often been accused. I was indicted by a whole body of accusers, and was looking down on them from my customary position in the dock of that courtroom. I saw Detective Inspector Ribble, a face with a permanent synthetic smile and known to me because his leering photograph had appeared so many times in the *Comet*'s pages. I saw Sergeant Dixon's stern and sullen countenance with his finger pointing at me derisively. And I saw the rest of the police investigations team standing behind them as a wave of blurred and indistinct faces.

The jury benches were now overcrowded with the figures of the twenty-five women who had been counselled by the wicked old witch Herself, since living with Her in that dense, dark and secret forest.

Her honour, the wicked old witch, was speaking to my accusers.

'Not only do you insist on wasting the court's time again with your ridiculous calumnies concerning women you see before your very eyes yet still claim have disappeared, but this time, you come as an assembled horde. What's the matter? Do you need to hold one another's hands?'

A titter of laughter rippled round the room.

She banged Her stuffed black cat down on the desk. Bang! Bang! Bang! *'Case dismissed! And I never want to see any of you in my courtroom ever again!'*

As the policemen were being ushered away, the court echoed with Sergeant Dixon's booming voice. 'This is a travesty of justice, your honour! John Smith is guilty of making those women disappear. I know it!'

Then he shouted directly at me. 'I don't like people disappearing on my patch, John! It bothers me and it gives me a great deal of work to do. I'll get to the bottom of this, John, I promise you that! Whatever's going on, I'll get to the bottom of it. If it's the last thing I do I'll have you in a real courtroom one day. You'll stand trial and you'll be convicted. You have my word on that, John!'

The big oak doors shut behind them against a babble of whispered murmurs from the public gallery.

Bang! Bang! Bang! Silence was restored straight away.

All eyes were on the wicked old witch but Her beady red ones, looking even more sinister and threatening than ever, were focused on me.

'That sniffing bloodhound won't give up, will he, Johnny Smith? But, never mind, soon your work will be done. Count the number!' She pointed a gnarled and leathery finger at the

figures in the jury box. *'Count the number of women you have directed to my cause. Well, do you not see, Johnny Smith – twenty-five! One more will make twenty-six. A magic number! A truly magic number! Do you know why, Johnny Smith, do you know why?'*

I shook my head.

'Because thirteen is the enchanted number of my coven and twenty-six will make two, Johnny Smith – two covens; and two is the number of completeness. Completeness as in marriage; the dominant female and the submissive male. The perfect alliance; the sacred combination; the inseparable complements. Remember that as you start the journey of your own marriage tomorrow. Honour your wife, Johnny Smith. Do not defile her with your foulness! But in all else, submit to her authority.

'Just one more. Send me just one more to complete my second coven, then your task will be done. And, anyway, it's getting too damned crowded down in my deep, dark and secret forest.

'Do as I say, Johnny Smith, and I will pardon you for all your past misdemeanours. It will make your mother proud of you. It will make her so very proud!

'Be on your way, Johnny Smith! But remember – the blood-hound still has your sniff about him!'

Bang! Bang! Bang! *'This court is now adjourned!'*

Dorothy and I were married on Saturday, October 21st, 1972 at the local register office. After the ceremony, the vast multitude of Dorothy's relations mingled with the dwindling remnants of my own adopted kin – Auntie Pat, Uncle George and a few anonymous cousins of my father's who came down from the north especially for the occasion and, of course, my best friends Tommy Callaghan and Tony Gallini who was also my best man.

The apprehensive bridegroom and his happy bride

went off on their honeymoon to Bournemouth where Dorothy spent the whole time trying to convince me that consummating our union wouldn't harm the unborn baby.

'Johnny,' she had pleaded, 'Dr Singh said it would be all right at least up to six months and even after that.'

But I pointed out she had probably got that wrong. After all, as Auntie Pat had said, you couldn't 'understand one single word he says'.

And so we returned to our matrimonial home; to the house of my childhood; the house of closeted ghosts and unpleasant dreams where, had it not been for the wonderful memories of a cherished father, I would have conjured up only singular remembrances of hatred and terror. During my lifetime, that poor old house had never witnessed one single display of physical affection, and neither would it still, even though newlyweds were now residing there.

But that belongs to the next part of my story.

Chapter 17

I think it was Pascal who once observed, 'The very last thing one settles in writing a book . . .' (and, I suppose, the same should apply even to a plain, ordinary story like mine) '. . . is what one should put in first.' So, I re-examined how my story starts and why I started it that way.

My first statement, 'This is my story', is a statement of truth. I am the only one with the authority to write it; the only one in possession of all the facts. I then say it is '. . . not my complete story . . .' Again, the truth. I begin the story when I am ten years old and, as far as I have got with it, I am but twenty-one – eleven years of life condensed into a little bundle of Imperial-typed pages with their inked-in 'i's. Writing one's complete story would inevitably make it sound like a schoolboy's daily diary. You know the kind of thing, 'Got up. It was raining. Had breakfast. Went to school . . .' 'Too ordinary to recount'? Yes, of course! But the complete story of any life, even a remarkable one, would be that, wouldn't it? In the case of my story, however, it is obvious from the first few paragraphs that I make an issue of its ordinariness. So why did

I do that? And, if it is so ordinary, why did I bother to write it at all?

I thought about these things and, having considered them, I still believe my life, up to the time about which I have written – and since this represents the sum total of my achievement – is no more than can be appraised in this respect to be ordinary and unremarkable. They often say to me, 'John', leaving aside the very questionable ethics of your actions, you have attained a certain amount of notoriety because of the things you have done. Your name has been made widely known through the media. Would you not consider this has marked your life as being remarkable and exceptional? Is that, perhaps, why you did those things?'

I suppose it all depends on how ordinariness is quantified. The spur to my success has always been the desire to achieve my mother's expectations, to gain her approval. I have a theory that, perhaps, the same is true even of those who achieve greatness. For example, were Einstein's wonderful accomplishments driven by some philanthropic cause? Or was his one and only motivation his constant endeavour to please his mother – a labour he might finally have achieved though he would have been the only one to know the answer to that. I believe every boy knows the criteria by which he may judge his own success because all boys are indoctrinated from early childhood with their mother's aspirations for them.

I knew what I had to do to purge the ordinariness of myself into the extraordinariness of more wholesome things and, despite the fact that I was convicted for that achievement, I honestly never did fulfil it. I was one short; so near yet so far. If I had accomplished my assignment, then I would have become as pure as refined gold. I would have been adjudged worthy in my mother's eyes – and, if what they tell me is true – in the eyes of my Mistress also, since they tell me They are one and the same thing. And who am I to argue? But be that as it may, if I had succeeded, I know my mother would finally have approved of me. Yet I failed and therefore remained within the category of 'ordinary and unremarkable', like most other boys who, despite growing into strong young men, find it impossible to achieve the distinction their mothers expect of them because most are set insurmountable goals.

'Well, we don't think your life has been ordinary!' they say and I thank them for their kindness but then I point out that I couldn't even achieve the ordinariness of consummating a marriage and fathering a child.

But did I do the things I did to mark my life as being remarkable and exceptional; to embellish the reality of my ordinariness? In the beginning, no. I simply rebelled against the natural order of things. I detested my lowliness and became a dissenter. I questioned my mother's innate authority and wanted to punish her and those I perceived to be like her. But what boy truly hates his mother; the woman who, through her suffering, gives him life?

'Did you hate your mother – really hate her?' they ask me again. I thought I hated her but aren't hate and love just different faces of the same old penny? I suppose if I really had hated my mother, I would have treated her with indifference but I never did that, did I? No, I tried to achieve what she really wanted of me – to be pardoned of my misdemeanours by the only One of true authority and power. Herself! And, if my conscious attempts to raise myself up from the depths of my ordinariness in my mother's honour makes me reprehensible, then yes, I admit I am guilty as charged.

'But do you not, then, believe in God, John?' That is another of their favourite questions. 'And if you do believe in Him, isn't He the only One of true authority and power and do you not consider Him to be the supreme One whose will should be done above the will of all others?'

God was never mentioned in our house. Like the other taboo subject of sex, religion was not part of my teaching. Death was never mentioned either. To me, people didn't die, they were 'taken'. And, to my indoctrinated mind, that meant they were taken by the witch either to work in Her service or to be gobbled up for Her supper. I had never knowingly witnessed death before, at least not in people. I once had a pet rabbit called Snowy whom I found one day lying motionless in his hutch. My father told me Snowy had died and was now in rabbit heaven. And it somehow seemed okay for the spirits of fluffy little rabbits, that had never hurt a fly, to float off to some nebulous paradise where they would be happy eternally. But people were different, I knew that, especially male people. They were subjects of the witch's justice, not God's. It was that same naive innocence which made me believe Ben was taken by the witch to be gobbled up for Her supper – a fate I was convinced would befall me if I carried on with the unforgivable practice of naughtiness. It never occurred to me that Ben had died tragically in a freak accident during a thunderstorm. And how could I have deduced my mother was going to my father's funeral? If I didn't perceive my father had died, I could hardly have known about a memorial to commemorate his death in the name of a God I didn't know about either, could I?

Then they ask me, 'What do you believe now?' and I simply answer, 'I don't know!' And, that being said, there is little else to say.

There is another curious question they often ask me. 'Did you know, John, in the Brothers Grimm stories your mother used to read to you, like Hansel and Gretel, that a little girl was captured by the wicked old witch too?' I always answer that I was unaware of this. 'Yes, John,' they continue, 'she – the little girl, that is – wasn't fattened up for the witch to eat because the witch wanted to keep her to do all the menial jobs that needed to be done around her cottage. Didn't your mother read that part in the stories she told you?'

No, she never did and I never read the stories in that book myself. Then they add, 'And did she not also read that the children weren't sent into the forest because they were naughty? Their father was a poor woodcutter and couldn't afford to feed them, that's why. It wasn't because of their disobedience.' And I say, 'No! She did say that the father was a poor woodcutter but, always, that the boy was a very naughty little boy who was rude to his mother and that's why the witch took him away!'

Thinking about it now, I suppose my mother falsified the original stories, and missed out any reference to the boy's sister for the same reason she never told me there were such things as teddy girls; a desire to somehow keep the superior female blameless of the misdemeanours and separate from the punishment of the deserving lowly male. I guess it was part of her education of me; a way of instilling respect for her sex.

'Do you blame her now, in any way, for the things you did?' Ah yes! That question always follows. And how can I answer it? After all, they are supposed to be the psychiatrists. They are the ones who are supposed to know all the answers.

I know I believe that, had I not been saddled with the

yoke of fulfilling my mother's expectations, my life's quest would have been a simple one; to find my Satisfaction House, that special place in the poem Mr Anderson read us all those years ago.

> *. . . It has a 'Welcome' mat*
> *Where sits a big fat cat,*
> *Which grins, 'Come in and have a gin,*
> *It's warm inside, I won't deride.*
> *For I'm a place that's special,*
> *I wasn't built with wealth,*
> *Love is me, in me you'll see*
> *That you can be yourself.'*

The halfway house didn't have a welcome mat. Neither did Auntie Pat and Uncle George have a cat; let alone a big fat one with a big wide grin. But they welcomed me nonetheless with a special warmth; a wonderful warmth generated by a love which showed no derision.

Yet, that feeling of inner peace still eluded me there. I knew it wasn't my Satisfaction House. I couldn't be myself there, you see. To find that part of me, I still needed to return to the house of my childhood with all its morbid fascinations and painful dreams. I still needed the house of my mother.

Could it be that those closeted ghosts were really trying to tell me the truth; that my mother made me endure her cruel discipline because she was trying to save me from my true self? If that is the case, the things she did were really a demonstration of her love for me, weren't they?

Perhaps that is my true remembrance of that place and that was its lure and its enchantment. I needed her love to be proved to me. I needed it so desperately.

And perhaps I needed that house for the same reason I needed to write my story (ordinary and unremarkable though it might be): to revisit my early life in search of evidence of a mother's love; something which would make me love her in return.

Now I was to live there again; with a wife I didn't love and a burden to a mission still unfulfilled.

Part Three

The Old House

Something borrowed, something blue,
The old house is now something new.
But still it guards the secret way,
And now a wife I must betray.

by Johnny Smith (aged 21)

Chapter 18

As I carried Dorothy's already expanding tummy over the threshold of 122 Melrose Rise, submissively compliant to her insistence on following the old-fashioned custom of bearing the new bride through the portals of her new matrimonial home, I was struck by the change in the atmosphere of the old place. It was as if I were entering a brand-new house for the very first time. It was more than just a feeling generated by the freshly painted white walls and woodwork – which generated an impression of space and airiness – and the orderliness of the now uncluttered lines, it was that this was the very first occasion I had entered that hallway without immediately encountering some remembrance of its past.

I lowered Dorothy to the floor and we wandered into the living room where the promised three-piece suite and colour television – wedding presents from Mr and Mrs Thatcher – greeted us in inarticulate welcome. Two cards, from our delighted parents, proudly stood on the mantelpiece hailing our return from honeymoon. The alcoves were now adorned with the two Canaletto prints Auntie Pat had picked up from a church bazaar for two pounds each and for which Dorothy had expressed an immense liking.

Yes, I distinctly remember how different the old house looked and felt, until I went into the kitchen, now fully fitted with pristine units and appliances – gifted to us by Auntie Pat and Uncle George – and looked out of the window onto the dreariness of the garden. It was only then I realised it was the same house; that beneath its new and fresh veneer it was still the house of my childhood, the house of fear and morbid enchantment. I felt suddenly cold and distant. Looking out on the skeleton of that sad old yew tree, I was transported back to a different time which seemed unchanging yet separated from the present by an eternity.

I felt Dorothy's arms around my waist and the bulge of her tummy pressing into the small of my back.

'It's lovely, isn't it, darling?' she cooed. 'A lovely new home and the start of a wonderful future together.'

Her arms tightened about me and her chin nestled on my shoulder. I knew she expected some kind of tender response but I was unable to give her one. Instead, I released her hold and turned to face her in an embrace of fabricated happiness. I held her close so Dorothy could not see my look of melancholy; the sadness of the knowledge that, for every second of every day, I would have to try and conceal my true feelings about a marriage that was both loveless and unwanted.

And, although I tried so desperately hard to forget it, the knowledge that Kevin Blowser's bastard was sprouting inside Dorothy's belly was a difficult thing to ignore. Like the foetus itself, my repugnance at the thought grew with the passing of every wretched and miserable moment.

More than ever, I wished for guidance from the man I

once called my father; coaching in coping with my selfishness, counselling in the fine and noble ways of munificence. I wanted to ask him how he endured, day after day, in bearing his deception for my sake as I now had to bear mine for the sake of Blowser's child. My one hope was that my feelings might change when the baby was born; that it might be so adorable, I couldn't help but grow to love it just as my father had once loved me. Yet, whatever happened, I knew I could never love its mother. But I could never tell Dorothy that; an awareness which only served to compound my despair. Then there was the further burden her presence presented, its handicap to the fulfilment of the commandment She had given to me: to show one more the secret way; to make up the numbers of the second sacred coven. That, above everything else, was the main reason for my misery.

Throughout that afternoon, Dorothy busied herself in her new kitchen preparing her very first meal as a wife for her new husband in her brand-new home. I tried to read, to catch up on back editions of the *Comet* which had been delivered while we were away. One headline read, 'Man Helps Police With Enquiries Into Where-Are-They-Women Disappearances'. However, in the paper the next day, I read he'd been released without charge. It turned out he was just a harmless, lonely, middle-aged bloke others thought a little odd because he chose to live in his own world of eccentricity, which just happened to fit Ribble's absurd 'psychological profile'. Other than that, the paper reported the police investigations were '. . . going nowhere fast.'

But try as I might, I couldn't settle. I wandered aimlessly about the house, more often than not getting in Dorothy's way, and sometimes just gazing out of the kitchen window into the forest. I could see the three recently dug patches, now profusely growing with foot-high shoots of young brambles already turning woody at their base. It was the restlessness of impatience I felt, and all the time I was pondering, trying desperately to conceive a plan which would enable me to conclude my assignment.

Dorothy noticed my agitation.

'Thinking about the work you've got to do out there, darling?' She looked at me lovingly. 'Don't worry yourself about that now, dear. Winter's coming. Frost has been forecast for tonight. The ground will soon be as hard as iron. I know you want to get on with it, Johnny, but there's not much point even thinking about it until spring at least.'

She came over to me and put an arm around my waist again.

'I'm cooking you a lovely dinner. I want tonight to be special – our very first night in our new home. I'll set the table and we'll use those lovely silver candlesticks my Aunt Maud gave us. I bought some candles to go in them. That will make it nice and romantic, won't it? Then I thought we could have an early night! What do you say, darling?'

She squeezed me harder.

Yes, an early night. I had been expecting that. Straight after dinner, she would smile sweetly, take my hand and guide me to our bed, where she would snuggle close and expect me to have sex with her. I knew the old excuses I had used successfully on our honeymoon would no longer appease Dorothy. Harming the unborn baby was the last thing on her mind. That night, the reality had to be faced. And the reality was I could not be aroused, despite all Dorothy's efforts.

'Honour your wife, Johnny Smith! Do not defile her with your foulness!' I heard Her voice, Her commandments to me, spinning round inside my head.

'It's the baby, isn't it? You don't want to make love to me because I'm carrying someone else's baby! No, Johnny! No, Johnny! Please tell me it isn't true!'

Dorothy was screaming. Then she turned away from me and burst into uncontrollable tears.

I remember pulling the bed covers up over her shoulders. I wanted to say something to dispel her fears just as much as she wanted to hear me say it. But, in the end, I could offer nothing. The best I could manage was to cuddle her till her sobs eventually became the slow, contented breaths of sleep.

But it was an unsettled rest. Her flickering eyelids and continual fitfulness told me she was dreaming. I still wonder what images were conjured up that night in the troubled reaches of her mind.

I eventually fell asleep myself but was suddenly woken up by the sounds of frenzied retching coming from the bathroom. I had become used to Dorothy's morning sickness but this sounded more violent than usual. When she came back into the bedroom, she looked ghastly and was holding herself below the bulge in her winceyette nightdress.

'I feel so sick, Johnny. And the pain – it's unbearable!'

I guided her to the bed and settled her, then asked if there was anything I could get – a drink, perhaps; a cup of tea?

Dorothy just moaned. 'Dr Singh! Call Dr Singh! Hurry!'

Chapter 19

'Mr Smith?' The doctor at the hospital showed me into his consulting room and offered me a chair before sitting down himself behind his desk. He picked up a large buff folder and spoke into it. 'I'm afraid your wife has miscarried. There was nothing we could do. I'm very sorry.'

The doctor looked up at me and smiled sympathetically before adding, 'But your wife is young and healthy, Mr Smith. There's no reason, absolutely no reason at all, why you can't try for another baby as soon as she has recovered.'

At that moment, I remember seeing in my mind's eye a scene from a television documentary I had watched on the artificial insemination of cows; a row of bovine backsides, their tails swishing, anxiously awaiting the insertion of the farmer's syringe. Dorothy's own backside was envisioned at the end of that row.

Yes, I know it was a callous thought to have, especially at the very moment my young wife was lying in a hospital bed suffering the emotional maelstrom of losing her first baby. But you have to understand the torment I, myself, was also feeling at that time. I knew we could not try for another baby. The doctor's prognosis had sounded so rudimentary and uncomplicated; so matter-of-fact, like throwing away a favourite old sweater when it becomes threadbare and buying a new one. Easy, natural: nothing to it!

But you see, although that baby had the hapless fate of being fathered by a nerd like Kevin Bowser, it represented the only chance Dorothy would ever get – assuming our marriage lasted and she remained faithful to me – of becoming a mother. Even those cows were more fortunate. They could be impregnated at the farmer's whim. I think my vision, insensitive though it was, reflected a sadness; the sorrow I genuinely felt for Dorothy.

The doctor's words also reminded me of my failure as a man. I guessed, too, that the experience would probably make Dorothy even more maternal and increase her insistence for us to try for another baby at the earliest opportunity; the impediment to our lovemaking removed, she would believe there was nothing to stop us making a baby that belonged to both of us, and us alone. I knew the simple act of going to bed each night would unfold into a terrible ordeal.

I also felt cheated; defrauded into offering Dorothy my hand in marriage because of a foolhardy and hasty impulse to emulate my father's selfless actions and take care of another man's child. Now that child was no more, but the consequences of my marriage had to be suffered and endured perpetually; day in, day out, worsening interminably.

'You can go up to the ward and see your wife, Mr Smith. She's feeling a bit low, of course. Try to cheer her up. She needs you now, Mr Smith - Mr Smith?'

'Er – thank you, doctor.'

I prepared myself to face my dejected wife and an anxious Mr and Mrs Thatcher and Auntie Pat and Uncle George, who were waiting in the corridor outside for news of Dorothy's condition.

After a brief announcement, we all trooped up to the ward where a nurse first showed me alone to Dorothy's bedside, announcing that '. . . only two visitors are allowed at any one time.' It was decided I would be granted my time on my own with her and then the others would visit in pairs.

Her eyes were watery and her expression pitiful. She attempted a smile as the nurse pulled back the curtain and I was revealed standing at the bottom of the bed. The nurse left us, enclosed within the privacy of the drapes and I sat beside her on the bed.

'Oh, Johnny! I'm so sorry!'

Dorothy collapsed into the sanctuary of my chest.

'What on earth are you sorry about?'

She looked up at me with her sad eyes and began to weep.

'I always let you down!' she sobbed. 'I remember saying to you a long time ago that I would hate you to marry me because you felt you had to. And what happened? I know I kind of forced you into proposing when I came to see you that night – I became pregnant by someone else; someone I never loved; someone I admit I led on because of my stupid vindictiveness – because I only wanted to hurt you!

'Yet you still asked me to marry you. You were wonderful about it, Johnny. I couldn't have asked for a more caring husband. And I want you to know that I don't blame you for not wanting to make love to me while I was carrying Kevin's baby. It must have been a constant reminder to you of my stupidity and my shame—'

She was sobbing so much by this time she couldn't talk any more. Levering herself up from my arms, she reached for a tissue from the box on her bedside cabinet, blew her nose, wiped her eyes and threw the used tissue into the little paper bag taped by the side of the bed. Then she nestled back into my embrace. Her voice became softer and more tranquil.

'Well, I've been lying here thinking about things. Hospital's a great place for that, y'know, Johnny. You lie here for hours on end feeling pretty miserable with yourself with nothing to do but think. I know I've let you down but I'll make it up to you, I promise. Even – even what happened to the baby—'

She briefly started sobbing again, then controlled herself.

'Well, what I mean is – I know this is a terrible thing to say but maybe it was all for the best. Our life together won't be messed up with reminders of my stupid past now, will it? When we have a baby, as I hope we will straight away, it will be ours, yours and mine, the way it should be, the way I always wanted it to be.'

Dorothy looked deep into my eyes.

I hated the moment. What could I say? I wanted the ground to swallow me up.

'Dorothy,' I tried to sound warm, loving and compassionate, 'you've been through a bad time. A horrible time! Just concentrate on getting well, please. We've got all the time in the world to talk about the future, haven't we? And anyway, I mustn't monopolise too much of you right now. You need your rest and . . .'

This was my chance. The chance of escaping from this

interminable interrogation. '. . . there are four other people who love you dearly, waiting to say 'Hi!' I'd better go and give your mum, dad, Auntie Pat and Uncle George the chance to come in and see you.'

She smiled; a coy, timid smile. 'Will you come this evening?'

'You just try and stop me.'

I kissed her on the lips and disappeared through the screen of curtains and, as they flapped shut behind me, I sighed with relief. My ordeal was temporarily ended. I trudged wearily down the ward to the group of chairs arranged along the wall near the entrance.

'How is she?' Mrs Thatcher enquired anxiously.

'A bit down, understandably. But otherwise okay. She wants to see you. Fifth bed down on the right. The one with the curtains pulled.'

Mr and Mrs Thatcher disappeared down the corridor and I was left alone with Auntie Pat and Uncle George. I sat down in the vacant chair beside Auntie Pat who leant towards me and gave me a cuddle.

'Poor Johnny!' she said in her own inimitable way. 'My poor, poor Johnny. I'm so sorry.'

'Yes, I know, Auntie Pat,' I responded, 'so am I. So am I.'

After that, we sat there without saying a word. When Mr and Mrs Thatcher returned and my foster parents went for their visit, the same stony silence prevailed. I was glad about that. I could be alone with my thoughts.

I searched outside of my own selfishness. I thought about the aborted life that had never known an existence outside of Dorothy's womb. The doctor had said there was no apparent physiological problem to cause the miscarriage and had put it down to '. . . just one of those very unfortunate things.' But Dorothy was so distressed by the conviction that the swelling in her belly was responsible for my impotence. I knew that anguish was the reason for her miscarriage. And suddenly, I felt so sad, I involuntarily started to cry. Huge great tears of genuine emotion flowed down my cheeks. I remember Mrs Thatcher looking up at me and smiling sympathetically. It was the first and only time she ever smiled at me in that way.

I visited Dorothy again that evening bearing a large bunch of early winter chrysanthemums. Fortunately, she seemed more cheerful, having been heartened by the news that she was to be allowed home in a couple of days.

She chatted to me endlessly about inconsequential trivia and showed me the baby clothes she had already started knitting from the wool and pattern her mother had brought in for her that afternoon. But, to my immense relief, that indirect allusion was the only reference she made to us 'starting another baby'.

I couldn't say what else she spoke of because I wasn't really listening. My mind was elsewhere, struck by a sudden and wonderful realisation; something the shock and upset had, until then, concealed from me. Her stay in hospital granted me liberty to complete my assignment – to show the last old crone the way to her salvation. Another two days! Yes, it was time enough.

I wanted to begin my search that very night but then realised I couldn't, having already accepted an invitation to have dinner at Auntie Pat's. I knew I couldn't rush away afterwards. She would insist on my staying on, just to chat over coffee and another chocolate cake. But, tomorrow night; yes, tomorrow night . . .

Mrs Thatcher was annoyed that I refused a similar dinner date with her husband and herself, feeling, I suppose, that she had somehow failed in her duty to supply the inept male's sustenance during her daughter's incapacity. But I told her I had already made plans for the following night to go out with Tommy Callaghan and Tony Gallini.

I visited the hospital early and found Dorothy a little depressed at the inordinately slow passage of time. 'I'm just getting impatient, Johnny,' she said. 'I want to be home with you, where I belong.'

It was around seven-thirty when I left her to make my way to a small club I had discovered in a sleazy part of a neighbouring town. Those dingy havens of iniquity all looked the same. If I were to bother repeating my description of the Blue Parrot, it could equally well apply to this new haunt. In fact, it was nothing more than a seedy little shit-hole down in the basement of a shadowy side street. I can't even remember its name now. But what does that matter? I didn't choose it for its charm, did I? Neither will I ever visit it again! Suffice it to say, for my purposes it was perfect.

Women, in their arrogant splendour, sojourned there in droves. I was hardly down the stairs into its basement gloom before a group of them converged on me, offering their favours. I settled on a girl in her late twenties with enormous breasts which her skimpy top, buttoning up at the front, did little to conceal.

I don't really know why I chose her. It had nothing to do with her very ample charms, of course. I suspect there was something in her manner which was even more contemptuous than the rest of them.

We had a couple of drinks.

'You from round 'ere?'

'Not far away.'

'So – what d'yer want?'

'Come back to my place?'

She thought for a short while. 'Cost yer ten quid. Money up front.'

I reached into my inside pocket, pulled out my wallet and withdrew two crisp five-pound notes which I handed her.

And so the deal for her deliverance was struck.

We left the club and hailed a cab. It was around nine-fifteen when we arrived at the house. After paying the fare and watching the taxi recede into the distance in an effluvium of exhaust fumes condensing on the cold November air, we went inside. It was warm and cosy. Immediately, she discarded her coat and draped it over the banisters.

'Nice!' she said, looking around.

Something made me pick up her coat and hang it in the hall closet before I showed her into the lounge. As we entered the room she glanced about, her gaze resting briefly on the two Canaletto prints hanging in the alcoves. She sat down on the couch and reached into her bag, pulling out a pack of cigarettes.

'I'd rather you didn't,' I said.

She looked at me derisively and replaced the cigarette pack. 'A man with no vices – except one, eh, love?'

She cackled a sarcastic snigger and gave me a knowing wink. 'Well! D'yer wanna get on wiv it? Here, or in the bedroom?'

I shrugged my shoulders. 'Here'll do as well as anywhere, I guess.'

She stood up and began unbuttoning her scanty top. In one well-practised movement, graced with the skill of many adept performances, the top was discarded and her hands were already behind her back, unclasping the clip of her brassiere. With its release, her breasts wobbled ponderously. Her stare was fixed on mine. She smiled smugly.

'The song says, diamonds are a girl's best friend but I tell you, luv – my tits are mine! Bring me in a lot of bus'ness, anyway.'

I noticed an ugly scar on her abdomen and, as she unzipped her skirt and began to wriggle out of it like a snake shedding its skin, I could see it extended below the line of her panties. She was aware of my scrutiny.

'Don't put you orf, does it, luv? Appendix. The bloody surgeon made an 'ash of it! Don't seem to put my uvver customers orf, any 'ow. But as they say – you don't look at the mantelpiece while you're poking the fire, do ya?'

She laughed her satirical cackle again.

My visitor was about to remove her knickers with the same unseemliness demonstrated by the rest of her kind, when the doorbell rang. She froze with one leg inelegantly cocked in mid-air.

'Blimey! It's yer bloody wife, ain't it?'

Of course, that was the one person I knew it couldn't be but I was, nonetheless, gripped with a terrible sense of foreboding.

'Get your clothes on! Quick! Wait in the kitchen. Through that door there.' I pointed to the route through the dining room to ensure she wouldn't venture out into the hallway.

The doorbell rang again. Its persistence was unrelenting.

'Go!' I said, in a subdued but resolute voice.

'Okay! Okay! But yer ain't 'avin' yer money back.'

She began to gather her clothing.

With the third ring, I watched her bottom wobbling towards the dining room, straightened up the cushions on the couch and went out into the hallway to open the door.

As my view opened up onto the porch, I was first aware of something being held, covered with a large chequered tea-towel. I looked up at the corpulent bearer of the load.

'You took a long time to answer the door, John!'

'Mrs Thatcher! I – I – must have nodded off on the couch.'

I looked behind her and spied Mr Thatcher sitting in the car in the road beyond, the engine still running. He waved a lazy hand in recognition.

'This is getting heavy, John. Aren't you going to invite me in?'

'Er – I'll take it, Mrs Thatcher.'

She released her burden into my hands and stepped past me into the hall.

'I don't suppose you've had anything to eat tonight. Just a few drinks with your friends in the pub, I expect. A snack, at the most. Am I right?'

She took back the anonymous weight with its chequered covering. 'Made you a lamb casserole. Least I could do with Dorothy in hospital. I know what you men are like when you have to look after yourselves. Didn't have any coriander though but I know Dorothy has some in her spice rack . . .'

With that, completely ignoring my vociferous stammering, 'but – but . . .', her enormous frame turned its back on me and sauntered off towards the kitchen door.

'Can't eat a lamb casserole without a sprinkling of some coriander on it. I'll just go into the kitchen and finish it off, then I'll pop it in the oven for a – good God!'

'Ello, luv! You 'is muvver, are yer?'

There was a loud crash as my lamb casserole hit the floor.

'John!' shouted an enraged Mrs Thatcher. 'Who is this – this – this person?'

'Oh! It's – it's Mrs – er, er, Johnson! Lives down the road! Knew Dorothy was in hospital. Had the same idea as you really! Offered to come in and cook me something. Very kind of her, in the circumstances, I thought—'

'And – does this Mrs – Johnson normally come visiting with the buttons of her blouse undone? At least, I assume you'd call it a blouse – it's so skimpy she might just as well not be wearing it!'

There was a long pregnant pause while Mrs Thatcher and my 'congenial neighbour' scrutinised each other.

'Er – I think this is where I vamoose! Where did yer put me coat?'

I followed her wiggling bottom into the hallway, retrieved her coat from the closet and showed her out through the front door, shouting, 'Well, thank you, Mrs Johnson, for your trouble this evening!'

I remember Mr Thatcher's head appeared through the open car window, his neck strained round and there was a look on his face which was part astonishment and part lechery. His eyes followed her voluptuousness as it disappeared up the road. And I sheepishly wandered back into the kitchen to suffer Mrs Thatcher's wrath. Her eyes were blazing. Her bulk wobbled with her anger. But, though her tongue was vicious, my ordeal was over quickly.

'I'm glad your dinner ended up on the floor, John! It's a fitting place for you to eat it!'

There were two loud bangs as first the kitchen then the front door crashed behind her. Then there was a silence which was heavenly.

Chapter 20

Insomnia governed my night. Try as I might, my anger, resentment and fear over the events of the evening simply would not leave me. In fact, the more I tried to suppress my thoughts, the more they rallied and regrouped to further frustrate my sleep.

I was irritated because of my unrecovered prepayment to the cow with big udders and at the untimely intrusion of a meddling mother-in-law, which I was convinced was nothing more than prying, under the deliberate sham of thoughtfulness. I was troubled by the unpleasant repercussions I thought must now follow because of what she would feel as a disagreeable but obligatory duty to inform her daughter of my indiscretion.

Yet, if these things were enough on their own to deny me the rest I so surely needed, they were nothing compared to the main reason for my fury and exasperation – the incensed frustration and bitterness at the squandering of the perfect opportunity and the improbability of fate ever contriving another. Mrs Thatcher had turned my assured and irrefutable victory into inglorious defeat and I knew I could never forgive her.

In those long and lonely hours of darkness, one overriding thought transcended all others; a repulsive and odious loathing of that bloated, interfering and contemptuous woman who, above all others, had demonstrated her seemliness to be the one to crown the sealing of the secret way. But I knew that was an impossible dream; a mere fantasy conceived in the sleeplessness of an endless night.

I was still tossing and turning with the futility of that thought when the shrillness of the alarm clock proclaimed it was ten o'clock. It was a Friday. I remember clearly because I intended to sleep in, savouring my last weekday of idleness before returning to work the following Monday.

As my hand reached out to switch it off, I was conscious of another ringing; a continual intermittent carillon of intrusion. I staggered out of bed and stumbled down the stairs into the hallway to answer the phone.

'Hello.'

There was a pause on the other end of the line.

'What time are you due to pick up your wife?'

The words *your wife* were emphasised as a purposeful reminder.

'Er – Mrs Thatcher! Er – they said around one o'clock.'

'Right! Mr Thatcher and I will be round to collect you in the car at twelve-thirty. After everything Dorothy's been through, it's not fair she should have to travel home from the hospital by bus.'

She paused again but I knew she wasn't finished.

'I want to tell you, John, that I don't intend to mention anything to her about last night's little episode. You don't deserve to be let off the hook and, believe me, my decision has nothing to do with your feelings in the matter. My concern is for Dorothy. She's in a highly emotional state and doesn't deserve to suffer any more upset, especially the upset of knowing that her pig of a husband – someone she deeply loves, though God knows why – was playing around while she was in hospital after losing the baby *you* gave her. Have you any idea what that means to a woman, John?'

The question was obviously rhetorical.

'But let me give you a warning – if you do anything else to hurt her, anything at all, I'll personally make life very unpleasant for you. Have I made myself clear?'

'But, Mrs Thatcher, it wasn't what it seemed. I—'

'Don't patronise me, John! And don't take me for a fool either. That woman was a strumpet! You couldn't wait for your wife, you had to go and pick up a common tart. Words fail me, John! Now I don't want to talk about it any more. Just be ready at half past twelve.'

The purring of the dialling tone told me she had hung up. Somehow, it was a sound of utter contentment, a sound which seemed to reflect the pleasure I knew she must have felt at fashioning another opportunity of rebuking me, again without hearing my defence. I hated her even more, especially now I had to treat her with a resolute kindness, knowing she had me by the proverbial short and curlies and the prejudice to pull at them hard if I put but one small step out of line.

I fantasised over the glorious vision of showing her to that deep, dark and secret forest. But, most of all, my fantasies echoed with the sublime screams of her anguish and her pain.

Our journey to the hospital was spent in rancorous silence. Even the normally agreeable Mr Thatcher solemnly concentrated on his driving without so much as a single word to me.

Dorothy was so happy to be going home she snuggled contentedly beside me on the back seat, much to the annoyance of her mother whose glaring eyes were reflected in the rear-view mirror which, seemingly unnoticed by her husband, she had obviously manoeuvred to keep me in her sights. But, I suppose for the sake of her unsuspecting daughter, normality otherwise prevailed and the women chatted on about inconsequential things against a crosstalk of comparable trivia conducted by Mr Thatcher and myself.

I made an overt display of welcoming Dorothy back to the house. The front door opened up to the delicious aroma of roasting chicken, which I had inexpertly stuffed and thrown into the oven just before I left. I sat Dorothy down in the lounge and fussed over her before making everyone a cup of tea, served with great aplomb on the silver tray, gifted to us by the Aunt Maud of the silver-plated candlesticks. And, afterwards, I busied myself in the kitchen peeling potatoes and performing other house-husbandly duties, leaving Dorothy to laud my caring qualities to her doting parents.

When it was time for Mr and Mrs Thatcher to leave, they all trooped into the kitchen to witness my endeavours where Dorothy's foot found the sticky residue of the previous night's lamb casserole.

'Yuk! What's this?' she exclaimed, examining the sole of her carpet slipper.

At that moment, Mrs Thatcher's eyes found mine and a droll smile formed on her lips.

'Er, just a little accident, dear. I'll clean it up properly in a minute.'

Dorothy giggled at this endearing evidence of the clumsiness and incompetence of the male but her mother's eyes held me with their malicious stare.

God, how I hated her!

While I was clearing away and washing up the dishes that evening, the telephone rang twice. It was gratifying to hear Dorothy extol my virtues of tenderness and compassion to Auntie Pat but I positively gloated when she repeated her praise to her meddling mother who felt it necessary to check up on the situation just a few short hours after witnessing at first hand my devoted attention to her cherished daughter. Her probing made me think of my childhood perceptions of the wicked old witch whose all-seeing eyes, as I was informed by my own obdurate mother, were constantly roving about the entire inhabited earth just looking for naughty little boys like me to take away and gobble up.

I realised Mrs Thatcher's all-seeing eyes, and her all-seeing other senses, for that matter, were homed in like finely tuned radar on one naughty boy in particular – the accused Johnny Smith – and she wouldn't rest until his misdemeanours were finally avenged.

In bed that night, Dorothy was tender and loving. In the darkness, and in the silence of our embrace, she whispered, 'Darling, do you remember the first time you brought me to this house?'

I was suddenly filled with apprehension.

'You know, when we were sixteen? I never did ask you how you managed to get the keys. I expect you managed to convince Miss Ramsbottom to lend them to you on some pretext or other.' She giggled and I nodded nervously, a gesture she seemed to sense even in the darkness.

'Yes, I thought so,' she continued, 'but I didn't ask you because I didn't really care. It was such a romantic thing to have done. You know, like something Romeo might have schemed to be alone with Juliet.' She giggled again. 'You were wonderful that night, Johnny. I think you realised I wasn't ready to make love to you. But I loved you enough even then to have had sex with you if that was what you wanted. I didn't want to lose you, you see. Do you remember what you said to me?' She paused for my answer.

'Tell me!'

'You said you respected me too much and we should wait till we were married. That was the first time you ever mentioned marriage to me. I was so happy that night, I cried myself to sleep with tears of joy. Does that sound silly?'

I didn't like to tell her that it did. But then I knew I would never understand the workings of the female mind. I simply shook my head, something which, again, she somehow perceived. I remember only my preoccupation with what all this feminine logic was leading to.

'Well, now we are married and I'm wonderfully happy! What's happened – I mean, losing the baby, and everything – was terribly sad but it wasn't your fault and I know the reason you've not made love to me has been because I was pregnant. Johnny, I've tried to put myself in your position – you know, asking myself the question how I would have felt if I were you. And I think I understand how you did feel about it all. It must have been terrible for you. But – well, sometimes, lying here with you like this, I've ached for you, darling . . .' I could sense her face strain round to look me in the eyes. I remember thinking, 'Thank God for the darkness!' '. . . and, well, sometimes I wonder – you do want me, don't you? You do want to make love to me – now – now I'm not pregnant any more?'

I searched my senses for the ability to utter simple falsehoods like, 'Yes, darling!' or 'Of course I do!' but, though I could form the words, my tongue seemed bonded to my palate as I tried to utter them. I turned and kissed her gently on the cheek, trusting in the old adage that actions speak louder than words, and wondering whether the same still holds true if the words you wish to speak are downright lies.

'Oh, Johnny!' She held me tight and kissed me sweetly. 'I want you so much – I wish . . .' She sounded embarrassed. '. . . I wish we could make love now. I want you so desperately! But they said I shouldn't have sex for another three to four weeks. But, we'll make up for the times we've missed, won't we, Johnny? We'll be making love so often I'll never want to let you out of bed. I'll wear you out with making glorious love to you!'

She giggled.

And I giggled too; not because I shared her joke. I didn't find what she said at all funny. No, mine was more of a nervous giggle, a titter of relief that I was to be given a period of grace before her thoughts of lovemaking would begin again in earnest. Then, we both slipped into the temporary diversion of sleep and dreamed our own dreams, together but separate, coupled but detached, just as we were in the course of our days.

I cannot tell you what Dorothy dreamt that night but I can clearly recall my own. I showed Mrs Thatcher the way to the deep, dark secret forest. It was a wonderful dream; an incredible, extraordinary fantasy culminating in her pitiful screams and my own glorious climax. I didn't want to wake. I wanted to dream that dream over and over again; lost in its rapture for ever. But, of course, I did awake. I awoke to the sombre realisation of truth and the greyness of a new November morning.

My onerous mother-in-law was a constant visitor to the house over that weekend. And, when she wasn't prying in person, she would be monopolising the telephone. If I answered, she would simply greet me with the unemotional statement, 'Get Dorothy for me!' It was an indifference which refused even to acknowledge me or call me by name.

Each night I willed myself to revisit that wonderful fantasy of showing her the secret way, of hearing her shrieks of terror. But instead she starred in a new version of an old dream; a dream which became a vile abomination. It was the wicked old witch's court and I was, once again, in the dock, accused of my customary naughtiness. But it was Mrs Thatcher who now led the army of my accusers, her obnoxious, raucous voice damning me of heinous atrocities. The accusers were all ushered from the courtroom, Mrs Thatcher protesting my guilt with a vicious malice, her penetrating voice still audible even after those huge oak doors had removed her from my sight.

The witch regarded me.

'So, another sniffing bloodhound has your scent, Johnny Smith, this one even more tenacious than all the rest! I want that one with me. That is the one you must send to complete the second coven. Send her to me, Johnny Smith! Send her to my deep, dark and secret forest, then your work will be done.'

When I dreamt that dream, I would awake in a sweaty clamour of delirium, screaming, 'Yes! Yes! I hear You – but how? How do I do it?' But my pleas remained unanswered and my despair was total.

I would stare for hours out into the forest and, always,

Dorothy would try to comfort me. 'Poor Johnny. Itching to make a start out there, aren't you? But try and forget about it till spring, my darling. It'll still be there then, you know!' she would say, smiling at me reassuringly. But the work I had in mind could not wait. I burnt for its fulfilment.

Chapter 21

'God! It's ten past nine!' I awoke with a start, realising I had forgotten to set the alarm clock. Of all the days I didn't want to be late for work, my first day back after matrimonial leave was surely the one.

I knew I would have to endure ribald jibes about all those nights of endless sessions 'on the nest' instead of on my back asleep. Heaven knows, even though my nights had been sexless, they had been disturbed enough to ring my eyes with dark circles; something I knew the office comedians would misconstrue and use to perpetuate their mirth. Now I would be at least an hour late, and although I knew I would not be disciplined for my tardiness on this occasion, I could hear in my mind their yells as I tried to creep into the office unnoticed.

'What's the matter, John! Wouldn't she let you get out of bed this morning?' 'Have to give her a couple of quickies before she'd get your breakfast, did you? Ha! Ha! Ha! Ha!'

If mine had been a normal honeymoon preluding a normal marriage, I could have tolerated their humour with the customary self-conscious look and embarrassed smile. But my bad mood made their ribaldry impossible to bear.

I told them to shut up which only made the situation worse, my sourness being attributed to, 'Oh dear! Honeymoon over already, is it?' and 'What's the matter, John? Didn't you get your *oats* for breakfast this morning?'

But somehow the day passed, slowly but surely, with an exclusive investigation into corrupt councillors accepting bribes for awarding contracts to preferred tenders. Fortunately, the enquiry took me away from the office for much of the day so I escaped their continued buffoonery.

When I got home that evening, I remember my mother-in-law sitting in her newly adopted armchair drinking tea and eating ginger cake. Her bloated body reclined with the enduring presence of a permanent resident.

The weeks passed and I realised her company was going to be the rule rather than the exception; something I resented more and more but could do nothing to prevent. I even had to endure Christmas in her company, a contention made bearable only by the presence of her affable, hen-pecked husband and my own dear Auntie Pat and Uncle George who came over on Christmas Day.

No coal fire was lighted in the grate that year, its black emptiness now replaced with a new gas fire. But my mind still recalled that hateful Christmas ten years before. I was struck with evidence of an inescapable fact – there was still no goodwill for me in that old house, either given or received. That Christmas, too, had to be spent in the company of a rancorous mother, even if she was someone else's.

But never was that certainty made clearer than on the night of Boxing Day when Dorothy decided the period of sexual abstinence, counselled by her doctors, was over.

'What's wrong, Johnny? Why are you doing this to me?'

She screamed, seemingly oblivious of her parents sleeping in the guest room. She would not be pacified.

'I want you, Johnny. What's so unreasonable about that? I am your wife, for God's sake! And I need you to want me as a wife but you don't even want to get close to me! Why don't you want me? Is it someone else? Are you getting it somewhere else?'

'Sshh, Dorothy! Your parents!'

'I don't care about them!' Her words wailed in long-drawn-out shrieks which accentuated every syllable. 'I – want – an – answer – Johnny – and – I – want – it – now!'

She jumped out of bed, snatched up the alarm clock and smashed it against the dividing wall between us and the guest room.

If the all-seeing, all-hearing senses of the slumbering old crone in the next room had been unaware of Dorothy's yells, that shattering crash would surely have awakened them.

Wasn't it William Congreve who penned the much-quoted observation, *'Heaven has no rage like love to hatred turned, Nor hell a fury, like a woman scorned'*?

I am convinced that such astute wisdom could not have been written unless Congreve himself had once been a hapless victim of an inflamed woman's wrath. But I am equally convinced, though I admit perhaps with ignorance and some bigotry, that no woman Congreve ever knew could have conjured up as much fury as Dorothy did that night.

It was an anger inconsistent with the normally placid Dorothy whose nature was more like the affable character of her father. For the first time, though certainly not the last, I recognised in her the inherited genes of her detested mother. She sat on the bed, visibly shaking with the strength of her fury. And, that night, I slept on the couch.

But the confrontation did not end there. Just as I was dozing in the discomfort of my temporary bed, wilfully beseeching the wonderful vision of Mrs Thatcher's deliverance to revisit my dreams, I was aware of the light being switched on and of being poked in the small of my back with a sharp object.

'What the—?'

I turned to see the point of an umbrella, brandished by the hated old crone herself, raised above me. Her eyes were flashing in a blaze of intense fire.

'My daughter might have been blinded by a loyalty which is totally misplaced but I know what you are. She won't tell me what you did tonight but I warned you. I warned you what I'd do to you if you ever hurt Dorothy again.'

I saw the umbrella wielded menacingly aloft. I had no choice but to defend myself. I jumped up, grabbing at the swinging arm, the weapon it brandished falling with a shattering crash onto Aunt Maud's silver-plated salver sitting on the sideboard. Mrs Thatcher stumbled and landed on her back, her fall broken by the ampleness of her backside and the lushness of the Wilton carpet she herself had insisted we purchase. My own landing was sweetness itself; onto the fluffiness of her pink woollen dressing gown which encased the softness of her belly. I pinned her to the ground.

Curiously, the intimate contact of my body with her own bloated carcass aroused my manhood. There and then, I think I could have committed the supreme act of defilement were it not for the authoritative words of the witch, learned by rote, having been played over and over in the unconsciousness of my dreams.

'Never – never again, Johnny Smith, aspire to gain carnal knowledge of any woman you discern is of my calling. I will permit none to be contaminated even with thoughts of your odiousness.'

But, before the remembrance of Her words reduced my arousal to the flaccidness of obeisance, Mrs Thatcher felt it. I know she felt it knocking at the door of her own foulness, demanding to come in. Her eyes blazed with hatred and her head twisted from side to side as she made muffled little gasping sounds of terror.

Her mouth was just a few inches from my own. It reminded me of the last time I had seen Miss Ramsbottom's mouth, forming its perfect letter 'O', the pinkness of her lips contrasting with her bleached, colourless face; just like that same cod on that same fishmonger's slab. I smelt that smell; that same odious smell.

How I restrained myself from showing Mrs Thatcher to that deep, dark and secret forest right there and then, I will never know. Perhaps it was the sound of slippered feet running down the stairs or my awareness of Mr Thatcher's hands on my shoulders or Dorothy screaming, 'Johnny! Johnny!'

I was hauled from her gibbering body. She staggered to her feet, her eyes engaging me in a cold, impassive stare.

'You debauched pig!' she spluttered, slavering saliva

gathering at the corners of her mouth. 'Dorothy once had a puppy which did that to my leg. I had it put down! What a pity I can't do the same thing to perverts like you. But I'll have you one day! I'll—'

'Shut up, you fucking old witch!'

Her eyes flashed with loathing and revulsion. I could feel Mr Thatcher's hands tighten around my shoulders. But he needn't have worried. I was suddenly seized with a sense of impeccable self-control. I looked at her and smiled mockingly.

'Mrs Thatcher, now we're in the mood for exchanging insults and threats, I'll simply say this to you – if you poke your snotty, meddling nose between Dorothy and me again, I'll do to you what, so far, I have only been able to do in the sweetness of my dreams!' I then added as a sublime afterthought, 'Oh, by the way, I think that poor puppy was better off where you sent it!'

She stormed out of the room, swiftly followed by her dutiful little husband. I heard her wrathful feet tramping up the stairs. Dorothy collapsed into a chair, her head held in her hands, the room echoing with her disconsolate sobs. I wanted to comfort her but I knew there was nothing I could do.

As Mrs Thatcher disappeared through our front door into the iciness of that winter's dawn, pursued by the servile Mr Thatcher, bearing her suitcase, my mother-in-law ordered her daughter to accompany her.

'I told you not to marry that pig. Didn't I tell you that?'

I remember Dorothy was sitting on the stairs then, her head still cupped in her hands, whimpering bitterly. She looked up at her mother and violently shook her head from side to side.

'No!' she screamed.

It was an act of extreme defiance.

For the next few days, Dorothy and I lived like Trappist monks, isolated in our own worlds of silence, maintaining separate lives under the one roof of our inimical home.

Most of the time, Dorothy stayed cocooned in her bedroom while I gazed wistfully out of the kitchen window at the hidden secrets of the forest, now made even more clandestine by a thick camouflage of snow. Its dreariness had been transformed into resplendence. I marvelled at nature's artifice, cloaking its putrefied decay with spotless purity.

We both felt the hopelessness of despair caused by the shattering of different dreams; a grief we could not share. As usual, Dorothy and I were together but separate, coupled but detached, though never had we been so indifferent to each other as we were during those days of dispassionate silence; a time made worse by the misconception that the rest of humanity was happily enjoying the revelries of the festive season.

I sometimes listened outside the bedroom door, heeding her wretched sobs but feeling powerless to comfort her. She became like a recluse, refusing even to see Auntie Pat and Uncle George when they visited after hearing a report of the family crisis, gloatingly and intolerantly recounted by the hated old crone herself.

'Mrs Thatcher said some terrible things about you, Johnny!' Auntie Pat passionately defended me, expressing horrid disbelief at the appalling accusations the other woman had made.

The one joy I had during that miserable time was answering the telephone and listening to the click and then the dialling tone as soon as I spoke. I knew who it was. Once she didn't hang up immediately. There was an exasperated little groan at getting my attentions yet again. I seized my opportunity. 'Is that the killer of poor, defenceless little puppy dogs?'

I gleefully listened to the immediate dialling tone, relishing its purr for a long while before replacing the handset. This time it was purring contentedly for me. The old crone didn't phone again.

It wasn't till the early hours of the first day of the new year that Dorothy and I spoke our first words to one another. I had stayed up, alone, with a bottle of Scotch, to see in the brand-new year – with the assured expectation it would continue in the same misery as the old one had ended – before retiring to the welcomed loneliness of my old room; the same room I had occupied in similar loneliness during my childhood.

I was concentrating hard on steadying my revolving head, or was it my revolving surroundings – for I have never been sure which is the reality – lying on my bed in the dark, waiting for unconsciousness to overcome me. Suddenly, I felt the pain of light on my eyelids and wondered whether I dared open my eyes to the full splendour of its brilliance.

'Johnny, we must talk.'

I bounced on the mattress as Dorothy's bottom descended on it and my head – or my surroundings, or possibly both – gyrated again.

Talk! There was nothing I wanted less. But I knew this moment had to come and supposed it might just as well be when my head was spinning anyhow; that way, I thought, I might not notice quite so much the dizziness caused by jumping onto the merry-go-round of trying to reconcile the irreconcilable (which, I suppose, is just a sober way of saying I was then too drunk to really care).

I gingerly levered myself up into a sitting position and leant back, sensing the security of the headboard behind my skull. Only then did I feel stable enough to expose my eyes to the blinding brilliance of the room light. I slowly lifted my eyelids. I concentrated on the blinding glow of the light hanging from the ceiling and my head stopped spinning.

I can't be absolutely sure because, as you can probably imagine, my recollections of that night are now somewhat hazy, but, as my eyes adjusted, I thought I noticed Dorothy smile. In the sadness of her despair, her face was graced with an endearing grin; probably at the spectacle of my drunken ineptitude. I shut my eyes. Then everything pirouetted again so I reopened them quickly.

Dorothy was gazing blankly at the bedclothes.

'Is there any truth in the things my mother said?'

'Depends exactly what it was she said!' (Which I think came out more like, 'Dephends exacthly what it wash she shled!')

I felt myself drifting off again into the contented world of wooziness. In an effort to stop myself, I blinked my eyes and next saw Dorothy staring at me. This time I was convinced I saw a cute little smile of attachment. Then her expression changed to one of aversion.

'When she came in to me – you know, after our row – I was crying. I didn't want to talk to her. She just called you a detestable low-life, Johnny! Then she rushed out of the room.'

I looked at her, trying hard to concentrate.

'Shlugs and shnails and phuppy dogs' tails!' I distinctly

remember saying that; it just came out, involuntarily. 'Your mother doesn'th like me very mush. She tried to hit me with her um – brhella.'

Dorothy looked bewildered. 'But why would she do that?'

'Becaush – she doesn'th like me very mush,' I reiterated with drunken silliness.

Dorothy was smiling again. I think I must have grinned back at her because her expression changed to one of counterfeit seriousness; but not for long. I suspect it was my inane, moronic leer which made her burst into uncontrollable giggles.

'You look ludicrous when you're drunk! My friend, Elaine, at the bank said, "If you want to know whether you really love your man, ask yourself that question when he's—"' she sounded embarrassed, '"—rat-arsed and incapable" was the expression she used.'

She smiled again. 'Well, now I have and, don't ask me why, but I still do love you, Johnny Smith. Even though you look ridiculous.'

She paused and observed my drunken leer before adding, 'I'm not going to get much sense out of you tonight, am I? We'll talk about this in the morning, shall we?'

Dorothy put an arm around me and helped me to my unsteady feet. 'Come to bed. My bed. Oh, don't worry. I'm not going to jump on you tonight. Even I know a hopeless cause when I see one. And by the way . . .' she looked deep into my partly closed eyes, 'Happy New Year, Johnny!'

'Happy New Year, Dorothly . . .'

I remember no more about that night.

*

In the morning we did talk. We talked for hours. Or rather, Dorothy did most of the talking. Her words reverberated through the hollowness of my throbbing head, empty yet still full of pounding timpanis put there during the night before. Nothing was resolved. But then, how could we even determine the indeterminable, let alone resolve it?

'But why does my mother hate you so much?' Dorothy pleaded.

At least I knew the old crone hadn't yet told her about the arrogant slut she'd caught me with while Dorothy was in hospital.

'And what did she mean about my puppy dog? What were you doing on top of her on the floor?'

But I guessed it was only a question of time before Dorothy would be gleefully informed, not only about the whore, but also about what Mrs Thatcher perceived as my attempted rape of her own bloated carcass.

'Dorothy, I fell on her. It was an accident. I was protecting myself from her bloody umbrella, for God's sake! What was I supposed to do? Let her hit me with it till I was black and blue?'

I remember Dorothy was silent then for a long while. Then she smiled. It was a weak, delicate smile, but a smile nonetheless.

'You're the first person I remember who's ever had the guts to stand up to her. I suspect that made her angry.'

Again, there was a silence as I noticed her weak smile evaporate.

'Johnny, there's no one else, is there? Tell me there's no one else!'

'I promise you. There is no one else.'

'Then – what are you going to do about your – problem? Will you go and see Dr Singh about it? Will you? Oh, say you will, Johnny! Please say you will!'

I promised I would. But, right then, I would have promised anything for my interrogation to be ended.

Things settled down for a while after that. Dorothy seemed to be heartened by her new belief that my 'problem' had a physiological cause which Dr Singh's wisdom could resolve. But she wouldn't let the matter drop and I eventually had to go through with the pantomime of going to his surgery.

It was a peculiar consultation. To this day, I do not know how much of what he said I really understood. I remember mostly answering with a simple yes or no, according to what seemed appropriate. But, as dear Auntie Pat had once said, '. . . you can't understand a single word he says!'

Over the next few weeks, we agreed an unspoken pact of tolerance. Dorothy returned to work and life trundled along with a semblance of resigned forbearance existing between us.

At the *Comet*, the story of the 'Where-Are-They-Women' had a temporary revival when it was discovered that another woman had joined their exclusive club. Though, of course, I knew she was only one of the original unidentified four whom someone had finally reported as missing.

I started driving lessons, passed my test first time and bought a cheap second-hand car. Dorothy and I would attempt to ease the tension between us by pleasant Sunday afternoon drives in the countryside, down little lanes in leafy bud unfolding in the warm spring sunshine. But our truce was uneasy and uncomfortable.

She had not spoken to her mother since the Christmas unpleasantness and the last she had talked to me on the matter was to say she had no intention of ever contacting her again. I felt relief at this. But it was a nervous comfort like the tenuous calm before an expected storm.

In March, I was notified of an appointment Dr Singh had arranged at the Urogenital Department of the local hospital to have my 'problem' investigated. Fortunately, or unfortunately as the case may be, it seems that someone understood what he was saying.

Dorothy was cheered by this news. But, of course, they found nothing wrong and could only suggest we visit the Marriage Guidance Bureau for professional counselling together. I refused to go; being ushered into a hospital toilet with a small glass bottle in which I was told to provide a sample of semen – something I could not have done at all were it not for my ability to envision the wonderful daydream of Mrs Thatcher's agonised face as I showed her the darkness of the secret way – was the very last ignominy I was prepared to suffer under the masquerade of saving an irreconcilable marriage.

Dorothy was incensed. I will never forget that night. She screamed and yelled at me with the strength of an enraged demon.

'All this time I've stuck by you! I've suffered the humiliation of your rejection. I've tried to understand how you could share my bed but not as a normal husband. I even blamed it on myself but it never was the baby, was it? All this time the problem was yours and you knew it and now we have a chance to sort it out, you tell me you won't go! Well, I've had enough, Johnny! I won't live this unnatural life any more. Do you hear me? I won't!'

Various missiles, including Aunt Maud's silver-plated

candlesticks, flew about the room. Whether they were aimed at me or the wall I cannot say, but neither did I particularly want to stay and find out.

As I climbed the stairs to seek the sanctuary of my childhood room, Dorothy's voice bellowed at me from the hallway below.

'And I'll tell you something else, shall I? Tomorrow I'm going to see my mother. I'll find out *why* she hates you. I'll have it out with her. All this time I've supported you. I cut her out of my life. Do you know why I did that? Do you know, Johnny? Because you're my husband. My husband! Huh, that's a laugh, isn't it? We've been married five months and you haven't even touched me! You're not a husband, Johnny! You're not even a man! My mother knows something about you, doesn't she, Johnny? Well, I'll find out what it is—'

I shut the bedroom door and listened to the golden silence. I knew tomorrow would be a different matter. After talking to her witch of a mother, she was bound to be infected with a new venom; a bitterness which would revitalise her tongue with a fresh and vibrant malevolence I would be powerless to resist.

But even God Himself, with all His awareness of His own seething creation, could not have anticipated the might of her wrath the following day. With the slamming of the front door, I felt its force.

'You bloody bastard! You screwed a tart! Right here in our house you screwed a tart while I was in hospital. Are you still screwing her? Or is it a different one now? Is that the only way you can get it off? With some slimy, disease-ridden slut?

'But no, that's not it, is it, Johnny? You tried to rape my mother! You tried to fuck my very own mother! In this very room! What kind of pervert are you? What depraved thoughts go on in that sick little mind of yours? Will any woman do? Is that it, Johnny? Any woman, just as long as it isn't your wife?'

I had never known Dorothy swear, except to quote someone else's expletives. And, even then, she would seem to prise the words from her tongue with an abashed unnaturalness. But, that night, obscenities flowed from her mouth with all the rustic vulgarity of a well-practised fishwife.

Her newfound earthiness had improved her aim as well. I ducked, trapped in a corner from which there was no escape. For a while, in fact until there were no more objects left on which she could lay an unerring hand, missiles flew around the room with alacrity. It was only when her ammunition was completely spent that she reverted to the use of her virulent tongue.

'You've always been a bloody weirdo!' she screeched. 'I can see that now but I was blinded by my stupid, misplaced love for you. Well – I've had it up to here . . .' she gestured the extent of her exasperation with a hand placed a foot or so above the top of her head, '. . . with your bloody warped and peculiar ways.'

Then she rested her tongue a while and pierced me with her blazing stare. How much like her mother she looked at that moment.

'I'm divorcing you, Johnny! Mummy made me see it was the only alternative I had.'

Yes, I bet she did!

'Now – get out of my sight, you disgusting, perverted bastard!'

So I obeyed the superiority of womankind and went; back up the stairs to the solitude of my room. In those long, sleepless hours of darkness, I thought of so many things. I thought about the consequences of what had happened. But the more I thought about them, the more I was gripped with a terrible fear; the kind which starts by knotting up your stomach then radiates a tingling sickness throughout the rest of your body. It was nothing specific, just an ominous foreboding; the fear of being a hapless victim of a female conspiracy, caught in the pincers of two rancorous women. One, my very own mother whose aspirations had assigned me an insuperable mission, and the other, the mother of my estranged wife, whom it was decreed should be both the providence and the adversary to that mission's fulfilment. She was dangerous; a treacherous and perfidious enemy.

I knew these events would have very serious repercussions, but what exactly? Sometimes it is the fear of the unknown which tips you over the edge. You know the machinations of destiny are conniving to get you and you are driven mad playacting different scenarios inside your head, contemplating their outcomes, over and over, without resolution. That night, I think I was visited by a temporary insanity. And there is a strange paradox because I am now a committed madman, writing my story incarcerated in one of Her Majesty's institutions for the criminally insane (known in this enlightened age as a high-security hospital).

I am not using these pages to meditate on the fairness of that judgement. The verdict is passed and I have already said this is where I want to be. And, anyway, it is over and done and I know it will never be undone. But I have never considered myself to be truly insane, if only because the deeds of which I was indicted were not acts of momentary rashness, committed whilst the balance of my mind was disturbed, but were premeditated and performed while I was fully conscious of my actions.

But I suspect the dividing line between sanity and insanity is a very thin and fragile one and there have been many who have crossed that line, if only temporarily. I know that is true of myself. I was visited by a temporary insanity that night in the tree house when Ben was taken, and also that night in the loneliness of my room, thinking and thinking about the things that had happened; things, I knew even then, that could only bring disaster.

Dorothy's rantings and ravings could have been heard streets away. I thought about that and what a shame it was that those nice old gentlefolk, Mr and Mrs Willmott, no longer lived next door. They were hard of hearing even when I lived there as a child. But (and I can say this now with an appreciation of what it truly means) they had died shortly before I returned to live in the house with Dorothy – he first, and she, like a languishing and lonely swan, only two weeks later. Our neighbours now were a Mr and Mrs Randall and their two young daughters.

In the beginning, Geoff Randall had seemed a friendly enough sort of guy. We would chat over the fence about the weather, football, and other trivial things. But since my fights with Dorothy had begun in earnest, he had become less friendly and had often remarked on the 'thinness of the dividing wall'. And not only that. He had begun to grumble about the state of our back garden and how the forest shoots were appearing on his side of the fence.

The forest! The divorce! The house! There would have to be a settlement. The house would have to be sold. The secret way would be a secret no more! My fear turned to terror. My terror turned to panic.

It was a strange irony that my marriage, which I

originally perceived as an obstacle to my mission, had now become the only way I could see of preserving it. Could I placate Dorothy? Was it possible to appease the maliciousness of her mother's hatred? Perhaps my sanity only returned to me that night because I clung to the slender chance that I could sweet-talk Dorothy out of her decision to divorce me. But I didn't realise then just how far she had been brainwashed by her prejudiced mother. And though it was not the first time her sweet and gentle nature had been recast into an inflamed madness, that night was the turning point. She was a Dr Jekyll who had been transformed into an unalterable Mr Hyde. Dorothy would never again display, to me at least, the reasonable, sensible side of her nature.

She refused to talk about things. In fact, she refused to talk to me at all. In due course, I received a letter from a solicitor informing me she was petitioning for divorce on the grounds of unreasonable behaviour. It stated, '. . . until the matter has been fully resolved, our client still wishes to live in the matrimonial home. We have advised her to do so only on the strict understanding that completely separate households can be maintained. We trust Mrs Smith will have your full co-operation in this matter and we have asked her to advise us if the arrangement becomes contentious or unworkable.'

When I think about the bizarre events that followed, I have wondered many times whether the final realisation that Dorothy could not be swayed from her decision to divorce me caused my temporary madness to return, this time to stay with me for ever.

But no, that is not the case. I know I am sane, even though you might be surprised I kept my sanity after reading about the events which happened next. But I know the things I am about to recount actually happened just as I have written. Though they may seem unbelievable and though they belong outside of my world of otherwise ordinariness, I swear they occurred; just as I swear I am not deranged.

CHAPTER 22

'I have heard your supplications, Johnny Smith! Do you dare to suggest that you cannot carry out my instructions to send me the woman I have asked for to my deep, dark and secret forest?'

The twenty-five lesser witches of the jury gasped an audible exclamation of horror.

'But – but your honour,' I stuttered, 'it is impossible! Everyone knows we hate one another. If I send her to You I will be suspected. There will be an investigation. Your deep, dark and secret forest will be discovered!'

The wicked witch rubbed Her gnarled old chin with a gnarled old hand. *'Mmm. I do see your predicament, Johnny Smith, but why should I concern myself with such trifling matters? You have been set an assignment in return for my granting you clemency, for all your past naughtiness to be absolved. Tell me, Johnny Smith, do you not desire to be exonerated of your heinous crimes?'*

'Yes! Yes, your honour. More than ever I wish for that! For my assignment to be completed and to receive Your magnanimous pardon. But – how, your honour? How? How can I achieve it without drawing attention to the secret way?'

The witch regarded me with Her red and beady eyes. Again Her gnarled old hand rubbed Her gnarled old chin as She considered the matter. *'Perhaps, Johnny Smith, perhaps there is a compromise. I have seen, in the bubbling abyss of my cauldron, that sapient visionary into all human things, that your wife, Dorothy, has developed a healthy interest in punishing the naughtiness of the degenerate and lowly male.*

'Indeed, it seems she has taken to the task with a newfound imperiousness which I admire. She is like her mother, Johnny Smith. She is like her mother! If the one is too difficult for you, send me the other. She will do, Johnny Smith! She will do very well in my fight against the disobedience of naughty little boys whose slugs and snails and puppy dogs' tails are ripe and juicy enough for gobbling. Yes – she will do very well indeed!'

'But – but, your honour! That is just as impossible, for the same reasons. I—'

The wicked old witch's gnarled, misshapen finger waggled as it pointed at me, standing in the dock. *'Enough, Johnny Smith, enough! You have heard my deliberations on the matter. I have conceded to your failings with extreme indulgence and that is my last word. One or the other, Johnny Smith, one or the other!*

'But, one word of warning. Do not try my patience for too long! You have one month. One more month to deliver the final one to my second coven. If you fail, Johnny Smith, not only will you not be pardoned for your misdemeanours but I will be forced to act myself and take matters into my own hands. For then, I and I alone will make the choice and see to the deliverance of the chosen one. And as for you, Johnny Smith, you will be disregarded! Treated with the lowly contempt you deserve, like something odious and detestable stuck to the bottom of my boots. You will be left to suffer the consequences of your misdemeanours on your own. Without my help

or my protection!' Bang! Bang! Bang! *'This court is now adjourned.'*

I awoke in a sweaty bedlam of terror; the bedclothes heaped about my feet. Perspiration stung my eyes as I slowly opened them onto the darkness of my lonely room.

Chapter 23

For the next few weeks, Dorothy and I settled down to the strict routine imposed by her under the instruction of her solicitors. And she insisted on interpreting to the ultimate letter that directive to maintain separate households under the same roof.

We cooked separate meals, we washed up separate dishes, made our separate beds in our separate rooms, without so much as one word to each other. She had even drawn up a rota for the use of the washing machine. I would do my laundry on Mondays and Fridays, she would do hers on Tuesdays and Saturdays, with the rest of the week left free on a first-come-first-served basis.

We talked only when absolutely necessary and, even then, it would be confined to obligatory topics of mutual relevance like, 'Have you paid the electricity bill?' Dorothy refused, absolutely and unequivocally, to talk about personal issues. A statement of extreme arrogance, 'You'll have to ask my solicitors,' being her only reply when I tried to broach any intimate matter with her.

Her one concession to our 'separateness' was to condescend to travel with me in the car when we went together for our weekly visits to the supermarket to buy our separate groceries to sustain our separate lives.

It was during one of these sustenance pilgrimages that Dorothy broke her own accustomed silence. I remember I was driving down the High Street past a small antique shop curiously called Let Bygones Be Bygones.

'Stop! Stop the car!'

'But, Dorothy, I can't stop here. There's nowhere to park and there's traffic everywhere. I—'

'Stop the car, damn you!'

I dutifully obeyed, even though it meant suffering the abuse of other drivers whose way I had blocked by double-parking so that Dorothy could get out.

I found a parking space and hurried down the street in the direction of Let Bygones Be Bygones. As I reached the shop window I saw a pair of hands reach in and remove a picture from its display on an artist's easel.

It was a painting I will never forget; done in oils on canvas, framed in heavily carved ebony looking as sombre and dismal as the painting itself. As it fleetingly passed before my eyes, I was bewitched by it; not because of its charm or because it possessed the inspired brushwork of a master. In fact, the artist was certainly unknown to me. I thought the picture was probably the work of one of the many unrenowned Victorian painters whose works frequently appear on the stalls of cheap bric-à-brac traders, and are offered to unsuspecting customers at very exorbitant prices.

But there was something about that painting which made it special. It had an austerity about it and a strange enchantment. Yet that was not all. There was something else I could not explain; something which made me perceive it as a work of singular and extraordinary importance. If I had been asked, at that time of first glimpsing it, the subject of the painting, I would simply have described it as a scene of a cottage in a dense wood or forest. There was a man – a woodcutter – in the foreground, chopping down a tree with an axe. That is all my eye perceived but my mind beheld much more; a perception of mystery and cryptic presence.

A little bell tinkled as I entered the shop. The painting was being wrapped in brown paper by a middle-aged shop assistant. He looked up.

'Won't keep you a minute, sir.'

'That's all right. We're together.'

Dorothy glanced round and examined me with a look of scorn, doubtless galled by the audacity of that statement. She took hold of the brown paper package tied with string and clasped it to her bosom as if it were priceless. With her other hand, she gave an undisclosed number of five-pound notes to the smiling, bespectacled assistant, who handed back some loose change with a 'Thank you very much, madam.'

'Had it long, have you? That painting?'

The assistant's gaze shifted warily to me. 'No. Actually, sir, an old lady brought it in to us only yesterday. I expect she wanted to sell it because she needed the cash. Can't identify the artist but it's a very fine piece of the Victorian period. Around eighteen-forty I would guess and in very good condition. If I might say so, sir, your wife has very fine taste. It's a lovely example of—'

'Old lady? What was she like? The old woman who sold it to you? Gnarled? Haggard? Decrepit? Big, hairy, warty nose? Little red beady eyes? Dressed all in black? Left her broomstick parked outside?' I interrupted.

The assistant examined me with a quizzical look, then

smiled. 'Well – I can't vouch for the broomstick, you understand, sir, but without wishing to seem unkind, I guess the rest is a pretty good description of her. Never seen her in the shop before though. Not one of our regulars, that's for sure.'

I felt a curious coldness. It was as if I were consumed with a foreboding of terror, perceived yet unimagined, abominated yet coveted. I had sensed that feeling only once before – again on an occasion when the wicked old witch had graced our ordinary human world with Her presence – up in the tree house with Ben on the night he was taken.

The shop assistant's further words shook me out of my reverie. 'You forgot these, madam! Your picture hooks.'

Dorothy was almost at the door. She turned, scuffled back to the counter where she almost snatched the little package from the shopkeeper's hand and made for the door again, her precious purchase still clasped to her breast. I had to catch my breath before I could follow her from the shop. Dorothy was scurrying down the street as I ran to catch her.

'Why did you buy that picture?' I said, spinning her round to face me.

She stopped and glared incredulously. 'Because I need it!'

It wasn't till later, when we were both staring at the painting hanging on the chimney breast, inappropriately framed on either side by the two Canalettos in the alcoves, that the strangeness of Dorothy's answer struck me. 'Because I need it!' She had sounded so impassioned. Her voice sounded as though she craved the painting, that it was as necessary as food, water or air to breathe. She was sitting in an armchair she had positioned especially and was gazing at the painting with a fixed, resolute stare. Her eyes were glazed in purposeful concentration.

I studied the picture. I looked at the cottage. It was then I first realised I had seen it somewhere before. Yes, I remembered. It was the gingerbread cottage in that big old book of fairy tales my mother used to read to me. That same cottage in the same clearing in the same forest, surrounded by those same eerie-looking trees which almost had faces etched into their gnarled old trunks, linking branches like arms joined in a charmed protective ring. I remember that my mother often used to turn the book around to show me that picture, pointing at it with her finger as I cowered in my little bed, listening to the grisly stories she would read me. 'This is where that wicked old witch lives,' she would say, 'and this is where she will take you to gobble you up, Johnny Smith, when you've been naughty one day – so naughty, that you'll deserve to be taken away to her little gingerbread cottage deep in this big old forest where nobody will ever hear you scream or be able to find you again.'

Then my eyes were drawn to the woodcutter. His axe was poised to strike at the base of a tree. I looked closely at his face, my eyes staring in complete disbelief. It was my father's face; there was no mistaking it. I examined the brushwork more closely. It was my father; I was sure of it. Even his manner, the way he bore his axe exactly as I remembered him on the back porch chopping up logs for firewood, was captured with accomplished mastery.

'. . . you will be taken from this place into my forest and work in my service as a woodcutter, making my firewood for me to cook those very naughty and very ordinary little boys whose

slugs and snails and puppy dogs' tails are tender enough for gobbling!'

The wicked old witch's words, recalled from a long-forgotten dream, resounded in my mind and that same coldness swallowed me whole.

I blinked my eyes and looked at Dorothy. She was staring at me, a curious smile etched on her face.

'It looks wonderful there, in that forest. I need to go there, Johnny! There's nothing left for me here. Show me the way! Please show me the way!'

'. . . *One or the other, Johnny Smith, one or the other!'*

I fought with the words of the Mistress's commandment to me. I would have shown her; I really would. Dorothy's request had sounded almost like a plea. I knew she desperately wanted to go. But I was halted by my own selfishness. The sniffing bloodhounds had my scent about them and I sensed they were close. Too close. It was fear that prevented me; the fear of being found out and punished by a subordinate justice which would never have understood the truth. I remember Dorothy's pathetic expression when I said I couldn't show her the way to her salvation. I was sad for her and told her I was sorry. But, without another word to me, she just turned her attentions back to the painting and I went up to my room, lost in the iciness of a terrible fear. Night came but I could not sleep. I made a supplication to the Mistress for me to be released from my dilemma but I was not taken to Her courtroom in a dream for my petition to be heard.

I remember the coldness of fear had dried my throat. I went downstairs for a drink and, in the glistening yellow moonlight shining through the living-room window, I saw Dorothy still sitting, staring at the spookiness of that painting; mesmerised in a hypnotic trance, gibbering feverously. I tried to coax her to bed but she would not be moved.

The next morning she was still there. I sat in another chair and watched her, seized by an inexplicable enchantment. The hours passed. Morning became afternoon, the afternoon became evening and the evening, night. But still she stared impassively into the sombreness of that canvas forest.

It was when I switched on a table lamp to try and dispel the eeriness that I first noticed it. I know what you will say. It was an imagining, nothing but a fanciful vision. Yet I know that wasn't so. I was distrustful myself at first but the more I stared into that picture, the more I was sure my senses weren't deceiving me.

There was my father, the witch's woodcutter, still in obedient service; his axe poised to strike at the base of the tree. Except it was a different tree, and a stump now stood at the spot where I had seen him before. I examined the painting closely. I even rubbed my finger over the new nuance, half expecting wet paint to appear on it. But the tree stump belonged. It conformed and harmonised with the rest, the small hairline cracks present in its varnish connecting with the web of other cracks in the rest of the picture. And, yes, there was another difference. A faint light was shining through the cottage windows and smoke was coming out of the chimney where I know there was no smoke before.

I sat down again, my head throbbing with shock and incredulity. Time passed. I cannot say how long I just sat there in my shocked, almost traumatised, state. I wasn't really conscious of anything until Dorothy moaned loudly and unexpectedly. It made me jump with fright. She got up from her chair, still entranced, as if controlled by a power outside of her own. By this time she was completely oblivious of my presence; in fact, I don't even think she could have been roused by a bomb exploding in the street outside.

Then, just as the carriage clock on the mantelpiece struck out its twelve strangled chimes to inform of midnight's advent, I remember observing her walk towards the painting. Yet it wasn't exactly walking, she kind of floated. That is the only way I can describe it. Her eyes were closed and she came to rest with her nose touching the canvas. As I looked on at this strange chimera, Dorothy became like the incredible shrinking woman, somehow levitating up within the very ether of the picture, as if she were suddenly captured within a rising translucent bubble, growing ever smaller, until its scantness became too diminutive to be contained and it silently burst into the intimacy of that strange canvas world, and she became a part of it.

I next saw her moving, actually walking between those gnarled old trees on the narrow path which led to the gingerbread cottage, lit only by the eeriness of the picture's native moonlight. I rushed over to the painting and tried to clutch her between my thumb and forefinger, to pluck her out of her new incarnation. But she had no more substance. Dorothy had somehow become as flat and formless as the rest of the things in that mystical aesthetic forest. She had no thickness I could grip, only the measured depth of a blob of smudged oil paints bonded to, yet somehow permitted to migrate along, their canvas foundation. I ran my finger over the strange embodiment of her favourite pink dress. I know she didn't feel my touch. It was as if the transmutation of her new self into her brand new world was now complete and absolute, untouched and uninfluenced by anything outside of it. She walked on regardless, as I watched, spellbound, in total bewilderment and stupefaction.

I saw her reach the cottage door, the light from the little windows either side of it illuminating the daub of her small painted face, a depiction so authentic yet peculiarly fraudulent. Then she opened up the door and went inside, immediately, without faltering, without question, as if she knew she belonged to the place in which she now found herself. I was so engrossed in observing this detail that it was a long while before I noticed the whole tableau again. And, when I did, I saw my father was no longer there.

I stayed in my chair for the next few days; was it two or three days? I don't remember. I didn't move. I didn't eat, neither did I drink. I wasn't even conscious of sitting in my own excrement. I simply watched, spellbound, at the changing nature of that canvas world. Early next morning, my father returned and the tree he was cutting was felled; I watched him move on to the next. As darkness fell on the forest I saw him walk behind the cottage, carrying his axe. I saw the gloom of the evening become transformed into the eeriness of a forest night and smoke reappeared from the chimney.

Then, one by one, twenty-six witches, all dressed in black, came out of the cottage and rode off into the night sky on besom brooms. I numbered them and counted the very same number return before daybreak. Although it was too dark to distinguish their faces, I knew who they were. Had it been light enough, I know I could have recognised each and every one of them.

The next day I watched it all again. I may have watched for a third day too; incredulously, unbelieving, too submerged in the bizarre vision to move away from it. But I swear the things I have said actually happened.

And I will tell you something equally unbelievable; something I can only accurately recount because I have conscientiously kept a diary of my life story, which is why I can write it now as it truly happened, in such detail and with such conviction and confidence. The day Dorothy disappeared into that painting was exactly one month and one day after I had dreamt of the wicked witch giving me but one month to fulfil my assignment. I have often thought of that fact and the admonition She gave me:

'. . . But, one word of warning. Do not try my patience for too long! You have one month. One more month to deliver the final one to my second coven. If you fail, Johnny Smith, not only will you not be pardoned for your misdemeanours but I will be forced to act myself and take matters into my own hands. For then, I and I alone will make the choice and see to the deliverance of the chosen one. And as for you, Johnny Smith, you will be disregarded! Treated with the lowly contempt you deserve, like something odious and detestable stuck to the bottom of my boots. You will be left to suffer the consequences of your misdemeanours on your own. Without my help or my protection!'

My undoing happened quite quickly after that though I remember very little of what actually occurred. For a while, I seemed to live in a world detached from reality; seemingly unconscious of real tangible things. If the telephone rang, I never knew. If someone came to the door, I acted in unwitting ignorance. If I ate and drank – and since I am still around to tell the tale, I presume I did – I was unaware of it. During the days that followed, there are not even any entries in my diary. It is for this reason, I can state, quite categorically, that my insensibility lasted two whole weeks; fourteen days of complete and utter nothingness. I was brought back to the real world by something which sounded more like an explosion than the front door being battered down.

'That's him! That's the low-life! What have you done with my Dorothy?'

It was the screaming voice of Mrs Thatcher. I slowly looked up to see her being physically restrained by a uniformed constable. A group of other faces surrounded her, just as they had appeared as the body of my accusers in the witch's courtroom. My eyes settled on Sergeant Dixon who was staring down at me with a smug, self-satisfied grin.

'Well, John! We meet again! It seems our paths continue to cross every few years or so, doesn't it?'

Chapter 24

'So, John, what's it going to be? Are you going to make things easy for yourself or not? I don't really mind either way. It's all part of the job to me. You get used to it—'

'Why don't you just ask the low-life what he's done with my daughter! That's why we're here, isn't it?' Mrs Thatcher screamed again.

Sergeant Dixon glared at her, then at the constable restraining her quivering bulk. 'Show Mrs Thatcher outside for a while, will you, constable.'

She was removed, still protesting about the inefficacious way Sergeant Dixon was conducting the inquiry.

The policeman's gaze slowly returned to my chair; the seat on which I had been slumped for the complete time of my obscure and unremembered senselessness. Sergeant Dixon looked for a while at my pitiful state then he crouched down so his head was level with mine.

The booming voice was subdued as he said, 'Where is she, John?'

I looked at him. I tried to speak but I was unable to.

'Where is she, John? Where is your wife? Mrs Thatcher

seems to think you've done something to her. Quite a forceful lady, your mother-in-law. Not the kind of woman to cross, is she?'

Sergeant Dixon stood up and looked around the room. 'It's a bit of a mess in here, John. Stinks too.' He sniffed. 'Have you shit yourself, John?'

'I – I—'

'I think we'd better get you cleaned up, don't you? Perhaps you'll feel better then. More able to talk. That sound okay to you, John?'

He nodded to another officer who helped me to my feet. I felt unsteady and stumbled. I remember he placed my arm around his shoulder and I was aided upstairs to the bathroom where I suffered the indignity of being assisted in my toilet and in changing my clothes. I remember hearing talking outside the bathroom door and noises coming from the bedrooms as other officers looked around the house. I was then escorted back to the living room. By this time my legs felt a little more as though they belonged to me.

Sergeant Dixon was examining the room when I returned. He looked up as I entered. 'Feeling better, John?'

I nodded.

'Now – sit down. Time we had a little chat, don't you think?'

I wasn't directed to the soiled chair in which I was found. The officer escorted me to the chair Dorothy had positioned in front of the painting. As I sat down, the picture loomed before me, its menacing presence jogging my memory into vibrant remembrances. I stared at it. It became my focus. It was all I could see. It was as if my eyes were blinkered; I had an awareness of nothing else.

As I stared at that painting, I noticed it had changed again. Everything was back as it originally was. There were no tree-stumps, just whole uncut trees, the woodcutter standing in his foremost position, his axe poised at the base of its initial target. I looked at the cottage. The chimney was smokeless. The painting was nothing more than an inanimate scene of a woodcutter's dwelling in a dense, dark wood.

'Do you like that painting, John?' Sergeant Dixon had obviously noticed my anchored gaze.

'No! I hate it! It was Dorothy's!'

'*Was* Dorothy's? I think you'd better tell me, don't you? Where is Dorothy, John? Where is she?'

I stared into the sergeant's eyes. 'I – she – she went away.'

I realised my answer had sounded a pathetic defence. But it was the truth, wasn't it? What else could I tell him anyway?

'Same old story, eh, John? Seems a lot of women you know decide to just get up and leave, doesn't it? And I suppose your wife didn't tell you where she was going either?'

I shook my head.

'But – you do know where she is, don't you, John?'

I didn't answer. I remember being surprised at the gentleness of Sergeant Dixon's interrogation. He wasn't questioning me with the same forcefulness he used those times at the halfway house. It made me think of the first time he had interviewed me, in my childhood bedroom of this very house, eleven years before, a few days after Ben was taken. I remember the fear his imposing figure evoked in me then. I still felt that fear; but now I realised it was the fear of his special knowledge of me and the astuteness of his mind.

'John.' His voice sounded almost compassionate. 'It will be better if you co-operate. You know that, don't you?'

Again I didn't answer. Sergeant Dixon's compassionate look changed to one of exasperation. He stared into my disconsolate face before adding, 'Look, John, I can see something has happened here. You're in quite a state. Perhaps it will make it easier if I tell you what we already know.

'Your mother-in-law has made quite a damning statement. In fact, we couldn't stop her talking. And I spoke to your neighbours before coming here.' He withdrew his notebook from his inside pocket and consulted it. 'Mr and Mrs Randall. They told us you and your wife aren't exactly the best of pals at the moment. Now – Mrs Thatcher's convinced you've done her daughter in but, if I listened to all the tales told by interfering mothers-in-law, I'd be running around the whole of my time doing nothing else but sorting out domestic squabbles.

'But the trouble is, John, your mother-in-law was most insistent and Mr and Mrs Randall confirmed that your rows were often very noisy and violent. And – well, John – you and I go back a long way now and I feel there are still a few matters we've left outstanding. You know – never quite got to the bottom of, so to speak. So I thought, why don't I just pop along and have another chat with John? Let's see if we can get everything sorted once and for all.

'So, what do you say, John? What do you say? Are we going to sort it out the easy way? What's happened to your wife, John? Has she left you? Is that why you're in this state?'

My mouth was so parched, I couldn't have uttered any words even if my mind was able to think of them. I remember I just looked at him with an expression of bewilderment.

Sergeant Dixon then exhaled a little gasp of resignation. 'Okay, John. Have it your own way!'

He reached into his other inside pocket and withdrew a large sheet of folded white paper.

'A search warrant, John. I'm going to turn this place inside out. It's the only option you leave me with.'

He strode over to a plain-clothes officer standing in the living-room doorway and said something to him which I didn't grasp. The man disappeared and I was next aware of a hubbub of commotion. I heard feet in the hallway and more feet climbing the stairs. There were other sounds of orders being given. I looked into the dining room, through the window into the garden and saw two veiled human shapes pass by the anaemic screen of its net curtains. Then they were gone from my sight.

I don't know why I glanced up at that painting then. Perhaps it was to seek some kind of reassurance. Perhaps it was because I really believed the secret way would be uncovered and I next expected to see the two policemen actually walking between the gnarled old trees on the narrow path leading to the gingerbread cottage. Or perhaps it was to entreat guidance and direction from the One who ruled over its domain. I really don't know why I looked up at that painting. I do not even know if my gesture had any motive at all, except the lure of its macabre enchantment.

But, whatever my reasons, I was totally unprepared for what I was to see. For there, standing right in the foreground, obliterating my father and the tree he was felling, was the hideous figure of the wicked old witch Herself. She was waggling Her aged, misshapen finger at me.

I heard Her laugh Her heinous cackle. I actually heard it; I swear I did. Then Her voice, Her hairy, warty voice, bellowed out to me from the dimensions of that canvas world, *'Didn't I warn you, Johnny Smith, that you will be disregarded! Treated with the lowly contempt you deserve, like something odious and detestable stuck to the bottom of my boots! Didn't I tell you that you'll be left to suffer the consequences of your misdemeanours on your own. Without my help or my protection!'*

Her abhorrent snigger reverberated through my head. It grew and grew until it consumed me completely and my senses were lost to it. I remembered no more for a while. I must have passed out. My first awareness, on coming to, was of an unknown male voice and face, above me.

'He's coming round.'

'Thanks, doc!' boomed the voice of Sergeant Dixon.

My eyes searched for him in the fuzzy blend of faces stooping above me. Then I remembered what had made me lose consciousness. The witch! The painting! I turned my head towards the chimney breast and saw it hanging there in all its dismal splendour.

It was back to normal; as I had first seen it in the window of Let Bygones Be Bygones. But I couldn't release my stare. I gazed in awe of its mysticism. I wanted it to animate in front of the sea of faces around me so I could shout, 'Look! Do you see it? Do you see it changing?'

But it didn't change. It just stared back at me, inert and lifeless; my father's axe locked in its unchanging sweep of suspended inanimation. I don't know how long I gaped at that painting but it was the sergeant's booming voice which finally recaptured my attention.

'What is it about that picture, John?'

I slowly turned my head and found him, my eyes engaging the coldness of his stare. 'You – you – wouldn't believe me if I told you.'

'Try me!'

There was an interminable pause while I tried to conjure up real words to explain the inconceivable. 'It – it –' I began, my stutterings interrupted by a breathless officer entering the room.

'Sarge! I think you'd better come and see this.' His words sounded compelling and urgent. Then he saw the police doctor among the group. 'You too, doc!' he added.

'Watch him!' Sergeant Dixon boomed instructions to a uniformed constable. His finger pointed at me. 'Don't let him out of your sight for a single second!'

The rest of the group disappeared, leaving me in the custody of the lone policeman; a young man, I remember, probably not much older than I was, who looked nervous as he approached my chair, his eyes glued to mine. I remember we just stared at each other in uncomfortable silence.

I have been trying to think what I was feeling at that moment. Fear? Hopelessness? Anger? With hindsight, I probably should have felt one or all of these things. But I really can't remember feeling anything. All I can recall about that time is the look of apprehension in that young policeman's eyes as they scrutinised me.

Suddenly, there was a babble of sounds from the kitchen. I could hear Sergeant Dixon's voice but it wasn't till he entered the hall that I could identify his exact words.

'—and I suppose you'd better call Ribble. I know he'll want to bask in the glory of this.'

He came into the living room alone. The constable looked relieved to see him. I remember that the sergeant's droll smile graced his face. It was a smile I had come to know well. He approached.

'Well, John!' He paused a while to scrutinise me. 'Seems you and I really *do* need to talk. A very serious talk, I would say!'

I couldn't look at him. Instead, my eyes wandered to the opened door of the living room where I watched several men carry large rolls of white sheeting and striped tape through the hall, into the kitchen, and out through the backyard door. When I looked back Sergeant Dixon was no longer there.

A short while later, more officers arrived bearing pick-axes and shovels. And, all the time, the eyes of that young constable never left me. Again, I don't remember feeling anything. I just sat there, dispassionate and unemotional. Occasionally, I would glance up at that painting; at the static figure of the woodcutter – my father. I studied his face. It was an unhappy face, grimacing with the toil of his labour. Both in this world, and in that, it seemed, his life was hard, lonely and sorrowful. Then, more than ever, I wanted to tell him I loved him.

I remember asking that young constable for permission to go into the kitchen to get a drink of water. He vigilantly accompanied me. As I filled my glass, I looked out of the window into the forest. I saw groups of men digging. I heard orders being shouted and the occasional cries of 'Here! Over here!'

I gazed upon the pristine whiteness of the sheeting, already erected to screen some areas of the garden. It reminded me of white, billowy bed-sheets hanging on the line to dry in the warm summer sunshine. It made me think of Mondays, washdays, and one Monday in particular when my mother was too busy to care about Ben and me planning our great adventure.

Then my gaze turned to the charred skeleton of that

big old yew tree, towering above the scene, like a phoenix rising from the ashes. That was my last remembrance of the forest; it was the last time I ever saw it.

And that was the last time I ever saw the house; that sad old house we had made something new, still standing as a silent but futile sentinel to a secret which was a secret no more.

CHAPTER 25

Before I end this part of my story there is one more thing I must recount for I have often considered my feelings for Dorothy as I watched her walk out of my unremarkable and ordinary life into the strange vista of her new incarnation. Did I feel sadness for her?

No, I don't think I ever did. And neither do I now. On the contrary, I believe I felt only envy and covetousness. For she had found her place of happiness – her Satisfaction House – that special place where she would be loved eternally and where she could truly be herself for ever more. And it was a further extraordinary blessing for Dorothy that she was personally chosen by the great and majestic mistress Herself.

Her obvious happiness only compounded my own misery. My birthright had condemned me to the unequitable unfairness of being born a lowly detestable boy who could only rise to guardianship of the secret way, without ever being granted the glory of passing through it.

No, I did not feel sadness for Dorothy. Not only was she accorded the honour of all these things but something else was proven; something which made me even more envious of her. You see, as much as I hated my mother-in-law, as much as I longed to send her myself through the portals of the secret way where she would be lost to me and I to her, as much as I knew she was the cause of exposing me and my deeds, I know that the odious Mrs Thatcher acted out of a sincere and honest motive – maternal love and a desire to protect her child – a virtue I had searched for so desperately in my own mother but never once found.

As I was led away from the house that day, handcuffed to Sergeant Dixon, and bustled into a waiting police car, I heard Mrs Thatcher speak to me. It was the first and only time I ever heard her voice display humility. The words she sobbed were only just audible above her great pitiable wails. There was no anger in her voice, only genuine agony and torment.

'You killed my baby! You killed my baby!'

That night, in the loneliness of my cell, I relived that moment in a fantasy. My ecstasy was sublime, made even more satisfying because Mrs Thatcher was agonising over a misconception. The imperious Mrs Thatcher had actually got something wrong.

I knew that, whatever else I would be accused of, there would be no evidence to charge me with Dorothy's demise. And anyway, it wasn't a demise at all, was it? Dorothy was exalted. Dorothy was happy. Mrs Thatcher should have been pleased for her. And grateful to the Mistress – her daughter's magnanimous deliverer.

Part Four

The Institution House

The most gracious gift
Is release from life's race.
Accepting what is;
Without want to replace.

by Johnny Smith (aged 37)

Chapter 26

Later that day, May 20th, 1973, I was read my rights and formally charged with the murders of, as yet, an undisclosed number of persons whose identities were still to be substantiated.

'You don't have to say anything but anything you do say will be written down and may be used in evidence against you. You may appoint a solicitor . . .'

I had heard those words, or similar ones, so many times in television detective series, I almost found myself reciting them in harmony with Sergeant Dixon's resounding boom. I think it was an image in my mind of the sergeant as his incongruous 'Dock Green' namesake which made me smile. Somehow, I found the vision farcical.

Sergeant Dixon stopped reading the words from the card and stared at me without emotion. 'Find something funny, do you, John? I'd advise against that! I would say having human remains buried in your garden is a pretty serious matter, wouldn't you?'

I stopped smiling. The sergeant read me my rights again. I didn't smile this time but listened in stony and sober silence. I decided I would not make a statement and asked for a solicitor to be appointed to me.

But Sergeant Dixon and Detective Inspector Ribble decided to question me for more than two hours without a solicitor present to represent me, nevertheless. The interview was recorded but my impassive voice declaring, 'I prefer not to comment until I have spoken to my solicitor' was the only statement transcribed from that tape despite their relentless cross-examination. I remember gazing fixedly at the clock on the wall, watching the undeviating sweeps of its red second hand yet noticing no movement of its other hands to confirm the passage of proper time. Like the watched kettle that never boils, I swear the slender black fingers of that watched clock never moved. That time seemed motionless and interminable.

I withdrew my gaze to the scratched and ring-stained table I was forced to sit behind at the police station, simply furnished with a telephone, an overflowing ashtray and three polystyrene coffee cups, still containing the cold dregs left behind from a previous interview. I concentrated on the vision of Ben's face imprisoned in his tomb of petrified whiteness.

They were asking their questions, one after the other. 'How many are there buried in your garden, John?' 'Are they those missing women? You may as well come clean, John, we'll find out eventually. And it will be better for you if you co-operate with us now, you know that, don't you?'

'I prefer not to comment until I have spoken to my solicitor.'

I saw those women's faces. I heard their agonised screams of terror. Why were they so afraid? I was only showing them where they wanted to go. They were defiled. It was their only salvation, and mine also. And now it was over, my assignment still unfulfilled.

'Where's Dorothy, John? Is she down there, in the garden? You may as well tell us. We'll find her eventually – come on, John, why don't you make it easy on yourself?'

That was the one time I nearly answered them. I wanted to tell them that they'd never find Dorothy; that she had been taken to that deep, dark and secret forest by the Mistress Herself, without trace, without my help. But I didn't.

'I prefer not to comment until I have spoken to my solicitor.'

'How did you kill them, John?'

Kill them? What did they mean 'kill them'? I showed them the secret way; the way to their eternal life, the way to their immortal incarnation in the service of the Mistress. It was only naughty little boys who died, those whose slugs and snails and puppy dogs' tails were juicy and tender enough for gobbling. They were the unfortunate ones. Boys like Ben. Those 'other little boys'!

'I prefer not to comment until I have spoken to my solicitor!'

This time my words were wrathful. I screamed them at my interrogators.

My mind recalled the spectacle of Ben's petrified face with such vividness, for a moment I was eleven years old again and it was that hot and humid July night up in the tree house. I saw the heinous gnarled and haggard vision of the witch's face plummet through that ring of fire. I saw Her opened mouth and a blackness which was illimitable, rimmed by a bracelet of drooling yellow teeth. I heard that same crunch of bone and that same nauseating repulsive belch. I saw Ben's headless body and I smelt that smell; that odious, repugnant smell. It was entrenched in my nostrils.

I saw it all so clearly, I screamed. I actually screamed out like a lunatic no longer in control of himself, then I remembered no more till I awoke in the sweaty darkness of a police cell. That was the very last time I recalled that image of Ben until I began to write my story. I suppose I just blotted it out. The memory of that night had become too painful. Especially then, I guess, when I was struck with the sudden realisation that I had failed in my oath to avenge his taking and in the assignment set for my own redemption. I knew then I would always be an ordinary boy, unpardoned, and destined to spend the rest of his miserable life in common and unremarkable unwholesomeness.

But, afterwards, when I woke up in that wonderful darkness, having relived that glorious moment in a dream when Mrs Thatcher wrongly blamed me for the taking of her daughter, I remember I felt nothing. I didn't feel anger or fear, or even sadness. I had surrendered myself completely to the inevitability of my fate. Wasn't this foretold – prophesied – by the only One of true authority? *'. . . And as for you, Johnny Smith, you will be disregarded! . . . You will be left to suffer the consequences of your misdemeanours on your own. Without my help or my protection!'*

I wasn't conscious of time passing and neither did I care that it was wasted in voluntary indifference. I have often thought about how I spent the rest of that night, the thoughts I had and the feelings I felt. But nothing is recalled so I assume it simply passed in the oblivion of obscurity.

To be truthful, I wasn't even conscious of the custody sergeant entering my cell. It was his voice, one single word, 'Breakfast!', which made me aware of him. That was all he said, then he was gone. I heard the clunk of the key turn in the lock.

I remember looking at the plate, at three sausages and some anaemic baked beans swimming in a greasy ooze. I felt sick and flushed the food down the toilet but I drank the mug of lukewarm coffee.

I can't be sure but it must have been some hours later when he next entered. I was still lying on my bunk doing nothing, thinking of nothing.

'Get up! Sergeant Dixon wants another little chat with you.'

I followed him down a dingy brick-lined corridor, up some iron stairs and into an interview room; a different room, smaller and airier. He directed me to a chair in front of a similar shabby desk and then sat down himself on a chair by the door.

There was an edition of the *Comet* lying on the table. I asked the policeman's permission to look at it. He neither granted nor denied my request so I picked it up and unfolded the front page.

'Where-Are-They-Women Are Found! Grisly graves uncovered in local garden – Man arrested!'

The headline was huge. I read the editorial.

'Police believe the case of the missing Where-Are-They-Women may finally be solved following the discovery of human remains in crude and shallow graves in a Melrose Rise back garden. The grisly finds were unearthed after police were called to the house to investigate a domestic incident. Detective Sergeant Dixon of the missing persons inquiry team set up to look into these curious and bizarre disappearances, said yesterday, "I can confirm we have found human skeletal remains and believe these to be of the missing women who have periodically disappeared over the last eleven years. But, as you will appreciate, we are still only in the very early stages of our investigations and I cannot say any more at this time except that a man is helping us with our enquiries."

'But the *Comet* can reveal the identity of the arrested man. He is John Smith who, until recently, was a colleague working as a reporter for this paper. Smith lived in the house in Melrose Rise as a child and returned to live there again following his marriage six months ago. His wife, Dorothy Smith, is believed to be numbered among the murdered women.

'As this reporter stood outside Smith's former home watching the macabre spectacle of large black bags containing the human remains being removed from the scene, I couldn't help but remember the strange and often eccentric young man who once lived there and, until recently, was a work colleague. It is because of its connection with the man now accused of the perpetration of these crimes that the *Comet* can print its exclusive insight into the mind of the Where-Are-They-Women murderer, written by those who knew him, those who once worked with him, day in, day out, often investigating the very incidents which have now made his name famous – or should I say infamous – as an item of news rather than a reporter of it.

'Over the next few days, the *Comet* will run its exclusive series of articles, "John Smith – The Man", featuring recollections by his work colleagues and interviews with other people who knew him. Remember, the *Comet* is the only paper with the special insight that enables it to reveal Smith's own disturbing yet fascinating story. (More details, page 2.)

'Reading about your exploits, John?'

I looked up into the cold, impassive eyes of Sergeant Dixon.

'You've become quite a celebrity!'

I didn't answer. I remember holding his gaze for a while before slowly lowering my head again to the front page of the newspaper spread out on the table. Suddenly, something was thrown down on top of it. I heard it thump. It was totally unexpected and I was startled.

My eyes focused on the incursion. I didn't recognise it at first. It was obviously some kind of book encased in a sealed transparent plastic bag; an old book, stained around the edges of its cover, well-worn and ravaged by the spoils of time. *My Favourite Book of Fairy Tales.* I stared at the title and the drawing of the silhouetted witch riding her broomstick across a bright yellow crescent moon.

Sergeant Dixon's hands appeared and removed the book from the bag. He placed it on the table again and flipped open the cover. And there, written on the flyleaf, were the words, 'To a very naughty and ordinary little boy, Johnny Smith, Christmas 1954. To be read to him as a warning. From Mummy.'

'Recognise this, John?'

I just stared at it in disbelief. The cover of that book will be remembered for the rest of my life as a thing of abject terror. It seemed that most of my early years were spent gawping at that picture of the wicked old witch on a sortie to gobble up another naughty little boy while I listened, spellbound yet with cowering dread, to my mother's hairy, warty voice tell its tales of horror. But, in all the years that book had sat on the top of the tallboy in my room, I had never once opened it. I had never read one single word printed in its pages.

I thought I had seen the last of that book eleven years ago. I thought it had been sent with my mother to that dark, deep and secret forest, never to be beheld again.

'Do you know where we found this, John? Buried in your garden under one of the bodies. Not much left of the body, of course, just a pile of old bones but the book – well, as you can see, it's quite well preserved really. Found it inside a plastic bag, you see, with the name "Cuthberts Grocery Store" printed on it. Used to be a Cuthberts in the High Street. Closed down in 1962. We haven't identified the body yet. We know it's female but do you want to know what I think, John? I think it's your mother! Am I right, John? Am I right?'

'I prefer not to comment until I have spoken to my solicitor.' I said after a long pause.

I remember asking myself why I had protected that hated book by placing it inside a plastic bag; why I hadn't condemned it to be irrevocably absorbed in the putrid decay of time. But I knew why. The answer was simple, wasn't it? That book was my authority. It was my Bible. Like anecdotes of the wrathful God of the Old Testament, stories were proffered from its pages of the ruthless punishment of disobedience. Its power was to be feared but also held in awesome respect. I revered that book. It had to be esteemed, protected on its journey to its last and final resting place just as the holy things of the Jews were protected inside the Ark of the Covenant on their journey through the wilderness.

I was aware of the sergeant's face appearing before me, his hands on the table, supporting his leaning body, his eyes no more than a few inches from my own.

'"To a very naughty and ordinary little boy, Johnny Smith, Christmas 1954. To be read to him as a warning.

From Mummy." Not the sort of thing a mother normally writes on a Christmas present, is it, John? Not very kind. Not very loving. Were you a naughty little boy, John? Were you?'

I stared into Sergeant Dixon's eyes with a look of complacent indifference. I felt no anger at his probing into my secret, just a dejection and a hopelessness because of an incomprehensible and inaccessible truth no words of logic or reason could ever explain.

'I must be good! I will be good, Mummy, I promise!' I heard myself whisper those words of allegiance, then I cried, great lamentable sobs of self-pity.

'John.' The sergeant's boom was more subdued. 'She wasn't very kind to you, was she? Your mother? Did she treat you badly? Is that why you killed her?'

I knew this new compassionate line of questioning was only a sham, simulated to break down my resistance and get me to confess. But confess to what? What had I done, except show them the way; the way to their salvation? I was their redeemer not their murderer. I had done nothing wrong. These thoughts only strengthened my resolve.

'I prefer not to comment until I have spoken to my solicitor.'

Sergeant Dixon looked exasperated. He stood upright and walked round behind my chair. 'We found your diaries, John! Very interesting reading, your diaries. A whole stack of 'em going back some twelve years or so. Do you want to tell me anything about those diaries, your dreams about the "wicked old witch" or the entries in red stating, "Showed one of them the secret way"?'

I recall thinking two things then. Firstly, how fortunate it was that I'd hidden those diaries in the old house and not in my bedroom at Auntie Pat's, where he would certainly have found them and the secret way would doubtless have been discovered a very long time ago. Then I thought how interesting it was that Sergeant Dixon had remembered the minutest detail of all these things without once having to refer to his notorious little black notebook. I wanted to ask him about that but, instead, I indifferently uttered my usual response.

'I prefer not to comment until I have spoken to my solicitor.'

The policeman walked round and faced me again. 'You know, John, you've caused me a lot of trouble. But that's all by the by now. My job is over as far as your little escapades are concerned. Do you know who I really feel sorry for now? Do you know who still has the hard work to do? The pathologists and the forensic guys. Funny though – they don't consider it hard work at all, fiddling around with bits of bodies, putting together the little pieces of the jigsaw. No accounting for taste, is there? I saw them just a short while ago, poring over the remains of those poor women, rushing around, putting little morsels under microscopes. Like kids with a new toy they were. It'll cost us a fortune in overtime though.

'Do you know what I like about scientists, John? Their dedication. Won't rest until they've solved the puzzle. They'll get there, John, make no mistake about that. They'll piece together identities from dental records, bits of jewellery, old X-rays – stuff like that. They'll prove scientifically that they are those missing women. They'll find out exactly how you killed them, even when. But then, your diaries tell us that, don't they? Very precise, your diaries, John! What I'm trying to say is – we'll get to the bottom of what happened, sooner or later, and that evidence will be used against you in court. But you could help us, John. You could save those poor guys a lot of trouble and the taxpayer a lot of money. I could then say you co-operated with us. It'll be better for you in the long run. Much better. We'll find out the hows and the whens but only you can really tell us the whys. Don't you see, John, how your co-operation now will help you later?'

I wanted to tell the sergeant how much I had admired his reasoned and persuasive discourse but I didn't think he'd appreciate my praise.

'I prefer not to comment until I have spoken to my solicitor.'

Sergeant Dixon raised his eyes in a gesture of irritated impatience. 'Okay, John, have it your own way. We'll appoint a solicitor for you. He'll be in to see you later today. But if you'll take my advice, you'll use the rest of today to think seriously about the things I've said.' He turned to face the uniformed sergeant sitting by the door. 'Take him back.'

The officer approached me, his hand placed on my elbow, guiding me to my feet. We had reached the door when Sergeant Dixon's boom stopped us in our tracks. I turned to face his roaring words.

'You know, John, I still remember the first time we met. You were just an unhappy little kid who'd been scared out of his wits. What really scared you, John? It wasn't just what happened to your pal Ben, was it?'

He paused for my response. But I remained silent.

'I felt sorry for you then; I feel sorry for you now. Think over what I said, John. Think it over carefully.'

Chapter 27

After that second interview with Sergeant Dixon, my time of isolation in the police cell gave new meaning to the expression 'being banged up'. The silence was almost palpable. I remember being aware of my own heartbeat as if it were a pulse of constant and resounding cannon fire. Those relentless bangs were my one and only reference to mark the passage of time. My wristwatch and other belongings had been removed when I was charged and there was no clock on the wall. Neither were there any windows to peer out of and glimpse the constant march of the day's advancing hours.

After thinking about Sergeant Dixon's words, my attitude was somehow different. At first, I could no longer allow that time to pass in voluntary ignorance. I can clearly recall I considered the things he said. I considered them ruthlessly. My brain was so fired with a confusion of thoughts and conceptions, I could not stop them crowding in on my disorder. It is strange that, when all reference to the passing of time is removed from you, it somehow makes you more conscious just how little time you have.

I began to feel hungry and longed for the uniformed

officer to bring in my lunch; not only so my hunger could be satisfied but also so I could learn how much of that valuable commodity, time, I had used constructively in the formation of my thoughts and how much of the day was now left to me.

The more I thought about this, the more my adrenaline flowed and my cannon-firing heartbeat boomed out the interminable seconds; lost seconds, squandered seconds, seconds marching incessantly on to their inevitable consequence. I think it was then, for the first time, I became fearful. I feared for my predicament. I feared for my very life.

My life! But that was irreclaimable, wasn't it? I remembered again the witch's last words to me, '*Didn't I warn you, Johnny Smith, that you will be disregarded! Treated with the lowly contempt you deserve, like something odious and detestable stuck to the bottom of my boots! Didn't I tell you that you'll be left to suffer the consequences of your misdemeanours on your own. Without my help or my protection!*'

And I think it was then I first realised that even my fear was pointless, that nothing really mattered any more. Because my one real objective – to be exonerated of my misdemeanours by the only One of true authority – was nothing but a hopeless dream. What was it Solomon the wise once said: '. . . everything is vanity, a striving after the wind!' It didn't matter what I thought; it didn't matter what I said. I was lost; I was dismissed; I was disregarded. Totally and for ever.

Then, suddenly, the passing of time didn't seem to matter any more either. My fear had run its course, my heartbeat slowed and the cannon stopped firing. I began to relax and slipped once more into the contentment of oblivion.

A constable came in with my lunch. I wasn't aware what food it was, I simply ate it to satisfy a bodily need. You see, even eating was nothing more than a meek submission to the preservation of my miserable and ordinary life. My hunger had dissipated with the rest of my vanities.

A different constable showed in my solicitor. I presumed the former one had finished his shift. I will never forget the look in Mr Thomas's eyes that first time he entered my cell. They say the eyes are the mirror of the soul and his eyes showed his soul was scared witless. Mr Thomas, as I remember, wore huge spectacles with concave lenses which magnified his fright into an intensified dread. He was a thin, gaunt Welshman who seemed at first to be totally unapproachable. He was timid and unassertive as well. Not exactly the type to inspire anyone in my situation with much confidence.

But, the more I saw of him over the next few days as he visited my cell to discuss my 'defence', the more I started to think my initial impressions were wrong. As time went on, he seemed more sympathetic and friendly, also keen and shrewd. And there were times when he proved he could be quite forceful when the need arose. Mr Thomas was a strange enigma. Despite his distant air, the more I talked to him the more I found him easy to talk to. I would talk to him for hours. And Mr Thomas listened, rarely interjecting, just listening, I thought with interest, making frequent and copious longhand notes.

As he became more at ease with me, I became more at ease with him. I began to tell of the more secret and mysterious things I had previously been unable to disclose to a single living soul. I told him of my mother and of the wicked old witch and the assignment She had set for my redemption. I told him of the secret way and the witches

I had sent there. I told him of Dorothy and the painting and the way the witch had summoned her personally into that dark, deep canvas forest. I told him all of these profound and confidential things and he appeared to listen with thoughtfulness and attention. In fact, I suppose I came to regard him as an ally and confidant – my only ally and confidant.

But I was wrong. I was deceived, deluded into believing he was being sympathetic. When I had finished, after finally finding the courage to recount the complete and unabridged strangeness of my truth, he simply looked up at me, indifferently and clinically, and said, 'Well, don't worry, Mr Smith. After what you've told me, I think we can make a plea of diminished responsibility. That'll make things better for you.'

He pretended to understand but really thought my story just the ramblings of a deranged lunatic. I became incensed, enraged that I could have been beguiled into trusting him. He was just like the rest.

I jumped up and leant across the table, grasping him by the lapels of his jacket and pulling his face to within a few inches of my own. Globules of spit sprayed his face as I screamed, 'You bastard! You bloody cynical, distrusting bastard! You don't believe a bloody word of what I've said, do you?'

I was restrained by the constable who was always present during our interviews and, before long, I felt other arms around me, dragging me back to my bunk. I remember the table was kicked over in our struggle, the solicitor's papers flying everywhere. It fell on top of Mr Thomas who stumbled backwards onto the floor when they pulled me away from him.

That night, when my anger had abated, I realised it was

a senseless thing to have done. I would now have an assault charge added to my list of offences and, more than that, it would probably be perceived as a practical demonstration of the unpredictable violence necessary for me to have committed the foremost crimes for which I had been accused. But then, I supposed none of this was of any real consequence.

No, it was of no consequence at all. It was senseless, just as everything else was senseless. Hadn't I conceded to the sublime wisdom of Solomon that *all* was nothing more than vanity, even one's right to feel anger at being betrayed?

It was my own fault anyway. I should have realised Mr Thomas was only indulging me, humouring me with his patronising charade. What was it he said during one of our little chats? Ah yes, I remember now. 'I must be frank with you, Mr Smith. You are being charged with the murder of your wife as well. May I ask you, did you kill—' He looked up at me and a condescending smile graced his thin anaemic lips. 'Er, I mean – did you show her the secret way too?'

'No!' I answered gullibly. 'It was the witch who showed her!'

But when he asked me that question, I thought I heard a little snigger burst from the lips of the constable who had always before sat disinterestedly and impassively in his chair by my cell door.

I suppose I knew then Mr Thomas didn't believe me; that, all the time, he was treating my strange verity as nothing more than a sick joke to be tattle-taled about the police canteen. But I chose to disregard my perceptions. I needed someone to share the heavy yoke of my truth, you see, and the lot fell upon the unfortunate Mr Thomas.

From that point on, the officers responsible for my custody, those who brought in my meals and escorted me to and from the station's interview rooms, eyed me strangely. In the beginning, they had treated me almost with a strange kind of respect; a fearful regard, as I suppose one might have for someone charged with such heinous crimes. But now, I could see in their eyes that I was nothing more than an object of derision. I knew what they were thinking, 'He's that madman who talks to witches and sees people disappear into paintings! Ha! Ha! Ha!'

Even Sergeant Dixon treated me differently. He wasn't disdainful, not exactly. But his manner during my interrogations was no longer forceful or aggressive. His questioning was more restrained, as if he was suddenly made aware he was dealing with someone to be pitied rather than feared.

I remember the last occasion I was called to his presence, along that well-trodden corridor and up that old iron staircase to my favourite small and airy interview room. Sergeant Dixon was already seated behind the table as I entered with my escort. He looked up at me and smiled.

'Sit down, John.'

I sat. The sergeant handed me a large bundle of paper stapled in the top left-hand corner.

'You'd better read this, John.'

'What is it?'

'The statement you made to your solicitor.'

I began to read. The clock on the wall showed ten past ten. When I finished reading, it showed ten thirty-five. During this time, Sergeant Dixon remained motionless, leaning back in his chair, his hands folded behind his head.

I handed the statement back to him.

'Well?' exclaimed the policeman.

'Well what?'

'Is that an accurate account of what you say happened, John?'

'I suppose so.'

I looked into his eyes. I saw an expression of sadness. He reached into his pocket and pulled out a fountain pen.

'You'd better sign it then.'

I took the pen, removed the cap and poised its nib above the document.

'John!' he said, scrutinising me; yes, there was definitely sadness in his eyes. 'Are you sure – absolutely sure – you want to sign that? I mean, are you positive it's an accurate account – your own account – of what really happened?'

'Yes! In as much as it's possible to put something like that into mere words.'

He stared at me for a long time before adding, 'And you don't want to rethink – reconsider your statement?'

'I don't think it could be stated much better than what's here already.'

Then he simply shook his head and shrugged his shoulders. I signed the document and handed it back to him. We sat in silence for a while.

'John.' His voice was now almost kindly. It reminded me of the way he spoke the first time I met him. 'You've never asked anything about what's going to happen to you. Don't you care?'

I remember I shrugged a gesture of indifference. 'I suppose I'll be disregarded. Treated with the lowly contempt I deserve!'

It was then he first looked at me oddly. It was a peculiar expression, not the look of disdain I regularly had from the other officers. It was a look of diffidence; a timid unsureness. The look one has on feeling something should be said but not knowing how to express it.

He shifted his eyes from my gaze. It was the first time I had ever known him appear uncomfortable under scrutiny. His eyes looked tired and heavy, not as clear and bright as I remembered them when he first came to see me after Ben was taken. And I knew it wasn't just the midnight oil Sergeant Dixon was burning over my little escapades which was responsible for his weariness. The years were beginning to show. Sergeant Dixon was looking much older. His hair had receded quite noticeably. Even the mellowing slug perched along his upper lip was looking jaded; it drooped now quite listlessly and was streaked with an enduring silver-grey.

He was staring at the ceiling when he said, 'Twenty-five, John! We've found twenty-five! We haven't identified them all yet but we do know none of them's Dorothy . . .' He suddenly looked me straight in the eyes.

'What have you done with her?' He asked the question almost forlornly; piteously, as if beseeching me.

'I've done nothing to her. It happened just as I said in the statement!'

Again that look. And a protracted pause. For a moment, I even began to believe he was debating with himself the credibility of my story.

'You know, John – I've even considered accepting the help of one of those clairvoyants. We've had lots of calls from them saying they can help us find her. What do you think, John? What do you think? You probably believe in all that mumbo-jumbo, don't you?'

I answered immediately. 'They'll never find her! No one will!'

'Still sticking to your same old story, eh, John?'

It was then I realised that Sergeant Dixon was really no different from the rest. True, he didn't openly express his scorn but I was still a thing of curiosity; an object to be paraded before him like a fairground side-show freak, to amuse and regale.

'Yes! And I always will!'

His eyes quickly shifted to the uniformed constable and, soon, I felt the other's customary hand on my elbow, guiding me to my feet and then to the door.

Once again, the sergeant's words stopped us before we left the room. The boom was back. 'Oh, John! I forgot to tell you. You're in court next week. But between you, me and the gatepost, it's a foregone conclusion you'll be held on remand. They'll take you to Broadmoor, I expect. In fact, that's pretty much a certainty. The guys there will want to have a little chat with you. 'Spect they'll want lots of little chats with you. Guess we won't be seeing much of one another from now on, eh? Good luck, John! Good luck.'

The next, and only other time I saw Sergeant Dixon, he was giving evidence at my trial at the Old Bailey.

After that, I seemed to be treated differently. I don't mean physically. I was still locked up all day. I was still constantly observed through the observation hatch of my cell doorway. And I had my belt and shoelaces removed, in case I took it upon myself to attempt suicide. No, the difference was one of attitude in those attending me. It was as if I was suddenly regarded more as a harmless simpleton than a fiendish serial killer. But it had its compensations. On many occasions, I had previously asked for daily papers to be given to me. Always, my request had been refused. But now it was granted. A selection of national dailies, and the *Comet*, were delivered to my cell each morning, along with my plate of fried breakfast ooze. The room service was very reliable and my body-clock soon became attuned to its arrival.

I had to endure the custody officers' sarcasm. 'How's the Witchfinder General today?' they would often ask as they handed me my tray. But I always remained silent and unemotional. Actually, I found their nickname quite amusing but it was nothing to the humorous ingenuity of my former employers.

'Witch Hazel-Nut To Go To Broadmoor!' The headline was emblazoned across the *Comet*'s front page the day after I first heard the news from Sergeant Dixon. I recognised the satirical wit of 'mild-mannered Clark'.

The article read, 'Since the arrest of John Smith for the sadistic murders of twenty-five women found in shallow graves in his back garden, and also the murder of his wife whose body is yet to be found, some "do-gooders" have accused this paper of conducting its own witch-hunt. And why has the *Comet* been so accused? Because it has been said that we have used our special knowledge of the man – who was once employed as a reporter with this paper – to conduct our own personal crusade against him. It is everyone's right, they say, to remain innocent until proven guilty in a court of law.

'We wish to make it clear that we, of course, do not disagree with this most basic principle of human rights and, in our reporting of this case, emphasise that we have never condemned Smith to be guilty of the atrocities of which he has been charged. We have simply reported the truth, the whole truth and nothing but the truth.

'And the truth is, by Smith's own admission, that he identified the murdered women as witches. So, we ask, who exactly is the one who should be accused of conducting a witch-hunt? Surely not the *Comet*! Perhaps the do-gooders who campaign for so-called fair play should canvass the opinion of the hostile crowd which gathers daily outside the police station where Smith is temporarily being held.

'But we stress *temporarily* because the *Comet* can exclusively report that, after the preliminary hearing into Smith's case on Friday morning, he will probably be taken to Broadmoor to undergo psychiatric examinations before his trial. In our headline, we have called Smith the "Witch Hazel-Nut". We make no excuses for this. And before you do-gooders out there write us more of your angry letters, why not consider the facts – the undeniable truths, which can be stated now without prejudice to Smith's pending trial. Smith hunted witches! Smith is to be sent to Broadmoor, one of this country's principal institutions where criminally insane "nuts" are incarcerated! And the hazel? Oh, did we omit to mention it before? Well, perhaps it simply slipped our minds – Smith has hazel eyes!'

Though I was convinced the headline came from the mocking wit of Ted Clark, the columns themselves shouted the unmistakable fierceness of Mr Garside's pen. I still admired that man even though I had now become his commodity rather than his colleague. I don't exactly know how the *Comet* got hold of this information before my trial though I'm pretty certain it wasn't divulged by Sergeant Dixon – yes, we might have had our differences over the years but I always considered him to be an honest and dedicated copper who played everything by the book.

Perhaps it was just another confidence Detective Inspector Ribble and Mr Garside exchanged at the nineteenth hole of the local golf course. Nowadays, of course, such an article would have been deemed prejudicial to my pending trial but, I guess, the constraints which exist today on the reporting of a case such as mine were not in place back then. Anyway, as far as I am aware, the *Comet* got away with it without even so much as a rap on the knuckles.

Their reports continued in the same vein for the next couple of days, but on the third day, I was not mentioned at all though the case itself continued to feature in the *Comet*'s pages.

'Crystal-Gazer Helps Find Missing Woman!' announced the headline. The following was reported:

'A clairvoyant has been enlisted to help the authorities locate Mrs Dorothy Smith, the missing link in the mysterious case of the Where-Are-They-Women. Police are baffled that, despite an exhaustive search, Mrs Smith's body was not unearthed in the quiet Melrose Rise garden, along with the remains of the twenty-five other missing women.

'Detective Sergeant Dixon, the official spokesman of the unit investigating the case, said yesterday, "We believe Mrs Smith's body may have been buried elsewhere but, although we have carried out extensive enquiries, her whereabouts are still a mystery."

'When asked whether he thought the clairvoyant's assistance would lead to Mrs Smith's body being located, Sergeant Dixon replied, "I can't really comment on that except to say that the help of such people has been successfully enlisted in the past. Frankly, I don't know if it will achieve results in this case but we have reached a stalemate. We are at a stage in our enquiries where anything is worth a try."

'Our reporter asked Sergeant Dixon if the clairvoyant had so far come up with any leads and received the reply, "No comment!" However, the *Comet* traced the clairvoyant, Mrs Molly Savante, who volunteered the following details. She said she "felt" Mrs Smith's presence in a deep wood or forest, somewhere very remote and isolated. "I saw dense, dark trees and an old lonely cottage. It looked quite eerie!" She further added, "But I do not sense sadness. Wherever she is, I believe she is happy."

'It seems that the bizarre case of the Where-Are-They-Women gets even more bizarre. For the best coverage of its progress, continue to follow the reports in the *Comet*.'

I couldn't help smiling when I read that.

Chapter 28

At my preliminary hearing, I was indeed bound over on remand and committed to spend some time in Broadmoor for psychiatric evaluation, just as Sergeant Dixon and the *Comet* had attested. Until my hospitalisation could be arranged, however, it was decided I should be sent to Wandsworth prison where I remained for six weeks, spending that entire time in the isolation wing, having no contact with the other prisoners, locked away in my forsaken little cell for twenty-two hours of each and every one of those neverending days. The other two hours were fastidiously spent in the humiliating pursuits of morning slopping out and being looked over by two burly warders in my lonely jaunts round the prison's exercise yard every afternoon.

It was on July 15th when I was finally taken from the depressing environs of Wandsworth to my new home on the outskirts of a pleasant little Berkshire town called Crowthorne. I must say, it was an enjoyable drive through the leafy roads of the Surrey and Berkshire countryside, the first time in months I had smelt the fresh naturalness of uncontaminated air.

I remember it was a hot and humid day and my mind struggled to release the memory of another sultry July day back in another time, another era, almost belonging to another life. But I couldn't place the remembrance and the moment passed.

I just sat back, my eyes closed, my face turned towards the partially opened window of the black maria, alive to the invigorating breeze on my face. We journeyed in complete silence. I did not speak to the officers sitting with me in the back seat and they did not speak to me.

There had been some unpleasantness when our little cavalcade left the prison building. An angry crowd had gathered outside and the media – reporters, cameramen and television crews – were waiting there in droves. I remember countless flashes as the photographers frantically, and optimistically, fired off shots through the van's windows, hoping to catch my villainous face frozen in a moment of gauche moronic horror. Eggs were thrown at the van and people were shouting. Their actual words were lost in the mêlée of pandemonium but I could see from the expressions on their wrathful faces, they weren't wishing me '*Bon voyage!*'

I can't explain why, but some involuntary compulsion – an inner knowledge we had arrived – forced me to open my eyes as we drove up the small winding approach to the 'hospital'. I saw Broadmoor's massively imposing perimeter wall and the huge wooden doors of its threshold; doors which seemed indomitable, immovable; doors that, once shut behind you, would remain shut permanently.

From the moment we drove into Broadmoor's inviolable realm, my recollections are somewhat hazy. All I can really say is that I became ensconced in a tremendous hubbub of activity, surrounded by unnumbered people who ushered me here, then there, then back again. I tried to familiarise myself with my new surroundings but there was never really time. It seemed I wasn't in one place long enough to record anything in the niches of my perception. That is, until I was shown to the privacy of my room.

I know there has been a recent outcry against the way in which lifetime inmates of high-security units, like I myself have now become, are housed. Many say we are kept in a style of luxury unbefitting the just deserts occasioned by our transgressions.

I have since learnt that Broadmoor Lunatic Asylum was originally built in 1863, using the labour of prisoners from Parkhurst prison on the Isle of Wight, after the Earl of Shaftesbury led a campaign in Parliament for the construction of a secure asylum to stem concern at the increasing public awareness of the plight of the 'madman'. It was the Mental Health Act of 1959, apparently, which changed it from an asylum to the more enlightened status of 'hospital'. The status of its inmates likewise changed to 'patients', and Broadmoor was refurbished to permit them to be accommodated as such.

Now I have a personal interest, I of course admit to being grateful to these reforms though I refuse to allow the pages of my story to attempt to justify, or otherwise, the relatively pleasant conditions in which we are kept. I will say, however, that I was extremely surprised when I first entered my room because, even in my wildest imagination, I had expected nothing like this. Although it could not be described as luxurious, even by my own modest standards, it was certainly airy, comfortable and complete with most of the amenities of home. This is why I deliberately refer to it now as a room; no longer a cell.

But do you know the first thing I noticed as I walked through its door? Daylight. Natural daylight streaming in through a large window, overlooking the hospital grounds. Barred that window may have been, but it was a window nonetheless; a hole into the world of normality, a world I once derided but now yearned to be a part of again.

I would spend many an hour just gazing through that hole watching the natural freedom of the animal world; the myriad varieties of birds, most unrecognised, the stray cats rummaging around the rubbish bins, the squirrels scampering about, seeming to be going nowhere in particular, and the rabbits with their powder puff backsides, unashamedly pilfering cabbages from the vegetable garden in the quietness of dawn and dusk. But it was the butterflies, just a profusion of multi-coloured dots from the distance of my view, which were observed with the greatest enchantment. Yet they sometimes evoked memories of 'the forest' and the sadness of an unclaimed redemption; momentary remembrances which filled me with a strange and languid melancholy.

I viewed these things with a brand new perception, completely absorbed in a newfound enchantment. I didn't really envy the freedom I saw outside. In fact, I was so engrossed in its magic, I often became oblivious of the bars on the window and the massive looming presence of the boundary wall which proclaimed the loss of my own liberty. I was just a spellbound observer who, for the first time in his life, had the time, with no other distractions, to observe nature's ways.

But I have given a false impression; the notion that I was left alone in that room with nothing else to do but gaze idly at another world which before had passed me by, unnoticed. And nothing could be further from the truth. In fact, it was the awareness that my time was controlled entirely by the whim of others which, above all else, acted as the principal reminder of my confinement. It would be more accurate to say that looking through that window was my one and only diversion when they had finally gone and left me in a tenuous and transient peace. It was my one digression. My one and only joy.

Early in the morning they would come and wake me from my turbid dreams and then it would begin; ceaselessly, unremittingly, their questions, fired with ruthlessness and tenacity. I became brainwashed by their undeviating punctuality, disciplined by their relentless routine of inquisition.

Sometimes, even the little self-will remaining would be taken from me, my interrogation being conducted under the effects of Sodium Pentothal, the 'truth drug'. 'Why are you doing this?' I would ask. 'I have never lied! I have only ever told you the truth! My answers will be exactly the same as before!' But they didn't listen. They heard again those same identical truths, the unbelievable facts of the strange, improbable story they had heard me recount endless times before.

They asked me about my mother; I told them I hated her. They asked about my childhood; I told them of my ordinary and unremarkable unwholesomeness. They asked me about the traumas I recalled of my juvenile years; I told them of my acne and falling off my bike. I told them everything I remembered; everything except the obliterated horror of a hot July night up in a tree house in an ordinary suburban garden.

They asked me about the women I had shown the secret way. 'Did you have sex with them, John? After they were dead? Is that why you murdered them, because you couldn't do it to them while they were still alive?'

They didn't understand and neither would they, ever! I became angry but, even though I shouted, I still answered them with words of truth. 'What are you suggesting? I'm not a necrophile! She would never permit that! And, anyway, I didn't kill them. I was their saviour! I showed them the way. The way to their deliverance! The way to their eternal life!'

'She? Who is she, John? The witch? The wicked old witch?'

'Yes!'

'Why wouldn't she permit you to have sex with them?'

'Because they were Hers! I couldn't defile Her agents with my foulness! Even though I wanted to – at least, in the beginning I wanted to, before She told me they belonged to Her.'

'You said that one of the women you showed the secret way ridiculed the size of your manhood. Are you embarrassed about your size, John? I mean, do you consider your penis to be smaller than the average man's?'

Yes, they sometimes even asked me questions like that. And what could I say? I am a virgin – then, now and always will be – and, whilst I admit to committing the occasional act of filthy self-abuse, I have otherwise only used my thing to pee out of. I honestly don't remember ever having consciously thought about whether it is big enough to satisfy my own ego and I certainly do not know, and neither do I care now, whether it is big enough to satisfy any of the unwholesome category of womankind. I must confess that, sometimes, when standing next in line to another pisser at a public urinal, I would occasionally glance down at the little guy next door; not, I hasten to add, to make a direct comparison. It is just something men and boys sometimes do – a lowly and detestable male thing – almost like an impulsive reaction, a condoned and sanctioned event in those places, an accepted way of passing the time during the pleasing moments of relieving the bladder. But, from what I have seen, I would guess the size of my own member is pretty much the norm.

When they asked me that question, however, I reacted as I suspect you would have reacted. I was incensed. Infuriated at their tactless probings into such intimate and sensitive things; matters which, to me, seemed as irrelevant to their enquiries as the size of their own repulsive little puppy dogs' tails.

'What kind of bloody stupid question is that?' I would scream. 'Is that all you can think of to ask me? Is that all they pay you for? What has that got to do with the things She told me to do? The women She told me to send Her?'

'Did she tell you to kill those women, John?'

'No! She only told me to send them. She needed them. And it was their salvation.'

'Why did she need them? Why did she tell you to send them to her?'

'For the boys. To find the naughty little boys She wanted to gobble up for her supper. Boys like – like – like—'

'Boys like who, John?'

My mind struggled to find one simple word. Ben! It struggled to envision an image of a face enveloped in a moment of terror. But all I saw was a fire lit in the grate of his shoulders; anonymous, unrecognised shoulders, and hands racked with immeasurable pain, rising as if to lift the wall of flame and reveal the unidentified face.

Then it was gone. The image faded and I opened my

eyes upon a sea of other nameless faces wearing shapeless white coats.

I cannot remember how many times that happened, how many times my interrogation ended with me trying to recall the vision of a petrified face I knew I could never forget. A vision I knew would live with me for ever yet, during those moments, was one which had deserted me; abandoned, shut out, because the pain of its memory was simply too agonising to bear. My own inescapable suffering exacted endurance enough.

I don't suppose it would have helped my cause if I could have told them about Ben. I suspect the psychiatric reports would still have damned me just as cruelly and with as much prejudice.

When I was about five or six years old, I remember asking my mother if every mummy read to their own little boys and girls those stories about the wicked old witch gobbling up those 'other little boys'.

I can still see her taunting smile as she said, 'No, Johnny. Little girls' mummies don't have to because little girls are never naughty. But every mummy who has the misfortune to have a little boy should read those stories to him as a reminder of how naughtiness is punished – though most do not. You see, Johnny, although it is very sad, some mummies do not seem to care about changing their little boys' slugs and snails and puppy dogs' tails into nicer, more wholesome things.

'But you are a lucky little boy, Johnny! You have a mummy who does care. You have a mummy to share this secret with. And a secret it must remain, Johnny Smith. For if you tell about the wicked old witch and the stories mummy tells you about her, no one will believe you. They will put you away. Yes, they will lock you up and throw away the key for telling lies about your wonderful mummy. That is, Johnny – that is, if the wicked old witch doesn't take you away and gobble you up first. She will do that if you are really naughty. You know that, Johnny, don't you?' Then she laughed; a heinous, vile snigger, just like the wicked old witch Herself.

Even though I was very young, those words of my mother have never left me. They are imprinted on my memory because, the very night she told me those things, the wicked old witch first visited me. It was a dream I will never forget. She was as I had first perceived her, like the funny old drawing on the cover of *My Favourite Book of Fairy Tales,* riding Her broom across a golden crescent moon.

But, in the same way that tales of harrowing fear came from the rancour of a mother's hatred and not from the innocuous words printed in the pages of that book, so the words the witch spoke to me that night did not originate from a mind of young innocence but from one already indoctrinated with the explication of a mother's hatred.

I watched the wicked old witch fly across that golden crescent moon, over our town and into my open bedroom window. I watched Her gaze at the little boy sleeping in that bed. Then I became that 'other little boy'. He was suddenly me – the naughty Johnny Smith – and the witch was speaking to him.

'Wake up, Johnny Smith! Let me show you what will happen to you if you ever tell naughty, disgusting lies about your wonderful mother! Let me show you these things as a warning.'

I was cowering in my bed. I remember pulling the covers up over my head but She pulled them back. I fearfully watched Her observe my skinny body, Her gnarled old hand reaching out towards me. She grasped the lapels of my pyjamas (they were the ones my daddy had bought me with the teddy bears on). Rip! The jacket was in Her hand. My torso was naked and She was smiling Her villainous smile. Then Her hand reached out for me again. It grasped my pyjama bottoms. Rip! I heard Her laugh mockingly at my shameful scrawny nakedness and saw Her point derisively at the puny limpness of my little puppy dog's tail. She laughed again, a terrible taunting snigger. I remember feeling exposed and vulnerable. Then She picked me up and flew me away with Her on Her broomstick.

We rose back up over our town, higher and higher into the dark night sky, across the golden crescent moon, and down into a deep, dark forest. I saw Her cottage. Smoke was coming from the chimney. But She didn't take me inside. She put me into a cage in a small clearing ringed by those gnarled old oaks that surrounded her gingerbread cottage. I could see those sombre-looking trees with their eerie faces etched into their contorted old trunks through the solid blackness of iron bars. I saw Her turn a key in the lock. I was still naked and I was cold. She stood observing me, laughing Her abominable snigger.

Daybreak came and bathed the denseness of that murky wood in a dim greyness. Then the wicked old witch held up the key in Her gnarled and haggard hand and threw it into the foggy gloom.

'That is what I do to naughty little boys who lie about their wonderful mothers, Johnny Smith! That is what I will do to you and there you will stay till you rot. You are not even scrummy or juicy enough to be gobbled up. You are just a naughty, ordinary little boy. A very naughty, ordinary little boy indeed!'

She bellowed out another heinous snigger; a wailing,

echoing snigger, and I awoke in the sweaty clamour of my screams. But my mother never came in to me. She always left me alone with my fear.

Sometimes, after those interrogations in the hospital, looking out through the window of my room before the magic of the world outside had removed its bars from my view, I remembered that dream. I knew the wicked old witch had heard me tell of my mother's tales of horror. I knew She had heard me reveal our secret.

I knew She would throw away the key.

Chapter 29

When I think of those weeks of perpetual inquisition, I often wonder how I survived; how it was that my sanity didn't desert me, and how it was they didn't actually drive me into the abyss of madness they were trying to prove I had already toppled into. I suppose it became a battle of wills, with mine emerging as the victor because of my commitment to facts I knew were gospel truths.

I was conditioned by their timetable. I would wake every day, it seemed at precisely the same time, wash and otherwise prepare myself. In those early days, the isolation rooms in Broadmoor had no integral toilets. It was part of the morning routine for a couple of orderlies to accompany me as I slopped out. But, this having been done, I would then just sit in the chair by the window, knowing I could count very slowly with the guaranteed assurance that, by the time I reached five hundred, the door to my room would be unlocked and in they would troop; a phalanx of figures in spotlessly white coats, bearing clipboards and strained expressions. Sometimes they would question me in my room but, more often than not,

I would be guided by two burly members of the hospital's escort staff to one of the special interrogation rooms where I knew the interviews were being recorded.

But, one morning, I had counted to five thousand before I dared confront the belief that they might not appear at all. The time passed. I stared out of the window, watching nature's pageant and the sun move on its undeviating path; the only reference I had to corroborate the passing of time.

It was quite high in the sky before I heard the clunk of the key in the lock. I turned suddenly but there was no shroud of white coats in the doorway, only the drabness of a single navy uniform, worn by a member of the nursing staff who bore a tray of food.

I asked about my inquisitors and was told they would not be coming. That day, and I think for the next four or five, though I cannot be absolutely sure, that nurse or an orderly, bearing sustenance three times a day, were the only human faces I saw. They discharged their duties quickly and silently, not permitting me to draw them into conversation.

Though I revelled in my solitude at first, I then began to yearn for the questioning of the psychiatrists. I longed for their barrage of words, for the very sounds of human contact which had previously driven me to distraction; I yearned for anything to break my solitary confinement.

It was as though I were suffering from a curious withdrawal symptom. I couldn't sleep, my night-time was spent almost entirely in the vacant act of peering from my window into the ghostliness of the moonlit world outside.

But even nature's spectacle had temporarily lost its enchantment. It wasn't that its familiarity had bred contempt, I had simply been brainwashed by a regime of persistent questioning which I suppose had become a peculiar drug to me. Now, I craved it; I craved the sound of a human voice and the authorisation to answer it.

I began to talk to myself, an act I know was overheard because I would often be startled by the grating noise of the observation-hatch in my door being slid open during my lonely monologues. I would then shout at the unidentified pair of eyes gawping at me through the narrow slit.

'Don't you have a mouth? Can't you talk to me? I know what you're thinking. You think I'm mad! You think I'm talking to myself because I'm insane! Don't you understand? I'm only talking to myself because there's no one else to talk to. Please answer me. Say something! Anything!' But the only sound I ever heard was the rasping of the hatch sliding shut.

Then, one day, the orderly did talk to me. 'Smith! The Medical Superintendent wants to see you.' It was curt and it was said from an expressionless face. He stood in the jamb and motioned for me to accompany him. Another orderly was waiting outside and, together, they escorted me down sundry corridors to the Medical Superintendent's office. I remember sitting in a chair outside his door, attended by two brawny guards, one seated each side of me. Eventually, I was shown inside. The Medical Superintendent was a puny little man whose head was only just visible over his huge walnut desk. His eyes lifted as I entered.

'Ah, Smith! Come in. Sit.' He gestured to a low chair placed in front of him. It was so low, I had to raise my head up to look into his eyes.

'We've got a date for your trial. October 10th. Three weeks from today.'

I remember thinking it must now be mid-September. I

tried to calculate how long I had been in this place but my brain was thrown into temporary confusion.

The little man stared at me; I think, anticipating a deluge of questions. It was strange. For the first time in days I had the opportunity to communicate, to convey my thoughts and fears, but I was unable to utter a single word.

'Is there anything you want to ask me?' he said after a long pause. 'You know – anything you want clarified?'

I remember I could only shake my head.

'Of course, your solicitor has appointed a barrister to represent you in court. We'll be arranging for him to come and see you here!'

He continued to stare into my expressionless face. 'Is there anything else, Smith?'

I wanted to speak. There were countless questions I wanted to ask but I remained dumbstruck.

'Very well, Smith. You can go.'

I stood up. His eyes shifted in a downward gaze to some papers on his desk. He picked up a pen, poised to write, then slowly, his eyes lifted again to stare at me standing before him.

'Still here, Smith?'

'Will they be coming again?' I stuttered.

There was a look of bewilderment on his face. 'Who, Smith? Will who be coming again?'

'Them! Them! Asking their questions!'

His look of bewilderment changed into a droll smile. 'Ah, the psychiatrists. No, Smith, I promise they won't be coming again. All the psychiatric reports have been concluded. You can relax now. They won't be bothering you any more.'

'But – but – I won't have anyone to talk to!'

I will never forget his incredulous expression. It was the kind of look which displayed astonishment and compassion all at once; a gaze which affirmed a judgement that I was nothing but a madman, an imbecile, willing to suffer the pain of interrogation just to have someone – anyone – to speak to.

'Your barrister will be coming soon. You can talk to him, Smith. He'll ask you all sorts of questions,' he started patronisingly, then his tone became more compassionate. 'Look, Smith, we've had repeated requests from a Mrs Wilkinson, your foster mother, I believe, to visit you. I can't make any promises, you understand, but I'll see what I can do to arrange it. Would you like that, Smith?'

I nodded. But to be honest, I wasn't sure if I wanted to see Auntie Pat, in this depressing place, with her knowing why I was sent here and me having to witness the shame of her humiliation. Yet, neither could I refuse her request. She must have been distressed enough already, there was no way I could add to that pain.

Three days later, I had my visit from Auntie Pat. We sat on opposite sides of a big table, without closeness, without contact, overlooked and continuously scrutinised by two orderlies whose prying eyes never left us. Our meeting didn't last long. She cried 'Oh, Johnny!' then she sobbed uncontrollably and was unable to speak another word. Helpless, she finally rushed from the room and I was taken back to my loneliness. That was the last time I ever saw her.

I think it was two days after that when I had my first interview with my barrister, a large craggy man who resembled the actor James Robertson Justice. The Medical Superintendent was wrong; he didn't ask me all sorts of questions. Yes, he talked. But mostly about trivial things like the weather and the football team he supported. When he did discuss my case, he conveyed the impression that his presence here was a mere formality which would serve no useful purpose at all.

'I'll put it quite plainly, Mr Smith, our only chance is to submit a plea of diminished responsibility. The psychiatric reports will certainly support our petition.'

My will had disintegrated. I had no anger or argument left. I simply nodded a surrendering compliance to my destiny. I saw him just three times; the last time on October 8th. I remember because he told me my trial was in two days. They were probably the longest two days of my life, both endured in a cold murky greyness. Nothing seemed to move in the world outside. I stared from my window onto a motionless calm and a persistent mist which hugged the ground till twilight merged its presence into the darkness.

On the evening before my trial, I was brought my black pinstripe suit, my favourite red tie and a crisp white shirt which the orderly hung up in the small built-in closet in my room. I spent hours that night just staring at those clothes, remembering the last time I had worn them; almost a year before. I saw myself standing again in that register office with Dorothy by my side, a radiant smile on her face and a noticeable bulge in her belly defacing the delicate contours of her pink satin dress.

She had looked so happy then and, for those moments when I allowed my mind to dwell on that time, I felt sadness for her. But then I realised that she was happier now than she had ever been in her whole life – even on her wedding day – living as she was in her little Satisfaction House in the bosom of those who really loved her. It was then that I realised she didn't warrant my sadness. She was redeemed and I should feel nothing but sincere genuine gladness for her.

It is odd that my thoughts that night were for Dorothy. As I sit here now, writing these words, I am trying to recall if I allowed myself the selfishness of any personal thoughts during the sleeplessness of those endless hours. But, do you know, I don't believe I did. I remember thinking only of how sweetness could change into acrimony and love into hatred. I realised that change was life's one true constant and our search for happiness our only true goal. It was only right and proper that Dorothy sought her new incarnation. She was happier now than she had ever been. But it was a bizarre irony that, tomorrow, I was to stand accused of her deliverance; not only an untruth but also an act perceived as a heinous wrongdoing.

I was still sitting on the edge of my bed, staring into the drab blackness of that closet, at 6 am when the same Medical Superintendent who first informed me of my pending trial – a man I fallaciously then called the governor, and, indeed, still do to this day – entered my room with two orderlies.

'Time to get ready, Smith,' he said.

In total silence, I washed and began to change into my worldly clothes. As I removed my trousers from their hanger, I remember noticing a few shreds of confetti flutter down from the turn-ups; brightly coloured scraps of wafting blue and pink which became little paper bells and horseshoes looking up at me from the carpet. How different, I thought, was the second occasion of wearing that suit going to be to the first. This time, there would be no radiant bride clutching my arm, no whoops of happy laughter or cheers of best wishes. True, that suit would again witness a sense of occasion but, instead, one of sober propriety and sombreness.

I knotted my tie and looked at myself in the small mirror above the hand basin. My face was still ordinary and unremarkable but now it looked lined and gaunt, belying its mere twenty-two years of life. I took a deep breath. I was as prepared for the coming events as I would ever be. I turned slowly and looked at the governor.

'Ready to go, Smith?' he said.

I nodded and they escorted me from my little room.

Chapter 30

'All Rise!'

Judge Walter T. Cattermole entered the courtroom with a purposeful flourish. It was as if he was determined to rid himself of the inconvenience of my trial so that he could get on with the more important things in life, like a worthwhile game of golf.

I remember he was a weedy little man with an aged face, a cheerless expression and a pontifical air who looked totally ludicrous in the pomp and circumstance of wig and gown. He also had a certain reputation as a judge and was nicknamed 'Black Cap Cattermole' because of his penchant for harsh decisions. I actually had reason to recall vividly a now famous remark he once made when sentencing a sixteen-year-old offender – a local boy accused of raping an under-age girl – when I covered the case for the *Comet.*

'If it were within my power, I would sentence you to have your privates surgically removed for the abominable act you have committed. But, since I cannot execute such a ruling, I will certainly give you the maximum sentence permitted to me by law though this is considerably less than you actually deserve—'

You can imagine how my heart sank when I saw his gloomy countenance enter the courtroom.

The chamber was packed. I looked around the becalmed waves of grimacing faces in the public gallery for a face to recognise but could identify none; though, for a moment – just one fleeting moment – it seemed that each and every one resembled the austere mask of my own implacable mother. And, suddenly, too, the jury was composed of the twenty-six witches' crones living in that deep, dark and secret forest. It seemed a portent to the sure and certain truth that my trial would not be conducted with impartiality and open-mindedness.

I will only transcribe the more interesting highlights of the trial. It was a long affair; the prosecution taking nearly three weeks to present its case. And, anyway, you already know the outcome. I was pronounced guilty of the murders of Helen Smith, Joyce Ramsbottom, Gertrude Jessop, Maria Gabrinsky, Patsy Kendall, Kate O'Malley, Jane Henderson, Marlene Rubens, Katherine Reilly, Josephine Mason, Janet Galbraith, Annie McIntyre, Anne Blake, Louise Kennedy, Alice Tooley, Alison Wilkes, Anita Rathbone, Yvonne Carlson, Kathleen Murphy, Karen Harvey, Maud Williams, Ann Thomas, Anne Smithson, Carole Wellermann, one other unidentified female and, of course, my wife, Dorothy Smith, *née* Thatcher. It felt strange hearing the long inventory of identities, most of which were previously unknown to me.

On the advice of my barrister, against my own judgement, I pleaded guilty to the lesser charge of manslaughter on the grounds of diminished responsibility. But it was the plea of a broken will.

The chief pathologist was asked to give evidence on the cause of the women's deaths. 'Apart from two, Helen

Smith and Patsy Kendall,' he replied, 'the causes of death could not be conclusively ascertained. The remains showed no positive evidence to verify how they died. You must understand, most had been dead a number of years and there were only skeletal remains left to examine. And, in most cases, these appeared quite complete and undamaged.'

'And the other two women? Helen Smith and Patsy Kendall?' continued the prosecution counsel.

'Mrs Smith's skull showed severe cranial damage, probably caused by repeated blows with the edge of a blunt implement. The indentations matched those which could have been produced by strikes with a spade found in the defendant's garden shed.'

'Show exhibit—' The barrister turned pages of the papers before him, '—G176!'

A court attendant wandered over to a table and picked out a tagged spade from the objects arrayed there, then he walked over and displayed it to the pathologist in the witness stand.

'Is that the spade in question?' continued the prosecution counsel.

The pathologist looked puzzled. 'To be honest, as they say, a spade is a spade. But if that's the one taken from the shed in the defendant's garden, then, yes, that is the spade.'

'Thank you. And Miss Kendall? How did she die?'

'Two vertebrae of her neck were dislocated. This is the kind of damage which can occur if the neck is pulled back, perhaps whilst an act of suffocation or strangulation is being performed.'

'And there is nothing you can offer to say how the other women died?'

'All we can say for certain is that the cause of death left the other victims with no identifiable injuries to their remains. There were—' He paused for a while, taking his reading glasses from his jacket pocket and putting them on, then he consulted his notes. 'There were some peculiarities in the cases of Anne Blake and Alice Tooley who respectively had a fractured tibia and femur. Obviously nothing to do with the cause of death but these injuries definitely happened after they had died. Interestingly, the position of their limbs when they were uncovered suggests the fractures were almost certainly caused during the act of burying them.' The pathologist took off his glasses and replaced them in his pocket.

'But – if, as you say, the injuries sustained by Miss Kendall were commensurate with those which might have been caused during suffocation or strangulation, is it not reasonable to assume that the women whose remains showed no discernible cause of death may have been suffocated or strangled as well?'

'Yes. I suppose that is a reasonable assumption. Though I would guess suffocation was the more likely cause because of the absence of damage to the neck vertebrae in any of the women other than Miss Kendall, and the fact that traces of material fibres were found in the mouth of another victim, Miss O'Malley, as though something, probably an article of clothing, was forced into her mouth.'

'And what of the clothing worn by the deceased women? Were they all fully clothed when they were buried?'

'Remnants of clothing found on the remains of Mrs Smith, Miss Ramsbottom and Mrs Jessop suggest they were fully clothed.' The pathologist again went through the motions of removing his glasses from his jacket pocket and putting them on, before referring to his notes once more. 'The evidence indicates they were wearing loose outer garments, probably dresses or tops and skirts of some kind. Various strands of fibres were found on each of their remains. And Mrs Jessop also wore a woollen cardigan. Fragments of wool fibres were identified.'

'And underwear?'

'Yes. It would appear those three women were all wearing underwear at the time of their deaths. Would you like the materials of the items classified?'

'No, that won't be necessary. But you say only those three women appeared to be fully dressed. What of the others?'

'Some appear to have been completely naked. No sign of any clothing on their remains at all. Others only had garments on the upper parts of their bodies. The remains of six of the women especially – those who appear to be the latest victims – still bore some articles of clothing which were, in some cases, quite well preserved. Some man-made fibres disintegrate only very slowly.' This time, the pathologist kept his glasses on.

'And what did these women appear to be wearing?'

He glanced again at his notes. 'One woman, the one who is still unidentified, was wearing a brassiere, the label "Marks & Spencer 36B" still plainly distinguishable. Another, Josephine Mason, only a short cotton slip. The rest, it would seem, appear to have been wearing only articles such as stockings or suspender belts or both.'

'But no panties? Can you confirm that, apart from Mrs Smith, Miss Ramsbottom and Mrs Jessop, the rest of the victims wore no panties?'

'Yes. As far as we can tell the evidence does suggest that. But I cannot say whether they had had sexual intercourse either before or after they died. There was no body tissue left for us to carry out that kind of test.'

'With respect, I did not ask you that question!'

'I'm sorry! I thought that was what you were implying.' He took his reading glasses off again, replacing them in his pocket. The expression on his face suggested the hope that they could now remain there.

'No it wasn't, though I understand you have ascertained that, apart from the first three women – that is, Mrs Smith, Miss Ramsbottom and Mrs Jessop – all the others were prostitutes?'

'I am a police pathologist, sir, not a detective. You will have to direct that question at someone with the authority to answer it!'

'Yes, Dr Ainsworth. My apologies, of course. I will address that to the appropriate person.'

Without cross-examination by my defence counsel, the pathologist was dismissed and Sergeant Dixon took the stand.

'Sergeant Dixon, am I correct in saying that you were the officer in charge of the missing persons investigations concerning these women?'

'For most of the period of the investigations, yes. But Detective Inspector Ribble led the inquiry team from August 1972.'

'So you would be the proper person to direct the question I inappropriately posed to Dr Ainsworth, the pathologist?'

'What question is that?'

'I asked him if he could confirm that, apart from Mrs Smith, Miss Ramsbottom and Mrs Jessop, and the woman still to be identified, of course, the rest of the women were all prostitutes.'

'Yes, with the exception of the women you specifically mentioned, I can confirm the rest were prostitutes.'

'So, it would not be unreasonable to suggest that the defendant invited those women to his home for the purpose of having sex with them?'

'Yes, I suppose that would be a reasonable assumption though it is something we could never actually confirm. The defendant has always denied this.'

'Thank you, Sergeant Dixon. But if that were not the reason for their invitation to the defendant's home, can you suggest another?'

The sergeant looked embarrassed.

'The defendant said in his statement to his solicitor – they were there because – because he identified them as witches.'

'Witches? Yes, of course, that is what he has said, isn't it?'

'Witches!' It was the strident voice of his honour, Judge Cattermole himself.

'Yes, m'lud. But I intend to deal with this unusual feature more fully during my questioning of the psychiatrists who undertook the defendant's psychiatric examinations at Broadmoor.'

His lordship grunted.

'Sergeant Dixon, there are also, I believe, some bizarre claims made by the defendant which surround a certain painting found hanging in his home? Would you care to comment on these?'

'I questioned the defendant on the whereabouts of his wife, Dorothy Smith. He said she had gone away. But, to his solicitor later, after his arrest, he claimed his wife had – had – disappeared into that painting. At the time, all I can confirm is that the defendant seemed preoccupied with it. He kept staring into it, engrossed, absorbed—'

'Disappeared into a painting? What kind of nonsense is this?' It was another of the harsh, pompous interruptions of his honour, the worshipful judge.

'If you please, m'lud, this is another issue which will be covered more fully during the prosecution's evaluation of the psychiatric reports. I merely want now to establish the circumstances just before the defendant's arrest and his state of mind at that time.'

Judge Cattermole grunted again and immediately imposed a luncheon adjournment.

When the trial resumed, the painting was held up before the court as exhibit H245. The judge was obviously not impressed with its artistry. 'The defendant claims his wife disappeared into that frightful monstrosity? It's hideous!'

'Yes, quite so, m'lud!'

Judge Cattermole grunted again and the prosecution counsel redirected his attentions to the policeman.

'Sergeant Dixon, how did the defendant seem when you first questioned him about the disappearance of his wife?'

'He was in a mess – upset – disorientated. He was sitting in his own excrement and, I believe, had been for some time.'

'Did he co-operate, answer your questions voluntarily?'

'No, not immediately. He didn't seem capable of anything at first. Just kept staring into the painting.'

'That painting? Exhibit H245? The painting he now claims his wife disappeared into?' The counsel pointed to the exhibit.

'Yes.'

There was a long pause while the jury assimilated this curious piece of evidence.

'But – despite the defendant's preposterous claims,

you did, of course, carry out extensive investigations into Dorothy Smith's whereabouts but her body has never been found. Am I right, Sergeant Dixon?'

I couldn't stand this manipulative slander of the truth any longer.

'I did not kill her! I did not kill any of them! I showed them the way to their deliverance! But not Dorothy. The witch took Dorothy Herself!'

'Silence!' Judge Cattermole's blast resonated around the courtroom. His cold stare engaged me. 'Another outburst like that and I'll have you for contempt! You will get your chance to speak later, at your counsel's discretion. But I will not, repeat *not*, tolerate any more of your tantrums while prosecution counsel is conducting his questioning. Do you fully understand?'

The counsel for the prosecution smiled, then continued. 'Sergeant Dixon, we'll leave that line of questioning for the moment. Let me ask you, when did Mrs Smith, the first victim, disappear?'

'That would be around March 1962.'

'And what were the circumstances of her disappearance?'

'There was no evidence at the time to make us suspect that her disappearance was suspicious. It happened shortly after her husband's death and it was thought she had gone away because of the sadness of her grief. The defendant, then a small boy of eleven, was found living alone at the family home.'

'By whom?'

'It was Gertrude Jessop who first reported the situation to us.'

'Who was later murdered? She was one of the victims later found buried in the garden, am I correct?'

'Yes, you are correct.'

'And the last identified victim, Carole Wellermann, when did she disappear?'

'Around September 1972, as far as we can establish.'

'So – these twenty-five women, beginning with Helen Smith and ending with Carole Wellermann, were buried in the defendant's garden over a period of ten years. The first, his mother, when the defendant was only eleven years old?'

'Yes!'

An audible intake of breath echoed around the courtroom.

'Sergeant Dixon, when asked the date of the disappearances of these poor unfortunate women, it is interesting that you say, quote, ". . . around March 1962" and ". . . around September 1972". But I understand that the defendant kept well-documented diaries which reliably record dates containing entries written in red, stating . . .' he regarded his notes, '. . . "showed one of them the secret way". Twenty-five such entries in total. Is that correct?'

'Yes, we did find such diaries.'

'And is it not also true that entries of ". . . Showed one of them the secret way" were recorded against the dates of March 11th, 1962 and September 2nd, 1972? Surely it is not unreasonable to assume these dates accurately represent the precise times these particular women met their deaths and that, over this ten-year period, the twenty-three other such entries bearing this strange phrase, precisely record the dates when he murdered the other women?'

'Yes – I mean, there were such entries recorded against the dates you mentioned, but we cannot conclusively prove from forensic testing those women actually died on the dates indicated.'

'Very well, Sergeant, I accept that point but would you not say it is a logical assumption?'

There was a long pause before Sergeant Dixon answered, 'Perhaps.'

'And what did the defendant say when confronted with the evidence of these diaries?'

'He refused to comment at first but then made a statement about them to his solicitor.'

'And what precisely can we now glean in the light of that statement as to what the phrase, "Showed one of them the secret way" actually means? Did he perhaps admit that, on the dates against which that phrase was written, he killed one of those poor women?'

'No, he didn't exactly admit to that though his signed statement does concede to the fact that, on the dates specified, he showed a woman to the . . .' he referred to his famous black notebook, turning pages as he did, then he looked up again to face the prosecution counsel, '". . . to the deep, dark, secret forest of the wicked old witch". They are his own words.'

'I see. And did he, perhaps, illuminate further on that point?'

'No, he didn't say anything else as clarification.'

There was a further audible intake of breath around the court.

'Witches again? What is all this talk of witches? Is this relevant? Perhaps you would care to explain where it is all leading.' It was the insufferably pretentious voice of his worship, Judge Cattermole.

'M'lud, this is a very strange and bizarre case and I beg your honour's indulgence in this matter. I submit it is relevant and it is my intention to clarify its significance when the psychiatric reports on the defendant are given in evidence.'

Judge Cattermole glared at the counsel. 'Very well then,' he said grudgingly.

That was on the fourth day of the hearing.

Sergeant Dixon remained in the witness stand for the rest of that day and some of the next. He was questioned on everything; his past interviews with me at the halfway house, the interrogations after my arrest and my assault of Mr Thomas. But one event that was never mentioned was the first time he interviewed me a few days after the taking of Ben. That was either forgotten about or considered as being of no relevance to the matters at hand.

But, when the questioning reverted to the diaries and, more specifically, my entries expounding my dreams in the wicked witch's court, Judge Cattermole once again expressed his exasperated displeasure in no uncertain vocabulary.

'I have already asked where all this talk of witches is leading to. It has still not been concisely explained to me, and yet here we go again with these time-wasting detours into the fanciful land of make-believe.'

After that, the prosecution counsel decided to liberate Sergeant Dixon from the witness stand, at least for the time being. My own counsel proffered no questions.

The next week was taken up entirely with an examination of the private, and previously undisclosed, lives of my twenty-six 'victims' and my relationship with them, where one existed. During that week, Mrs Thatcher took the stand and spoke of my marital strife and violent rows with her daughter. She also condemned me for the act of sexual perversion she claimed I attempted on her own fat carcass; a deed seemingly supported by her misrepresentation of the time she caught me with the whore during her surprise visit to the house while Dorothy was in hospital. She spoke gleefully, almost gloatingly, watching me standing in the dock out of the corners of beady little eyes which looked like black, bottomless ponds sunken in the corpulent meadows of her face and triple chin. Oh, how I hated her.

On the third day of that week, a surprise witness was called.

'Call Miss Watson!' The shout was echoed through the courtroom door into the hallway outside. A large woman was shown to the witness stand and sworn in.

'You are Miss Isobel Watson of 5 Florentine Court?'

'I am.'

'And, until her disappearance on September 17th, 1966, you shared a flat with Joyce Ramsbottom at the property in Florentine Court where you still live?'

I remember thinking, so this is Miss Ramsbottom's lesbian lover. I imagined them entwined in an intimate embrace. Curiously, I found the thought quite arousing.

'Yes, I did,' she replied, in a voice sounding robust, almost masculine.

'Can you confirm to the court that the late Miss Ramsbottom was a social worker assigned to the case of the defendant, John Smith?'

'I can.'

'And did she ever discuss John Smith's case with you?'

'Yes, she did. Even when he was no longer on her case list.'

'No longer on her case list? Would you kindly explain what you mean by that, Miss Watson?'

'Johnny – er – the defendant, was assigned to her when he was eleven, right after he was found living alone. She remained assigned to him for about a year or so after he was fostered by his aunt, Mrs Wilkinson. I think that was the name Joyce – er – Miss Ramsbottom, said. But then he was removed from her case list because he was no longer considered to require a social worker. He obviously had a good home with people who cared for him and wasn't in any danger or in need of protection.'

'But, Miss Watson, we have heard evidence that Miss Ramsbottom last visited the defendant just a few days before her disappearance. Let me see, that would be some four years after she stopped being his official case worker, when the defendant was sixteen. Can you tell the court why she continued – how shall we say? – to take an interest in him and his affairs?'

'She – she used to talk about Johnny – the defendant – a lot. He was almost an obsession with her. She was convinced he knew something about his mother's disappearance. "I'm sure he knows more than he's told us", she would often say. She thought there was something sinister about the boy.'

'Sinister? She used that very word, sinister, to describe him?'

'Yes, often!'

'Can you explain in exactly what way she thought him sinister?'

'She said it was hard to explain. Something in his eyes. Something in his mannerisms. I know she considered him odd. "I can't define exactly what it is. Johnny is an interesting case . . ." she would say, ". . . but, whatever it is, I'm determined to find out." So, she kept on going round there to see him.'

'You mean as a sleuth? Carrying out her own line of investigation?'

'If you put it like that, yes.'

'And do you know if she discovered anything? Was there anything at all she confided to you?'

'Yes! It was the evening before she disappeared. She was very excited when she came home. "I'm seeing Johnny tomorrow!" she said. "I've taken a set of house keys from the safe. I'm meeting him at his old house. He said it might jog his memory if he went back there. You know, help him remember what his mother said before she went away. Then we might finally be able to trace her." I remember telling her it was a stupid thing she was doing. And I was proved right, wasn't I? But she didn't listen to me.'

'Miss Watson, why did you never divulge this information to the police when they questioned you after Miss Ramsbottom's disappearance?'

'Because – because she shouldn't have done it! It was against all the rules of procedure. What she did, taking those keys and arranging to meet a sixteen-year-old boy alone in an uninhabited property, was wrong. She might have lost her job. I suppose I was protecting her. That's all. I know it was silly but, at the time, it was done with the best of intentions and – well, as time went on, it became more difficult to disclose the truth. So I never did – till now, that is.'

'And what made you finally decide to come forward with this information?'

'I – I thought about it for a long time. And, well, I know I left it late in the day, but I realised I had to come forward. I owed it to Joyce.'

'I understand that the disappearance of those keys to

the property at 122 Melrose Rise wasn't actually discovered until some two years later, due to an oversight in office monitoring procedures.'

'I'm afraid I know nothing of that!'

'I am not suggesting you do, Miss Watson. But your evidence does clear up the little mystery for us as to who took them, and when, doesn't it? It would also explain how the defendant managed to get hold of them to continue murdering so many more unfortunate victims and concealing their bodies in the garden of that house.' He stopped abruptly, turning and directly addressing the jury benches. 'Yes, ladies and gentlemen of the jury, the defendant, John Smith, must have taken those house keys from Miss Ramsbottom after he had brutally killed her – before committing her body to the desecration of its shallow grave where it lay undiscovered for more than five years. And there can only be one reason why he took those keys – to have access to the garden, and what he called the secret way, so he could deposit more unfortunate victims alongside the unconsecrated remains of Miss Ramsbottom and his own mother.'

He turned back to face Miss Watson in the witness stand. She was, by this time, wiping away a crocodile tear with an index finger. 'Thank you, Miss Watson. I'm sorry to have distressed you. I have no further questions.'

She began to leave the stand. But my counsel rose to his feet. For the first time he spoke.

'Miss Watson, please remain where you are. I have a few questions for you. Er, you lived with Miss Ramsbottom. Is that correct?'

'Yes.'

'May I ask – what was your relationship with her?'

Miss Watson looked flustered.

'Objection, m'lud!' intervened the prosecution counsel. 'What possible relevance can a past relationship have to this case?'

My own barrister replied. 'M'lud, a clear insinuation has been put forward that my client lured those unfortunate women to the house for the purpose of having sexual intercourse with them. I am endeavouring to prove that, not only is this postulation incorrect in this instance but, on the contrary, the arranged meeting was at Miss Ramsbottom's instigation.'

Judge Cattermole considered the matter for some while before declaring, 'Objection overruled.' I sensed that he did so somewhat reluctantly.

My counsel turned again towards the witness stand.

'Miss Watson, let me put the question to you more directly. Were you and Miss Ramsbottom lovers?'

Miss Watson was silenced.

'I must direct you to answer the counsel's question, Miss Watson,' ordered the voice of his worship.

Poor Miss Watson looked more flustered than ever, her manly sounding voice rising up a pitch or two. 'I – we – we lived together!'

'That is not exactly an answer, is it, Miss Watson? People sometimes live together without being emotionally or physically involved, so let me help you by rephrasing the question. Did you sleep in the same bed as Miss Ramsbottom?'

There was a long pause. 'Yes.' Her answer was almost inaudible.

'So, you were lovers?'

'Yes,' she said in the same whisper, after another long pause.

'And is it not also true that, a few days before Miss

Ramsbottom's disappearance, you rowed with her because of your suspicions that Miss Ramsbottom had begun a new relationship? You had heard a hurtful rumour, hadn't you, Miss Watson, that this new friend was not another woman but a man? And a young man at that. In fact, nothing more than a mere boy. You were incensed, weren't you?'

'Yes.' It was an even quieter whisper.

'Speak up, Miss Watson.'

'Yes.'

'I put it to you that you believed this young man to be none other than John Smith and that you further believed your lover had arranged her assignation at the house for the sole purpose of being alone with him and not for the reason she gave you.'

Miss Watson did not answer. She visibly reddened and lowered her head.

'I further put it to you that you argued with her again the night before she disappeared because you confronted Miss Ramsbottom with your suspicions. In fact, I suggest your reason for not divulging this information before now was not out of some misguided loyalty to your former lover but because your anger and jealousy prevented you from coming forward. You felt scorned and didn't want any information made known which could possibly help her, did you?'

'Objection, m'lud!'

'Overruled. Please answer the question, Miss Watson.'

'May I remind you, you are still under oath.' My counsel had the sudden steadfastness of a foxhound sensing a kill. I wondered where he had dug up the information that enabled him to play this discrediting trump card.

Miss Watson stared at my counsel for a long while before answering. It was a cold, impassive stare; a stare of insolence. 'No! That is not true!' Her response was almost a scream.

The barrister looked at her. 'Miss Watson, I will ask you that question again. But before you reply to it for the second time, I think it only fair to warn you that the defence has secured a witness who will, if necessary, testify to this court that you did argue with Miss Ramsbottom the night before she disappeared and that you did indeed confront her with your suspicions that Miss Ramsbottom had engineered the assignation with the defendant at that house for the purpose of being alone with him. You see, Miss Watson, Miss Ramsbottom confided this information to a close friend on the very morning of the day she went missing. This witness, Miss Watson, is a person who has not been available to give a statement before now because she has been living in New Zealand.'

Miss Watson was reduced to sobbing; loud, unyielding and uncontrollable sobbing. Suddenly, she stopped her whimpering and stared at my counsel defiantly.

'Yes!' she was almost shouting now. 'We did row! She fancied Johnny Smith all right! She admitted it, the night before she disappeared. I knew then that was why she kept going round to see him. That was the real reason. In the beginning I suppose it might have had something to do with her finding out the truth about his mother's disappearance, but then it became nothing more than—' She stopped to remove a handkerchief from the pocket of her charcoal-grey suit. Then she blew her nose, loudly and gauchely. 'That was what she wanted of him. That was the reason for her excitement the night before she went to that house. Lust! Nothing but lust. She lusted after a sixteen-year-old. And a boy, at that! And I hated her! I hated her!'

'Thank you, Miss Watson. I don't think I have any further questions to ask you.'

Miss Watson then broke down completely and, still sobbing, was escorted from the witness stand.

I could hardly believe the evidence of my own ears. I remember feeling bemused. The first impulses I had had that day, and dismissed because they seemed so improbable, were perfectly right. Even hearing it direct from the mouth of her lesbian lover, it was hard to accept that one of the imperious kind of female could ever really have fancied me. So I was wrong. Miss Ramsbottom wasn't really wholesome after all. And she wasn't sent by the Mistress as a temptress to seduce me into the trap of Her retribution. I felt lightheaded; awed, almost honoured, that a woman of Miss Ramsbottom's seeming wholesomeness actually wanted to sample the foulness of my lowly and detestable little puppy dog's tail.

The next day, a Friday, my presence at the court was not required. The jury was bused to 122 Melrose Rise so they could witness the secret way personally. Or, as the *Comet* reported it in their own inimitable manner, 'Jury taken to Where-Are-They-Women House of Horrors'.

The first few days of the final week were devoted almost entirely to the evidence of the psychiatric reports. The Broadmoor psychiatrist responsible for my case took the stand.

'You are Dr Sigmund, the psychiatrist in charge of the defendant's psychiatric reports conducted at Broadmoor?'

I remember thinking how apt his name was and, despite the severity of my predicament, I couldn't help smothering a controlled titter.

'I am,' the man replied, wisps of long, unruly hair fringing the shininess of his bald dome and falling over his eyes with the intensity of his affirmative nod.

'Dr Sigmund, we have heard in this court a great deal of evidence pertaining to the defendant's – how shall I say? – communication with a spectre he refers to as "the wicked old witch". Can you throw any light on this matter for us please?'

As the prosecution counsel was speaking these words, he was observing Judge Cattermole's reaction to his question and, as if to try and pre-empt any unhelpful remarks by the judge, he quickly added, 'M'lud, I think this is where my previous reference to the matter of witches will be made clear and the significance of this line of questioning explained. I beg your worship's indulgence once again.'

At this, Judge Cattermole merely proffered his customary grunt; it sounded like a contented pig. And, happy that his honour would not interrupt, at least for a while, the prosecution counsel then nodded to Dr Sigmund to give his response to the question.

'Smith sees the wicked old witch as a symbol of authority, just like a deeply religious person may perceive God – a power whose will must implicitly be obeyed otherwise severe consequences will follow. His many dreams set in her courtroom attest to her authority.'

'You mean, he believes the witch is capable of exacting retribution for what he perceives as disobedience of her will?'

'Oh yes! Indeed yes!'

'And what does the defendant believe this witch will do to him if he disobeys her – her – what shall I call them, do you think? Her commandments?'

'Yes. I think commandments is as good a word as any. As I have said, the witch holds almost a god-like significance to Smith. He believes her power to be supreme. But he considers he has already been immutably sentenced for his shortcomings. In his own words, ". . . to be locked up and the key thrown away!"'

'And what exactly does he believe he has done to deserve this punishment?'

'He believes he has failed in an assignment she set him for his redemption.'

Judge Cattermole banged his gavel. 'Perhaps the learned gentleman did not fully comprehend my previous observations on these absurdities. I will, therefore, make myself abundantly clear. I will not allow my courtroom to be used as a vaudeville spectacle. It may well be that the verdict of this court is for the defendant to be locked up and the key thrown away but that is for the court to decide. The defendant's own beliefs or wishes have no bearing on the outcome at all. Now, for the last time, what is the point of this continual line of questioning.'

'With the greatest respect, m'lud, with the evidence of the examining psychiatrists, I am endeavouring to establish the motive for these crimes. That the defendant perceived he was, in fact, acting in submission to the dictates of his authority figure – the witch, m'lud. I would say it is of paramount importance to the case.'

Judge Cattermole spent a few seconds considering this before the penny eventually dropped. 'Are you trying to tell me it is your conjecture that the defendant committed these crimes because he believed a *witch* told him to?'

'Yes, m'lud, that is precisely my conjecture.'

'Incredible!' spluttered the judge. 'You'd better proceed

then – er – is it something you think you can conclude before the luncheon adjournment?'

The counsel examined his watch. 'Regrettably not, m'lud.'

'Very well, we will take an early luncheon.'

The judge staggered to his feet as the clerk shouted. 'All rise!'

The afternoon of the fourteenth day saw a resumption of the psychiatrist's examination.

'Dr Sigmund, you will recall mentioning an assignment the defendant believes the witch set for his redemption. Can you please tell us the nature of this assignment?'

'Yes. To send women to her deep, dark and secret forest to complete two covens. Twenty-six women. Two lots of thirteen.'

'Do you conclude he believed this spectre ordered him to kill these women?'

'It is our opinion that the exact means of secreting them to her abode was never specifically alluded to. Nothing the defendant has said leads us to believe the witch gave that precise instruction. In fact, Smith has always denied knowledge of killing them at all, maintaining instead that he sent them to their eternal life. But such is a common conviction when one is deluded into thinking that one is acting under what, for all intents and purposes, is nothing short of divine judgement. And, as I have said, since he saw the witch's authority as absolute, that is precisely the way he would have perceived it.'

'You mean that any means would have justified the end because he perceived the power instructing him was omnipotent?'

'Well, yes, that may be the assumption of a rational mind but Smith's mind at the time might not have been capable of conceiving that kind of reasoned logic in carrying out the mandates of his authority figure. I would say it is probably more a question that he carried out the instructions without any regard or thought for the consequences.'

'I see. Or, to be honest, maybe I don't. But I am just a simple man with a simple understanding of such matters. Perhaps the jury are grasping this better than I am. However, let us move on, if we may. Tell me, Dr Sigmund, we have heard that the defendant buried a book of fairy tales with the body of his mother. Do you have any theories as to why he did this?'

The psychiatrist smiled. 'His mother used to read to him from that book when he was a small child. Or rather, she pretended to. But, instead, the stories she recounted were of her own creation – stories of terror; extreme terror. She used her tales to inculcate obedience. She told him if he wasn't a good boy, the wicked old witch would take him away and gobble him up. He became indoctrinated into believing this. That book was the manifestation of his mother's influence and the witch's power. He buried it with his mother's body in an attempt to rid himself of the authorities in his life, both the real and the symbolic.'

'And what of the diaries, Dr Sigmund? This court has heard the defendant's own written words from those diaries about how the witch came to him in dreams and instructed him. In your experience, is it a usual occurrence in such cases for an imagined voice of perceived omnipotence to appear in this way to people suffering from the same kind of delusions as the defendant?'

'They are the classic symptoms of schizophrenic paranoia. Voices – not always in dreams, often they come when the subject is awake. But the voices are always commanding, authoritative and unrelenting. When the subject is under their influence, he relinquishes all control of his own self-will.'

'That would explain then, would it not, the defendant's curious and perplexing claims concerning the painting, exhibit H245, and the witch appearing from within it.'

'Indeed it would! The voice came to him whilst he was awake; that is the only difference. It is not at all unusual. He admitted the painting reminded him of an illustration in that book of fairy tales. That remembrance acted as the trigger to create the image of the witch and her voice in his mind. He truly believes he saw her and heard her voice.'

'And what of his claim that his wife disappeared into that painting? What, if anything, can we conclude from this testimony?'

'Because of the similarity of the painting to the illustration in that book, it became the reality – the tangible manifestation of the deep, dark, secret forest where the wicked witch lived. It became the real place to which he sent those women. His wife disappearing into it is just an extension of this symbolism.'

'Thank you, Dr Sigmund, I have no further questions.'

The judge first looked relieved, then greatly irritated as my own counsel rose and began his cross-examination.

'Dr Sigmund, you have given a very concise explanation of the part played by the painting in this unusual and bizarre case. Now, we have already established that the painting was purchased by Mrs Smith and not by the defendant himself. Would you say it is possible that that innocent and guileless act could have been directly responsible for Dorothy Smith's apparent death? And, please bear in mind that, until a verdict is passed, her death must remain an assumption in view of the absence of her actual physical remains.'

'If Mrs Smith is dead, I would speculate that the painting could have acted as provocation for Smith to have perpetrated that act. It would certainly have acted as a reminder to Smith of an unfulfilled assignment. Remember, his wife is thought to be the twenty-sixth victim – the accomplishment of the second coven, according to the witch's instructions.'

'But, if that is the case, why do you suppose there are so many differences surrounding Dorothy Smith's disappearance to the disappearances of the rest? For example, the other twenty-five women were, by Smith's own admission, dispatched to the secret way by Smith himself. They were all found buried in the same place – his back garden. Yet he claims he was not responsible for Dorothy Smith's disappearance. And, indeed, her body has so far not been found. She was not buried with the others. Tell me, Dr Sigmund, don't you find this inconsistency odd?'

'Yes, to be honest I do. That is the one atypical feature of this entire case. Having established the ceremony of dispatching these women to the witch, I would have expected him not to deviate from it. In other words, his garden, which incidentally he referred to as the forest, was the way to the deep, dark forest of the witch as far as he was concerned. If his wife is buried somewhere else, I cannot explain why. It doesn't follow the usual conventions in a case such as this.'

'Then, possibly, we can speculate that something else was responsible for Dorothy Smith's disappearance, as the defendant has repeatedly claimed.' The remark was made as a rhetorical aside. He gave the psychiatrist no time to answer. 'We have also heard that the defendant was . . .' the lawyer consulted his notes, '". . . found sitting in his own excrement". Obviously, he was in a state of severe shock and, it would seem, had been for some time. Can you give any explanation for this?'

'No, not really. When he was questioned on that specific point he answered . . .' the psychiatrist turned pages of transcripts on the rostrum before him. There was a delay before he found the relevant passage, '". . . so would you have been sitting in your own shit if you'd seen what I had seen."'

A little titter of laughter echoed around the public gallery.

'But you would agree that, whatever happened to cause the defendant's condition, it would seem to have been a trauma of some significance?'

'Yes, I would agree with that.'

'Thank you, Dr Sigmund. M'lud, I will be questioning Dr Sigmund again during my presentation of the case for the defence. But I think that will be all for now.'

That night, my barrister came to see me in my cell at Wandsworth prison, the dismal place I was taken back to each evening during the term of my trial at the Old Bailey.

'Mr Smith, I know you do not want me to put your foster mother, Mrs Wilkinson, on the stand but I still think she will be a valuable character witness.' He looked at me and a sincere smile graced his craggy face. 'Tomorrow, we begin our defence. Won't you please reconsider your decision? She is willing to testify, you know, if you would like her to. But she is leaving that entirely up to you.'

I simply shook my head. I had refused his request

because I couldn't allow Auntie Pat to suffer any more at my hands. 'No. Tell her thanks, but I don't think so. It wouldn't do any good. But – there is something I would like to ask you. How did you find out about Miss Ramsbottom and Miss Watson?'

The lawyer smiled again. 'Your foster mother hired a private detective to scratch around. That's what he came up with. Don't know if it'll do any good but it was worth a try, eh? Mrs Wilkinson's still fighting for you, you know. Shame you won't let her testify. But it's your decision. I'll respect what you say. See you tomorrow, Mr Smith.'

He left and the guards left with him. I remember the echoing sound of the key turning in the lock and the clunk of the light switch being thrown outside my cell. The darkness was immense, cavernous.

Chapter 31

The next morning, my counsel began his defence, rising to his feet and staring into the face of the policeman who was once again in the witness stand.

'Sergeant Dixon, I promise I won't keep you there as long as my learned friend did, but I'm afraid I do have a couple of questions for you. I'd like to start with the clairvoyant – er – Mrs Molly Savante, wasn't it, whose help I believe you recruited to find the body of Dorothy Smith? I understand you showed Mrs Savante the painting which has been exhibited and much talked about during this trial. Can you please confirm that you did show her the painting?'

'Yes, I did show the painting to her.'

'And what was her reaction when she saw it?'

The sergeant turned over pages in his little black notebook. He said, 'She stared at it, almost mesmerised, and said, "Yes, that is the place I have seen in my mind. Dorothy is there. Inside that cottage. It is in some deep, dark and secret forest but I cannot place where. Find that cottage, Sergeant, and you have found your woman." I then asked her if she discerned whether Mrs Smith was dead and she replied, "I cannot see. It is misty and dark. But I sense she is happy. She is happy to be where she is. That's all I can tell you."'

'Hmm. I suppose my first question for you is did you take her remarks seriously? I mean, did you try and discover the location of the scene in that painting, or did you perhaps simply disregard her remarks as being of no consequence? A load of hogwash?'

'We went to great lengths in an attempt to find the location. The painting was examined by several art experts to see if they could identify the artist. We thought, if we could discover who he was, it might be known whether he had a favourite district where he often painted. In this way, we hoped we might be able to pinpoint the area quite precisely.'

'And?'

'We drew a blank. The artist could not be identified. We even had the trees in the painting examined by eminent tree experts in case they were uncommon trees which only grew in a certain place. But they were thought to be oak trees and hornbeams. Do you have any idea how many oak and hornbeam forests there are in the country and how many acres they occupy? And, added to that, although the age of the painting could not be estimated with any accuracy, it was thought to be quite old. Maybe the forest which is depicted doesn't exist any more. Or perhaps it was just a figment of the artist's imagination in the first place! Who knows?'

'Yes, Sergeant, I do appreciate the problem. But let's return to the clairvoyant's statement for a moment. She sees a scene in her mind, before she sees the painting, which she describes to you quite accurately. You show her the painting. Perhaps you were prompted to do this because the scene she described portrayed that in the picture very reliably. It's a strange coincidence, don't you think? Tell us, Sergeant, exactly how did these events occur?'

'Mrs Savante approached us and offered her help. She had previously helped the Warwickshire police locate a missing body some years earlier. She asked for an article of clothing belonging to the missing woman, something she was fond of and wore frequently. Mrs Smith's mother helped us identify such an item and this was given to Mrs Savante. She then described the scene in the forest and the old cottage and, yes, I agree the description was similar enough for me to show her the painting in the hope that the precise location could be identified. It is a strange coincidence, if that is what it is. I cannot comment on the logic of all this. I prefer to keep an open mind.'

'Perhaps you might think it is all too much of a coincidence to be believed as one. And, what of Mrs Savante's remarks that Mrs Smith is happy? What was it she said exactly? "But I sense she is happy. She is happy to be where she is." What do you make of this, Sergeant Dixon?'

'To be honest, I don't know. Mrs Savante didn't exactly say she was still alive, did she?'

'No, she didn't. But neither did she say she was dead. Though obviously you considered you had enough evidence to charge the defendant with her murder.'

'I would say twenty-five other bodies is evidence enough to charge him!'

'Maybe so, Sergeant, maybe so. But Dr Sigmund, the psychiatrist, distinguished in his field, has told of his own misgivings surrounding the disappearance of Dorothy Smith. And Mrs Savante who, as we have learnt, has used her very special and unusual powers to help the police before, has also indicated some doubt about the circumstances in Dorothy Smith's case. Also, the defendant himself has stated many times under interrogation that he did not kill her. I am merely pointing out that, regardless of the circumstantial evidence, there must exist an element of doubt about Mrs Smith. Maybe she is still alive. Maybe she simply left her husband and is living in that cottage or elsewhere. It's not uncommon for wives to leave husbands, is it? Thank you, Sergeant. I have no further questions.'

As Sergeant Dixon left the witness stand and walked away from the court and my life, he glanced up at me briefly. There was no look of triumph on his face, only a poignant sadness which tacitly disclosed that the battle he had won was nothing but a pyrrhic victory. He looked much older now. His face was lined and gaunt, yet I somehow perceived something more than that. I suddenly realised that the jacket, waistcoat and trousers of his smart three-piece suit no longer fitted him snugly. They hung loosely about him as if the power of the man inside was wasted through a depleting and enervating weariness. I was saddened as those big old courtroom doors separated him permanently from my very ordinary and unremarkable existence. In my mind he became the spent, dejected image of my father – on the very last time I ever saw him in the flesh – as he listlessly trudged from our living room to take to his bed, awaiting his summons from the wicked old witch to be taken from this life into Her service as Her woodcutter.

Two months later I learnt from an article in the *Comet* that Sergeant Dixon had taken early retirement. The paper reported, 'Detective Sergeant Ted Dixon, the officer who for many years was in charge of the investigation into the Where-Are-They-Women horrors, left the local force last Friday. Although he requested his leaving should remain a quiet affair, the *Comet* feels it must join with his work colleagues in honouring the devotion to duty of an extremely loyal and dedicated police officer. We all wish him well in the peaceful life he has chosen for his retirement with his wife Christine in the little Dorset town of Winkton near the seaside resort of Bournemouth.

'Sergeant Dixon's associates feel it was probably the harrowing time he spent investigating the Where-Are-They-Women murders which was primarily responsible for his decision to take early retirement from the force. We say to him, "Good luck to you, Ted, and enjoy your retirement! The whole community is in your debt for bringing the Where-Are-They-Women murderer to book. You thoroughly deserve to take things easy from now on."'

I have never heard anything more about Detective Sergeant Ted Dixon. I often wonder how things have turned out for him. Although I saw him little – and got to know him even less – during his few spasmodic appearances in my life, there aren't many others who have had more of a direct bearing on its outcome. I didn't even know Sergeant Ted Dixon was married. But, for what it's worth, I wish him well because, even though we were adversaries, I believe I grew to respect and like the man. He must be in his seventies now. The homage paid to him in those columns of the *Comet* is fully endorsed by me and I would like to express my own personal hope that his retirement is indeed proving to be both peaceful and happy.

My counsel called just one other witness, Dr Sigmund, the Broadmoor psychiatrist.

'Doctor Sigmund, how many times did you interrogate

the defendant during his stay at the hospital?'

'I don't exactly know. I could count the occasions from the transcripts, I suppose.'

'No, doctor, that won't be necessary. But would it be true to say that there were very many occasions?'

'Yes, it would.'

'And sometimes these examinations were carried out under the influence of Sodium Pentothal, were they not?'

'Yes, they were.'

'Pentothal what?' barked the voice of Judge Cattermole.

'Pentothal, Sodium, m'lud. It is known as the "truth drug". It induces truthful responses under questioning.'

His lordship grunted.

'And, tell me, doctor, did the defendant's answers under the influence of this drug ever deviate from those he gave without it?'

'No, they didn't. His responses were always very consistent.'

'And what does this convey to you?'

'That he is convinced about his account of what happened. He isn't lying. Whatever the real truth about his bizarre story, he really believes it occurred just the way he said.'

'And does this surprise you?'

'In what respect?'

'That he genuinely believes all the separate episodes in his curious and bizarre story to be true?'

'Not especially. Schizophrenics always accept their versions of things, often quite passionately, no matter how ridiculous they may seem to a rational mind. It is a symptom of the personality change. And convincing them to adopt a different reality is one of the difficulties in successfully treating the condition.'

'Dr Sigmund, this is a court of law; a place exclusively devoted to the exchange of facts. It is the job of this court to weed out the facts from the speculation, the definites from the maybes. I'll tell you what I consider the facts to be, shall I? John Smith has never lied in recounting his interpretation of the truth, bizarre though it might be. He has admitted showing those other women the secret way, as he calls it. And they were found exactly where he perceived that route to be. I am not condoning that and I am sure the verdict of this court will recognise the seriousness of what he has done.

'But he has always denied his wife was numbered among those other women. And the facts do seem to corroborate his testimony, would you not agree, Dr Sigmund?'

'I have already admitted that is the one anomalous feature of this case. That is really all I can say on the matter.'

'Then I suppose that will have to do, won't it, doctor? Oh, just one more question before I finally let you go. Would the defendant's condition, and the change in his personality during those periods when he felt he was under the influence of this omnipotent figure he referred to as the wicked old witch, in any way interfere with his capability to distinguish between what he perceived as right and wrong?'

'Probably. As I have said, in the defendant's case, the witch represents the ultimate authority. She is very powerful to him. If she had told him it was her will, and therefore right to show those women the way to her, he would readily have accepted that. His own ethics, or any misgivings he might normally have had over what he was doing, would have been overriden.'

'And is it possible that this overriding of logical reasoning could have remained with him even when his personality appeared to return to a more stable state?'

'In his case, I believe that is possible. He might always have been under that influence, even during those times when he might have appeared to regain a more balanced state of mind. In fact, it is probably accurate to say that Smith only ever felt a sense of righteousness and self-worth if he was constantly serving his authority faithfully and carrying out what he perceived to be her will, even during periods of absences when the witch did not actually manifest herself to him.'

'So, John Smith might never have perceived he was doing wrong – I mean, anything which was against the law?'

'The witch *was* his law. Her court was his only authority. He would do whatever he believed she told him to do, without any regard for the proper law of the land.'

'Thank you, Dr Sigmund. I have no further questions for you.'

The summation of the prosecution counsel was, as you would expect, quite damning. He made a great issue of disparaging my own counsel's remarks by stating, 'Ignorance of the law, either through innocence, naiveté or any other reason, is no excuse for escaping the force of its judgement.

'My learned friend has based his entire defence on the supposition that the defendant was not aware of the seriousness of his actions or even that he was doing anything wrong at all. But our history books are full of accounts of people who have justified heinous inhuman acts on the basis of all sorts of misguided reasonings. Adolf Hitler is but one example. Some still say his motives were misunderstood.

'Ladies and gentlemen of the jury, if you were deciding

on the evidence at Hitler's trial, would it be reasonable to conclude there are mitigating circumstances which have to be considered when reaching your verdict? Of course not! I am sure you would agree that such a conclusion would be preposterous even though Hitler may sincerely have believed his deeds were perfectly right and just. Precisely the same situation exists in the case you are deliberating on here today. I submit there is absolutely no doubt Smith murdered the twenty-five women whose remains were found buried in his garden and, indeed, the counsel for the defence has offered no real disagreement to these charges. They were acts of cold, inhuman and calculated brutality.

'But you have heard that, in the case of Dorothy Smith, the defendant's wife, the body has never been found. His honour will no doubt direct you that, under law, the evidence of a body is not required to return a verdict of guilty of murder. And the evidence submitted at length during this trial, and the memory of the poor, innocent victim who still lies buried in an unconsecrated grave somewhere, scream out for you to return that verdict. Ladies and gentlemen of the jury, let that justice be done!'

In his own summing up, my counsel did not say anything I haven't already told you. There was no impassioned plea for mercy or forbearance, just a forceful and reasoned reiteration of the fact of my consistent testimonies and how my account of Dorothy's disappearance was borne out by the evidence of certain witnesses. I felt quite sorry for him. He tried his best under impossible circumstances. I think he was an honest and sincere man and I liked him.

As I have already said, I was found guilty on all twenty-six counts of murder. I was told to rise as Judge 'Black Cap' Cattermole passed sentence.

'You have been found guilty of the cold-blooded slaying of twenty-six women. In all my years on the bench, I have never had to preside over a more hideous and macabre case. To kill one is outrageous; to kill twenty-six is carnage. But your counsel has submitted a plea of diminished responsibility and I admit it is with reluctance that I have to accept that submission.

'Nevertheless, the fact remains you are a danger to innocent women everywhere and your reasons for committing these atrocious crimes are of no consequence to the way I must deal with that. I can never allow you to walk the streets and endanger the lives of decent law-abiding citizens ever again.

'My one concession to your counsel's plea is to accept the fact that, for the time being at least, you need constant psychiatric attention. You will therefore be taken from this place to a high-security institution for mentally ill offenders where, for as long as is deemed necessary, you will spend time in their charge. But that does not mean I can put any time limit on your sentence because, if the day ever dawns when it is felt you can be transferred from the hospital to a prison, I intend to see to it that you remain locked up for the rest of your life. And rest assured, Mr Smith, when I say life I mean just that. You will spend the remainder of your natural days safely secured behind bars where you will never again be given the chance to commit the kind of atrocities we have heard about in this courtroom over the past few weeks.

'I can find no more words to say on this matter. I suspect the entire court is glad this case is finally over. Just thinking about the appalling deeds you have done makes me feel sick in the pit of my stomach. Take him down!'

And so it was, on November 11th, 1973, I was returned to Broadmoor, a committed psychopath, unjustly accused both of murder and insanity. You may think that is the end of my story but in many ways it is only just beginning.

As usual, the wicked old witch had the last laugh; or, should I say, the last abominable snigger.

Chapter 32

Time passed. And as it passed, I seemed to endure it more passively. Before my trial, each day in this place seemed interminable to me, moving on to the sameness of the next, sluggishly and ponderously, burdened as I was by the encumbrance of resentment at the way I was forced to endure them. I have my rigorous routines to bear now, just as I did then, but there is one difference; the difference which gives me the strength to carry on and makes each day seem typical instead of an eternity. Time is no longer incessant or painful, aided I'm sure by my daily medication which they say is to relax me. I cannot deny I have formed some reliance on drugs but there is more to my forbearance than that. You see, with the passing years, I have gradually learnt the art of resignation; of submissively yielding to the relinquishment of hope, of not coveting a miracle which might change my fortune. It was the conscious abdication of my former life which finally made my new existence bearable.

They still come to me, my psychiatrists. But now I don't regard them as antagonists; I see them more as friends. I am no longer their guinea pig. To most, I have become more a thing of academic interest; a twentieth-century Elephant Man whose hideous brain, rather than hideous countenance, is deemed worthy of study.

One who used to come is a committed Christian. He sometimes came to me alone, in his own free time. To him, I was a sinner to be saved. He begged me to renounce my former life, make my peace with God and Christ, repent and turn around. He gave me a Bible and I have read it many times. We often discussed the book which, to him, is the inspired word of the Almighty and, to me, is nothing but a mystery. He never did convince me to change my allegiance but I am still relatively young and who knows what the measure of my remaining years will accomplish? He talked of his God as being compassionate and loving, not at all like the exacting mistress I've striven to serve. He appeared so joyous that, sometimes, I wished I could find his faith. So perhaps I haven't stopped coveting that miracle after all.

I am kept separate from the other patients and not allowed visitors, so I used to look forward to our little chats. Not that anyone else would want to come and see me now, except for Auntie Pat, of course, but I know that would distress her greatly so I'm pleased the restriction has been imposed. But she writes to me often and sends the occasional copy of the *Comet*. And, on my birthday, many years ago now, she applied for permission to make me a present of a portable colour television set which now sits on my bedside table.

I cannot complain at the way I am treated. I have most things I could ever want. When I first told them I was thinking of writing my story they agreed to let me keep my diaries for a while and even arranged to have transcripts of my trial photocopied for me.

Talking of writing my story, I found out from one of Auntie Pat's letters that a Sunday tabloid had contacted her, offering a very large sum of money for my own exclusive account of the Where-Are-They-Women murders. One day I might write it but, of course, it would be a very different story from this one. I know what they want: sensationalism; sex; gory accounts of gory acts. And I think I have enough imagination to embellish the ordinariness of the truth to give them what they want – the kind of stuff that will sell their paper by the truckload.

In case you are wondering, I think I have finally accepted that I did kill those women; except Dorothy, of course, for I will never confess to that. But, even so, I was not the kind of serial killer you sometimes read about these days. You know, the kind who kills with a wanton malicious savagery like the character of Hannibal Lecter in Thomas Harris's book *The Silence of the Lambs*, who ate his victims' organs and made masks from their skin. The women I sent Her were not humiliated and neither did I mutilate them, for She would certainly have adjudged such things as unforgivable. And I still say I acted with the enlightenment of an exalted knowledge. Death to them was nothing more than a momentary sting, to be endured before the glory of their resurrection by the Almighty One. For that is what happened. I know they still live. And I know the life they lead is one of eternalness. How can I be so sure of this? Because I have seen these things with my own eyes.

I am actually staring now into the sombre drabness of the most fantastic thing the psychiatrists have granted me: the painting. The picture I loathed yet viewed with a morbid and irresistible fascination. I asked to have it, I must admit, without much hope, but it now holds pride of place on the pale green wall which once served as a chimney breast to an open fire before the central heating was installed.

I know that giving me that painting was not entirely selfless. They use it as an aid to study my condition. We often stand as a group and stare into that canvas forest.

'What do you see in the painting now, John?' they ask me.

'It's the same as it was when I first saw it,' I answer.

And that is the truth. Whenever they come and see me, it always reverts to the inanimate scene of a woodcutter, standing outside a cottage in the clearing of a dense wood, cutting down a tree – his axe unalterably poised in suspended animation.

'But it changed again last night,' I add.

Again that is the truth; for when they finally leave me, and the darkness outside suspends my vigil at the window, watching the antics of the rabbits in the vegetable garden, I become a voyeur into the domain of the Mistress. She graciously allows me the privilege of insight into the affairs of Her world.

There are now so many differences in that canvas forest, it is almost unrecognisable. I was shocked the first night that picture hung on my wall and I sat before it, watching the scene change into the reality of its contemporary time. Although it was night and I saw the forest lit only by an eerie moonlight, I noticed that the moonbeams seemed more penetrating, that they were somehow able to pierce the dense branches of those gnarled old trees which before had seemed to link their boughs into a thick impervious cover. I noticed, too, that the little gingerbread cottage was almost basking in the moonlight, no longer protected by the profuse impenetrable foliage of those mighty oaks.

Then, as my eyes became accustomed to the night, I saw the reason why. There were no trees any more, just stumps. Row upon row upon row upon row of stumps, their rings of growth now disclosing, in inglorious nakedness, the centuries those old trees had stood there as silent sentinels.

The picture looked less threatening and, at first, I felt a strange sense of comfort; a kind of reassuring consolation. But, later that night, and indeed on every night I have watched since, the old sensation of sinister presence returned when I saw the lesser witches ride their brooms across that moonlit sky. They came back long before a watery sun dappled its rays upon the vista. Though it was still quite dark, I was sure they carried naughty little boys into the cottage with them.

When dawn finally came, from somewhere I heard a cock crow and saw my father trudge his weary way from behind the cottage. I wondered exactly where it was he laid his spent and wasted body for his few short hours of peace before the rooster summoned him to begin each new day's toil.

His face looked grim and his figure wretched and racked with the pain of constant labour. I watched his unhappy form tramp across the picture, his axe slung over his shoulder. Then he was gone, beyond the tableau the ebony framework allowed me to see. How far he had to walk to find the denseness of virgin forest and more trees to fell, I will never know. Some evenings he would return pushing a wooden wheelbarrow heaped with logs which he would stack outside the cottage door to fuel the continual column of greyish smoke I saw rising from the chimney every night. And sometimes, a female face I recognised vaguely, would appear at that door. She would stoop, pick up some of the logs and take them back inside with her.

The seasons moved on in that forest just as they did in the world outside my own window. But, come rain, come shine, come sleet or snow, every day my father obediently went about the service of his ruthless mistress, always tireless, never once being permitted a day to rest.

During the years I have been an observer into that covert world, I have seen my father trudge his weary way through scenes transformed by a knee-deep covering of snow and in a summer's heat so intense I could almost smell the sweat of his toil. And, always, he was faithful. Always, he served the Mistress with a steadfast and unswerving devotion.

'So, what happened in the painting last night, John?' they ask me and I bring them up to date. Often, there is nothing of interest to tell them, nothing they haven't heard before. Life, even in the deep, dark and secret forest, has its ordinariness just like everywhere else. But I tell them anyway, even if I do repeat some of the things I told them the day before. They don't seem to mind or get bored. They always listen keenly, without derision, making notes of the things I say.

I tell them of my father, the woodcutter, and how sorry I feel for him. 'Do you still miss your father then, John?' 'Yes I do!' I admit. 'And I always will.'

Such were the conventions of our time together, established by the passing years. But it was two years ago, almost to the day, nearly twenty-one years since the start of my lifetime incarceration, when new and even stranger things began to happen in the forest. I suppose I was pleased I had new truths to engage their interest.

I remember it was summer and a hazy sun was still

shining when my father returned to the cottage. His approach was announced by a ponderous rumbling; just a distant, almost inaudible, sound at first which slowly increased as he drew nearer. As he entered from the left-hand side of the picture frame, I could see his back was bent with the labour of pulling something extremely heavy. Then a large wooden cart was gradually revealed, stacked with roughly hewn planks and larger timbers. It was a burden enough for the power of a carthorse to pull and I screamed out in sympathy at my father's agony.

I could sense his suffering as he unloaded the cart and stacked the timbers in a levelled clearing next to the cottage. Then he was gone, back to his secret place of seclusion and peace.

That night, as usual, the black shapes rode their besoms and, when they returned, more 'other little boys' were ushered into the cottage. The next day I told the psychiatrists of these things and they wrote them down on pads attached to their clipboards.

It was a couple of days after that I received a letter from Auntie Pat, together with a week-old copy of the *Comet.* She apologised for not writing for a while but explained she had been ill with a heavy cold. I read her letter, already unsealed and examined by the hospital authorities, then opened up the folded newspaper. The headline hit me immediately.

'Nationwide Hunt for Missing Boys!' Intrigued, I read the columns.

'A nationwide enquiry is being launched into the curious cases of young boys who have disappeared in unexplained circumstances over the past few years. The exact extent of the incidents is still in doubt and police authorities are trying to co-ordinate their efforts and match cases in an attempt to make some sense out of the conundrum. Incidents have been reported as far afield as Plymouth, Aberdeen and Norwich.

'A spokesman said yesterday, "We are not dealing here with simple cases of runaways which, unfortunately, are all too common these days. Kids run away from home for a variety of reasons and some are never heard from again. Though those cases are tragic, we can normally identify that they happen because of a definite cause, like an argument at home, for example. No, we are talking here about disappearances which have no rhyme or reason. It is almost as if these particular boys have been sucked into some black hole. And, because they appear to be nationwide occurrences, and not confined to a specific area, it has taken a tremendous co-ordination of effort to fit the pieces together. In fact, if it were not for a new computer, installed centrally to log cases of juvenile disappearances, the similarity of these cases might never have come to light.'

When asked about the total number of cases involved, the spokesman added, "There are currently around two hundred cases being investigated which seem to fit the circumstances I have described, and what makes the situation even more curious is that they all involve male children between the ages of seven and fifteen."

'One case is of particular interest because it concerns a local boy, Timothy Ross, aged 10. We spoke to his distraught mother, Eileen Ross, at her home in Cranleigh Towers yesterday. While trying to restrain her tears, Mrs Ross told our reporter, "Timmy just disappeared. He went to bed around eight o'clock and when I went to wake him next morning his bed was empty, though it had been slept in." She wept bitterly as she added, "What makes this worse is that Timmy was sent to bed without any supper because he was naughty and now he has gone. I just want him to know I'm not angry with him any more. I love him and want him back!"

'Although this case may seem simple, having all the ingredients of a juvenile running away because his parents were angry with him, it is clearly not as simple as that. Cranleigh Towers is a high-rise block and Timmy lived on the eleventh floor.

'He obviously could not have got out of the bedroom window, even though his mother told us it was a warm night and she had left his window open. And, because of the spate of recent burglaries in the area, his father had fitted a deadlock to the front door. In the morning, the door was still deadlocked and the key still in place in the keyhole. How Timmy left the flat is, therefore, a mystery. He also seems to have disappeared wearing only his pyjamas. No clothes or other belongings were found to be missing.

'All the other cases similarly classified as unexplained, some now going back several years, happened in equally mysterious circumstances. To quote the final words of the police spokesman, "It is almost as if we are dealing with a new phenomenon like the Bermuda Triangle. We euphemistically refer to it as the Plaberwich Triangle to depict the furthermost points at which these disappearances have so far occurred."'

I could hardly believe it. When my friends arrived, I rushed to them. 'Look! Look at this!' I screamed.

They read the article. 'And what do you think has happened to those boys, John?'

'Don't you see? Don't you get it? The two covens of witches who fly out of the cottage every night. I've told you over and over again! They come back with boys – naughty little boys to eat for their supper!'

'Oh, we see,' one replied, 'and you think the witches are taking those boys?'

'Of course!' I bellowed excitedly. 'It's the only explanation.'

'So what exactly happened in the painting last night, John?'

'I – I – don't know! I fell asleep.'

Sometimes I did. No matter how hard I tried to keep my nightly vigil, I would usually doze off at some point. Normally, I would keep awake for my father to return home and sometimes I would wake up in my uncomfortable chair, in time to see the witches return from their nightly sortie. It seemed my mind was somehow attuned to that moment. But, for the past two nights, I had given in to my exhaustion completely, sleeping soundly, without observing any event in the canvas forest at all.

'So you didn't see what your father, the woodcutter, did with the timber he brought back to the cottage?'

'No, I didn't see anything. I went to bed. I was exhausted. But when I looked this morning, there was even more timber stacked in that clearing. But he wasn't there. I guess he was working somewhere else in the forest.'

'Well, John, I'll tell you what we'll do. You try and stay awake tonight and tell us tomorrow what is going on there. Then we'll decide what we're going to do about all this. Does that sound okay to you, John?' It was the voice of Dr Sigmund. 'Tell you what, let's look now, John, shall we?'

We stared into the painting; at the inanimate scene of a solitary woodcutter with his axe poised to strike at the base of a tree. Of course, there were no longer any tree stumps and the levelled clearing beside the cottage had magically regrown with thick, gnarled and luxuriantly foliaged oaks.

'But you know this doesn't work! It's always the same when you're here. The painting goes back to the way it was.'

There was a long pause, then Dr Sigmund spoke again. 'We'll leave you then, John. You've got paper and a pencil. Watch what happens this afternoon, and tonight if you can. Write down everything you see and tomorrow morning we'll all decide what we'll do about the witches and the little boys, shall we?'

'You mean, tell the police?'

'If that is the right thing to do, yes.'

He smiled at me. Then they left and I began my watch. The picture immediately changed before my gaze. I sat in that chair and my eyes never left the painting for a single moment. An orderly brought in my lunch and set it down on the table. While he was there, the picture instantly froze, back to its original form.

My lunch went cold, untouched. I would guess it was around four in the afternoon and I remember my eyes were becoming heavy with their constant scrutiny. It was faint at first but after a while I was sure it was there; the rumble of the huge cart I had seen my father pull into the picture a couple of days before. The rumble grew louder. His head appeared, then his arched back, straining to pull the unwieldy burden. I saw the cart, not loaded with timber this time, but stone. Roughly hewn granite, gathered from some unknown quarry in the depths of that unknown forest.

He pulled it to the levelled ground beside the cottage,

wiped his brow and leant on those huge cart-handles for a while. Then he looked skywards, his left hand placed on his pained and aching back. It was a look of utter despair. He began to unload the cart. Stone after stone was stacked beside the timber. I counted fifty-six huge boulders. How he lifted them I swear I will never know. Then he walked behind the cottage and out of my view.

At first, I thought he might have gone for the night but he returned a few minutes later with a pickaxe and a shovel. He paced an area of the clearing, then began to dig. I watched the drudgery of his labour and I wept. I cried loud sobs and through them wailed unheeded words. 'Daddy! I'm so sorry. Oh, Daddy! Oh, Daddy!'

I don't know how long I watched his toil or how much I actually observed. Whatever happened was seen through tear-filled eyes. I was suddenly aware it was getting dark. I wiped my eyes and saw my father trudge back to his unseen bed to rest his weariness. During the time he laboured, he had erected four huge posts in the corners of the clearing and had nailed some other planks to support them and keep them stable in their beds of wet concrete. I saw, too, along one side of the structure, that some of the stones had been cemented together to the height of my father's waist. But I saw no more, not the witches ride their besoms nor their return, bearing their cargo of naughty little boys. I threw my body on the bed and cried myself to sleep. When consciousness returned, the sun was streaming through my window.

I rushed into the bathroom then straight to my chair in front of the painting. My father had obviously been labouring for hours. He had erected a wooden scaffold around the stonework and was pulling the stones up to his platform by means of a crude hoist. The structure had risen far beyond his own height, tapering as it ascended. It was clear he was constructing a stone chimney stack. I rushed to get some paper and a pencil and drew a rough sketch.

My breakfast arrived and, as the orderly entered, the picture reverted to its original scene, as if an unseen hand had magically drawn a safety-curtain on which the first was painted. I ate with a ravenous appetite and, as the orderly went out, the scene reverted just as magically, and I watched the play continue with my father resuming his toil. About fifteen minutes or so later, the lock clunked again and in came the psychiatrists. Immediately, the painting assumed its usual inactive state.

'So, John – tell me what happened.'

I showed them my sketch. 'This is what my father is building in the clearing next to the cottage.'

My drawing was passed from one to the other.

'Looks as if he's building another cottage, doesn't it, John?' Dr Sigmund smiled. 'Any ideas why?'

I shook my head.

'What about the witches? Did they ride again last night?'

I shook my head again. 'I don't know. I was asleep.' I felt ashamed, like a watchman admitting he'd dozed off on duty.

Dr Sigmund's smile grew wider. 'Well, never mind. You know, it's a pity it doesn't allow anyone else to see it. We could take it in turns then, couldn't we, John? Give you a break?'

'What about the boys?' I asked. 'What are we going to do about them?'

'What do you want us to do about them, John? Do you care about those boys?'

I shook my head once more. No, I never did care about those 'other little boys', did I? Just as long as I wasn't one of them.

'Well, in that case,' continued the kindly voice of Dr Sigmund, 'why don't we leave it a while longer? Then you can tell us if anything else happens, can't you? You know, just to confirm we're not barking up the wrong tree, as it were.'

I agreed. After all, why would the police listen to anything I had to say? Dr Sigmund was right. We had to be sure. But I knew the true reason I had renounced my conviction so readily, why my concern had been so half-hearted. I could not betray the wicked old witch. I was still Her submissive servant.

'John, you've been cooped up in here for a long time now. Maybe you've been a little too preoccupied with the painting. Why don't I get the escort staff to take you into the grounds for a while? It's a lovely day outside, the fresh air will do you good. The picture will still be here when you get back, you know.'

Dr Sigmund always said that when he didn't know what else to say.

That evening the new cottage's fireplace and chimney were finished. My father had also begun to construct a stone damp-course around the foundations and a door-frame stood, alone, in the middle of the front aspect. I did doze after that but I awoke in time to see the witches return. Several little boys were taken into the old cottage.

Still, we decided to do nothing. Dr Sigmund and the rest agreed we couldn't present any substantial evidence on which the police could act. I did not contest their decision.

Three weeks later, my father had finished the walls – using smaller stone blocks cemented together, faced with clinkered timber planks – put in glazed window-frames, and was busily working at thatching the roof. A few days after that, the second cottage was all but finished.

When I think about the events that followed, I feel confused as to exactly how they fit in to the passage of time. It seems that, every day, something occurred which is significant to my account but it is difficult to tell it all sequentially. In the forest, my father often appeared at the new cottage, carrying in pieces of exquisitely made furniture; chairs, beds and other items and, each day, I would tell of these new happenings.

I received two letters from Auntie Pat, within the space of a couple of weeks, both containing editions of the *Comet.* In both letters she remarked that the papers contained something which might interest me.

I found the first article she referred to. It was on page seven, only a column, and was headed, 'Plaberwich Triangle Widens'. Auntie Pat had ringed it with a red pen.

'The riddle of the unexplained disappearances of young boys seems to be taking on an international flavour with similar incidents being reported from as far away as Stockholm in Sweden and Lyons in France. Many theories have been put forward, from the wildly fanciful abductions by aliens, to a sinister conspiracy of a global child kidnapping or paedophile ring.

'"I am not trying to detract from the seriousness of these tragic cases but some people are regarding them almost with mystical hysteria!" said Chief Constable Ernest Goodson of the Metropolitan Police. "That just isn't logical. And it's a policeman's job to deal in logical facts. Each of these cases is specific and, as such, each must be treated as a separate and independent incident. There can be no universal force doing these things. That is a ridiculous postulation. And let's get these disappearances into some kind of perspective. The number of cases which can be described as 'unexplained' represents only a relatively small percentage of the total number of boys who go missing every year under what can only be described as more usual circumstances. It is possible too that, following the extensive investigations each and every case will receive, either by police forces in this country or our colleagues overseas, it will be discovered that most of these so-called 'mysterious' disappearances have a correspondingly more rational explanation."

'But still, disappearances which can only be described as irrational continue to occur, baffling police authorities around the world.'

I didn't even bother showing them that article. I knew the truth. I knew the inescapable fate of those little boys and that nothing could be done to help them even if I could make the authorities believe me. The wicked old witch was beyond their law, beyond that travesty of justice which had unfairly condemned me. I knew there was no such thing as justice, neither man's nor the witch's. But I had still told them the truth. If they chose to disregard it, that was up to them. They would come to me in the end. They would eventually believe me because their enquiries would get them nowhere and they would have to treat the things I said with more seriousness. It was only a matter of time. And I had all the time in the world, hadn't I?

But it appeared that one of them believed me, even then: the Christian. Or, at least, he believed me after a fashion. He came to see me one night. Curiously, I remember I had observed my father come out of the new cottage, having finished his day's toil, to trudge his weary way back to his place of rest. I had then turned on the television to watch a documentary programme about the mysterious disappearance of those young boys. They had coined the same phrase used by the press, the broadcast being called *The Plaberwich Triangle – An Investigation.*

We watched the programme together, totally absorbed and fascinated. It confirmed that the disappearances had but one common denominator; they were all totally inexplicable, the boys vanishing as if into thin air. As far as could be ascertained, about three hundred and fifty cases had been reported in the United Kingdom alone, many of the boys disappearing from institutions such as Borstals and remand homes. In fact, the report estimated that at least seventy per cent of the missing boys were confirmed young offenders. It highlighted this as a 'curious but undeniable fact' and concluded that it only added to the peculiar circumstances that these boys could so easily disappear from 'secured' premises, though it did not deduce any conclusions from this evidence.

'Now do you believe what I've been saying?' I asked when the programme had finished.

The Christian, whose name was David Kelsall, nodded. 'Yes, John, I do. Though I don't think it happens quite the way you believe it does.' He smiled and paused before adding. 'Do you remember us discussing Armageddon and the way the world will become before that occurs?'

I nodded. But, to be honest, we had talked about so many things in the Bible, there was much I hadn't remembered. He must have sensed my confusion because he continued, 'There was that scripture we read in the Second Book of Timothy, Chapter 3, which talks of an increase in the number of children being disobedient to their parents. Do you remember that, John?'

I said 'Yes' though, to be truthful, I couldn't recall it.

'Well,' he persisted, 'don't you see? This is the start of it!'

'The start of what? Are you suggesting it's God doing those things? Taking those boys?'

'No, not exactly. But God has used His agents to do His bidding in the past.'

'That's crap! It's the bloody witch, I tell you, and Her subordinate crones. She's not an agent of your God! Even if your God does exist He can't be as strong as She is otherwise he would stop it, wouldn't he? You're mad! Why don't you go and see a bloody psychiatrist!' I exploded with the impassioned knowledge of truth.

An orderly rushed into my room at hearing my enraged shouts, the Christian was ushered out and the lock clunked behind him. I never saw David Kelsall again. I suspect he asked to be withdrawn from my case. The next morning when the other psychiatrists came to see me, the incident wasn't mentioned. Neither did they say why Dr Kelsall wasn't with them.

I remember I watched the picture intently over the next few days. I slept very little. By day, I saw my father hanging curtains in the new cottage and painting the window frames and other woodwork. He took a massive cauldron in through the door and returned later bearing water, which I assume he drew from some well outside of the picture, in two wooden buckets suspended by chains to a huge wooden yoke which he wearily hauled over his wasted shoulders. Many times he trudged to and fro bearing those buckets of water to fill that cauldron, which I imagined hanging in the well of the great fireplace I had seen him construct. Then he came with his wheelbarrow loaded with logs. Later that day, I saw grey smoke rising from the new chimney.

And by night, I watched the witches' sortie and their return with their haul of naughty little boys. They took them into the old cottage and the column of grey smoke from that chimney continued to billow out into the autumnal night air.

But there was one afternoon I will never forget; an afternoon when I observed an event which made all those constant hours of sleepless vigilance worth every agonising moment. I remember the psychiatrists had just left for the day and, even in my weariness, I resisted the temptation to throw myself onto the bed because of some strange premonition that something unmissable was about to happen. I don't know why I felt this awareness of insight. To this day I believe it was graciously given me by the Mistress Herself.

When I think of the momentous significance of the happening, I sometimes feel it should have been heralded by a fanfare of trumpets, as befits events of circumstance. But nothing announced it. I remember my eyes were heavy, the act of staying awake becoming oppressive.

Suddenly, a blue veil obliterated the painting. In the beginning, it just seemed to flash before me as an out-of-focus shape. It floated before my eyes and into the picture, becoming the outline of a figure walking down the little path between the tree stumps leading to the cottages. As it retreated, I recognised it as the back view of a woman in a long blue dress. There was no mistaking that corpulent backside and, as her full form became visible, I recognised the massive bulk of her bloated body. And the dress. It was one of her favourites. I had seen that dress recline in its favourite armchair in my living room at the old house with Dorothy enough times to believe it had taken up permanent residence.

I watched in a state of excited jubilance as the figure walked to the door of the first cottage. She waited outside and, a few moments later, the door opened. I saw Dorothy and my mother standing there. They embraced the new arrival, accompanied her to the new cottage, and went inside. Later Dorothy and my mother returned to the original cottage. My eyes were glued to the picture, spell-bound. I willed myself to stay awake. And later, on the stroke of midnight, the twenty-six witches from the old cottage were joined by the one from the new, riding their besoms into the black night sky. I saw no more that night. But, before I gave in to sleep, it all became abundantly clear. I knew why the wicked old witch had commanded my father to construct the new cottage. She was inaugurating new covens in that dark, dense and secret forest. That new initiate, whose imperiousness She Herself had told me She admired, was just the first of many more She would summon there.

The next morning, I simply told my friendly inquisitors they would soon hear news of another disappearance – a woman whose identity would surprise them.

'And who is this woman, John?' asked Dr Sigmund.

'Oh, you'll find out soon enough!' I replied.

He noted my remarks and smiled. 'So, we'll wait to be surprised then, shall we, John?'

It was five days later when the second edition of the *Comet* I've already mentioned arrived from Auntie Pat. Enclosed with it was a letter which simply said, 'My Dear Johnny, At least they can't blame you for this one. Read the *Comet*'s headline. I've always known you were innocent.

Now perhaps they'll listen. Love, as always, Auntie Pat XXX'.

I unrolled the paper. The headline hit me at once. It was huge, occupying the whole front page. 'Mother of Murdered Girl Disappears In Equally Mysterious Circumstances.' I remember I laughed out loud.

CHAPTER 33

'How did you know Mrs Thatcher would disappear, John?' Dr Sigmund looked puzzled. He scratched his bald dome, eagerly waiting for my answer.

'I saw her walk into the painting, down the little path leading to the cottages. The wicked old witch summoned her, just as She summoned Dorothy.'

I remember Dr Sigmund just looked at me for a long time. It was a strange look, a look of deep reflection allied with dejection.

'Do you have any friends on the outside, John?'

'No, not any more.'

'What about before? Before you were arrested? Did you ever talk to anyone about the wicked old witch? About the women you identified as the ones she told you to send to her? The ones, perhaps, you thought you'd like to send to her, like the mother-in-law you hated?'

'What are you suggesting? That I've got an accomplice on the outside? Someone who's taking over where I left off? Don't you understand? It's the wicked old witch Herself! She took the bloated old crone just as She took Dorothy. And there'll be more. Why do you think She had my father build the second cottage? Why don't you see it? Why don't you understand?' I was angry.

'Calm down, John! Calm down. I'm only demonstrating what the police will say if we tell them what you saw. They won't understand how you were able to see these things, will they? They deal in facts, John. Only facts. And the painting won't allow them to see into the forest, will it?'

I calmed down. I understood the soundness of what he had said.

'They'll never find Mrs Thatcher. Just like they've never found Dorothy. What will they think about that? They can't blame me for it, can they? I've got the perfect alibi!'

Dr Sigmund smiled. 'Yes, John, that's true. You've got the perfect alibi this time.' His smile disappeared. 'But sometimes, you know, after a case like yours, someone else, perhaps someone who sympathises with the way you feel, imitates the events. Copy-cat killings they call them.'

I became angry again. 'But they're not dead! None of them! They're all living in the forest. I saw Dorothy there. And my mother. They're happy. They're happy!' I shouted.

'I know, John, I know. But that's the theory the police are working on. They're convinced Mrs Thatcher has been abducted or murdered by someone with a special interest in your case; someone who studied it and identified your mother-in-law as the next victim. A sympathiser or someone who wants the publicity for himself.'

My anger turned to apathetic indifference. 'Why should I care anyway? I'm glad she's there. It's where I always wanted to send her. There's nothing they can do anyway, either about her or the others who'll follow. And there will be others, you know. And the more the witch calls, the more those naughty little boys will disappear as well, never to be seen again.'

We looked at each other in silence for a while.

'Has anything else happened in the forest, John? Anything else you'd like to tell me about?'

'No! Nothing else has happened. Don't know how many boys have been taken. I've slept right through these past few nights.'

'John – you've been cooped up in here for a long time now. Maybe you've been a little too preoccupied with the painting. Why don't I get the escort staff to take you into the grounds for a while? It's a lovely day outside, the fresh air will do you good. The picture will still be here when you get back, you know.'

Obviously, Dr Sigmund could think of nothing more to say.

Six months passed. More copies of the *Comet* and, sometimes, editions of the national dailies, arrived from Auntie Pat. My former employers had resurrected the title of the Where-Are-They-Women and the headline at that time read, 'Whereabouts Of New Where-Are-They-Three Still Baffles Police'. But they, of course, were only viewing the tally in terms of local disappearances.

Some of the tabloids, however, reported a countrywide perspective, stating there were now fifteen women throughout the country who had recently gone missing in mysterious circumstances, and speculating that the copycat 'Witch Murderer' was seeking his victims nationally.

By this time, I could personally attest to eleven new initiates walking down the narrow path between those tree stumps to become inhabitants of the new cottage.

It was about this time that I also witnessed something else I had never seen in all the years that painting hung in my room. Why I missed it before I cannot say. I can only presume I had fallen asleep on every previous Hallowe'en night before the profane ceremony started. But now I have seen it. In fact, I have seen it twice. On the first occasion, thirty-seven witches cavorted naked round a huge fire my father had lit in a clearing before he retired for the night. The flames illuminated them perfectly. I recognised many of their faces and the shameless immodesty of their ugly, unclothed bodies in the light of the bright blazing bonfire which, though it consumed everything else in its wake, left the canvas completely unscathed.

I saw things I can only suppose are normally carried out behind closed doors, inside the clandestine cottages which serve as their dwellings, where I have never been allowed the privilege of scrutiny. I learnt that witches do other things to those naughty little boys before they gobble them up.

They commit acts of indescribable perversion and degradation which I could never narrate; acts that sickened even me, literally making me vomit. I learnt that witches are not wholesome; witches are capable of even more foulness than disgusting lowly males. My mother never told me about these things just as I have never told Dr Sigmund or his colleagues.

Even though I was disgusted by what I saw, I know I will watch the spectacle again next October 31st, on the eve of All Saints' Day – Hallowe'en – and on every year following for as long as I am able to. I made a note in my diary there and then to be sure I would not forget. Yes, the sight was disgusting. Yes, it was offensive and sickening. But I was drawn to it by the same morbid and saturnine compulsion which had hauled me back to the old house after destiny had liberated me from it.

I know what Dr Sigmund would say if I ever told him of the sights I had witnessed during those Hallowe'en night spectacles.

'Tell me more about your mother, John? Did she ever abuse you when you were a little boy?'

Sometimes, I think I begin to recall things. Incidents which start to unfold in the faculties of remembrance and understanding. Then I feel a sense of panic, of dread and terror, and I let the memories fade because the pain of them becomes too dreadful. But, always, the last image in my mind is of my mother's nakedness and her outstretched arms pulling me towards her. And her face, wearing an expression which is strange, and the noises she made, short, sharp gasps of breath and curious little moans.

And sometimes, for the briefest of instants, I think I begin to behold another vision. It is an image of blackness, of stubbly, jet black hairs like those growing off the warts on the witch's hooked nose; sinister and menacing. I am being pulled towards them. I smell a smell, a horrible smell. It is entrenched in my nostrils and I taste that smell on my lips and in my mouth. I am being held to that blackness and there is no escape. I know I do not want to be held there. I cannot breathe. I feel those stubbly hairs in my mouth and I begin to choke on them. It is horrible and I force the remembrance from me.

Then, there are other fleeting memories. Like being pinned across my mother's knees, feeling indescribable pain in my bare bottom and my mother's voice shouting, 'This is what you get for your disgusting acts of foulness! It is that revolting and offensive little puppy dog's tail that controls you, Johnny Smith. It controls all of your lowly kind!' I try to shout back, 'But I couldn't help it! I didn't want to do it! You made me. You made me!'

No, I cannot tell Dr Sigmund about any of these things. But I will tell you this. When I witnessed the witches cavort around their fire on the Hallowe'en night just passed, there were fifty-two of them – four covens of thirteen. And earlier that day, I watched my father haul his huge handcart, loaded with more planks and timbers which he stacked in another levelled clearing beside the second cottage. The following day, All Saints' Day itself, I began writing my strange tale.

And I suppose it is now nearly finished, except you know that isn't really true. It will probably never end, will it? Because, as I began to collect my thoughts before loading the first tongue of clean white paper into Dr Sigmund's typewriter beneath its row of curved silver teeth, a curious realisation came to me. Something I had not perceived before.

On all the countless occasions I had stared into that canvas forest, watching the events unfold in that strange, dark world of witches, seeing them ride off into the night sky in their constant search for more naughty little boys, and recognising the illuminated faces of many of them as they capered around on their special nights of celebration, I never once saw the face of their mistress, the wicked old witch Herself. She was never with the rest.

As I considered this fact, I wondered about it. Had She moved on, perhaps, leaving the covens She had established there to initiate more in some other dark and secret forest? And, if so, how many were now thriving in the depths of other unknown places of mystery and seclusion, unobserved and denied by the inferior authorities of humankind? Where would it end? Would it ever end?

I wish I had thought to ask Her these things when I had the opportunity. Because, for one last time, She graciously granted me the privilege of audience. It was about two weeks ago now. I was seated at my table writing my story when, I supposed at first for inspiration, but now with hindsight I know it was because it was Her will, I turned and glanced at the painting.

She was there, standing on the foremost tree stump, pointing Her gnarled and haggard old finger at me.

'Johnny Smith!' She bellowed, *'I know you are writing of me. But no matter. Have your litttle indulgence. No one will believe you. It is just as your wonderful mother once said. They will think you are telling lies again. And you are serving the sentence of that misdemeanour even now, aren't you, Johnny Smith? Locked up and the key thrown away. For, mark my words, there you will spend the rest of your days. Till you rot, Johnny Smith. Till you rot!*

'But – in your own way, you have tried your best to be a true and loyal servant and I am not ungracious. Of your own free will, though your reasoning was fallacious, you began the enlistment to my cause. A work which I, myself, am now continuing and will endure until my purpose is complete.

'Your own wonderful mother has petitioned me on your behalf and, although I have told her I cannot grant you clemency, I have decided to give you the one thing for which you have always striven. And I can reward you with that, Johnny Smith, even there, in that grim, dismal dwelling that has become the place in which you will end your days.

'Have patience, Johnny Smith, have patience! It will be granted to you soon. You will have your sense of comfort and

peace. Where you have come to live will become your own special place. You will want for nothing else. And this I will do because your own wonderful mother has requested it. Yes, Johnny Smith, she has proved her love for you. What more can a lowly detestable boy ask for? Yes, indeed! What more can a lowly detestable boy ask for?

'You have always been a lucky boy, Johnny Smith! You will never know just how many times you were so nearly taken away and gobbled up for your disgusting acts of naughtiness. But I always spared you because I knew you had it in you to be special – to change your slugs and snails and puppy dogs' tails into more wholesome things.

'This is the last time I will grant you audience, Johnny Smith. But you will need me no more. Your job is done and now it is time for you to bask in the reward of your endeavours. Enjoy your incarceration, Johnny Smith, there in your own little Satisfaction House!'

I heard Her abominable snigger one last abominable time, then She was gone. And I have seen Her no more.

That night, goaded by an inexplicable sadness, I began to think about the wonderful thing my mother had done for me – petitioning the wicked old witch to ensure the rest of my days would be filled with happiness. Then I remembered long-forgotten words I had overheard my Auntie Pat say to Uncle George, about how my mother was abused – raped by her own father – incessantly violated, something which must rank as one of the most lowly and detestable acts ever committed by a lowly and detestable male. And I began to understand something of her own dreadful unhappiness and the reasons why she treated me like she did. She was just as much a victim of circumstance as I was. It was as if I were suddenly seeing light pervade a tunnel of consummate darkness. In the silence of my thoughts, I heard myself whisper, 'I love you, Mummy! I love you!' Then I cried. I cried until I was spirited away in the contentment of a deep and dreamless sleep. The next morning I awoke to an all-consuming peace and serenity which has never really left me since.

Before I finally end my story, I will bring you up to date with the current situation in the world outside of my own. The most concise report I have read was an article in *The Times*, a cutting of which was, of course, sent to me by my faithful Auntie Pat. It was entitled, 'Disappearance Mysteries Deepen – World Hunt Under Way', and said the following:

'A worldwide committee is being set up to investigate the disturbing epidemic of disappearances which have baffled police authorities in many countries throughout the world. It is to be an international body made up of representatives of law enforcement and other agencies from all over the globe. The first meeting of this new organisation, BEWITCHED, an acronym of ***B**oard of **E**mergency **W**orld **I**nvestigations **T**eam for **C**ase **H**istories of **E**nigmatic **D**isappearances*, is to be convened in Paris, on December 2nd.

'Its chief purpose is to research the spate of unsolved and unexplained missing persons enquiries which seem to have hit epidemic proportions. One of the primary objectives of the committee will be to correlate all such incidents to provide accurate statistics on the extent of the mystery which some estimates have said involves thousands of persons worldwide. A curious aspect of the case histories being investigated is that they are made up entirely of women over the age of twenty-one and young boys between the ages of six and sixteen. No other classification of persons is involved.

'The committee is to consist of experts in all areas of psychic research as well as specialists in forensic sciences and top people from investigation agencies. "We are leaving no stone unturned in our analysis. No theory will be too wild for our consideration, even paranormal ones. The situation is getting grave and we must find the answer to this baffling phenomenon," said Jacques Bordaine, a BEWITCHED spokesman. It is perhaps strange that this story breaks on a day when, in Paris alone, we have read in the papers of the unexplained disappearances of five more women and ten small boys.'

I have often mused over the name chosen for that committee. I am sure the term BEWITCHED was engineered by the contemptuousness of the wicked old witch Herself; Her way of cocking a snook at the puny human attempts to solve Her insoluble enigma.

I have mused over many other things besides. It gets dark early now winter has arrived. There is nothing I can observe from my window after the gloom of dusk has cast its dismal cloak and, by that time, I have long since watched my father trudge his weary way to his place of rest, having laboured all day long constructing the third cottage. There is nothing of interest to observe even in the forest except the dim light from the windows of the cottages and the wispy columns of grey smoke rising from the chimneys. That is, until the stroke of midnight when the posse of witches rides. So there is nothing to do but lie on my little bed and think until the welcome diversion of sleep overcomes me.

And there is one issue which, recently, has never really left my mind. I keep remembering the last words David Kelsall, the Christian, said to me before he was ushered from my room by an orderly anxious for his life.

'There was that scripture we read in the second book of Timothy, Chapter 3, which talks of an increase in the number of children being disobedient to their parents. Do you remember that, John?'

I looked up that scripture in the second book of Timothy and have now re-read it countless times. In full, it says:

'This know also, that in the last days perilous times shall come. For men shall be lovers of themselves, covetous, boasters, proud, blasphemous, disobedient to parents, unthankful, unholy, without natural affection, truce-breakers, false accusers, inconsistent, fierce, despisers of those that are good, traitors, heady, high-minded, lovers of pleasures more than lovers of God, having a form of Godliness but denying the power; thereof from such turn away. For this sort are they which creep into houses and lead captive silly women laden with sins, led away with diverse lusts. Ever learning and never able to come to the knowledge of the truth.'

I do not even pretend to know the full portent of those words but I see confirmation of all these evil characteristics of mankind in almost every article I read in the daily papers. It is a sad, desperate world out there and one which seems to be getting worse.

Then I pondered a curious speculation, fuelled by further words said to me by Dr Kelsall: 'Do you remember us discussing Armageddon and the way the world will become before that occurs?' and 'But God has used His agents to do His bidding in the past.'

I then began to wonder, what if the witch is God's agent and He is using Her to purge the world of boys disobedient to their parents, and women laden with sins, led away with diverse lusts, the covetous, the proud, the 'lovers of pleasures'? Would the world then be rid of its undesirables, leaving only the more righteous to multiply and fill the earth, leading to the fulfilment of God's original purpose? Maybe that is His Armageddon. But, then again, maybe not. After all, who am I, a committed psychopath, to speculate on the grand scheme of the Almighty? As David Kelsall once told me, 'His ways are often mysterious! The mills of God grind slow but they grind incredibly fine!'

But, as I have said, there is much I contemplate in my isolation. Just the ramblings of a deranged lunatic, I almost hear you say. And I expect you are right. As for me, I do not know. And, what is more, I do not really care. I am now no part of that world. I don't have to live in it, do I? I am, at least, glad of that. All I am sure of is that the wicked old witch has been true to Her word. I do not know if they will ever believe me or treat the things I say with any seriousness but neither do I even care about that. You see, I am happy. I now have that inner sense of comfort and peace She promised me. I have found that place where I can truly be myself and I never want to leave here. And, when I consider that it has all happened because of my mother's will, I also realise that no lowly detestable boy could ever have received more of a demonstration of a mother's love. I have come to realise that she loves me, just as I have come to realise that I love her.

A short while ago, I wrote to Auntie Pat and asked her to send me a WELCOME mat. It now sits outside my door. And there is a cat – one of the strays I used to see rummaging around the rubbish bins outside – which has been adopted by the hospital. It often sleeps on that mat, wearing a kind of wide self-satisfied grin.

Tonight is Christmas Eve. And tomorrow, Dr Sigmund has promised he will come to my room with a bottle of gin and some tonic. I know we will discuss my beliefs. And I know he won't deride the things I say. He will listen patiently, as he normally does, and we will debate the problem of the wicked old witch, the novices being conscripted to Her cause and the disappearances of those naughty little boys.

I must admit I do sometimes feel sad. There are occasions when those old and painful memories crowd in on me; like the times, especially, when I remember Ben and the night up in the tree house when he was taken. And it seems that, now my mind has relived the event, I remember it more and more often. I will never reconcile myself to its injustice but who am I to question it? Her law, just like Herself, is all-powerful and omnipotent. But otherwise I am happy. Yes, I am happy. Truly happy. You see, at last I have found my Satisfaction House – my special place where I can be myself – and I know I will live in its comfort and peace for the rest of my very ordinary and unremarkable days.

'. . . It has a "Welcome" mat
where sits a big fat cat,
which grins, "Come in and have a gin,
It's warm inside, I won't deride.
For I'm a place that's special,
I wasn't built with wealth,
Love is me, in me you'll see
That you can be yourself."'